D1081855

AUSTIN PUBLIC LIBRARY

FEARFUL SYMMETRIES

EDITED BY ELLEN DATLOW

FIRST EDITION

Distributed in Canada by
HarperCollins Canada Ltd.
1995 Markham Road
Scarborough, ON M1B 5M8
Toll Free: 1-800-387-0117
e-mail: hcorder@harpercollins.com

Distributed in the U.S. by
Diamond Comic Distributors, Inc.
10150 York Road, Suite 300
Hunt Valley, MD 21030
Phone: (443) 318-8500
e-mail: books@diamondbookdistributors.com

Library and Archives Canada Cataloguing in Publication

Fearful symmetries : an anthology of horror / Ellen Datlow, editor.

Issued in print and electronic formats.
ISBN 978-1-77148-193-9 (pbk.).--ISBN 978-1-77148-194-6 (pdf)

1. Horror tales. 2. Short stories. I. Datlow, Ellen, editor of compilation

PN6120.95.H727F43 2014 808.83'8738 C2014-900778-7
C2014-900779-5

CHIZINE PUBLICATIONS
Toronto, Canada
www.chizinepub.com
info@chizinepub.com

Edited by Ellen Datlow
Copyedited and proofread by Michael Matheson and Sandra Kasturi

We acknowledge the support of the Canada Council for the Arts which last year invested $20.1 million in writing and publishing throughout Canada.

Published with the generous assistance of the Ontario Arts Council.

Printed in Canada

FEARFUL SYMMETRIES

AN ANTHOLOGY OF HORROR

EDITED BY
ELLEN DATLOW

ChiZine Publications

ALSO EDITED BY ELLEN DATLOW

A Whisper of Blood
Alien Sex
Blood is Not Enough: 17 Stories of Vampirism
Blood and Other Cravings
Darkness: Two Decades of Modern Horror
Digital Domains:
A Decade of Science Fiction and Fantasy
Hauntings
Inferno: New Tales of Terror and the Supernatural
Lethal Kisses:
19 Stories of Sex, Death and Revenge
Little Deaths
Lovecraft Unbound
Lovecraft's Monsters
Naked City: Tales of Urban Fantasy
Nebula Awards Showcase 2009
Off Limits: Tales of Alien Sex
Omni Best Science Fiction:
Volumes One through *Three*
Omni Books of Science Fiction:
Volumes One through *Seven*
OmniVisions One and *Two*
Poe: 19 New Tales Inspired by Edgar Allan Poe
Supernatural Noir
Tails of Wonder and Imagination: Cat Stories
Telling Tales:
The Clarion West 30th Anniversary Anthology
The Best Horror of the Year:
Volumes One through *Five*
The Dark: New Ghost Stories
The Del Rey Book of Science Fiction and Fantasy
Twists of the Tale: An Anthology of Cat Horror
Vanishing Acts: A Science Fiction Anthology

WITH TERRI WINDLING

After: Nineteen Stories of Apocalypse and Dystopia
Queen Victoria's Book of Spells
Salon Fantastique:
Fifteen Original Tales of Fantasy
Sirens and Other Daemon Lovers
Teeth: Vampire Tales
The Year's Best Fantasy and Horror:
First through Sixteenth Annual Collections

The Adult Fairy Tale Series

Black Heart, Ivory Bones
Black Swan, White Raven
Black Thorn, White Rose
Ruby Slippers, Golden Tears
Silver Birch, Blood Moon
Snow White, Blood Red

Children's Fairy Tale Series

A Wolf at the Door:
And Other Retold Fairy Tales
Swan Sister: Fairy Tales Retold
Troll's Eye View: A Book of Villainous Tales

The Mythic Series

The Beastly Bride: Tales of the Animal People
The Coyote Road: Trickster Tales
The Faery Reel: Tales from the Twilight Realm
The Green Man: Tales from the Mythic Forest

WITH KELLY LINK AND GAVIN J. GRANT

The Year's Best Fantasy and Horror:
Seventeenth through Twenty-First Annual Collections

WITH NICK MAMATAS

Haunted Legends

CONTENTS

INTRODUCTION
11

A WISH FROM A BONE
GEMMA FILES
13

THE ATLAS OF HELL
NATHAN BALLINGRUD
39

THE WITCH MOTH
BRUCE MCALLISTER
60

KAIJU
GARY MCMAHON
70

WILL THE REAL PSYCHO IN THIS STORY PLEASE STAND UP?
PAT CADIGAN
76

IN THE YEAR OF OMENS
HELEN MARSHALL
99

THE FOUR DARKS
TERRY DOWLING
114

THE SPINDLY MAN
STEPHEN GRAHAM JONES
134

THE WINDOW
BRIAN EVENSON
146

MOUNT CHARY GALORE
JEFFREY FORD
151

BALLAD OF AN ECHO WHISPERER
CAITLÍN R. KIERNAN
168

SUFFER LITTLE CHILDREN
ROBERT SHEARMAN
181

POWER
MICHAEL MARSHALL SMITH
206

BRIDGE OF SIGHS
KAARON WARREN
219

THE WORMS CRAWL IN,
LAIRD BARRON
235

THE ATTIC
CATHERINE MACLEOD
253

WENDIGO NIGHTS
SIOBHAN CARROLL
268

EPISODE THREE: ON THE GREAT PLAINS, IN THE SNOW
JOHN LANGAN
278

CATCHING FLIES
CAROLE JOHNSTONE
310

SHAY CORSHAM WORSTED
GARTH NIX
322

ACKNOWLEDGEMENTS
334

ABOUT THE AUTHORS
335

COPYRIGHT ACKNOWLEDGEMENTS
342

KICKSTARTER BACKERS
343

INTRODUCTION

Fearful Symmetries was funded by Kickstarter, a crowd funding mechanism that has in the last few years increased in popularity. Why did I do this rather than use a traditional approach to publishing an anthology? I've rarely had problems selling theme anthologies to book publishers. Before a publisher commits to buying a book (novel, single-author collection, or anthology) the publisher must sell the book to its marketing and sales people, who in turn have to sell it to bookstores. But non-theme anthologies have always been a hard sell, and it's even more difficult in today's publishing climate.

Using Kickstarter was an experiment. I've donated to several Kickstarter projects, but had never been involved with one before. I approached Brett Alexander Savory and Sandra Kasturi, owners of the Canadian ChiZine Publications, to partner with me on the project. I thought they'd be a good match for what I had in mind because I enjoy what they publish and I love their production values and commitment to good-looking books. They also have excellent distribution, which means their books are available in most bookstores. This is important, so that the book is available to the general reading public, not only our several hundred backers. I was delighted (and relieved) when we reached our goal, and shocked when we went above it. The one thing we'd forgotten to factor into our financial estimates was the percentage paid out to Amazon, who handled our payments, and to Kickstarter itself. So the money that went over our initial requirements went for that.

I solicited some of the writers I've worked with in the past and also a few whose work I've admired but never published before. And in a break from my usual working method, Brett, Sandra, and I decided to hold a month-long open reading period. We promised to keep at least a couple of slots open for unsolicited stories submitted during that period. We received 1,080 submissions. There were several readers, including Sandra and a prominent Australian publisher/editor. Of those 1080 submissions, 119 were passed on to me. I ended up buying four.

Every anthology is a balancing act, be it reprint or original, theme or unthemed. While I love editing themed anthologies, there's something especially challenging and fun molding an anthology with fewer boundaries. The editor has to be even more aware of varying tones, themes, voice, and locale in the stories she acquires.

So what can you look forward to in *Fearful Symmetries*? There are monsters—human and non-human. There are children—those who victimize, and those who are victims. There are supernatural horrors, psychological terrors, noirish dark fantasies, and downright weird fictions.

Come on in, and make yourself a cozy little nook in the dark, and enjoy.

—Ellen Datlow, New York, 2014

A WISH FROM A BONE

GEMMA FILES

War zone archaeology is the best kind, Hynde liked to say, when drunk—and Goss couldn't disagree, at least in terms of ratings. The danger, the constant threat, was a clarifying influence, lending everything they did an extra meaty heft. Better yet, it was the world's best excuse for having to wrap real quick and pull out ahead of the tanks, regardless of whether or not they'd actually found anything.

The site for their latest TV special was miles out from anywhere else, far enough from the border between Eritrea and the Sudan that the first surveys missed it—first, second, third, fifteenth, until updated satellite surveillance finally revealed minute differences between what local experts could only assume was some sort of temple and all the similarly coloured detritus surrounding it. It didn't help that it was only a few clicks (comparatively) away from the Meroitic pyramid find in Gebel Barkal, which had naturally kept most "real" archaeologists too busy to check out what the fuck that low-lying, hill-like building lurking in the middle distance might or might not be.

Yet on closer examination, of course, it turned out somebody already *had* stumbled over it, a couple of different times; the soldiers who'd set up initial camp inside in order to avoid a dust storm had found two separate batches of bodies, fresh-ish enough that their shreds of clothing and artefacts could be dated back to the 1930s on the one hand, the 1890s on the other. Gentlemen explorers, native guides, mercenaries. Same as today, pretty much, without the "gentlemen" part.

Partially ruined, and rudimentary, to say the least. It was laid out somewhat like El-Marraqua, or the temples of Lake Nasser: a roughly half-circular building with the rectangular section facing outwards like a big, blank wall centred by a single, permanently open doorway, twelve feet high by five feet wide. No windows, though the roof remained surprisingly intact.

"This whole area was underwater, a million years ago," Hynde told Goss. "See these rocks? All sedimentary. Chalk, fossils, bone-bed silica and radiolarite—amazing any of it's still here, given the wind. Must've formed in a channel or a basin . . . but no, that doesn't make sense either, because the *inside* of the place is stable, no matter how much the outside erodes."

"So they quarried stone from somewhere else, brought it here, shored it up."

"Do you know how long that would've taken? Nearest hard-rock deposits are like—five hundred miles thataway. Besides, that's not even vaguely how it looks. It's more . . . unformed, like somebody set up channels while a lava-flow was going on and shepherded it into a hexagonal pattern, then waited for it to cool enough that the up-thrust slabs fit together like walls, blending at the seams."

"What's the roof made of?"

"Interlocking bricks of mud, weed, and gravel fix-baked in the sun, then fitted together and fired afterwards, from the outside in; must've piled flammable stuff on top of it, set it alight, let it cook. The glue for the gravel was bone-dust and chunks, marinated in vinegar."

"*Seriously,*" Goss said, perking up. "Human? This a necropolis, or what?"

"We don't know, to either."

Outside, that new chick—Camberwell? The one who'd replaced that massive Eurasian guy they'd all just called "Gojira," rumoured to have finally screwed himself to death between projects—was wrangling their trucks into camp formation, angled to provide a combination of look-out, cover and wind-brake. Moving inside, meanwhile, Goss began taking light-meter readings and setting up his initial shots, while Hynde showed him around this particular iteration of the Oh God Can Such Things Be travelling road-show.

"Watch your step," Hynde told him, all but leading him by the sleeve. "The floor slopes down, a series of shallow shelves . . . it's an old trick, designed to force perspective, move you farther in. To develop a sense of awe."

Goss nodded, allowing Hynde to draw him towards what at first looked like one back wall, but quickly proved to be a clever illusion—two slightly overlapping partial walls, slim as theatrical flats, set up to hide a sharply zigzagging passage beyond. This, in turn, gave access to a tunnel curling downwards into a sort of cavern underneath the temple floor, through which Hynde was all too happy to conduct Goss, filming as they went.

"Take a gander at all the mosaics," Hynde told him. "Get in close. See those hieroglyphics?"

"Is that what those are? They look sort of . . . organic, almost."

"They should; they were, once. Fossils."

Goss focused his lens closer, and grinned so wide his cheeks hurt. Because yes yes fucking YES, they were: rows on rows of skeletal little pressed-flat, stonified shrimp, fish, sea-ferns, and other assorted what-the-fuck-evers, painstakingly selected, sorted, and slotted into patterns that started at calf-level and rose almost to the equally creepy baked-bone brick roof, blending into darkness.

"Jesus," he said, out loud. "This is *gold*, man, even if it turns out you can't read 'em. This is an Emmy, right here."

Hynde nodded, grinning too now, though maybe not as wide. And told him: "Wait till you see the well."

The cistern in question, hand-dug down through rock and paved inside with slimy sandstone, had a roughly twenty-foot diameter and a depth that proved unsound-able even with the party's longest reel of rope, which put it at something over sixty-one metres. Whatever had once been inside it appeared to have dried up long since, though a certain liquid quality to the echoes it produced gave indications that there might still be the remains of a water table—poisoned or pure, no way to tell—lingering at its bottom. There was a weird saline quality to the crust inside its lip, a sort of whitish, gypsumesque candle-wax-dripping formation that looked as though it was just on the verge of blooming into stalactites.

Far more interesting, however, was the design scheme its excavators had chosen to decorate the well's exterior with—a mosaic, also assembled from fossils, though in this case the rocks themselves had been pulverized before use, reduced to fragments so that they could be recombined into surreally alien patterns: fish-eyed, weed-legged, shell-winged monstrosities, cut here and there with what might be fins or wings or insect torsos halved, quartered, chimerically repurposed and slapped together to form even larger, more complex figures of which these initial grotesques were only the pointillist building blocks. Step back far enough, and they coalesced into seven figures looking off into almost every possible direction save for where the southeast compass point should go. That spot was completely blank.

"I'm thinking the well-chamber was constructed first," Hynde explained, "here, under the ground—possibly around an already-existing cave, hollowed out by water that no longer exists, through limestone that *shouldn't* exist. After which the entire temple would've been built overtop, to hide and protect it . . . protect *them*."

"The statues." Hynde nodded. "Are those angels?" Goss asked, knowing they couldn't be.

"Do they *look* like angels?"

"Hey, there are some pretty fucked-up looking angels, is what I hear. Like—rings of eyes covered in wings, or those four-headed ones from *The X-Files*."

"Or the ones that look like Christopher Walken."

"Gabriel, in *The Prophecy*. Viggo Mortensen played Satan." Goss squinted. "But these sort of look like . . . Pazuzu."

Hynde nodded, pleased. "Good call: four wings, like a moth—definitely Sumerian. This one has clawed feet; this one's head is turned backwards, or maybe upside-down. *This* one looks like it's got no lower jaw. This one has a tail and no legs at all, like a snake. . . ."

"Dude, do you actually know what they are, or are you just fucking with me?"

"How much do you know about the Terrible Seven?"

"Nothing."

"Excellent. That means our viewers won't, either."

They set up in front of the door, before they lost the sun. A tight shot on Hynde, hands thrown out in what Goss had come to call his classic Profsplaining pose; Goss shot from below, framing him in the temple's gaping maw, while 'Lij the sound guy checked his levels and everybody else shut the fuck up. From the corner of one eye, Goss could just glimpse Camberwell leaning back against the point truck's wheel with her distractingly curvy legs crossed, arms braced like she was about to start doing reverse triceps push-ups. Though it was hard to tell from behind those massive sun-goggles, she didn't seem too impressed.

"The Terrible Seven were mankind's first boogeymen," Hynde told whoever would eventually be up at three in the morning, or whenever the History Channel chose to run this. "To call them demons would be too . . . Christian. To the people who feared them most, the Sumerians, they were simply a group of incredibly powerful creatures responsible for every sort of human misery, invisible and unutterably malign—literally unnameable, since to name them was, inevitably, to invite their attention. According to experts, the only way to fend them off was with the so-called 'Maskim Chant,' a prayer for protection collected by E. Campbell Thompson in his book *The Devils and Evil Spirits Of Babylonia, Vol.s 1-2* . . . and even that was no sure guarantee of safety, depending just how annoyed one—or all—of the Seven might be feeling, any given day of the week. . . ."

Straightening slightly, he raised one hand in mock supplication, reciting:

"They are Seven! They are Seven!

"Seven in the depths of the ocean, Seven in the Heavens above,

"Those who are neither male nor female, those who stretch themselves out like chains . . .

"Terrible beyond description.

"Those who are Nameless. Those who must not be named.

"The enemies! The enemies! Bitter poison sent by the Gods.

"Seven are they! Seven!"

Nice, Goss thought, and went to cut Hynde off. But there was more, apparently—a lot of it, and Hynde seemed intent on getting it all out. Good for inserts, Goss guessed, 'specially when cut together with the spooky shit from inside. . . .

"In heaven they are unknown. On earth they are not understood.

"They neither stand nor sit, nor eat nor drink.

"Spirits that minish the earth, that minish the land, of giant strength and giant tread—"

("*Minish*"?)

"Demons like raging bulls, great ghosts,

"Ghosts that break through all the houses, demons that have no shame, seven are they!

"Knowing no care, they grind the land like corn.
"Knowing no mercy, they rage against mankind.
"They are demons full of violence, ceaselessly devouring blood.
"Seven are they! Seven are they! Seven!
"They are Seven! They are Seven! They are twice Seven! They are Seven times seven!"

Camberwell was sitting up now, almost standing, while the rest of the crew made faces at each other. Goss had been sawing a finger across his throat since *knowing no care*, but Hynde just kept on going, hair crested, complexion purpling; he looked unhealthily sweat-shiny, spraying spit. Was that froth on his lower lip?

"The wicked *Arralu and Allatu*, who wander alone in the wilderness, covering man like a garment,
"The wicked *Namtaru*, who seizes by the throat.
"The wicked *Asakku*, who envelops the skull like a fever.
"The wicked *Utukku*, who slays man alive on the plain.
"The wicked *Lammyatu*, who causes disease in every portion.
"The wicked *Ekimmu*, who draws out the bowels.
"The wicked *Gallu* and *Alu*, who bind the hands and body . . ."

By this point even 'Lij was looking up, visibly worried. Hynde began to shake, eyes stutter-lidded, and fell sidelong even as Goss moved to catch him, only to find himself blocked—Camberwell was there already, folding Hynde into a brisk paramedic's hold.

"A rag, *something*," she ordered 'Lij, who whipped his shirt off so fast his 'phones went bouncing, rolling it flat enough it'd fit between Hynde's teeth; Goss didn't feel like being in the way, so he drew back, kept rolling. As they laid Hynde back, limbs flailing hard enough to make dust angels, Goss could just make out more words seeping out half through the cloth stopper and half through Hynde's bleeding nose, quick and dry: rhythmic, nasal, ancient. Another chant he could only assume, this time left entirely untranslated, though words here and there popped as familiar from the preceding bunch of rabid mystic bullshit—

Arralu-Allatu Namtaru Maskim
Asakku Utukku Lammyatu Maskim

Ekimmu Gallu-Alu Maskim
Maskim Maskim Maskim

Voices to his right, his left, while his lens-sight steadily narrowed and dimmed: *Go get Doc Journee, man! The fuck's head office pay her for, exactly?* 'Lij and Camberwell kneeling in the dirt, holding Hynde down, trying their best to make sure he didn't hurt himself till the only person on-site with an actual medical license got there. And all the while that same babble rising, louder and ever more throb-buzz deformed, like the guy had a swarm of bees stuck in his clogged and swelling throat . . .

ArralAllatNamtarAssakUtukkLammyatEkimmGalluAlu MaskimMaskimMaskim
(Maskim)

The dust storm kicked up while Journee was still attending to Hynde, getting him safely laid down in a corner of the temple's outer chamber and doing her best to stabilize him even as he resolved down into some shallow-breathing species of coma.

"Any one of these fuckers flips, they'll take out a fuckin' wall!" Camberwell yelled, as the other two drivers scrambled to get the trucks as stable as possible, digging out 'round the wheels and anchoring them with rocks, applying locks to axles and steering wheels. Goss, for his own part, was already busy helping hustle the supplies inside, stacking ration-packs around Hynde like sandbags; a crash from the door made his head jerk up, just in time to see that chick Lao and her friend-who-was-a-boy Katz (both from craft services) staring at each other over a mess of broken plastic, floor between them suddenly half-turned to mud.

Katz: "What the *shit*, man!"

Lao: "I don't know, Christ! Those bottles aren't s'posed to *break*—"

The well, something dry and small "said" at the back of Goss's head, barely a voice at all—more a touch, in passing, in the dark.

And: "There's a well," he heard himself say, before he could think better of it. "Down through there, behind the walls."

Katz looked at Lao, shrugged. "Better check it out, then," he suggested—started to, anyhow. Until Camberwell somehow turned up between them, half stepping sidelong and half like she'd just materialized, the rotating storm her personal wormhole.

"I'll do that," she said, firmly. "Still two gallon cans in the back of Truck Two, for weight; cut a path, make sure we can get to 'em. I'll tell you if what's down there's viable."

"Deal," Lao agreed, visibly grateful—and Camberwell was gone a second later, down into the passage, a shadow into shadow. While at almost the same time, from Goss's elbow, 'Lij suddenly asked (of no one in particular, given *he* was the resident expert): "Sat-phones aren't supposed to just stop working, right?"

Katz: "Nope."

"Could be we're in a dead zone, I guess . . . or the storm . . ."

"Yeah, good luck on that, buddy."

Across the room, the rest of the party were congregating in a clot, huddled 'round a cracked packet of glow-sticks because nobody wanted to break out the lanterns, not in this weather. Journee had opened Hynde's shirt to give him CPR, but left off when he stopped seizing. Now she sat crouched above him, peering down at his chest like she was trying to play connect-the-dots with moles, hair, and nipples.

"Got a weird rash forming here," she told Goss, when he squatted down beside her. "Allergy? Or photosensitive, maybe, if he's prone to that, 'cause . . . it really does seem to turn darker the closer you move the flashlight."

"He uses a lot of sunscreen."

"Don't we all. Seriously, look for yourself."

He did. Thinking: *Optical illusion, has to be* . . . but wondering, all the same. Because—it was just so clear, so defined, rucking Hynde's skin as though something was raising it up from inside. Like a letter from some completely alien alphabet; a symbol, unrecognizable, unreadable.

(***A sigil***, the same tiny voice corrected. And Goss felt the hairs on his back ruffle, sudden-slick with cold, foul sweat.)

It took a few minutes more for 'Lij to give up on the sat-phone, tossing it aside so hard it bounced. "Try the radio mikes," Goss heard him tell himself, "see what kind'a bandwidth we can . . . back to Gebel, might be somebody listening. But not the border, nope, gotta keep off *that* squawk-channel, for sure. Don't want the military gettin' wind, on either side. . . ."

By then, Camberwell had been gone for almost ten minutes, so Goss felt free to leave Hynde in Journee's care and follow, at his own pace—through the passage and into the tunnel, feeling along the wall, trying to be quiet. But two painful stumbles later, halfway down the tunnel's curve, he had to flip open his phone just to see; the stone-bone walls gave off a faint, ill light, vaguely slick, a dead jellyfish luminescence.

He drew within just enough range to hear Camberwell's boots rasp on the downward slope, then pause—saw her glance over one shoulder, eyes weirdly bright through a dim fall of hair gust-popped from her severe, sweat-soaked working gal's braid. Asking, as she did: "Want me to wait while you catch up?"

Boss, other people might've appended, almost automatically, but never her. Then again, Goss had to admit, he wouldn't have really believed that shit coming from Camberwell, even if she had.

He straightened up, sighing, and joined her—standing pretty much exactly where he thought she'd've ended up, right next to the well, though keeping a careful distance between herself and its creepy-coated sides. "Try sending down a cup yet, or what?"

"Why? Oh, right . . . no, no point; that's why I volunteered, so those dumbasses *wouldn't* try. Don't want to be drinking *any* of the shit comes out of there, believe you me."

"Oh, I do, and that's—kinda interesting, given. Rings a bit like you obviously know more about this than you're letting on."

She arched a brow, denial reflex-quick, though not particularly convincing. "Hey, who was it sent Lao and what's-his-name down here, in the first place? I'm motor pool, man. Cryptoarchaeology is you and coma-boy's gig."

"Says the chick who knows the correct terminology."

"Look who I work for."

Goss sighed. "Okay, I'll bite. What's in the well?"

"What's *on* the well? Should give you some idea. Or, better yet—"

She held out her hand for his phone, the little glowing screen, with its pathetic rectangular light. After a moment, he gave it over and watched her cast it 'round, outlining the chamber's canted, circular floor: seen face on, those ridges he'd felt under his feet when Hynde first brought him in here and dismissed without a first glance, let alone a second, proved to be in-spiralling channels stained black from centuries of use: run-off ditches once used for drainage, aimed at drawing some sort of liquid—layered and faded now into muck and dust, a resinous stew clogged with dead insects—away from (what else) seven separate niches set into the surrounding walls, inset so sharply they only became apparent when you observed them at an angle.

In front of each niche, one of the mosaicked figures, with a funnelling spout set at ditch-level under the creature in question's feet, or lack thereof. Inside each niche, meanwhile, a quartet of hooked spikes set vertically, maybe five feet apart: two up top, possibly for hands or wrists, depending if you were doing things Roman- or Renaissance-style; two down below, suitable for lashing somebody's ankles to. And now Goss looked closer, something else as well, in each of those upright stone coffins . . .

(Ivory scraps, shattered yellow-brown shards, broken down by time and gravity alike, and painted to match their surroundings by lack of light. Bones, piled where they fell.)

"What the fuck *was* this place?" Goss asked, out loud. But mainly because he wanted confirmation, more than anything else.

Camberwell shrugged, yet again—her default setting, he guessed. "A trap," she answered. "And you fell in it, but don't feel bad—you weren't to know, right?"

"We found it, though. Hynde, and me . . ."

"If not you, somebody else. Some places are already empty, already ruined—they just wait, long as it takes. They don't ever go away. 'Cause they *want* to be found."

Goss felt his stomach roil, fresh sweat springing up even colder, so rank he could smell it. "A trap," he repeated, biting down, as Camberwell nodded. Then: "For us?"

But here she shook her head, pointing back at the well, with its seven watchful guardians. Saying, as she did—

"Naw, man. For *them*."

She laid her hand on his, half its size but twice as strong, and walked him through it—puppeted his numb and clumsy finger-pads bodily over the clumps of fossil chunks in turn, allowing him time to recognize what was hidden inside the mosaic's design more by touch than by sight: a symbol (***sigil***) for every figure, tumour-blooming and weirdly organic, each one just ever-so-slightly different from the next. He found the thing Hynde's rash most reminded him of on number four, and stopped dead; Camberwell's gaze flicked down to confirm, her mouth moving slightly, shaping words. *Ah*, one looked like—*ah, I see*. Or maybe *I see you*.

"What?" he demanded, for what seemed like the tenth time in quick succession. Thinking: *I sound like a damn parrot*.

Camberwell didn't seem to mind, though. "Ashreel," she replied, not looking up. "That's what I said. The Terrible Ashreel, who wears us like clothing."

"Allatu, you mean. The wicked, who covers man like a garment—"

"Whatever, Mister G. If you prefer."

"It's just—I mean, that's nothing like what Hynde said, up there—"

"Yeah sure, 'cause that shit was what the Sumerians and Babylonians called 'em, from that book Hynde was quoting." She knocked knuckles against Hynde's brand, then the ones on either side—three sharp little raps, invisible cross-nails. "*These* are their actual *names*. Like . . . what they call *themselves*."

"How the fuck would you know that? Camberwell, what the hell."

Straightening, shrugging yet again, like she was throwing off flies. "There's a book, okay? The *Liber Carne*—'Book of Meat.' And all's it has is just a list of names with these symbols carved alongside, so you'll know which one you're looking at, when they're—embodied. In the flesh."

"In the—you mean *bodies,* like possession? Like that's what's happening to Hynde?" At her nod: "Well . . . makes sense, I guess, in context; he already said they were demons."

"Oh, that's a misnomer, actually. 'Terrible' used to mean 'awe-inspiring,' 'more whatever than any other whatever,' like Tsar Ivan of all the Russias. So the Seven, the *Terrible* Seven, what they really are is angels, just like you thought."

"Fallen angels."

"Nope, those are Goetim, like you call the ones who stayed up top Elohim—*these* are Maskim, same as the Chant. Arralu-Allatu, Namtaru, Asakku, Utukku, Gallu-Alu, Ekimmu, Lammyatu; Ashreel, Yphemaal, Zemyel, Eshphoriel, Immoel, Coiab, Ushephekad. Angel of Confusion, the Mender Angel, Angel of Severance, Angel of Whispers, Angel of Translation, Angel of Ripening, Angel of the Empty . . ."

All these half-foreign words spilling from her mouth, impossibly glib, ringing in Goss's head like popped blood vessels. But: "Wait," he threw back, struggling. "A 'trap' . . . I thought this place was supposed to be a temple. Like the people who built it worshipped these things."

"Okay, then play that out. Given how Hynde described 'em, what sort of people would *worship* the Seven, you think?"

". . . terrible people?"

"You got it. Sad people, weird people, crazy people. People who get off on power, good, bad, or indifferent. People who hate the world they got so damn bad they don't really care what they swap it for, as long as it's *something else*."

"And they expect—the Seven—to do that for them."

"It's what they were made for."

Straight through cryptoarchaeology and out the other side, into a version of the Creation so literally Apocryphal it would've gotten them both burnt at the stake just a few hundred years earlier. Because to hear Camberwell tell it, sometimes, when a Creator got very, verrry lonely, It decided to make Itself some friends—after which, needing someplace to put them, It contracted the making of such a place out to creatures themselves made to order: fragments of its own reflected glory haphazardly hammered into vaguely humanesque form, perfectly suited to this one colossal task, and almost nothing else.

"They made the world, in other words," Goss said. "All seven of them."

"Yeah. 'Cept back then they were still one angel in seven parts—the Voltron angel, I call it. Splitting apart came later on, after the schism."

"Lucifer, war in heaven, cast down into hell and yadda yadda. All that. So this is all, what . . . some sort of metaphysical labour dispute?"

"They wouldn't think of it that way."

"How *do* they think of it?"

"*Differently*, like every other thing. Look, once the shit hit the cosmic fan, the Seven didn't stay with God, but they didn't go with the devil, either—they just went, forced themselves from outside space and time into the universe they'd made, and never looked back. And that was because they wanted something angels are uniquely unqualified for: free will. They wanted to be us."

Back to the fast-forward, then, the bend and the warp, till her ridiculously plausible-seeming exposition-dump seemed to come at him from everywhere at once, a perfect storm. Because: *misery's their meat, see—the honey that draws flies, bi-product of every worst moment of all our brief lives, when people will cry out for anything who'll listen. That's when one of the Seven usually shows up, offering help—except the kind of help they come up with's usually nothing very helpful at all, considering how they just don't really get the way things* work *for us, even now. And it's always just one of them at first, 'cause they each blame the other for having made the decision to run, stranding themselves in the here and now, so they don't want to be anywhere near each other . . . but if you can get 'em all in one place—someplace like here, say, with seven bleeding, suffering vessels left all ready and waiting for 'em—then they'll be automatically drawn back together, like gravity, a black hole event horizon. They'll form a vector, and at the middle of that cyclone they'll become a single angel once again, ready to tear everything they built up right the fuck on back down.*

Words words words, every one more painful than the last. Goss looked at Camberwell as she spoke, straight on, the way he didn't think he'd ever actually done, previously. She was short and stacked, skin tanned and plentiful, eyes darkish brown shot with a sort of creamier shade, like petrified wood. A barely visible scar quirked through one eyebrow, threading down over the cheekbone beneath to intersect with another at the corner of her mouth, keloid raised in their wake like a negative-image beauty mark, a reversed dimple.

Examined this way, at close quarters, he found he liked the look of her, suddenly and sharply—and for some reason, that mainly made him angry.

"This is a fairy tale," he heard himself tell her, with what seemed like over-the-top emphasis. "I'm sitting here in the dark, letting you spout some . . . Catholic campfire story about angel-traps, free will, fuckin' misery vectors. . . ." A quick head-shake, firm enough to hurt. "None of it's true."

"Yeah, okay, you want to play it that way."

"If I *want*—?"

Here she turned on *him,* abruptly equal-fierce, clearing her throat to hork a contemptuous wad out on the ground between them, like she was making a point. "Look, you think I give a runny jack-shit if you believe me or not? *I know what I know.* It's just that things are gonna start to move fast from now on, so you need to know that; *somebody* in this crap-pit does, aside from me. And I guess—" Stopping and hissing, annoyed with herself, before adding, quieter: "I guess I wanted to just say it, too—out loud, for once. For all the good it'll probably do either of us."

They stood there a second, listening, Goss didn't know for what—nothing but muffled wind, people murmuring scared out beyond the passage, a general scrape and drip. Till he asked: "What about Hynde? Can we, like, *do* anything?"

"Not much. Why? You guys friends?"

Yes, damnit, Goss wanted to snap, but he was pretty sure she had lie-dar to go with her Seven-dar. "There's . . . not really a show, without him," was all he said, finally.

"All right, well—he's pretty good and got, at this point, so I'd keep him sedated, restrained if I could, and wait, see who else shows up: there's six more to go, after all."

"What happens if they all show up?"

"All Seven? Then we're fucked, basically, as a species. Stuck back together, the Maskim are a load-bearing boss the likes of which this world was not designed to contain, and the vector they form in proximity, well—it's like putting too much weight on a sheet of . . . something. Do it long enough, it rips wide open."

"*What* rips?"

"The crap you think? Everything."

There was a sort of a jump-cut, and Goss found himself tagging along beside her as Camberwell strode back up the passageway, listening to her tell him: "Important point about Hynde, as of right now, is to make sure he doesn't start doin' stuff to himself."

". . . like?"

"Well—"

As she said it, though, there came a scream-led general uproar up in front, making them both break into a run. They tumbled back into the light-sticks' circular glow to find Journee contorted on the ground with her heels drumming, chewing at her own lips—everybody else had already shrunk back, eyes and mouths covered like it was catching, save for big, stupid 'Lij, who was trying his level best to pry her jaws apart and thrust his folding pocket spork in between. Goss darted forward to grab one arm, Camberwell the other, but Journee used the leverage to flip back up onto her feet, throwing them both off against the walls.

She looked straight at Camberwell, spit blood and grinned wide, as though she recognized her: *Oh, it's you. How do, buddy? Welcome to the main event.*

Then reached back into her own sides, fingers plunging straight down through flesh to grip bone—ripped her red ribs wide, whole back opening up like that meat-book Camberwell had mentioned and both lungs flopping out, way too large for comfort: two dirty grey-pink balloons breathing and growing, already disgustingly over-swollen yet inflating even further, like mammoth water wings.

The pain of it made her roar and jackknife, vomiting on her own feet. And when Journee looked up once more, horrid grin trailing yellow sick-strings, Goss saw she now had a sigil of her own embossed on her forehead, fresh as some stomped-in bone-bruise.

"Asakku, the Terrible Zemyel," Camberwell said, to no one in particular. "Who desecrates the faithful."

And: "God!" Somebody else—Lao?—could be heard to sob, behind them.

"Fuck Him," Journee rasped back, throwing the tarp pinned 'cross the permanently open doorway wide and taking impossibly off up into the storm with a single flap, blood splattering everywhere, a foul red spindrift.

'Lij slapped both hands up to seal his mouth, retching loudly; Katz fell on his ass, skull colliding with the wall's sharp surface, so hard he knocked himself out. Lao continued to sob-pray on, mindless, while everybody else just stared. And Goss found himself looking over at Camberwell, automatically, only to catch her nodding—just once, like she'd seen it coming.

"—like *that*, basically," she concluded, without a shred of surprise.

Five minutes at most, but it felt like an hour: things narrowed, got treacly, in that accident-in-progress way. Outside, the dust had thickened into its own artificial night; they could hear the thing inside Journee swooping high above it, laughing like a loon, yelling raucous insults at the sky. The other two drivers had never come back inside, lost in the storm. Katz stayed slumped where he'd fallen; Lao wept and wept. 'Lij came feeling towards Camberwell and Goss as the glow-sticks dimmed, almost clambering over Hynde, whose breathing had sunk so low his chest barely seemed to move. "Gotta *do* something, man," he told them, like he was the first one ever to have that particular thought. "*Something*. Y'know? Before it's too late."

"It was too late when we got here," Goss heard himself reply—again, not what he'd thought he was going to say, when he'd opened his mouth. His tongue felt suddenly hot, inside of his mouth gone all itchy, swollen tight; strep? Tonsillitis? Jesus, if he could only reach back in there and *scratch* . . .

And Camberwell was looking at him sidelong now, with interest, though 'Lij just continued on blissfully unaware of anything, aside from his own worries. "Look, fuck *that* shit," he said, before asking her: "Can we get to the trucks?"

She shook her head. "No driving in this weather, even if we did. You ever raise anybody, or did the mikes crap out too?"

"Uh, I don't think so; caught somebody talkin' in Arabic one time, close-ish, but it sounded military, so I rung off real quick. Something about containment protocol."

Goss: "*What*?"

"Well, I thought maybe that was 'cause they were doing minefield sweeps, or whatever—"

"When *was* this?"

"... fifteen minutes ago, when you guys were still down there, 'bout the time the storm went mega. Why?"

Goss opened his mouth again, but Camberwell was already bolting up, grabbing both Katz and Hynde at once by their shirt-collars, ready to heave and drag. The wind's whistle had taken on a weird, sharp edge, an atonal descending keen, so loud Goss could barely hear her—though he sure as hell saw her lips move, *read* them with widening, horrified eyes, at almost the same split-second he found himself turning, already in mid-leap towards the descending passage—

"*—INCOMING, get the shit downstairs, before those sons of bitches bring this whole fuckin' place down around our goddamn—*"

(ears)

Three hits, Goss thought, or maybe two and a half; it was hard to tell, when your head wouldn't stop ringing. What he could only assume was at least two of the trucks had gone up right as the walls came down, or perhaps a shade before. Now the top half of the temple was flattened, once more indistinguishable from the mountainside above and around it, a deadfall of shattered lava-rock, bone-bricks and fossils. No more missiles fell, which was good, yet—so far as they could tell, pinned beneath slabs and sediment—the storm above still raged on. And now they were all down in the well-room, trapped, with only a flickering congregation of phones to raise against the dark.

"Did you have any kind of *plan* when you came here, exactly?" Goss asked Camberwell, hoarsely. "I mean, aside from 'find Seven congregation site—question mark—profit'?"

To which she simply sighed, and replied—"Yeah, sort of. But you're not gonna like it."

"Try me."

Reluctantly: "The last couple times I did this, there was a physical copy of the *Liber Carne* in play, so getting rid of that helped—but there's no copy here, which makes *us* the *Liber Carne*, the human pages being Inscribed." He could hear the big I on that last word, and it scared him. "And when people are being Inscribed, well . . . the *best* plan is usually to just start killing those who aren't possessed until you've got less than seven left, because then why bother?"

"Uh huh . . ."

"Getting to know you people well enough to *like* you, that was my mistake, obviously," she continued, partly under her breath, like she was talking to herself. Then added, louder: "Anyhow. What we're dealing with right now is two people definitely Inscribed and possessed, four potential Inscriptions, and one halfway gone. . . ."

"Halfway? Who?"

She shot him that look, yet one more time—softer, almost sympathetic. "Open your mouth, Goss."

"Why? What f—oh, you gotta be kidding."

No change, just a slightly raised eyebrow, as if to say: *Do I look it, motherfucker?* Which, he was forced to admit, she very much did not.

Nothing to do but obey, then. Or scream, and keep on screaming.

Goss felt his jaw slacken, pop out and down like an unhinged jewel-box, revealing all its secrets. His tongue's itch was approaching some sort of critical mass. And then, right then, was when he felt it—fully and completely, without even trying. Some kind of raised area on his own soft palate, yearning down as sharply as the rest of his mouth's sensitive insides yearned up, straining to map its impossibly angled curves. His eyes skittered to the well's rim, where he knew he would find its twin, if he only searched long enough.

"Uck ee," he got out, consonants drowned away in a mixture of hot spit and cold sweat. "Oh it, uck *ee*."

A small, sad nod. "The Terrible Eshphoriel," Camberwell confirmed. "Who whispers in the empty places."

Goss closed his mouth, then spat like he was trying to clear it, for all he knew that wouldn't work. Then asked, hoarsely, stumbling slightly over the words he found increasingly difficult to form: "How mush . . . time I got?"

"Not much, probably."

"'S what I fought." He looked down, then back up at her, eyes sharpening. "How you geh those scars uh yers, Cammerwell?"

"Knowing's not gonna help you, Goss." But since he didn't look away, she sighed, and replied. "Hunting accident. Okay?"

"Hmh, 'kay. Then . . . thing we need uh . . . new plan, mebbe. You 'gree?"

She nodded, twisting her lips; he could see her thinking, literally, cross-referencing what had to be a thousand scribbled notes from the margins of her mental grand grimoire. Time slowed to an excruciating crawl, within which Goss began to hear that still, small voice begin to mount up again, no doubt aware it no longer had to be particularly subtle about things anymore: ***Eshphoriel Maskim, sometimes called Utukku, Angel of Whispers . . . and yes, I can hear you, little fleshbag, as you hear me;***

feel you, in all your incipient flowering and decay, your time-anchored freedom. We are all the same in this way, and yes, we mostly hate you for it, which only makes your pain all the sweeter, in context—though not quite so much, at this point, as we imitation-of-passionately strive to hate each other.

You guys stand outside space and time, though, right? he longed to demand, as he felt the constant background chatter of what he'd always thought of as "him" start to dim. *Laid the foundations of the Earth—you're megaton bombs, and we're like . . . viruses. So why the hell would you want to be* anything *like us? To lower yourselves that way?*

A small pause came in this last idea's wake, not quite present, yet too much there to be absent, somehow: a breath, perhaps, or the concept of one, drawn from the non-throat of something far infinitely larger. The feather's shadow, floating above the Word of God.

It does make you wonder, does it not? the small voice "said." ***I know I do, and have, since before your first cells split.***

Because they want to defile the creation they set in place, yet have no real part in, Goss's mind—*his* mind, yes, he was *almost* sure—chimed in. *Because they long to insert themselves where they have no cause to be and let it shiver apart all around them, to run counter to everything, a curse on Heaven. To make themselves the worm in the cosmic apple, rotting everything they touch . . .*

The breath returned, drawn harder this time in a semi-insulted way, a universal "tch!" But at the same time, something else presented itself—just as likely, or un-. Valid as anything else, in a world touched by the Seven.

(Or because . . . maybe, this is all there is. Maybe, this is as good as it gets.)

That's all.

"I have an idea," Camberwell said, at last, from somewhere nearby. And Goss opened his mouth to answer only to hear the angel's still, small voice issue from between his teeth, replying, mildly—

"Do you, huntress? Then please, say on."

This, then, was how they all finally came to be arrayed 'round the well's rim, the seven of them who were left, standing—or propped up/lying, in Hynde and Katz's cases—in front of those awful wall-orifices, staring into the multifaceted mosaic-eyes of God's former *Flip My Universe* crew. 'Lij stood at the empty southeastern point, looking nervous, for which neither Goss nor the creature inhabiting his brain-pan could possibly blame him.

While Camberwell busied herself moving from person to person, sketching quick and dirty version of the sigils on them with the point of a flick-knife she'd produced from one of her boots. Lao opened her mouth like she was gonna start crying even harder when she first saw it, but Camberwell just shot her the fearsomest glare yet—Medusa-grade, for sure—and watched her shut the fuck up, with a hitchy little gasp.

"This will bring us together sooner rather than later, you must realize," Eshphoriel told Camberwell, who nodded. Replying: "That's the idea."

"Ah. That seems somewhat . . . antithetical, knowing our works, as you claim to."

"Maybe so. But you tell me—what's better? Stay down here in the dark waiting for the air to run out only to have you celestial tapeworms soul-rape us all at last minute anyways, when we're too weak to put up a fight? Or force an end now, while we're all semi-fresh, and see what happens?"

"Fine tactics, yes—very born-again barbarian. Your own pocket Ragnarok, with all that the term implies."

"Yeah, yeah: clam up, Legion, if you don't have anything useful to contribute." To 'Lij: "You ready, sound-boy?"

"Uhhhh . . ."

"I'll take that as a 'yes.'"

Done with Katz, she swapped places with 'Lij, handing him the knife as she went, and tapping the relevant sigil. "Like that," she said. "Try to do it all in one motion, if you can—it'll hurt less."

'Lij looked dubious. **"One can't fail to notice you aren't volunteering for impromptu body-modification,"** Eshphoriel noted, through Goss's lips, while Camberwell met the comment with a tiny, bitter smile.

Replying, as she hiked her shirt up to demonstrate—"That'd be 'cause I've already got one."

Cocking a hip to display the thing in question where it nestled in the hollow at the base of her spine, more a scab than a scar, edges blurred like some infinitely fucked-up tramp stamp. And as she did, Goss saw *something* come fluttering up behind her skin, a parallel-dimension full-body ripple, the barest glowing shadow of a disproportionately huge tentacle-tip still up-thrust through Camberwell's whole being, as though everything she was, had been and would ever come to be was nothing more than some indistinct no-creature's fleshy finger-puppet.

One cream-brown eye flushed with livid colour, green on yellow, while the other stayed exactly the same—human, weary, bitter to its soul's bones.

And Camberwell opened her mouth to let her tongue protrude, pink and healthy except for an odd whitish strip that ran ragged down its centre from tip to—not exactly *tail*, Goss assumed, since the tongue was fairly huge, or so he seemed to recall. But definitely almost to the uvula, and: oh God, oh shit, was it actually splitting as he watched, bisecting itself not-so-neatly into two separate semi-points, like a child's snaky scribble?

Camberwell gave it a flourish, swallowed the resultant spit-mouthful, then said, without much affect: "Yeah, that's right—'Gallu-Alu, the Terrible Immoel, who speaks with a dead tongue . . .'" Camberwell fluttered the organ in question at what had taken control of Goss, showing its central scars long-healed, extending the smile into a wide, entirely unamused grin. "So say hey, assfuck. Remember me now?"

"You were its vessel, then, once before," Goss heard his lips reply. **"And . . . yes, yes, I do recall it. Apologies, huntress; I cannot say, with the best will in all this world, that any of you look so very different, to me."**

Camberwell snapped her fingers. "Aw, gee." To 'Lij, sharper: "I tell you to stop cutting?"

Goss felt "his" eyes slide to poor 'Lij, caught and wavering (his face a sickly grey-green, chest heaving slightly, like he didn't know whether to run or puke), then watched him shake his head, and bow back down to it. The knife went in shallow, blunter than the job called for—he had to drag it, hooking up underneath his own hide, to make the meat part as cleanly as the job required. While Camberwell kept a sure and steady watch on the other well-riders, all of whom were beginning to look equally disturbed, even those who were supposedly unconscious. Goss felt his own lips curve, far more genuinely amused, even as an alien emotion-tangle wound itself invasively throughout his chest: half proprietorially expectant, half vaguely annoyed.

"We are coming," he heard himself say. **"All of us. Meaning you may have miscalculated, somewhat . . . what a sad state of affairs indeed, when the prospective welfare of your entire species depends on you not doing so."**

That same interior ripple ran 'round the well's perimeter as 'Lij pulled the knife past "his" sigil's final slashing loop and yanked it free, splattering the frieze in front of him; in response, the very stones seemed to arch hungrily, that composite mouth gaping, eager for blood. Above, even through the heavy-pressing rubble-mound which must be all that was left of the temple proper, Goss could hear Journee-Zemyel swooping and cawing in the updraft, swirled on endless waves of storm; from his eye's corner he saw Hynde-whoever (***Arralu-Allatu, the Terrible Ashreel,*** Eshphoriel supplied, helpfully) open one similarly parti-coloured eye and lever himself up, clumsy-clambering to his feet. Katz's head fell back, spine suddenly hooping so heels struck shoulder-blades with a wetly awful crack, and began to lift off, levitating gently, turning in the air like some horrible ornament. Meanwhile, Lao continued to grind her fisted knuckles into both eyes at once, bruising lids but hopefully held back from pulping the balls themselves, at least so long as her sockets held fast. . . .

(Ekimmu, the Terrible Coaib, who seeds without regard. Lamyatu, the Terrible Ushephekad, who opens the ground beneath us.)

From the well, dusty mortar popped forth between every suture, and the thing as a whole gave one great shrug, shivering itself apart—began caving in and expanding at the same time, becoming a nothing-column for its parts to revolve around, an incipient reality fabric-tear. And in turn, the urge to rotate likewise—just let go of gravity's pull, throw physical law to the winds, and see where that might lead—cored through Goss, ass to cranium, Vlad Tepes style, a phantom impalement pole spearing every neural pathway. Simultaneously gone limp *and* stiff, he didn't have to look down to know his crotch must be darkening, or over to 'Lij to confirm how the same invisible angel-driven marionette hooks were now pulling at *his* muscles, making his knife-hand grip and flex, sharp enough the handle almost broke free of his sweaty palm entirely—

(Namtaru, the Terrible Yphemaal, who stitches what was rent asunder)

"And now we *are* Seven, without a doubt," Goss heard that voice in his throat note, its disappointment audible. **"For all your bravado, perhaps you are not as well-educated as you believe."**

Camberwell shrugged yet one more time, slow but distinct; her possessed eye widened slightly, as though in surprise. And in that instant, it occurred to Goss how much of herself she still retained, even in the Immoel-thing's grip, which seemed far—slipperier, in her case, than with everybody else. Because maybe coming pre-Inscribed built up a certain pad of scar tissue in the soul, in situations like these; maybe that's what she'd been gambling on, amongst other things. Having just enough slack on her lead to allow her to do stuff like (for example) reach down into her other boot, the way she was even as they "spoke," and—

Holy crap, just how many knives does this chick walk around with, exactly?

—bringing up the second of a matched pair, trigger already thumbed, blade halfway from its socket. Tucking it beneath her jaw, point tapping at her jugular, and saying, as she did—

"Never claimed to be, but I do know *this* much: Sam Raimi got it wrong. You guys don't like wearing nothin' *dead*."

And: *That's your* plan? Goss wanted to yell, right in the face of her martyr-stupid, *fuck all y'all* snarl. Except that that was when the thing inside 'Lij (Yphemaal, its name is Yphemaal) turned him, bodily—two great twitches, a child "walking" a doll. Its purple eyes fell on Camberwell in mid-move, and narrowed; Goss heard something rush up and out in every direction, rustle-ruffling as it went: some massive and indistinct pair of wings, mostly elsewhere, only a few pinions intruding to lash the blade from Camberwell's throat before the cut could complete itself, leaving a shallow red trail in its wake.

(Another "hunting" trophy, Goss guessed, eventually. Not that she'd probably notice.)

"No," 'Lij-Yphemaal told the room at large, all its hovering sibling-selves, in a voice colder than orbit-bound satellite-skin. **"Enough."**

"We are Seven," Eshphoriel Maskim replied, with Goss's flayed mouth. **"The huntress has the right of it: remove one vessel, break the quorum, before we reassemble. If she wants to sacrifice herself, who are we to interfere?"**

"Who *were* we to, ever, every time we have? But there is another way."

The sigils flowed each to each, Goss recalled having noticed at this freak-show's outset, albeit only subconsciously—one basic design exponentially added upon, a fresh new (literal) twist summoning Two out of One, Three out of Two, Four out of Three, etcetera. Which left Immoel and Yphemaal separated by both a pair of places and a triad of contortionate squiggle-slashes; far more work to imitate than 'Lij could possibly do under pressure with his semi-blunt knife, his wholly inadequate human hands and brain.

But Yphemaal wasn't 'Lij. Hell, this very second, *'Lij* wasn't even 'Lij.

The Mender-angel was at least merciful enough to let him scream as it remade its sigil into Immoel's with three quick cuts, then slipped forth, blowing away up through the well's centre-spoke like a backwards lightning rod. Two niches on, Katz lit back to earth with a cartilaginous creak, while Lao let go just in time to avoid tearing her own corneas; Hynde's head whipped up, face gone trauma-slack but finally recognizable, abruptly vacated. And Immoel Maskim spurted forth from Camberwell in a gross black cloud from mouth, nose, the corner of the eyes, its passage dimming her yellow-green eye back to brown, then buzzed angrily back and forth between two equally useless prospective vessels until seeming to give up in disgust.

Seemed even angels couldn't be in two places at once. Who knew?

Not inside time and space, no. And unfortunately—

That's where we *live*, Goss realized.

Yes.

Goss saw the bulk of the Immoel-stuff blend into the well room's wall, sucked away like blotted ink. Then fell to his knees, as though prompted, only to see the well collapse in upon its own shaft, ruined forever—its final cosmic strut removed, solved away like some video game's culminative challenge.

Beneath, the ground shook, like jelly. Above, a thunderclap whoosh sucked all the dust away, darkness boiling up, peeling itself away like an onion till only the sun remained, pale and high and bright. And straight through the hole in the "roof" dropped all that was left of Journee-turned-Zemyel—face-down, from a twenty-plus-foot height, horrible thunk of impact driving her features right back into her skull, leaving nothing behind but a smashed-flat, raw meat mask.

Goss watched those wing-lungs of hers deflate, thinking: *she couldn't've survived*. And felt Eshphoriel, still lingering, clawed to his brain's pathways even in the face of utter defeat, interiorly agree that: ***It does seem unlikely. But then, my sister loves to leave no toy unbroken, if only to spit in your—and our—Maker's absent eye.***

Uh huh, Goss thought back, suddenly far too tired for fear, or even sorrow. *So maybe it's time to get the fuck out too, huh, while the going's good? "Minish" yourself, like the old chant goes. . . .*

Perhaps, yes. For now.

He looked to Camberwell, who stood there shaking slightly, caught off-guard for once—amazed to be alive, it was fairly obvious, part-cut throat and all. Asking 'Lij, as she dabbed at the blood: "What did you *do*, dude?"

To which 'Lij only shook his head, equally freaked. "I . . . yeah, dunno, really. I don't—even think that was *me*."

"No, 'course not: Yphemaal, right? Who sews crooked seams straight . . ." She shook her head, cracked her neck back and forth. "Only one of 'em still *building* stuff, these days, instead of tearing down or undermining, so maybe it's the only one of 'em who really *doesn't* want to go back, 'cause it knows what'll happen next."

"Maaaaybe," 'Lij said, dubious—then grabbed his wound, like something'd just reminded him it was there. "Oh, *shit*, that hurts!"

"You'll be fine, ya big baby—magic shit heals fast, like you wouldn't believe. Makes for a great conversation piece, too."

"Okay, sure. Hey . . . I saved your life."

Camberwell snorted. "Yeah, well—I would've saved yours, you hadn't beat me to it. Which makes us even."

'Lij opened his mouth at that, perhaps to object, but was interrupted by Hynde, his voice creaky with disuse. Demanding, of Goss directly— "Hey, Arthur, what . . . the hell *happened*, here? Last thing I remember was doing pick-ups, outside, and then—" His eyes fell on Journee, widening. "—*then* I, oh Christ, is that—who *is* that?"

Goss sighed, equally hoarse. "Long story."

By the time he was done, they were all outside—even poor Journee, who 'Lij had badgered Katz and Lao into helping roll up in a tarp, stowing her for transport in the back of the one blessedly still-operative truck Camberwell had managed to excavate from the missile-strike's wreckage. Better yet, it ensued that 'Lij's backup sat-phone was now once again functional; once contacted, the production office informed them that border skirmishes had definitely spilled over into undeclared war, thus necessitating a quick retreat to the airstrip they'd rented near Karima town. Camberwell reckoned they could make it if they started now, though the last mile or so might be mainly on fumes.

"Better saddle up," she told Goss, briskly, as she brushed past, headed for the truck's cab. Adding, to a visibly gobsmacked Hynde: "Yo, Professor: you gonna be okay? 'Cause the fact is, we kinda can't stop to let you process."

Hynde shook his head, wincing; one hand went to his chest, probably just as raw as Goss's mouth-roof. "No, I'll . . . be okay. Eventually."

"Mmm. Won't we all."

Lao opened the truck's back door and beckoned, face wan—all cried out, at least for the nonce. Prayed too, probably.

Goss clambered in first, offering his hand. "Did we at least get enough footage to make a show?" Hynde had the insufferable balls to ask him, taking it.

"Just get in the fucking truck, Lyman."

Weeks after, Goss came awake with a full-body slam, tangled in his sleeping bag and coated with cold sweat, as though having just been ejected from his dreams like a cannonball. They were in the Falklands by then, investigating a weird earthwork discovered in and amongst the 1982 war's detritus—it wound like a harrow, a potential subterranean grinding room for squishy human corn, but thankfully, nothing they'd discovered inside seemed (thus far) to indicate any sort of connection to the Seven, either directly or metaphorically.

In the interim since the Sudan, Katz had quit, for which Goss could hardly blame him—but Camberwell was still with them, which didn't make either Goss or Hynde exactly comfortable, though neither felt like calling her on it. When pressed, she'd admitted to 'Lij that her hunting "methods" involved a fair deal of intuition-surfing, moving hither and yon at the call of her own angel voice-tainted subconscious, letting her post-Immoelization hangover do the psychic driving. Which did all seem to imply they were stuck with her, at least until the tides told her to move elsewhere . . .

She is a woman of fate, your huntress, the still, small voice of Eshphoriel Maskim told him, in the darkness of his tent. ***Thus, where we go, she follows—and vice versa.***

Goss took a breath, tasting his own fear-stink. *Are you here for me?* he made himself wonder, though the possible answer terrified him even more.

Oh, I am not here at all, meat-sack. I suppose I am . . . bored, you might say, and find you a welcome distraction. For there is so much misery everywhere here, in this world of yours, and so very little I am allowed to do with it.

Having frankly no idea what to say to that, Goss simply hugged his knees and struggled to keep his breathing regular, his pulse calm and steady. His mouth prickled with gooseflesh, as though something were feeling its way around his tongue: the Whisper-angel, exploring his soul's ill-kept boundaries with unsympathetic care, from somewhere entirely Other.

I thought you were—done, is all. With me.

Did you? Yet the universe is far too complicated a place for that. And so it is that you are none of you ever so alone as you fear, nor as you hope. A pause. ***Nonetheless, I am . . . glad to see you well, I find, or as much as I can be. Her too, for all her inconvenience.***

Here, however, Goss felt fear give way to anger, a welcome palate-cleanser. Because it seemed like maybe he'd finally developed an allergy to bullshit, at least when it came to the Maskim—or this Maskim, to be exact—and their fucked-up version of what passed for a celestial-to-human pep-talk.

Would've been perfectly content to let Camberwell cut her own throat, though, wouldn't you? he pointed out, shoulders rucking, hair rising like quills. *If that—brother-sister-whatever of yours hadn't made 'Lij interfere . . .*

Indubitably, yes. Did you expect anything else?

Yes! What kind of angels are *you, goddamnit?*

The God-damned kind, Eshphoriel Maskim replied, without a shred of irony.

You damned yourselves, is what I hear, Goss snapped back—then froze, appalled by his own hubris. But no bolt of lightning fell; the ground stayed firm, the night around him quiet, aside from lapping waves. Outside, someone turned in their sleep, moaning. And beyond it all, the earthwork's narrow descending groove stood open to the stars, ready to receive whatever might arrive, as Heaven dictated.

. . . there is that, too, the still, small voice admitted, so low Goss could feel more than hear it, tolling like a dim bone bell.

(But then again—what is free will for, in the end, except to let us make our own mistakes?)

Even quieter still, that last part. So much so that, in the end—no matter how long, or hard, he considered it—Goss eventually realized it was impossible to tell if it had been meant to be the angel's thought, or his own.

Doesn't matter, he thought, closing his eyes. And went back to sleep.

THE ATLAS OF HELL

NATHAN BALLINGRUD

"He didn't even know he was dead. I had just shot this guy in the head and he's still standing there giving me shit. Telling me what a big badass he works for, telling me I'm going to be sorry I was born. You know. Blood pouring down his face. He can't even see anymore, it's in his goddamn eyes. So I look down at the gun in my hand and I'm like, what the fuck, you know? Is this thing working or what? And I'm starting to think maybe this asshole is right, maybe I just stepped into something over my head. I mean, I feel a twinge of real fear. My hair is standing up like a cartoon. So I look at the dude and I say, 'Lay down! You're dead! I shot you!'"

There's a bourbon and ice sitting on the end-table next to him. He takes a sip from it and puts it back down, placing it in its own wet ring. He's very precise about it.

"I guess he just had to be told, because a soon as I say it? Boom. Drops like a fucking tree."

I don't know what he's expecting from me here. My leg is jumping up and down with nerves. I can't make it stop. I open my mouth to say something but a nervous laughs spills out instead.

He looks at me incredulously, and cocks his head. Patrick is a big guy; but not doughy, like me. There's muscle packed beneath all that flesh. He looks like fists of meat sewn together and given a suit of clothes. "Why are you laughing?"

"I don't know, man. I don't know. I thought it was supposed to be a funny story."

"No, you demented fuck. That's not a funny story. What's the matter with you?"

It's pushing midnight, and we're sitting on a coffee-stained couch in a darkened corner of the grubby little bookstore I own in New Orleans, about a block off Magazine Street. My name is Jack Oleander. I keep a small studio apartment overhead, but when Patrick started banging on my door half an hour ago I took him down here instead. I don't want him in my home. That he's here at all is a very bad sign.

My place is called Oleander Books. I sell used books, for the most part, and I serve a very sparse clientele: mostly students and disaffected youth, their little hearts love-drunk on Kierkegaard or Salinger. That suits me just fine. Most of the books have been sitting on their shelves for years, and I feel like I've fostered a kind of relationship with them. A part of me is sorry whenever one of them leaves the nest.

The bookstore doesn't pay the bills, of course. The books and documents I sell in the back room take care of that. Few people know about the back room, but those who do pay very well indeed. Patrick's boss is one of those people. We parted under strained circumstances a year or so ago. I was never supposed to see him again. His presence here makes me afraid, and fear makes me reckless.

"Well if it's not a funny story, then what kind of story is it? Because we've been drinking here for twenty minutes and you haven't mentioned business even once. If you want to trade war stories it's going to have to wait for another time."

He gives me a sour look and picks up his glass, peering into it as he swirls the ice around. He'd always hated me, and I knew that his presence here pleased him no more than it did me.

"You don't make it easy to be your friend," he says.

"I didn't know we were friends."

The muscles in his jaw clench.

"You're wasting my time, Patrick. I know you're just the muscle, so maybe you don't understand this, but the work I do in the back room takes up a lot of energy. So sleep is valuable to me. You've sat on my couch and drunk my whiskey and burned away almost half an hour beating around the bush. I don't know how much more of this I can take."

He looks at me. He has his work face on now, the one a lot of guys see just before the lights go out. That's good; I want him in work mode. It makes him focus. The trick now, though, is to keep him on the shy side of violence. You have to play these guys like marionettes. I got pretty good at it back in the day.

"You want to watch that," he says. "You want to watch that attitude."

I put my hands out, palms forward. "Hey," I say.

"I come to you in friendship. I come to you in respect."

This is bullshit, but whatever. It's time to settle him down. These guys are such fragile little flowers. "Hey. I'm sorry. Really. I haven't been sleeping much. I'm tired, and it makes me stupid."

"That's a bad trait. So wake up and listen to me. I told you that story for two reasons. One, to stop you from saying dumb shit like you just did. Make you remember who you're dealing with. I can see it didn't work. I can see maybe I was being too subtle."

"Patrick, really. I—"

"If you interrupt me again I will break your right hand. The second reason I told you that story is to let you know that I've seen some crazy things in my life, so when I tell you this new thing scares the shit out of me, maybe you'll listen to what the fuck I'm saying."

He stops there, staring hard at me. After a couple seconds of this, I figure it's okay to talk.

"You have my full attention. This is from Eugene?"

"You know this is from Eugene. Why else would I drag myself over here?"

"Patrick, I wish you'd relax. I'm sorry I made you mad. You want another drink? Let me pour you another drink."

I can see the rage still coiling in his eyes, and I'm starting to think I pushed him too hard. I'm starting to wonder how fast I can run. But then he settles back onto the couch and a smile settles over his face. It doesn't look natural there. "Jesus, you have a mouth. How does a guy like you get away with having a mouth like that?" He shakes the ice in his glass. "Yeah, go ahead. Pour me another one. Let's smoke a peace pipe."

I pour us both some more. He slugs it back in one deep swallow and holds his glass out for more. I give it to him. He seems to be relaxing.

"All right, okay. There's this guy. Creepy little grifter named Tobias George. He's one of those little vermin always crawling through the city, getting into shit, fucking up his own life, you don't even notice these guys. You know how it is."

"I do." I also know the name, but I don't tell him that.

"Only reason we know about him at all is because sometimes he'll run a little scheme of his own, kick a percentage back to Eugene, it's all good. Well one day this prick catches a case of ambition. He robs one of Eugene's poker games, makes off with a lot of money. Suicidal. Who knows what got into the guy. Some big dream climbed up his butt and opened him like an umbrella. We go hunting for him but he disappears. We get word he went further south, disappeared into the bayou. Like, not to Port Fourchon or some shit, but literally on a goddamn boat into the swamp. Eugene is pissed, and you know how he is, he jumps and shouts for a few days, but eventually he says fuck it. We're not gonna go wrestle alligators for him. After a while we just figured he died out there. You know."

"But he didn't."

"That he did not. We catch wind of him a few months later. He's in a whole new ballgame. He's selling artifacts pulled from Hell. And he's making a lot of money doing it."

"It's another scam," I say, knowing full well it isn't.

"It's not."

"How do you know?"

"Don't worry about it. We know."

"A guy owes money and won't pay. That sounds more like your thing than mine, Patrick."

"Yeah, don't worry about that either. I got it covered when the time comes. I won't go into the details, 'cause they don't matter, but what it comes down to is Eugene wants his own way into the game. Once this punk is put in the ground, he wants to keep this market alive. We happen to know Tobias has a book that he uses for this set-up. An atlas that tells him how to access this shit. We want it, and we want to know how it works. And that's *your* thing, Jack."

I feel something cold spill through my guts. "That's not the deal we had."

"What can I tell you."

"No. I told . . ." My throat is dry. My leg is bouncing again. "Eugene told me we were through. He told me that. He's breaking his promise."

"That mouth again." Patrick finishes his drink and stands. "Come on. You can tell him that yourself, see how it goes over."

"Now? It's the middle of the night!"

"Don't worry, you won't be disturbing him. He don't sleep too well lately either."

I've lived here my whole life. Grew up just a regular fat-white-kid schlub, decent parents, a ready-made path to the gray fields of middle-class servitude. But I went off the rails at some point. I was seduced by old books. I wanted to live out my life in a fog of parchment dust and old glue. I apprenticed myself to a bookbinder, a gnarled old Cajun named Rene Aucoin, who turned out to be a fading necromancer with a nice side business refurbishing old grimoires. He found in me an eager student, which eventually led to my tenure as a librarian at the Camouflaged Library at the Ursulines Academy. It was when Eugene and his crew got involved, leading to a bloody confrontation with a death cult obsessed with the Damocles Scroll, that I left the Academy and began my career as a book thief. I worked for Eugene for five years before we had our falling out. When I left, we both knew it was for good.

Eugene has a bar up in Midcity, far away from the t-shirt shops, the fetish dens and goth hangouts of the French Quarter, far away too from the more respectable veneer of the Central Business and the Garden Districts. Midcity is a place where you can do what you want. Patrick drives me up Canal and parks out front. He leads me up the stairs and inside, where the blast of cold air is a relief from a heat which does not relent even at night. A jukebox is playing something stale, and four or five ghostlike figures nest at the bar. They do not turn around as we pass through. Patrick guides me downstairs, to Eugene's office.

Before I even reach the bottom of the stairs, Eugene starts talking to me.

"Hey fat boy! Here comes the fat boy!"

No cover model himself, he comes around his desk with his arms outstretched, what's left of his gray hair combed in long, spindly fingers over the expanse of his scalp. Drink has made a red, doughy wreckage of his face. His chest is sunken in, like something inside has collapsed and he's falling inward. He puts his hands on me in greeting, and I try not to flinch.

"Look at you. Look at you. You look good, Jack."

"So do you, Eugene."

The office is clean, uncluttered. There's a desk and a few padded chairs, a couch on the far wall underneath a huge Michalopoulos painting. Across from the desk is a minibar and a door which leads to the back alley. Mardi

Gras masks are arranged behind his desk like a congress of spirits. Eugene is a New Orleans boy right down to his tapping toes, and he buys into every shabby lie the city ever told about itself.

"I hear you got a girl now. What's her name, Locky? Lick-me?"

"Lakshmi." This is already going badly. "Come on, Eugene. Let's not go there."

"Listen to him now. Calling the shots. All independent, all grown up now. Patrick give you any trouble? Sometimes he gets carried away."

Patrick doesn't blink. His role fulfilled, he's become a tree.

"No. No trouble at all. It was like old times."

"Hopefully not too much like old times, huh?" He sits behind his desk, gestures for me to take a seat. Patrick pours a couple of drinks and hands one to each of us, then retreats behind me.

"I guess I'm just trying to figure out what I'm doing here, Eugene. Someone's not paying you. Isn't that what you have guys like him for?"

Eugene settles back, sips from his drink, and studies me. "Let's not play coy, Jack. Okay? Don't pretend you don't already know about Tobias. Don't insult my intelligence."

"I know about Tobias," I say.

"Tell me what you know."

I can't get comfortable in my chair. I feel like there are chains around my chest. I make one last effort. "Eugene. We had a deal."

"Are you having trouble hearing me? Should I raise my voice?"

"He started selling two months ago. He had a rock. It was about the size of a tennis ball but it was heavy as a television set. Everybody thought he was full of shit. They were laughing at him. It sold for a little bit of money. Not much. But somebody out there liked what they saw. Word got around. He sold a two-inch piece of charred bone next. That went for a lot more."

"I bought that bone."

"Oh," I say. "Shit."

"Do you know why?"

"No, Eugene, of course I don't."

"Don't 'of course' me. I don't know what you know and what you don't. You're a slimy piece of filth, Jack. You're a human cockroach. I can't trust you. So don't get smart."

"I'm sorry. I didn't mean it like that."

"He had the nerve to contact me directly. He wanted me to know what he was offering before he put it on the market. Give me first chance. Jack, it's from my son. It's part of a thigh bone from my son."

I can't seem to see straight. The blood has rushed to my head, and I feel dizzy. I clamp my hands on the armrests of the chair so I can feel something solid. "How . . . how do you know?"

"There's people for that. Don't ask dumb questions. I am very much not in the mood for dumb questions."

"Okay."

"Your thing is books, so that's why you're here. We tracked him to this old shack in the bayou. You're going to get the book."

I feel panic skitter through me. "You want me to go there?"

"Patrick's going with you."

"That's not what I do, Eugene!"

"Bullshit! You're a thief. You do this all the time. Patrick there can barely read a *People* magazine without breaking a sweat. You're going."

"Just have Patrick bring it back! You don't need me for this."

Eugene stares at me.

"Come on," I say. "You gave me your word."

I don't even see Patrick coming. His hand is on the back of my neck and he slams my face onto the desk hard enough to crack an ashtray underneath my cheekbone. My glass falls out of my hand and I hear the ice thump onto the carpet. He keeps me pinned to the desk. He wraps his free hand around my throat. I can't catch my breath.

Eugene leans in, his hands behind his back, like he's examining something curious and mildly revolting. "Would you like to see him? Would you like to see my son?"

I pat Patrick's hand; it's weirdly intimate. I shake my head. I try to make words. My vision is starting to fry around the edges. Dark loops spool into the world.

Finally, Eugene says, "Let him go."

Patrick releases me. I slide off the desk and land hard, dragging the broken ashtray with me, covering myself in ash and spent cigarette butts. I roll onto my side, choking.

Eugene puts his hand on my shoulder. "Hey, Jack, you okay? You all right down there? Get up. Goddamn you're a drama queen. Get the fuck up already."

It takes a few minutes. When I'm sitting up again, Patrick hands me a napkin to clean the blood off my face. I don't look at him. There's nothing I can do. No point in feeling a goddamn thing about it.

"When do I leave?" I say.

"What the hell," Eugene says. "How about right now?"

))) ● (((

We experience dawn as a rising heat and a slow bleed of light through the cypress and the Spanish moss, riding in an airboat through the swamp a good thirty miles south of New Orleans. Patrick and I are riding up front while an old man more leather than flesh guides us along some unseeable path. Our progress stirs movement from the local fauna—snakes, turtles, muskrats—and I'm constantly jumping at some heavy splash. I imagine a score of alligators gliding through the water beneath us, tracking our movement with yellow, saurian eyes. The airboat wheels around a copse of trees into a watery clearing, and I half expect to see a brontosaurus wading in the shallows.

Instead I see a row of huge, bobbing purple flowers, each with a bleached human face in the center, mouths gaping and eyes palely blind. The sight of them shocks me into silence; our guide fixes his stare on the horizon, refusing even to acknowledge anything out of the ordinary. Eyes perch along the tops of reeds; great kites of flesh stretch between tree limbs; one catches a mild breeze from our passage and skates serenely through the air, coming at last to a gentle landing on the water, where it folds in on itself and sinks into the murk.

Our guide points, and I see a shack: a small, single-room architectural catastrophe, perched on the dubious shore and extending over the water on short stilts. A skiff is tied to a front porch which doubles as a small dock. It seems to be the only method of travel to or from the place. A filthy Rebel flag hangs over the entrance in lieu of a door. At the moment, it's pulled to the side and a man I assume is Tobias George is standing there, naked but for a pair of shorts that hang precariously from his narrow hips. He's all bone and gristle. His face tells me nothing as we glide in toward the dock.

Patrick stands before we connect, despite a word of caution from our guide. He has some tough-guy greeting halfway out of his mouth when the airboat's edge lightly taps the dock, nearly spilling him into the swamp, arms pinwheeling.

Tobias is unaffected by the display, but our guide is easy with a laugh and chooses not to hold back.

Patrick recovers himself and puts both hands on the dock, proceeding to crawl out of the boat like a child learning to walk. I'm grateful to God for the sight of it.

Tobias makes no move to help.

I take my time climbing out. "You wait right here," I tell the guide.

"Oh, *wye*," he says, shutting down the engine and fishing a pack of smokes from his shirt.

"What're you guys doing here?" Tobias says. He hasn't looked at me once but he can't peel his gaze from Patrick. He knows what Patrick's all about.

"Tobias, you crazy bastard. What the hell do you think you're doing?"

Tobias turns around and goes back inside, the Rebel flag falling closed behind him. "Come on in I guess."

We follow him inside, where it's even hotter. The air doesn't move in here, probably hasn't moved in twenty years, and it carries the sharp tang of marijuana. Dust motes hang suspended in spears of light, coming in through a window covered over in ratty, bug-smeared plastic. The room is barely furnished: there's a single mattress pushed against the wall to our left, a cheap collapsible table with a plastic folding chair, and a chest of drawers. Next to the bed is a camping cooker with a little sauce pot and some cans of Sterno. On the table is a small pile of dull green buds, with some rolling papers and a Zippo.

There's a door flush against the back wall. I take a few steps in the direction and I can tell right away that there's some bad news behind it. The air spoils when I get close, coating the back of my throat with a greasy, evil film that feels like it seeps right into the meat. Violent fantasies sprout along my cortex like a little vine of tumors. I try to keep my face still, as I imagine coring the eyeballs out of both these guys with a grapefruit spoon.

"Stay on that side of the room, Patrick," I say. I don't need him feeling this.

"What? Why?"

"Trust me. This is why you brought me."

Tobias casts a glance at me now, finally sensing some purpose behind my presence. He's good, though: I still can't figure his reaction.

"Y'all here to kill me?" he says.

Patrick already has his gun in hand. It's pointed at the floor. His eyes are fixed on Tobias and he seems to be weighing something in his mind. I can tell that whatever is behind that door is already working its influence on him. It has its grubby little fingers in his brain and it's pulling dark things out of it. "That depends on you," he says. "Eugene wants to talk to you."

"Yeah, that's not going to happen."

The violence in this room is alive and crawling. I realize, suddenly, why he stays stoned. I figure it's time we get to the point. "We want the book, Tobias."

"What? Who are you?" He looks at Patrick. "What's he talking about?"

"You know what he's talking about. Go get the book."

"There is no book!"

He looks genuinely bewildered, and that worries me. I don't know if I can go back to Eugene without a book. I'm about to ask him what's in the back room when I hear a creak in the wood beyond the hanging flag and someone pulls it aside, flooding the shack with light. I spin around and Patrick already has his gun raised, looking spooked.

The man standing in the doorway is framed by the sun: a black shape against the brightness, a negative space. He's tall and slender, his hair like a spray of light around his head. I think for a moment that I can smell it burning. He steps into the shack and you can tell there's something wrong with him, though it's hard to figure just what. Some malformation of the aura, telegraphing a warning blast straight to the root of my brain. To look at him, as he steps into the shack and trades direct sunlight for the filtered illumination shared by the rest of us, he seems tired and gaunt but ultimately not unlike any other poverty-wracked country boy, and yet my skin ripples at his approach. I feel my lip curl and I have to concentrate to keep the revulsion from my face.

"Toby?" he says. His voice is young and uninflected. Normal. "I think my brother's on his way back. Who are these guys?"

"Hey, Johnny," Tobias says, looking at him over my shoulder. He's plainly nervous now, and although his focus stays on Johnny, his attention seems to radiate in all directions, like a man wondering where the next hit is coming from.

I could have told him that.

Fear turns to meanness in a guy like Patrick, and he reacts according to the dictates of his kind: he shoots.

It's one shot, quick and clean. Patrick is a professional. The sound of the gun concusses the air in the little shack and the bullet passes through Johnny's skull before I even have time to wince at the noise.

I blink. I can't hear anything beyond a high-pitched whine. I see Patrick standing still, looking down the length of his raised arm with a flat, dead expression. It's his true face. I see Tobias drop to one knee, his hands over his ears and his mouth working as though he's shouting something; and I see Johnny, too, still standing in the doorway, as unmoved by the bullet's passage through his skull as though it had been nothing more than a disappointing argument. Dark clots of brain meat are splashed across the flag behind him.

He looks from Patrick to Tobias and when he speaks I can barely hear him above the ringing in my head. "What should I do?" he says.

I step forward and gently push Patrick's arm down.

"Are you shitting me?" he says, staring at Johnny.

"Patrick," I say.

"Am I fucking cursed? Is that it? I shot you in the face!"

The bullet-hole is a dime-sized wound in Johnny's right cheekbone. It leaks a single thread of blood. "Asshole," he says.

Tobias gets back to his feet, his arms stretched out to either side like he's trying to separate two imaginary boxers. "Will you just relax? Jesus Christ!" He guides Johnny to the little bed and sits him down, where he brushes the blond hair out of his face and inspects the bullet hole. Then he cranes his head around to examine the damage of the exit wound. "Goddamn it!" he says.

Johnny puts his own hand back there. "Oh man," he says.

I take a look. The whole back of his head is gone; now it's just a red bowl of spilled gore. What look like little blowing cinders are embedded in the mess, sending up coils of smoke. Most of Johnny's brains are splashed across the wall behind him.

"Patrick," I say. "Just be cool."

He's still in a fog. You can see him trying to arrange things in his head. "I need to kill them, Jack. I need to. I never felt it like this before. What's happening here?"

Tobias pipes up. "I had a job for this guy all lined up at The Fry Pit! Now what!"

"Tobias, I need you to shut up," I say, keeping my eyes on Patrick. "Patrick, are you hearing me?" It's taking a huge effort to maintain my own composure. I have an image of wresting the gun from his hand and hitting him with it until his skull breaks. Only the absolute impossibility of it keeps me from trying.

My question causes the shutters to close in his eyes. Whatever tatter of human impulse stirred him to try to explain himself to me, to grope for reason amidst the bloody carnage boiling in his head, is subsumed again in a dull professional menace. "Don't talk to me like that. I'm not a goddamn kid."

I turn to the others. The bed is now awash in blood. Tobias is working earnestly to mitigate the damage back there, but I can't imagine what it is he thinks he can do. Brain matter is gathered in a clump behind them; he seems to be scooping everything out. Johnny sits there forlornly, shoulders slumped. "I thought it would be better out here," he said. "Shit never ends."

"The atlas," I say.

"Fuck yourself," Tobias says.

I stride toward the closed door. If there's anything I need to know before I open it, I guess I'll just find out the hard way. A hot pulse of emotion blasts out at me as I touch the handle: fear, rage, a lust for carnage. It's overriding any sense of self-preservation I might have had. I wonder if a fire will pour through the door when it's opened, a furnace exhalation, and engulf us all. I find myself hoping for it.

Tobias shouts at me: "Don't!"

I pull it open.

A charred skull, oily smoke coiling from its fissures, is propped on a stool in an otherwise bare room no bigger than a closet. Black mold has grown over the stool, and is creeping up the walls. A live current jolts my brain. Time dislocates, jumping seconds like an old record, and the world moves in jerky, stop-motion lurches. A language is seeping from the skull—a viscous, cracked sound like breaking bones and molten rock. My eyes sting and I squeeze them shut. The skin on my face blisters.

"*Shut it! Shut the door!*"

Tobias is screaming, but whatever he's saying has no relation to me. It's as though I'm watching a play. Blood is leaking from his eyes. Patrick is grinning widely, his own eyes like bloody headlamps. He's violently twisting his right ear, working it like an apple stem. Johnny is sitting quietly, holding his gathered brains in his hands, rocking back and forth like an unhappy child. My upper arms are hurting, and it takes me a minute to realize that I'm gouging them with my own fingernails. I can't make myself stop.

Outside a sound rolls across the swamp like a foghorn: a deep, answering bellow to the language of Hell spilling from the closet.

Tobias lunges past me and slams the door shut, immediately muffling the skull's effect. I stagger toward the chair but fall down hard before I make it, banging my shoulder against the table and knocking Tobias's drug paraphernalia all over the floor. Patrick makes a sound, half gasp and half sob, and leans back against the wall, cradling his savaged ear. The left side of his face is painted in blood. He's digging the heel of his hand into his right eye, like he's trying to rub something out of it.

"What the fuck was that!"

I think it's me who says that. Right now I can't be sure.

"That's your goddamn 'atlas,' you prick," Tobias says. He comes over to where I am and drops to the floor, scooping up the scattered buds and some papers. He begins to assemble a joint; his hands are shaking badly, so this takes some doing.

"A skull? The book is a skull?"

"No. It's a tongue inside the skull. Technically."

"What the Christ?"

"Just shut up a minute." He finishes the joint, lights it, and takes a long, deep pull. He passes it over to me.

For one surreal moment I feel like we're college buddies sitting in a dorm. It's like there's not a scorched, muttering skull in the next room, corroding the air around it. It's like there's not a man with a blown-out skull moping quietly on the bed. I start to laugh, and I haven't even had a toke.

He exhales explosively, the sweet smoke filling the air between us. "Take it, man. I'm serious. Trust me."

So I do. Almost immediately I feel an easing of the pressure in the room. The crackle of violent impulse, which I had ceased to even recognize, abated to a low thrum. My internal gauge ticked back down to highly frightened, which, in comparison to a moment before, felt like a monastic peace.

I gesture for Patrick to do the same.

"No. I don't pollute my body with that shit." He's touching his ear gingerly, trying to assess the damage.

"Patrick, last night you single-handedly killed half a bottle of ninety-proof bourbon. Let's have some perspective here."

He snatches it from me and drags hard on it, coughing it all back out so violently I think he might throw up.

Johnny laughs from his position on the bed. It's the first bright note he's sounded since his head came apart. "Amateur!"

I notice that Johnny's head seems to be changing shape. The shattered bone around the exit wound has smoothed over and extended upward an inch or so, like something growing. A tiny twig of bone has likewise extended from the bullet wound beneath his eye.

"We need to get out of here," I say. "That thing is pretty much a live feed to Hell. We can't handle it. It's time to go."

"We're taking it with us," Patrick says.

"No. No we're not."

"Not up for debate, Jack."

"I'm not riding with that thing. If you take it you're going back alone."

Patrick nods and takes another pull from the joint, handling it much better this time. He passes it back to me. "Okay, but you gotta know that I'm leaving this place empty. You understand me, right?"

I don't, at first. It takes me a second. "You can't be serious. You're going to kill me?"

"Make up your mind."

For the first time since his arrival at my shop last night, I feel genuine despair. Everything to this point has had some precedence in my life. Even this brush with Hell isn't my first, though it's the most direct so far. But I've never seen my own death staring back at me quite so frankly. I always thought I'd confront this moment with a little poise, or at least a kind of stoic resignation. But I'm angry, and I'm afraid, and I feel tears gathering in my eyes.

"Goddamn it, Patrick. That doesn't make any sense."

"Look, Jack. I like you. You're weak and you're a coward, but you can't help those things. I would rather you come with me. We take this skull back to Eugene, like he wanted. We deliver Tobias to his just reward. You go back to your little bookstore and all is right with the world. But I can't leave this place with anybody in it."

Tobias doesn't seem to be paying attention. He's leaning back against the bed, a new joint rolled up and kept all to himself. I can't tell if he's resigned to his own death or if he's so far away he doesn't even know it's being discussed.

I can't think of anything to say. Maybe there isn't anything more to be said. Maybe language is over. Maybe everything is, at last, emptied out. I still feel the skull's muted influence crawling through my brain. It craves the bullet. I anticipate the explosion of the gun with a terrible relish. I wonder, idly, if I'll hold onto myself long enough to feel myself flying.

The bellow from the swamp sounds again. It's huge and deep, like the ululating call of a mountain. It just keeps on going.

Johnny smiles. "Brother's home," he says.

Patrick looks toward the flag-covered doorway. "What?"

Tobias holds his hand aloft, finger extended, announcing his intention to orate. His eyelids are heavy. The joint he'd made for himself is spent. "There's a hell monster. Did I forget to tell you?"

I start to laugh. I can't stop myself. It doesn't feel good.

Johnny smiles at me, mistaking my laughter for something else. "It appeared the same time I did. Toby calls it my brother." He sounds wistful.

Patrick uses the gun barrel to open the flag a few inches. He peers outside for a few moments, then lets it fall closed again. He looks at me. "We're stuck. The boat's gone."

"What? He left us?"

"Well . . . it's mostly gone."

I take a look for myself.

The airboat is a listing heap of bent scrap metal, the cage around its huge propeller a tangled bird's nest. Our guide's arm, still connected to a hunk of his torso, rests on the deck in a black puddle. The thing that did this is swimming in a lazy arc some distance away, trackable by the rolling surge of water it creates as it trawls along. Judging by the size of its wake, it's at least as big as a city bus. It breaches the surface once, exposing a mottled gray hide and an anemone-like thistle of eye stalks lifting skyward. The thing barrel-rolls until a deep black fissure emerges, and from this suppurated tear comes that stone-cracking bellow, the language of deep earth that curdles something inside me, springs tears to my eyes, brings me hard to my knees.

I scramble weakly away from the door. Patrick is watching me with a sad, desperate hope, his intent to murder momentarily forgotten, as though by some trick known only to me this thing might be banished back to its home, as though I might fix this scar that Tobias George, that mewling, incompetent little thief, has cut into the world.

I cannot fix this. There is no fixing this.

Behind us both, locked in its little room, the skull cooks the air.

It's the language that hurts. The awful speech. While that thing languishes in the waters out front, we're trapped inside. It seems to stay quiet unless it's provoked by some outrage to its senses: an appearance by one of us, or—we believe, since none of us heard the attack on the airboat and our guide—the effects of the skull in the room. As long as we're quiet and hidden, we seem to be safe.

"Why would you do that to a man?" Patrick says. We're all sitting in a little huddled circle, passing the joint around. We might have been friends, to someone who didn't know us. "Why would you send him a piece of his own dead son?"

"Are you serious? No one deserves it more than Eugene. He humiliated me. He made me feel small. All those years sending him a cut from money I earned, or doing errands for him, or tipping him off when I hear shit

I think he should know. Never a 'thank you.' Never a 'good job.' Just grief. Just mockery. And his son was even worse. He would lay hands on me. Slap the back of my head. Slap my face, even. What am I going to do, challenge Eugene's son? So I became everybody's bitch. The laughing stock."

Patrick shakes his head. "You didn't, though. Truth is we barely ever thought about you. I didn't even know your name until you knocked over that poker game. Eugene had to remind me."

This is hard for Tobias to hear. He stares hard at the floor, the muscles in his jaw working. He looks at me. "See what I mean? Nothing. You just have to take it from these guys, you know? Just take it and take it and take it. It was one of the happiest days of my life when that kid finally got wasted."

He goes on. We have nothing but time. He robbed the poker game in a fit of deranged anger and then fled south, hoping to disappear into the bayou. The reality of what he'd just done was starting to sink in. He's of the vermin class in criminal society, and vermin come in multitudes. One of his vermin friends told him about this shack where his old granddaddy used to live. He gets a boat and comes out here, only to find a surprise waiting for him.

"The skull was in a black, iron box," he says, "sitting on its side in the corner. There's a hole in the bottom of the box, like the whole thing was meant to fit around someone's head. It had a big gouge in the side of it, like someone had chopped it with something. I don't know what cuts through metal like that though. And inside, this skull . . . talking."

"It's one of the astronauts," Johnny says.

I rub my fingers in my eyes. "Astronauts? What?"

Johnny leans in, grateful for his moment. He tells us that there are occasionally men and women who wander through Hell in thin processions, wearing heavy gray robes and bearing lanterns to light their way. They are invariably chained together, and led through the burning canyons by a loping demon: some malformed, tooth-spangled pinwheel of limbs and claws. They tour safely because they are shuttered against the sights and sounds of Hell by the iron boxes around their heads, which gives them the appearance of strange, prison-skulled astronauts on a pilgrimage through fire.

"I recognized the box," Johnny says. "This is one of those guys. The box was broken, so I guess something bad happened to him."

"Where is it?"

Tobias shrugs. "I threw it out in the bayou. What do I need a broken box for? I started asking for things, and it sent them. The rock, the shard of bone."

"Hold on. How did you know to ask it for things? You're leaving something out."

Tobias and Johnny exchange a look. The burning embers in the back of Johnny's head seem to have gathered more life: little tongues of flame spit into the air from time to time, as though a small fire has kindled. The extending bone around his head has grown further, opening out as though a careful hand has begun to fashion a wide, smooth bowl. The bone growing from his face has grown little offshoots, like a delicate branch.

Patrick picks up on their glance, and retrieves his gun from the floor, holding it casually in his lap.

"Everything that's brought here has a courier," Tobias says. "That's how Johnny got here. He brought the bone. And there was one already here when I found the skull. It told me."

"It?"

"Well . . . it was a person at first. Then it changed. They change over time. Evolve."

Patrick gets it before I do. "The thing in the water."

"Holy Christ. You mean Johnny's going to turn into something like *that*?" I look again at the fiery bowl his head is turning into.

"No no no!" Tobias holds out his hands, as if he could ward off the very idea of it. "I mean, I don't know. I'm pretty sure that's only because the other one never went away. I think it's the proximity of the skull that does it. There was one other courier, the girl who brought me the rock. I sent her away."

"Jesus. Where?"

"Just . . ." He waves, vaguely. "Away. Into the bayou."

"You're a real sweetheart, Tobias."

"Well come on, I didn't know what to do! She was just—there! I didn't know anybody was going to be coming with it! I freaked out and told her to get out! But the important thing is I never saw any sign that she changed into anything. I haven't seen or heard anything from her since. You notice how the plants get weird as you get close to this place? It's gotta be the skull's influence."

"That's not exactly airtight logic, Tobias," I say. "What if it's not just from the skull? What if it comes from them too? I could tell something was fucked up about Johnny as soon as I saw him."

"Well I'm taking the fucking chance! If there are going to be people coming out, they need to have a chance at a better life. That's why I got Johnny here a job. He'll be far away from that skull, so maybe he won't change into anything." He looks at his friend and at the lively fire that's crackling inside his head. "Well, he wouldn't have if you guys hadn't fucked it all up. I've got this all worked out. I'm going to find them jobs in little places, in little towns. I got money now, so I can afford to get them set up. Buy them some clothes, rent them out a place until they can start earning some money of their own. A second chance, you know? They deserve a second chance."

He's getting all worked up again, like he's going to break down into tears, and I'm struck with a revelation: Tobias is using this skull as a chance to redeem himself. He's going to funnel people out of Hell and back into the world of sunlight and cheeseburgers.

Tobias George may be the only good man in a fifty-mile radius. Too bad it's the most doomed idea I've ever heard in a life rich with them. But there are several possibilities for salvaging this situation. One thing is clear: Eugene cannot have the atlas. The level of catastrophe he might cause is incalculable. I need to get it back to my bookstore and to the back room. There are books there that will provide protections; at least I hope so.

All I need is something to carry it in.

I know just where to get it.

"Patrick. You still want to bring this thing to Eugene?"

"He's the boss. You change your mind about coming?"

"I think so, yeah. Tobias, we're going into the room."

He goes in gratefully. I think he feels in control in this room in way that he doesn't out there with Patrick. It's almost funny.

The skull sits on the moss-blackened stool, greasy smoke seeping from its fissures and polluting the air. The broken language of Hell is a physical pressure. A blood vessel ruptures in my right eye and my vision goes cloudy and pink. Time fractures again. Tobias moves next to me, approaching the skull, but I can't tell what it's doing to him: he skips in time like I'm watching him through strobe lights, even though the light in here remains a constant, sizzling glare. I try not to vomit. Things are moving around in my brain like maggots in old meat.

The air seems to bend into the skull. I see it on the stool, blackening the world around it, and I try to imagine who it once belonged to: the chained Black Iron Monk, shielded by a metal box from the burning horrors of the world he moved through. Until something came along and opened the box like a tin can, and Hell poured inside.

Who was it? What order would undertake such a pilgrimage? And to what end?

Tobias is saying something to me. I have to study him to figure out what.

The poor scrawny bastard is blistering all over his body. His lips peel back from his bloody teeth.

"Tell it what you want," he says.

So I do.

The boy is streaked with mud and gore. He is twelve, maybe thirteen. Steam rises from his body like wind-struck flags. I don't know where he appears from, or how; he's just there, two iron boxes dangling like huge lanterns from a chain in his hand. I wonder, briefly, what a child his age had done to be consigned to Hell. But then, it doesn't really matter.

I open one of the boxes and tell the boy to put the skull inside. He does. The skin bubbles on his hands where he touches it, but he makes no sign of pain.

I close the door on it, and it's like a light going out. Time slips back into it groove. The light recedes to a natural level. My skin stops burning, the desire to commit violence dissipates like smoke. I can feel where I've been scratching my own arms again. My eye is gummed shut with blood.

When we stumble back into the main room, Patrick is on his feet with the gun in his hand. Johnny is sitting on the bed, the bony rim of his open skull grown further upward, elongating his head and giving him an alien grace. The fire in the bowl of his head burns briskly, crackling and shedding a warm light. Patrick looks at me, then at the boy with the iron boxes. "You got them," he says. "Where's the skull?"

I take the chain from the boy. The boxes are heavy together; the boy must be stronger than he looks. Something to remember. "In one of these. If it can keep that shit out, I'm betting it can keep it locked in, too. I think it's safe to move."

"And those'll get us past the thing outside?"

"If what Johnny said is true."

"It is," Johnny says. "But now there's only one extra box."

"That's right," I say, and swing them with every vestige of my failing strength at Patrick's head, where they land with a wet crunch.

He staggers to his right a few steps, the left side of his face broken like crockery, and he puts a hand into the rancid scramble of his own brain. "I'll go get it," he says, "I'll go."

"You're dead," I tell him gently. "You stupid bastard."

He accepts this gracefully and collapses to his knees, and then onto his face. Dark blood pours from his head as though from a spilled glass. I scoop up the gun, which feels clumsy in my hand. I never got the hang of guns.

Tobias stands in shock. "I can't believe you did that," he says.

"Shut up. Are there any clothes in that dresser? Put something on the kid. We're going back to the city." While he's doing that, I look at Johnny. "I'm not going to be able to see. Will you be able to guide me out?"

"Yes."

"Good," I say, and shoot Tobias in the back of the head.

For once, somebody dies without an argument.

I don't know much about the trip back. I open a slot on the base of the box and fit it over my head. I am consumed in darkness. I'm led out to the skiff by Johnny and the boy. The boy rides with me, and Johnny gets into the water, dragging us behind him. Fire unfurls from his head, the sides of which are developing baroque flourishes. His personality is diminished, and I can't tell if it's because he mourns Tobias, or because that is changing too, developing into something cold and barren.

The journey takes several hours. I know we pass the corpse flowers, the staring eyes and bloodless faces pressing from the foliage. I am sure that the creature unleashes its earth-breaking cry, and that any living thing that hears it hemorrhages its life away, into the still waters. I know that night falls. I know the flame of our new guide lights the undersides of the cypress, runs out before us across the water, fills the dark like the final lantern in a fallen world.

I make a quiet and steady passage there.

Eugene is in his office. The bar is closed upstairs and the man at the door lets us in without a word. He makes no comment about my companions, or the iron boxes hanging from a chain. The world he lives in is already breaking from its old shape. The new one has space for wonders.

Eugene is sitting behind his desk in the dark. I can tell he's drunk. It smells like he's been here since we left, almost twenty-four hours ago now. The only light comes from the fire rising from Johnny's empty skull. It illuminates a pale structure on Eugene's desk: a huge antler, or a tree made of bone. There are human teeth protruding along some of its tines, and a long crack near the wider base of it reveals a raw, red meat, where a mouth opens and closes.

"Where's Patrick?" he says.

"Dead," I say. "Tobias, too."

"And the atlas?"

"I burned it."

He nods, as though he'd been expecting that very thing. After a moment he gestures at the bone tree. "This is my son," he says. "Say hi, Max."

The mouth shrieks. It stops to draw in a gasping breath, then repeats the sound. The cry is sustained for several seconds before stuttering into a sob, and then going silent again.

"He keeps growing. He's going to be a big boy before it's all over."

"Yeah. I can see that."

"Who're your friends, Jack?"

I have to think about that before I answer. "I really don't know," I say, finally.

"So what do you want? You want me to tell you you're off the hook? You want me to tell you you're free to go?"

"You told me that before. It turned out to be bullshit."

"Yeah, well. That's the world we live in, right?"

"You're on notice, Eugene. Leave me alone. Don't come to my door anymore. I'm sorry things didn't work out here. I'm sorry about your son. But you have to stay away. I'm only going to say it once."

He smiles at me. He must have to summon it from far away, but he smiles at me. "I'll take that under advisement, Jack. Now get the fuck out of here."

We turn and walk back up the stairs. It's a long walk back to my bookstore, where I'm anxious to get to work on the atlas. But I have a light to guide me, and I know this place well.

THE WITCH MOTH

BRUCE MCALLISTER

The Black Witch moth can grow up to 16 cm. and is known as "La Mariposa de la Muerte."
—*Encyclopedia Americana*

The Black Witch moth should be seen at night when it cannot be seen because it is so black. In the daylight it is a hole in the universe, one that leads to a world where there is no light.

The first Black Witch moth I ever saw was in the sunlight of Balboa Park, when I went there for a dahlia show to keep my grandmother company—which I did often when I was ten because my grandmother's love kept me from darkness in my family, where my mother's spells could reach us all.

The moth flew from a hydrangea bush I had rustled with my hand, hoping something might burst from it—a lizard or butterfly perhaps. At first I didn't understand what the darkness was. A small rubber bat on the end of a child's string? A black handkerchief given life by a spell? Or was it just my eyes playing tricks on me, blinded by the sunlight that made the flowers so bright?

It limped through the air and disappeared into the hole it had made in the universe. My grandmother had stopped because I had. "Are you all right?" she asked.

"I don't know," I answered. I often said such things to her, but she didn't mind. She knew that all light carried shadow and that there were things in the world—and in every family—you couldn't see even if you had the entire sun to see them by.

"You saw something," she said, as if she knew exactly what it was and where everything was going to end.

"Yes."

"I'm sure you did, but if it's important you will see it again; and if not like this, then later, when you need it even more. Let's go look at the dahlias now. We can come back here later if you want, if you haven't seen it somewhere else in the park by then."

I nodded. She was right. I would find it again if I needed to, and if not today, then sometime, in some way.

Some people who love see only the light. My grandmother saw the darkness, too, and still loved. That made me feel safe in a world where, she'd once told me, "There are more witches than even the witches know. . . ."

Because we lived on a Navy base, one that hugged the bayside of the peninsula, I took my little brother, who was six, with me when I went to the tallest piers, to their oily pilings and oily planks, which you could smell. He felt safer when we went to the floating docks, because the water was close to you. You didn't have far to fall. But the boats there were small—patrol boats, skiffs, and a sailboat or two for the personal use of officers. We both liked the great steel ships—which could only dock at the tallest piers—and if I promised we would stay in the middle when we walked on them, Tommy could come with me. I held his hand so tight it hurt him sometimes, but I did it because I was scared for him. I didn't want him running to the edge of the pier and falling to the water far below, which sometimes happened when I dreamed. I wouldn't be holding his hand tight enough in the dream. He'd pull away and, screaming, run to the edge and not stop running. He'd go over, and the screaming would stop only when he hit the water. It was as if this was what someone wanted (and I knew who). To drown him. To make him go away. To make *us all* go away.

Even when we walked down the very middle of the pier, he could look down and see the green, oily water far below through the narrow cracks between the planks. I'd tell him not to look, but sometimes he would, and it would stop him. He'd sit down on the planks, oily as they were, and he wouldn't move no matter how hard I pulled. He'd start crying. "She's going to get me, Jimmy!" he'd say. "She's going to put me in the trash cans, or drown me." He meant our mother, and he was right—spells can pull you through cracks—but what could we do? She was our grandmother's daughter, and (so our grandmother said) *a witch who didn't know she was one—or didn't want to know . . . because it was easier that way.*

I thought he might start screaming, like the dreams, but he didn't. He would instead cry in hopelessness, in the most terrible sadness I had ever heard. I'd have to pick him up and carry him a ways to get him to forget the water.

When I told our grandmother, who lived with us, how Tommy behaved on the pier, she stopped her ironing and said to me: "My little brother did the same thing. His name was Ralph. He had curly hair and died when he was six, taken away by a stranger. He was adorable, and I loved him very much. I don't think I've ever told you about him, have I?"

"No, Grandma. He must have been special."

"He was. He would get scared of falling through the cracks. He would carry on and on, sitting there on the pier and looking down through them."

"It's so silly, isn't it. Grandma. To be scared like that."

She looked at me. "No, it isn't. Your little brother has reason to be scared. I do what I am able, but she never stops. She does it in her sleep, too. She's just too strong."

"I hold Tommy's hand so hard it hurts him."

"I know, Jimmy. You love him, but sometimes that's not enough. Sometimes they die anyway, even if you don't want them to. Sometimes people take them away, if not in a stranger's car then in a dream that is no dream—one you don't know is coming. . . ."

We would go out to the end of the biggest pier, Tommy and me, because there we could look out at the whole bay and to our right and left the steel ships were tied with immense ropes to metal cleats taller than I was. Sometimes a sailor would be there, one we got to know. He would be at the end of the pier looking out at the bay, too, but he would be waiting for something.

He had a rope tied to a cleat that no one used for anything. He wanted something to take what was on the end of it. The first time we met him he said: "Know what's at the end of this rope?"

"No," I answered.

"They shouldn't be this huge this far into the bay, but surfers down on the Strand disappear every once in a while. You never know what's in the sea—even in a bay."

"I guess not," I said.

Tommy seemed scared of the sailor, but I held his hand tight and finally he stopped pulling.

"You live in one of the quarters by the banyan tree?" the sailor asked.

"Yes."

"Must be nice."

It was—except for the smells at night, and how our father cried. But I didn't say this. I wanted him to tell us more about the rope and what was down there in the water.

He kept looking out at the bay. His hands were slick with something I'd seen on my own hands before. Fish scales and fish slime. You couldn't fish without getting it on you, but where was his catch?

"I've got a tuna hook on that rope, and I put a whole mackerel on it, case you're interested. You boys fish?"

I nodded.

"Thought so. I've pulled in a lot of leopards and blues out here. Eight-footers and ten-footers. Even a twelve-foot mako. There's a four-foot steel leader. They can't get through it—even the big ones."

I nodded again. I didn't know what else to do. I loved to catch things. I loved fishing, even if it smelled. It was a different odor from the one that filled the streets around our quarters at night, under the biggest banyan tree anyone had ever seen.

The next time we went, the sailor wasn't there. It was as if he'd never been there—never existed—but I knew that wasn't true. I knew what was real and what she could take away. I'd always known. That was why (Grandma said) she hated me so.

Tommy was frightened of how empty the end of the pier was, so we came home.

The time after that, the sailor was putting a live mackerel on a hook that was wider than our father's hand. He let Tommy touch the hook.

Tommy touched it without getting scared. He just stared at it, eyes wide, and touched it more than once.

I knew she would have put Tommy on that hook if she could, but I was watching Tommy, and my grandmother was watching me even when she wasn't around.

The next time, the sailor was leaning over and making a sound. When we got up to him, we almost left. He was throwing up.

He looked at us and straightened up, embarrassed. His eyes were red, like he'd been crying.

The rope was gone.

He looked so sick.

"You all right?" I asked. My parents and grandmother had raised me to be courteous.

He didn't answer that. Instead he said: "I found a dog, a pretty big one, over by the barracks. He was starving to death." He stopped talking and bent over again, but didn't throw up. "That's what I used. He didn't fight me. He was weak. I don't know why I did it. I knew something was out there, something bigger than twelve feet, and I wanted it. . . ."

He pointed to the cleat where the rope had been.

"It took the whole thing. What would it have to be to take the rope, the whole thing, like that?"

I didn't know what to say.

"I keep seeing that dog. I had a dog once when I was little. . . ."

I saw Tommy on the hook—because that was what she wanted. But she'd have to find another hook. This one I was watching.

The next time we went out, and the four times after that, the man was gone. When I asked another sailor—one that worked in the metal shops by our quarters—he said he didn't know any sailor like that.

"He was out at the end of the first pier a lot," I said.

"A swabbie catching sharks?"

"It was after work," I said. "On weekends, too. I think his name was Curt."

"He'd have been with the metal shops. No one by that name here. You sure he was a sailor?"

"He wore blues," I said.

"You must have been imagining things," he said suddenly, and for a moment he sounded just like our mother. He *was* our mother. Her voice, her body just below his skin. Not in our heads, but completely *real*—because that is what witches do. She could do things like this, I knew, and she knew I knew.

I looked away. I didn't want to see his eyes, which weren't his. I took Tommy home. I led him down the street between the machine-shop Quonset huts to the dirt path, past the goldfish pond and the greenhouses, into our house with all its rooms, holding his hand tightly because he was my brother.

I missed talking to the sailor, the one with the rope and the hook, even though Tommy had nightmares about the dog. The nightmares stopped. I had bad dreams, too, but they helped me remember that I had a dog—a little one, a fox terrier named Walter. How I'd forgotten him, I didn't know, or I did, but didn't want to think about it—that she'd taken him away without my knowing.

I asked her—I was feeling brave—but, busy as she was with her schoolwork, she just looked at me with those black eyes of hers, the ones that wanted to kill someone or something, and I finally went away—which is what she wanted.

I didn't tell anyone I missed the sailor, but my grandmother knew.

"You missed him because he was a piece of you, Jimmy. You'd made him one. You both loved fishing. But he wasn't scared enough. You've got to be scared sometimes."

I asked her about our dog. She didn't know either. It bothered her. "Sometimes things die and you just don't know they have," she said, looking up at the ceiling as she folded our clothes, trying to remember our dog, not able to, upset. "She's getting worse, Jimmy. She's my daughter. I don't know what to do. . . ."

My father would cry when he got home from the submarine warfare laboratory he directed—the one high on the peninsula, looking down on the bay.

He hadn't always cried like this. He'd started crying a month before, the day our mother started screaming about how she had a right to be happy but how could she with all of us?

He'd take off his uniform, which smelled like him (I loved that smell), and he'd go upstairs to his bedroom, shut the door, and start crying. Sometimes he wouldn't come down for dinner. I thought my mother would take him his meal, but she said no, he could come down if he wanted it.

When I tried to take it to him once, she knocked the plate out of my hand and started shouting about how she was going to leave us one way or another.

I tried to do it another time, too, and she slapped my face. She wanted to do more than that, but Grandma's voice—she was at her card group in town, but she was in the room somehow—said: "No, Martha. *Do not* . . ."

Later, when she couldn't see me, I stood by his door and listened to the crying. I wanted to think it was headaches—"migraines" could make a grown man cry—but it wasn't. He was just very sad. Grandma said he'd never gotten over his mother's death when he was little, in that epidemic that killed so many in the world, but we knew it wasn't that really. It sounded, the way he cried, like someone who was dying—because she wanted him to, I knew—and he was remembering what it was like before, and he missed it, so he cried.

We had the quarters we had—a tennis court, a little beach, a sailboat tied to the floating docks, a big front lawn—because my father's boss didn't want them. He was an admiral and, like all admirals, liked to give parties. He wanted to live up by the laboratory, in a modern house, looking down on the lights of the bay and the long island in the middle of it where Navy jets landed and took off day and night. He could have parties on the patio there, looking down at everything, he said.

There were other quarters like ours, though not quite as nice, on the other side of the old banyan tree. Another captain and his family lived there. He had a wife and a daughter who was "slow."

The terrible smells at night, after Taps played and night covered the base—and the sailors were in their barracks—didn't come from the buildings or the banyan tree or the streets that wound among the metal-shop buildings, the two quarters and the great tree. They came from the gray dumpsters and trash cans everywhere.

I thought at first it was dead fish. It might have been at first, but not later. The other captain's wife—in the other quarters—liked to fish, but she hated to clean the creatures she caught. Even when they were twenty-or thirty-pound Black Sea Bass, she would dump them in whatever garbage cans she came across that weren't near her quarters.

This was when the bay was still young and the peninsula was still pretty wild. You could see coyotes at night moving like ghosts in packs up by the laboratory. You could catch big fish in the bay, as if no one had ever fished for them before, and so they trusted and bit and you pulled them in. But to catch something as beautiful as a thirty-pound Black Sea Bass and throw it away was a terrible thing.

When I told my grandmother about it, she said, "You play with her daughter—the girl who is slow but is also so happy when she makes a basket, the way you've taught her to make one, laughing like a baby even though she is fourteen and becoming a young woman and doesn't know she bleeds. That brings you happiness, too—to help her like that. But what is it like for the captain's wife, who didn't expect a child like Diane, who thought life would bring something else. Why clean a wonderful fish when your daughter will never grow up the way you want her to, never tell with her own life the story you, her mother, want so much to have told in yours? It would make you scream and shout, wouldn't it? It would make you catch and let die and then throw the most beautiful creatures away, wouldn't it? Does this sound familiar, Jimmy? Do you know someone else like this? A mother and a special boy—one who sees what he shouldn't see, knows what his mother is doing and gets in her way, and she can't stand it?"

I didn't understand what she was saying, but I could tell from her eyes—which were blue and bright and crinkled when she smiled—that it didn't matter. It didn't matter because I would when I was grown up, a man, understand.

When Taps sounded at sunset through the loudspeakers all over the base, I had to stop playing on our front lawn. I had to put my hand over my heart and wait. Standing there as the world got dark, I could smell the odors even worse. When the bugle stopped, I could move again, and I went looking for them. I looked for them every night for a week.

I started in the dumpsters by the machine shops because they were closest. One had the smell, and one didn't. It wasn't fish, but it was definitely something dead *because she wanted it to be.* If it was a dog or a cat or a rat, one dumpster or trash can made sense, but it wasn't just one. I walked on under the electric lights on wires strung over the street and found another dumpster that reeked even worse.

The third one was just a garbage can. It smelled too, and of the same thing. I knew what was in it, but I also didn't know. I was afraid to think of it—of what it was—even though I knew. It was a *person.* A boy whose hand I held every day. I did not want to remember his name . . . *because she does not want you to.*

How could it be *someone*? How could a smell in a garbage can or dumpster be *someone* and someone I knew?

The next one—a tiny gray dumpster—smelled the same, and I knew who it was even though I wasn't supposed to. It burned my nose, but that wasn't why I was crying. I was very sad, sad as he was, knowing that he was dying and crying because of it.

Something stirred in the eighth dumpster and called my name. I knew the voice—it wanted to help me. It wanted to stop the witch, but how? How does a mother stop a daughter she has to love?

When I stepped up to it, the voice stopped. Only the smell, the rotting, stayed.

I was crying now just like my father, and I was scared that someone would find me like that. MPs patrolled in their cars at night—not many, but sometimes. They would take me back to our quarters and say, "We found him crying by a dumpster. Why would your son be crying on a military base street at night, by a place where people put garbage?"

After they left, my mother would slap me. It wouldn't matter. I would be waiting for my father to come downstairs, but he wouldn't be able to. He would be crying and so could not come down, and her slap would be about that as much as how I'd embarrassed her with the military police.

Later, with their door closed, she would tell my father, "They found him crying. Why can't you both go away?"

She wouldn't slap him because there would be no need to. He would already be crying.

"They're all dead!" my mother was shouting. We were in an apartment—a dirty and tiny one—not our quarters on the base. Why were we here? I couldn't hear anyone else in the apartment.

"How can they all be dead?" I asked, but I knew. *She wanted them to be dead.* She wanted to be alone because only then, she believed, could she be happy. But she wasn't completely alone yet.

What to do about Jimmy? she was thinking, and it was like a scream that wouldn't stop.

I was shivering. I could barely breathe. The air smelled like fried fish, old and burnt. I'd said something to her about my grandmother, and she'd said, "Your grandmother died when you were two! What is wrong with you?" And then, though I hadn't mentioned him, she said, "You never had a little brother! You couldn't possibly have held his hand. And the piers—those are on the navy base. You've never even been there."

I hadn't mentioned the piers.

"And you couldn't possibly hear him crying."

"Who?"

"Your father. He's dead, too. He died three years ago, leaving me like this—with *you*—what was he thinking!

How would my mother do it? I didn't know, but I could feel her gathering from the air around us, room by room, every shadow, every light, what she needed in order to do it. It would take her a little while, and then it would happen.

Would I just disappear? Would I become something else? Would it hurt?

That night she kept shouting to herself in the living room of the apartment, and I waited. There was nothing to do. Then, as I lay in my bed, in the dark, the Witch Moth appeared at my window. I couldn't see it, but I could hear it. I got up and let it in and felt its velvet hand against my face. It landed somewhere in the darkness. I knew who it was, and why she'd come. *One witch to stop another*, a voice had whispered—*one who doesn't know she's one . . . or doesn't want to know.*

The others came then, too, their wings whispering in the dark even if my mother had killed them and always would.

I opened my bedroom door because they wanted me to. They flew to her, and in a moment she stopped shouting. She didn't make a sound. I don't think she was there anymore.

Later, my grandmother, sitting on a chair in my bedroom under an old floor lamp she'd always liked, said, "Your mother—my only daughter—shouted a lot, and did even more terrible things than that, but you don't have to worry now. I shouldn't have waited. In this world—listen to me carefully, Jimmy—she went away three years ago, just ran away, leaving the four of us to enjoy these beautiful quarters. Everything is fine now. . . ." She paused. She took a breath. "I love you. I've always loved you more than anything else, Jimmy, but you know that."

She was smiling. She was looking right at me under the lamp's light, more real than anything I'd ever known. Her eyes—which were like black velvet, not blue glass—were crinkling. The red spot on her nose was like a tiny flower. "Death is no more frightening than life," she said with a little laugh. "So why shouldn't we smile, Jimmy?"

I nodded, and I smiled—and, as I did, everyone who really mattered came back to me on black wings.

KAIJU

GARY MCMAHON

Diving deep, something large moves and writhes with the currents, heading into the comforting darkness. The waters become cold, the water pressure increases. A sleek, muscled body drives on, speeding ever downwards, moving fast towards the bottom of everything.

Jeff pulled up at the kerb and stared out of the side window at the remains of his house. The army took down the road blocks a few days ago, the useable highways were being patrolled by the police and the Territorial Army, and things were slowly making their way back towards some kind of normality.

He didn't want to leave the car. He felt as if it offered him some kind of protective bubble from the world. Not in any literal sense, of course—nobody felt safe now, not after what happened—but inside the car, behind a layer of metal and glass, he could at least compartmentalise his thoughts.

There was no point in staying here, though. He had no choice but to get out. He needed to be sure there were no survivors.

He shifted his gaze to the windscreen and watched a young woman picking her way through the rubble a few yards up ahead. She was dressed in a blue boiler suit, like the kind worn by staff on the factory floor where he used to work, and her hair was pulled back severely from her face. Her pale cheeks were smudged with dirt. Her tiny white hands looked steady enough, but her gait was ungainly as she moved carefully through the broken bricks and shattered timbers that had once formed a home—presumably hers, or that of someone she knew.

Jeff felt like crying. He had lost so much. Everybody had. He didn't know a single person who remained untouched by the events of the past three weeks. When that thing attacked, it brought with it only destruction. Like a biblical plague, it wiped out everything in its path.

That thing . . . the beast . . . the monster . . .

Thinking of it now, he felt stupid. It was a child's word used to describe something he struggled to label in an adult world. Everything changed the day it arrived; even the rules of physics were twisted out of shape, along with the precarious geometry of his own existence.

When he was a boy, he loved reading comics and watching films about monsters. Now he was a man, and he had seen the proof that monsters really existed, he could not even begin to fathom what his younger self had found so fascinating about them.

He opened the door and got out of the car. Night was falling but it was still light enough to see clearly. There was a slight chill in the air. The woman was closer now to his position, and she wasn't as young as he'd initially thought. Middle aged: possibly in her early forties. The mud on her face clouded her features, at first hiding the wrinkles and the layers of anguish that were now visible.

"Have you seen them?" She approached him as she spoke, stumbling a little as she crossed onto the footpath. He saw that the heel of one of her shoes—the left one—had snapped off during her travels. The woman hadn't even noticed.

"I'm sorry?"

"We all are . . . we're all sorry. But have you seen them? My children."

He clenched his fists. Moments like these, situations in which he could smell and taste and just about touch someone else's loss, made him nervous. He felt like a little boy again, reading about mythical creatures from a large hardback book.

"No. No, I haven't."

"They're still alive. Somewhere." She glanced around, at the wreckage of the neighbourhood." Her eyes were wide. Her lips were slack. "They let me come back here to try and find them. They were in the cellar when it . . . when it hit. The Storm . . ."

That's what they called it: the Storm. The name seemed fitting. He couldn't remember who first coined the term, probably some newspaper reporter.

"I . . ." He stopped there, unable to think of anything that might help the woman come to terms with her loss.

"I got out, but they stayed down there. The army truck took me away—they wouldn't let me go back for them. They were trapped, you see . . . by the rubble. The Storm trapped them inside, underneath. I have to find them."

She reached out and grabbed his arm. He could barely feel her grip, despite her knuckles whitening as her fingers tightened around his bicep. "Could you help me look for them?" Her smile, when it struggled to the surface, was horrible. Jeff thought he'd never seen an expression so empty.

"I have to . . . I have things to do. This was my house." He pointed to the pile of bricks and timbers and the scattered glass shards; the piles of earth; the pit formed by a single foot of the Storm.

"We were neighbours?" She peered at him, trying to focus. "Before it happened?"

"I guess so." He'd never seen her before in his life. This woman was a stranger but they were all supposed to be connected by their shared tragedy. Jeff had never felt that way. He was alone with his ghosts.

They stood there for another moment, as if glued together by some sticky strands of time, and then he pulled away. Her arm remained hanging there, the fingers of her hand curling over empty air.

"My children . . ."

He looked into her eyes and saw nothing, not even an echo of her pain. She was stripped bare, rendered down to nothing but this mindless search for things that were no longer here. He couldn't tell her, she wouldn't be told. She needed to discover the truth for herself.

"Good luck," he said, and he meant it.

Jeff walked away, heading towards the ragged hole in the earth where his house had once stood, the great footprint of the beast that had once passed this way. He wished he'd seen it happen. It must have been an amazing sight, to see the buildings flattened by the gigantic beast as it charged through the neighbourhood and towards the city.

He heard the woman's scuffling footsteps behind him as she moved away. He wished he had it in him to help her. He hoped she would find her children alive, but doubted she ever would. Not even the bodies would remain. Not even bloodstains.

The Storm came, and that was all. There was no reason for its arrival. It wasn't like the old movies he'd seen as a kid, where an atomic detonation or the constant experimentation of mankind caused a rift in the earth or a disturbance in the atmosphere, and out stumbled a stop-motion nightmare. No, it was nothing like that. The Storm came, it destroyed whatever it encountered, and it went away again, sated.

They were unable to fight it. The authorities didn't know what to do; the army and navy and air force were at a loss: none of their weapons had any effect on the Storm. So they waited it out, hoping the thing would either wear itself out and tire of the rampage, or move on, crossing the border into another country. Fingers hovered over the buttons of nuclear launch systems. Members of parliament voted in secret chambers. The nation prepared for a great and terrible sacrifice.

He remembered those first surprisingly clear pieces of footage transmitted on the Internet, and then again on the news channels: HD quality CCTV pictures of some great lizard-like beast emerging from the shadows on the coast, a B Movie come to life. But this was not a man in a suit, or a too-crisp GCI image. It was colossal, the height of two tower blocks, one standing on top of the other. Its arm span was a half a mile across, but it barely needed to stretch them so far to tear down a church, a town hall, a factory warehouse. . . . Bullets and bombs simply bounced off its thick, plated hide to create more damage to the surrounding area. Its call was the trumpet of Armageddon. When it opened its mouth to roar, the sound was unlike anything humanity had heard before.

Nobody knew what the creature was, where it came from, why it appeared. The scientists mumbled in jargon, talked about tectonic plates, seismic events, and then finally, they went quiet. They locked themselves into deep underground laboratories to try and invent something that would kill the thing.

And then . . . then it went away, slinking back into the ocean, the waves covering it like a blanket. The sea bubbled. Ships capsized. The coastal barriers fell. The Storm passed.

But the Storm could return at any time. They all knew this, but it went unspoken. There were celebrations, the blockades came down, people started to rebuild what had been ravaged. But somewhere back in the shadows, or under the dark waters, the Storm waited. Perhaps it even watched.

Jeff walked across the roughly turned earth, his boots hard and solid as he made his way towards the hole in the ground. When he reached it, he went down onto his knees and peered over the rim. It was deep, with standing water gathered at its base, and in each of the toe prints. There was no sign of a body, or of body parts. His family were wiped out, deleted, removed without trace from the face of the earth.

He smiled, gritting his teeth.

As a boy he'd loved monsters. As a man, he wasn't so sure how he felt.

If it were not for the Storm, he would have been forced to think of some other way to dispose of them, but the monster answered his desperate prayers and came to cleanse him, to remove the evidence of his crimes.

He wondered . . .

If he hoped hard enough, wished for long enough, might it come back? There were other people he wanted to get rid of. It was a nice thought, but he knew it was a fantasy. The situation had nothing to do with him; it was simply a handy coincidence. Even now, it amused him to think something this absurd had saved him from being found out. It was as if one of those childhood comic books had come to life.

Jeff got to his feet and moved slowly away from the ruins. The breeze turned into a light wind, and it whipped up a mass of litter, sending papers and packets and scraps of material scampering into the gutter. Jeff watched them as they tussled. He remembered the way his family struggled: Katherine and the girls, fighting for their sad little lives. It was like watching a movie, only less real. The actors didn't even look like the people they were trying to portray.

They'd never looked like his family, those actors. The woman he'd married, the daughters he'd fathered, were at some point replaced by strangers. That was why they had to go. It all seemed so clear, and then, without thinking, he'd done it: he had ended them. There was no memory of planning, or running through it all in his mind. There was only the act itself, and the mess left behind.

The wind died down. The litter went still. He smelled old fires and diesel fumes. He tasted bitterness at the back of his throat. Something huge loomed against the horizon, its form unclear, fluttering and unstable.

Jeff walked back to the car, climbed inside, turned on the engine, and waited. He watched the woman as she made her way across the street, towards yet another ruined house. He smiled. Inside his head, he heard the voice of the Storm.

The roaming woman sat down in the rubble, staring at the ground. She clenched and unclenched her hands and then started rooting in the dirt, as if she might find her lost children there, somewhere beneath the disturbed top soil. He imagined her brushing away gravel to see a face staring up at her, eyes closed, lips sealed shut on a silent scream.

Clouds moved behind her, shifting across the low red sky. Something dark shimmered beyond them, like a promise straining to be fulfilled. He thought of giant butterfly wings, and then of the opening mouth of the Storm.

Jeff started the car but waited a few moments—still watching the woman—before driving away. He didn't turn on the radio. All they ever talked about was the Storm.

As he headed down the road, towards some unidentified place he'd never been before, he thought about this new world and wondered how everyone would cope with the way things were now, the changes happening in the wake of the monster. Jeff had stepped through the veil, but the rest of the world followed behind him.

He drove all night, and then he stopped the car in a lonely place to sit and look up at the sky. Trees stirred like wraiths against the breezy evening. The stars pulsed, the darkness bulged, threatening to burst open like a ripe melon, and he tried to catch a glimpse of the old world, the one they'd all left behind. After a long time, he gave up trying.

And at the bottom of the sea, curled up among the old wrecks in a long, deep, nameless trench, something yawns and blinks its eyes before drifting back into a deep, soundless slumber. It dreams of screams and bloodshed, and finds comfort in the sweet memory of Man's fear.

WILL THE REAL PSYCHO IN THIS STORY PLEASE STAND UP?

PAT CADIGAN

Back in the day, nobody liked Tom Clement, not even his parents.

They made him stay in the cellar. If they even let him inside, that is—a lot of times, they'd lock him out overnight. He'd have to sleep under the sagging porch of their rented house on Second Street. If he couldn't get inside the next morning to wash up and change his clothes, he'd just go to school and clean up as best he could in the boys' bathroom, hurrying to get out of there before the jocks caught him and beat him up for being a fag.

That was the Sixties—peace and love, anti-war and civil rights, but a guy could still get his ass kicked for being a fag. Or even just looking like a fag, which, by virtue of his slight, delicate build, soft voice, and quiet disposition, was Tom Clement's crime against high school masculinity. That's a capital offence in places like the old home town.

I'd never been especially fond of the place myself. It was no scenic New England village—factories outnumbered schools and churches. It was a small, dirty town and I yearned to live in a real city, like Boston.

I used to hope that my father would find us so we'd have to move again, the way he had a few times after we'd made our middle-of-the-night escape from the trailer park. I was a little over four then but I remembered it vividly, along with what had happened *before* we left; still do. There were no shelters for battered women in those days. A woman fleeing an abusive husband was more likely to be returned to her abuser and told to be a better wife, the kind a man didn't want to smack every time she opened her mouth.

The night we pulled off the highway into the Thunderbird Motel parking lot, I'd thought it was just another brief stopover. But either we'd finally managed to lose my father or looking for us cut into his drinking time too much, because there were no threatening middle-of-the-night phone calls. My mother got a job, we moved into a fourth-floor walk-up, and I had to accept the fact that this was home until I got myself out.

That probably makes me sound like a stuck-up brat. I was. In the old home town, that was no distinction.

Catholic school meant wearing uniforms. Sounds awful but it wasn't really so bad if your parents couldn't afford much in the way of new clothes. The women in my mother's office had a round-robin thing going with hand-me-downs. Stuff like dungarees and t-shirts wore out pretty quickly but dressier things could survive up to five different kids. The moms liked it but wearing stuff three or four or even five years out of date quite frankly sucked. "Second Hand Rose" was funny if you were Barbra Streisand, not if you were Rose. Yeah, I was an ingrate. What teenager isn't?

Well, not Tom Clement. The school provided his uniform; everything else came from clothing drives. Tom was so grateful he wrote thank-you notes to the parish. Someone found one once and passed it around in the cafeteria. Kids screamed with laughter to know that every night, Tom knelt down and thanked God for somebody's cast-off underwear.

Kids like Tom had a limited number of ways to cope. They could drop out and become juvenile delinquents, they could hide in the library and study, or they could turn to God. Tom was hardly cut out for a life of crime; his first five minutes in juvenile hall would have been his last and most miserable moments on earth. The library had limited value as a refuge—the world was still waiting outside after it closed at six, nastier than ever. There was nowhere he could go except heaven, or at least as close as he could get without dying. Tom had made no secret that after graduation, he was joining the Brothers of Mercy (basically male nuns for you non-Catholics), for a life of prayer and service in Clarence, New York (wherever *that* was).

Adolescence had awakened my inner skeptic, which hadn't been sleeping all that soundly anyway. But when I saw that kid struggling through the halls between classes, dodging blows from passing jocks or trying to pick up the scattered books and papers some Neanderthal had knocked out of his arms while the rest of the school walked over them pretending not to see, I thought there had *better* be a God, because He *owed* Tom Clement. *Big* time.

Not everyone walked over Tom's scattered books and papers—I didn't and neither did most other girls, not even in-crowd queens and cheerleaders (unless they were in a hurry, of course). Guys couldn't do anything. The only kindness any guy could safely show Tom Clement was not bothering to punch him.

All things considered, I'm more likely to be the psycho in this story than Tom Clement. But I'm not. Although I could be wrong.

We were in the middle of lunch in the cafeteria when Joyce Kilburn said she wanted to go to the prom with Tom Clement. I thought she was making a cruel joke, which wasn't like her at all. She'd been my best friend since kindergarten. *Cruel* wasn't in her vocabulary.

"Close your mouth, Ruth, before something flies in," she said. "I really like him. He's a nice guy."

She sat back, looking around as if waiting for someone to contradict her. It was the usual foursome at the table—her, me, Kate St. Denis, and Mary McCoy. Kate had gone all through school with us, but Mary had transferred last year from San Diego and she was both culture-shocked and homesick for the weather.

"I *know* he's a nice guy," I said. "But if you really *do* like him, why would you want to subject him to something like that?"

"Something like *what*? I'm a nice person *and* a fun date," Joyce said defensively. "And I'm not a dog, either." True enough—she was dark-haired and dark-eyed, and unlike most of us, she had perfect skin, no acne. She also had a nice body—chubby by today's standards, blossoming back then.

"I don't mean it like that." I glanced at Kate and Mary, who were both wide-eyed. "What do you think will happen if he goes to the prom?"

Joyce lifted her chin belligerently. "We'll dance, everybody'll get their picture taken, and either Theresa Guilfoyle or Debbi Belliveau'll be prom queen. Then everyone goes out to eat or to a party."

I wanted to shake her. "Have you missed what's been happening to him every day for the last four years?"

"But all the guys'll be in *tuxedoes*," Mary offered, a bit timidly.

"*Rented* tuxedoes," Kate added. "They'd have to pay for any damage—"

"So they'll pay," I snapped. "You think they're afraid of having to cough up for a few rips or bloodstains?"

"But Ruthie, their dates'll *kill* them if they get all messed up," Mary said. She was the only person allowed to call me *Ruthie*.

"Only if they do it *before* the photo."

Joyce folded her arms. "I already talked to my folks about it. They said they'd pay for his tux and everything."

I shook my head. "If you *really* want to do a good deed, join the Girl Scouts and read to the blind. If you go through with this, all you're gonna do is get Tom Clement *killed*."

"Not if we double with you and Jack," she said slyly and with that, she defeated me. I couldn't refuse to double-date with my best friend and she knew we weren't already doubling with someone else. Jack and I had met last summer working at the Crazyland Amusement Park. Now he was a freshman at the local teacher's college, which made him as invulnerable as Superman; the laws of our particular jungle weren't even real to him. I was becoming less real to him myself as we grew apart and I knew it. But he never pressured me for sex and he was gallant enough not to break up with me till after my graduation. He's definitely not the psycho in this story, although he was cute enough to have made a particularly creepy one.

Jack agreed we had to double with Joyce and Tom just to make sure the poor guy didn't end up getting his head flushed in the men's room. High school bullies wouldn't pick on anyone with a friend who could fight back. I praised his insight and compassion.

"I do appreciate your keen perception of my character," he laughed, "but maybe I won't have to play bodyguard. He might say no."

That hadn't even occurred to me. "You're right," I said with a relieved sigh. "If I were him, I wouldn't go if my date were the Virgin Mary and we were doubling with Jesus."

"That sounds like a fun car to be in," Jack said dryly. He was unfettered by matters of faith, which was so refreshing. "If Tom says no, introduce Joyce to the Big JC. I just hope the Virgin Mary's already got a date, though, or you got a dress for nothing."

By the time Joyce actually asked Tom Clement to the prom, it was all over the school. That didn't surprise me; what did was how little the grapevine had distorted it. Perhaps it was so juicy that even the biggest gossips were stumped for a way to embellish it. Or maybe it was just the girl involved.

Joyce, like me, Kate, and Mary, belonged to that group of kids who were neither in-crowd popular like cheerleaders and jocks, nor preyed-on outcasts like Tom Clement, which meant we were almost never talked about. But this was something else. A girl asking a boy out at all was iffy. But *Tom Clement*? To the *prom*? That was more than outrageous, it was unprecedented. There was no telling what could happen.

When the movie *Carrie* came out a few years later, I imagined a lot of my former classmates sitting in a dark movie theatre, staring up at pale, delicate Sissy Spacek and thinking, *Shit, that's Clement in a dress!* And maybe one or two nudging each other and saying, *Damn, why didn't* we *think of that?* when the blood came down.

Tom Clement said yes, Joyce told me breathlessly. She looked happy, thrilled even, but also a bit taken aback. Had *she* thought all along that Tom would say no, I wondered . . . or maybe even hoped he would?

"He was *so sweet* when I asked him," she said as we headed over to her house after school. "So *shy*, so *cute*. He's never been on a date, you know. And then he insisted on giving me these—" She showed me two tiny gold-colored crosses. Cheap little charms, no better than something you'd get out of a Crackerjacks box. Catholic Crackerjacks; there were a few tiny bumps on the surface of each cross that was supposed to be the body of Christ. "One for you and one for me. As a token of his appreciation and for good luck, he said. Isn't that *sweet*?" She barely paused for breath as she dropped one into my pocket. "You *have* to go shopping with me. Help me pick out a dress that's different from yours but won't clash. So we'll all look nice together."

She went on about stuff in fashion magazines, apparently oblivious to the other kids walking past us in twos and threes. They'd part to go around us, walking fast to get ahead before looking over their shoulders and talking to each other.

The weird thing was, hardly any of them were laughing. A few were, and there were some disdainful sneers and withering looks but most kids just seemed kind of spooked. When my mother looked like that, she'd say, *Goose walked over my grave*.

All the while Joyce continued prattling about empire waists and sweetheart necklines and dotted Swiss as if we were the only two people on the street, or even in the whole town. Finally, I couldn't stand it anymore and asked her if she really didn't know people were staring.

"Oh, for God's *sake*!" Joyce rolled her eyes. "Of *course* I know, I'm not stupid. Hey, *you*! Yeah, the three musketeers up there!" she yelled just as three big guys ahead of us looked over their shoulders. "Take a picture, it lasts longer!"

There was never a bottomless pit to fall into when you really needed one, I thought miserably. But to my surprise, they only walked faster, dropping their heads and hunching their shoulders like they were afraid someone—Joyce? Me? Both of us?—might hit them. Joyce looked back and gave a single harsh laugh. "Aw, whatsamatta—you guys forgot *your* cameras, too?"

I peeked over my own hunched shoulder. A small gaggle of girls behind us had slowed down so suddenly that some boys had run right into them. Books and ring-binders hit the sidewalk, shedding papers; a timely gust of wind scattered them in every direction. Well, except for the ones they stepped all over—accidentally, of course. The lucky few who hadn't dropped anything were dodging traffic to get across the street as fast as possible.

"Yeah, now we know why the chickens crossed the road—because they're *chicken*," Joyce laughed. "Come on, Ruth. And close your mouth before something flies in." My shoulders were up around my ears but the taunts I was waiting for never came. I should have been more relieved than I was but my best friend suddenly intimidating people was too weird.

"Didn't any of that bother you at all?" I asked after a bit. "Even just a little?"

Joyce laughed, her hair bouncing around her non-hunched shoulders. "Doesn't what happens to Tom Clement every day bother *you*?"

"But the way everyone was staring—"

"Are you *kidding*?" Joyce elbowed me. "That's *nothing* compared to what he gets *all the time*. If you can't handle it, maybe we'd better not double."

"But we've already decided—"

"We can *un*-decide. I'll get my dad to drive us. Maybe that'd be better anyway."

"No, come on, Joyce, you already told Tom we're doubling, right? Don't change plans without even talking to him about it. He might not want to go if it's just you two alone."

She hesitated. "You're right. He wouldn't say yes till I told him we'd be going with you and Jack."

I felt guilty for wishing she hadn't told me that, but not as guilty as I should have.

Two Saturdays before the prom, Joyce and I went downtown to LaFleur armed with a swatch my mother had cut from a seam of my dress. LaFleur had the largest formal/bridal wear department in town. Joyce had no intention of buying anything from them—by now it was too likely someone else would have the same dress. But we figured we might as well see what everyone else would be wearing.

Joyce and I were slightly-more-than-budding feminists but there was still enough little girl in us to love playing dress-up. We were so busy with all the lace and velvet and general fluffiness that it took a while before we noticed no one had come over to ask if we needed help.

That *never* happened. If you were a teenager, you couldn't walk into a store without a sales person pouncing before the door shut behind you. Because teenagers stole, everyone knew that. Neither Joyce nor I had ever shoplifted but stony-faced clerks followed us even when we were with a parent. This did have one advantage—we never had to wait for service. Except that day.

Joyce noticed before I did. After a lot of fabric-feeling, color-comparing, and mind-changing, she picked out three dresses to try on. But instead of going into the changing room, she paced back and forth holding the hangers high in the air so the hems wouldn't drag on the carpet. I thought she was just dithering some more until she said, "Do you see a sales clerk anywhere?"

There weren't even any other customers around. It was a few moments before I finally spotted a small cluster of sales clerks and shoppers in the accessories department, whispering to each other over a display case. Some I recognized from school but a few were adults—*real* adults, with gray in their hair. All of them had the same sour expression of disapproval pinching their lips together.

Joyce and I looked at each other. Then she hung the dresses on the nearest hook and we marched out the front door together.

"Can you believe that?" she said when we were outside.

"No," I said honestly. I couldn't. Since when did grown-ups care about high school crap? What was wrong with them? "For a minute there, I thought you were gonna throw those dresses on the floor."

"I was tempted," she said. "But then they'd have had a reason to throw us out. And then maybe they'd bill my mom for damaged merchandise."

Damaged merchandise. The fluttery chill I felt—if that was a goose walking over my grave, it was a pretty big goose.

"The hell with this—let's go to Worcester," Joyce said suddenly. "Mom'll let me take the car. There'll be a better selection."

Joyce was right. No one stared at us except sales people and only for the usual reasons. We had lunch out and Joyce found a dress that made me wish my mother hadn't already made mine.

It was Jack's idea for Tom Clement to spend all of prom weekend at his house. A few days before, he stopped by after school, had me point Tom out, and talked to him. Tom looked awestruck as he nodded; I don't think he said a word. *That's my boyfriend*, I thought, watching from a short distance away with Joyce. I'd never liked Jack so much as I did right then and there. Would I ever feel the same about anyone else? The question was a brief, secret pang.

My feelings about my best friend, on the other hand, were more mixed. I wondered if she'd ever realize that however much she thought she was doing for Tom Clement, Jack was actually doing more.

Or was I just jealous because I had to share my boyfriend's attention? We weren't just going to the prom any more, we—or to be honest, Jack—also had to protect Tom.

It was like Jack and I had been drafted for someone else's fight and it wasn't going to be pretty. Maybe I'd just been watching too much Vietnam on the news, I thought; lately the metaphor seemed all too apt for so many things.

"*Ruth*." My mother made two syllables out of my name—*Roo*-uth. That and the way she stood in the doorway of my room with her hands on her hips usually meant I was in trouble. "What's this I hear about you going to the prom with some guy named Tom Clement?"

It was the morning of the prom and I was going nuts trying to put my hair up in rollers. I'd been letting it grow since last September's Great Hair

Disaster—what the hairdresser had called a "lamp cut"—and it seemed to be all odds and split ends. "*I'm* not going with Tom Clement," I said, meeting her gaze in the mirror. "I'm going with *Jack*. You know that. *Joyce* is going with Tom."

"In the same car. And I've heard this boy is . . ." she hesitated, her face troubled. "*Not* from a very good home."

"It's not his fault. I've told you about him." I started to summarize the torments he had been put through by kids who *were* from good families.

"*That's* the boy?" she broke in, horrified. "But surely his family won't—"

I told her about Jack's inviting him to stay the weekend.

"And Jack's parents don't mind?" my mother asked, incredulous.

Jack had recently moved into an apartment with a roommate, a bit of information I'd decided she could live without. "Well, he's over at Jack's now," I said, hoping I sounded casual.

Her troubled expression deepened as she sat down on my bed. "I've managed to maintain a spotless reputation since we came here and that's no small thing. In a small town, people are always ready to gossip about a single mother. And you've been a good girl, a good student, the best daughter anyone could ask for. Why do you want to jeopardize everything by associating with this boy? Once you lose your reputation, you *never* get it back."

Oh, hell, not the bad-reputation talk again, I thought. "Good thing I'll be a hundred miles away at UMass next year. Things like that are why I don't want to stay here a second longer than I have to." I told her about shopping in LaFleur.

"No wonder everyone was staring at me the last time I went in there!" she snapped. "I thought I was imagining things. God only knows what they were whispering."

"What *could* they say—that I'm going to the prom?" I said. "It's true, I'm going to the prom. So what?"

"Guilt by association! Lie down with dogs and you'll get up with fleas!"

Suddenly I was so angry I wished Tom Clement really *was* my date. "What does *that* mean—if I ride in the same car with Tom Clement, my mother's just like his? She drinks and smacks me around and locks me out of the house all night, too?" She started to say something but I talked over her. "If you really *were* a good person, you'd *help* Tom Clement, take him in, even. *We'd* be his *foster family*—"

The next thing I knew, she had the front of my bathrobe in one hand and was about to backhand me with the other.

Now, my mother had *never* hit me. She had never *threatened* to hit me, she'd never even *joked* about hitting me. I'm not sure whether she caught sight of herself in the mirror or just saw me flinch, but she snatched her hands away and put them behind her back. Then she sat down on the bed again, looking horrified and like she was about to throw up. I rushed over and put my arms around her.

We held each other and she stroked my hair like I was a little kid again, neither of us speaking for I don't know how long. Then she cleared her throat. "First thing Monday morning, I'll call the welfare office and tell them that boy needs help. If they say they can't do anything, I'll call every number I can find in City Hall, all the way up to the mayor. Then I'll move on to the county and even the state if I have to."

I gave her a squeeze.

"But *don't* say anything to the Clement boy. Let him be a normal teenager for a weekend. And don't tell Joyce or Jack, either," she added, ushering me back to the bureau so she could put my hair up for me. "You know what *my* mother always used to say—the only way two people can keep a secret is if one of them is dead."

The old joke couldn't have been less funny. I wasn't sure whose grave the goose was walking over but I thought it might be more than one.

I suspect this never happens to psychos.

Joyce invited me to get dressed at her house rather than limp down four flights of steps in a gown and heels. Her parents invited my mother, too. Between the cube flash on her Instamatic and Mr. Kilburn's Polaroid Land monster, Joyce and I were practically blind by the time Jack and Tom showed up. Then they were blinded too, while all the parents oohed and aahed over what handsome couples we were. Joyce's dress and mine looked great together and the wrist corsages were perfect.

But the surprise success was Tom Clement's tuxedo. Jack had taken charge and the two of them turned up in Edwardian velvet jackets, Tom's a rich brown, Jack's a wine-dark maroon. Jack looked wonderful but Tom seemed transformed—the tux did more for him than any of us might have imagined. His frail delicacy became an all but aristocratic elegance. When I looked at the photos years later, it was still there. Three of us were going to a prom; the fourth could have been on his way to a reception for visiting royalty. *As* the royalty.

Joyce was bowled over. So was I; I felt that heart-skip stirring sensation that always came with the start of a crush and had to remind myself not to look at him too much. While Joyce's parents were saying *One more, honey, okay? And now just one more, pleeeeeeeze?* I got into the car with Jack.

"You're wonderful," I said, scooting over next to him as he slid behind the wheel. "You're the most wonderful guy in the world." I kissed him on the cheek but when I pulled back, I was surprised to see that he didn't look very happy. "Something wrong?"

"Nah. I don't know. Nothing really. I just—" he shrugged, wincing. "I've been feeling kinda weird since last night. Maybe I'm coming down with something."

"Puke on this dress and I'll kill you with my bare hands." I was only half-kidding.

"Nah, it's not like that. It's more like a headache—"

"I've got some Bufferin in my bag." It was actually Midol but what he didn't know wouldn't hurt him.

"In that silly little thing?" Jack nodded at my clutch purse. "That's not big enough for a stick of gum."

"You'd be surprised at what I can get in here," I said solemnly. "Besides Mi—ahem, *my Bufferin*, I've got lipstick, a pack of tissues, moist towelettes, a Swiss Army knife, two road flares, and a set of jumper cables."

I thought for sure that would make him laugh but he only managed a brief smile. "No, it's more like a headache I don't have yet," he said. "I'll let you know if that changes. I just feel . . . I don't know, *funny*. Out of focus. I bet when the pictures come back, I'll be all blurry." He shrugged. "Maybe it's an allergy. All the flowers." He looked at my wrist corsage and I immediately moved my arm so it was farther away from him. Then Joyce and Tom got into the car and we headed off for our big night at the Merritt-Andersen Country Club.

The MACC, as most people called it, was twenty minutes outside of town, in an area of mixed woodlands and fields, most of it privately owned. It was a pretty drive but my nerves were jumping before we passed the city limits. Halfway there, I suddenly wanted to beg Jack to take us somewhere else, anywhere else. *Hey, really, what the hell*—anyone *can go to a prom but* we *could go dancing in Worcester.* Boston *even!*

I glanced at Jack; his attention was on the road. In the rear view mirror, I saw Joyce and Tom sitting like a shy couple on a living room sofa. Each had a hand resting on the space between them. If one of them moved an inch, they'd have been touching; neither did.

I sneaked another look at Jack. This time he caught me and gave me a quick smile before resting his arm on the back of the seat, inviting me to cuddle up. I did, heart sinking. Just as well that I didn't have the nerve to suggest skipping the prom. They'd think I'd lost my mind and neither Jack nor Joyce would believe I'd been kidding. They'd go at me until I confessed I was scared something bad would happen. And I'd have to say it all to Tom Clement's face.

All my worrying about the prom being ruined would have been for nothing. I'd have done it myself, before we even got there.

Maybe *I* needed some Midol, I thought, and opened my silly little purse. I really did have tissues, moist towelettes, and a Swiss Army knife but I was dismayed to see I'd forgotten my lipstick. Well, maybe Joyce would loan me hers. Or the chaperones would have some, along with other emergency supplies (everybody knew you were most likely to get your period while wearing a light-colored evening gown at the prom). I was about to close the bag again when a small gold glint caught my eye. Tom Clement's chintzy little cross was wedged so firmly in one corner that I couldn't pull it out without tearing the lining. Weird; I didn't remember putting it in there but then I didn't remember leaving my lipstick on the dresser, either. Oh, well, I thought, at least I hadn't forgotten the Midol.

Nobody gave us a second look when we got out of the car in the parking lot. Two MACC staff members were checking people in at a table outside the ballroom. They smiled as they found our names on their list and told us how stunning we all looked. I knew they were saying that to everyone but they sounded like they really meant it and it gave me a thrill in spite of myself.

When we went in, a hush did not fall over the entire room and people did not stare in disbelief. The only person who did any staring was me—I was goggling at the giant chandelier hanging down from the high domed ceiling. It was all spirals, spirals around spirals and spirals within spirals—I almost went cross-eyed.

"I'd hate to be the guy who has to clean that thing," Jack chuckled.

"Close your mouth, Ruth, before something flies in," Joyce added, which broke the spell immediately.

"Unh-unh-unh," I said, wagging my finger. "You can't say that on weekends. I hope you brought something less annoying to use till Monday."

"Sounds like somebody's jaws weren't fast enough," Joyce replied, fake-haughty.

Tom Clement burst into hearty laughter, something I'd never heard him do in all the time I'd known him.

"That's another day for talking about it and one more because you should've known better," I told her. "We'll just tell everyone you came down with lockjaw till Thursday."

"Wednesday," Joyce corrected me.

"Now it's Friday, because you can't count." That made Tom laugh even harder.

All at once, Jack was pulling a chair out for me, saying, "I hope this is all right with everyone."

"It's perfect," Joyce said as Tom did the same for her.

"Perfect," he echoed, sitting on her left.

Instead of making another joke, I heard myself say, "Perfect." Because it was.

Each table seated eight and it was early enough that we had this one all to ourselves. We took the seats by the window, which looked out on the garden. It was gorgeous but my attention was divided between it and the other four chairs. *Please, God, don't let any of the real assholes sit there,* I prayed silently. *Please let all the really* big *shitheads get here while there are plenty of other places to sit.*

I wasn't sure what was sillier—begging the Deity to deliver me from assholes and shitheads or reverting to prayer, period. Apparently, my inner skeptic had taken the evening off.

My gaze fell on Tom Clement. He was smiling at me, a small, private smile, like we shared a secret. Like he'd caught something of what I was thinking.

Which had to be my stupidest idea ever. Maybe my brain was out for the night, too.

Things kept not going wrong. The Deity or dumb luck had decided to give me a break and steered Linda O'Shea and Jane Vaccha our way. Linda and Jane were nice but even better, their dates both went to college with Jack. It wasn't long before we were all chatting away, like this was what we always did on Saturday night.

There was a finger-food buffet; I managed not to wear any of it. The eight elegantly dressed chaperones were country club members; they called themselves hosts when they stopped at each table to say hello. As the buffet was being disassembled, someone dropped one of the steel trays; there was no jeering, no sarcastic applause. Two of the chaperones rushed to help. Nice people, I thought. By the time we got up to dance, I'd practically forgotten I'd ever been worried about anything.

The music was a little on the syrupy side and the singer really wanted to be Sinatra. The MACC house band—or house bland, I thought; *music you won't remember for a night you'll never forget*. I was about to share my brilliant wit with Jack in the middle of another slow one but the expression on his face stopped me.

"What's wrong?" I said.

"Huh?" He looked startled, as if he'd forgotten I was there. "Nothing, everything's great. Well, the band kinda bites. Other than that, everything's fine." He smiled and all at once I felt wistful. My whole life was about to change and while that was what I'd always wanted, it wouldn't be easy. I wasn't in love with Jack but the thought of breaking up was sad. If only I could sleep through it, or just skip over it, like in a movie: *Jack and Ruth dance, smiling at each other, fade out; fade in six months later as Ruth exits dormitory at UMass, where a light snow is falling.*

Oh, sure. When a light snow was falling in hell, maybe.

Something else occurred to me. "Where's Tom?" I asked, looking around.

Jack tilted his head to my right; Tom and Joyce were dancing about ten feet away. None of the couples around them gave them a second look.

"I think he'll be all right," Jack said.

If only I could believe that, I thought, looking at the tables to see if any of the guys sitting this one out were paying too much attention to Tom and Joyce, or whispering as if they were up to something.

"*Ruth*." Jack didn't quite make two syllables out of it. "You're so tense, it's like dancing with a board. Take it easy, already. You're *my* date, not *his* babysitter." Pause. "Unless you'd rather be *his* date."

"Don't be ridiculous!" But I felt my face get warm all of a sudden, which made me even more embarrassed. "I don't want to be here with anyone but you," I said, lowering my voice.

For answer, Jack ushered me off the dance floor and out the now-open patio doors at the far end of the room. The sun was down and the glow in the west was almost gone. Other couples were taking a stroll in the garden, in the cool and the dark and the quiet. *Very* quiet—despite the open doors, the music was barely audible. As we moved onto one of the pathways, Jack put his arm around me and I felt some of the tension go out of my shoulders.

"I just did it to make you happy," he said. "Having that guy stay over with me. You've been telling me about Tom Clement since we started going out and to be honest, I thought you were exaggerating at first. But I've got classes with a couple of guys who graduated from your school last year and now I know you weren't." He shook his head. "Nothing like that ever happened where I went to school. It's not like I really wanted to be his self-appointed bodyguard but I figured what the hell. Guy deserves a break and it would make you happy."

"I *am* happy," I said. "But if you really don't feel well, say so and we'll leave. I won't get mad—"

He gave me a squeeze. "What about Joyce and Tom?"

"They'll understand—"

"Then they're nicer than me." He gave me another squeeze. "Maybe they are. I'm afraid I'm not the great guy I want you to think I am. Or that *I* want to think I am."

"What are you talking about?" I asked, baffled.

"One hour of Tom Clement in my apartment and I wanted to pound his head in."

I drew back, shocked. There was just enough light from the country club windows to let me see his pained expression. "What did he do?"

"Absolutely nothing. He's a nice guy—not queer, by the way. He likes girls. This is his first ever date. He said now that he has some idea of what he's giving up, it'll be even harder. But that's good, because the greater the sacrifice, 'the more pleasing it is unto the Lord.'" He sighed. "In case you're wondering, that's *not* why I wanted to punch him."

"So what is?" I asked.

"Damned if I know." Jack sighed again. "He's a nice kid who never got a chance at life. He's poor, his family—shit, I don't know why they aren't in *jail*. Your church is always collecting for starving people overseas, but there's a kid right here in town whose parents lock him out all night. They could do more than just give him used jockey shorts."

I thought of what I'd said to my mother earlier. Just before she had almost hit me. "How do you feel now?"

Jack's shoulders rose and fell heavily. "I'm fine out here," he said unhappily, "but when I go back inside, I still won't like him and I still won't know why."

"When we were all talking at the table, I didn't think anything was bothering you."

"There were six other people, I didn't have to pay attention only to him."

We strolled along in silence for a little bit. "What about tomorrow?" I asked finally. "We're supposed to go to Crazyland so Joyce and I can ride the roller coaster till we puke."

Jack didn't quite groan. "I'll manage."

"You could say you don't feel well and stay home, the three of us'll go."

Jack gave a short laugh. "Over my dead body. Crazyland isn't the prom—people don't *have* to behave themselves. And I don't just mean the bad boys in your class. They're actually pretty tame next to the guys from Tri-County, even the ones that actually graduate. You know what *their* parents give them for graduation? Bail."

"That was my guess after tattoos," I said. We laughed together and for a few moments, everything was how it used to be. Then we were walking back toward the ballroom and a sudden, profound melancholy went through me.

Sensing something, Jack put his arms around me like he thought I might fall. "You okay?"

"Yeah, it's just getting pretty dark out here."

The MACC employees from the check-in table stood on either side of the doorway, sans smiles. Apparently we were the last couple to come back in and they'd been waiting to close the doors, which they did rather noisily.

I turned to say something to Jack but he was staring past me, his face grimmer than ever. "Oh, shit. Stay here." He waved me back as he strode toward our table. I started to follow him anyway but Linda O'Shea and Jane Vaccha materialized on either side of me and held my arms.

"Don't," said Linda. She barely cleared my shoulder even in heels but she was stronger than she looked. "The cops are coming."

"The *cops*?" I looked from her to Jane who was holding my left arm even more tightly. "What's going on?"

"Nothing good," Jane said. "That poor kid."

A couple of chaperones were trying to usher kids out to the lobby but most of them just stood on the dance floor, probably right where they'd been when the band had stopped playing, staring at the scene unfolding at our table.

The table itself had been shoved out of position and some chairs overturned, no doubt by the large man looming over Tom Clement. He had Tom backed up against the wall in such a way that he was bent sideways over a corner of the table. It was an extremely awkward position; Tom would have fallen except the man was holding him up by his throat. His other hand was clamped on Joyce's forearm and she was crying in pain or fear or both. Jack was nowhere to be seen.

"I can't believe Clement's drunken father would actually bust in and ruin everything like this," Linda said. "Why is he even here? Who let him in?"

"He works in the kitchen," Jane said.

A chaperone in floaty pink chiffon started pulling at us, saying everyone had to get out of the room but I wasn't about to leave my best friend. I dug in my heels; so did Jane and Linda. The chaperone insisted; we wouldn't budge. She was fluttering around us in a pink chiffon cloud, alternately pleading and demanding when Joyce bent over the hand on her arm and sank her teeth into it.

The man bellowed so loudly I thought I heard the crystals in the chandelier rattle. He let go of both Joyce and Tom, who immediately fled in opposite directions. Suddenly Linda and Jane were telling me we had to *go*, right *now*, come *on*, but the man had finally turned around so I could see him clearly. He sat down heavily on a nearby chair, holding his arm and sobbing with drunken heartbreak. I knew that sound.

I also knew the drunken father making it wasn't Tom Clement's. And before long, everyone else knew it, too.

Decades later, I still can't tell you what pissed me off more: my father's crashingly bad timing or his mistaking Joyce for me. Like I said, Joyce was pretty—okay, prett*ier*, but I wasn't a dog by comparison, even with my less-than-perfect complexion. And while we both had dark brown hair and brown eyes, we didn't look like we were related.

But I could remember my father saying I looked just like his youngest sister when she was small. Maybe I grew up to look completely different; maybe he picked the prettiest girl who fit my general description. Or maybe he was just so trashed by then he didn't know the difference.

Anyway, that was it for the prom. The chaperones kept telling everyone to go home but no one wanted to miss this freak show. We waited in the lobby for the police, listening to the wails of despair coming through the closed doors from the ballroom. Sometime after cops arrived but before they escorted my still-weeping drunken father out to their patrol car, Jack reappeared with Joyce and Tom. Jack had wrapped his coat around Joyce; she was shivering so much her teeth were chattering. When she pulled the coat tighter around herself, I saw a hand-shaped bruise was already coming up on her arm. Tom looked like he'd just taken a blow to the head and was too stunned to know it. I could see a perfect imprint of my drunken father's thumb right under his jawline.

The MACC employees wanted to call an ambulance for Joyce but she insisted she just wanted to go home. If she'd said yes, everyone would have stayed to watch that, too, and she knew it. No one suggested Tom Clement might need medical attention.

Jack said he'd take Joyce home and then, without a word even to me, drove straight to the hospital emergency room. I thought Joyce would have a fit but she never made a sound, not even when Jack picked her up and carried her inside. While they treated her, he called her parents.

I sat for half an hour with Tom Clement before he was examined. The nurse who came to get him did a double-take and said, "Oh, Christ, Tom, not *again*."

"Not exactly," he coughed, following her to an examination room. He was back five minutes later with a box of Sucrets, free to go.

When Joyce's parents arrived, they didn't speak to any of us. They didn't even look at us. They just gathered Joyce up and left.

My mother met me at the door with a big mug of hot chocolate and a blanket. Jack had phoned her, too. I made a mental note to thank him for calling her before she got some wild, third-hand story. But that didn't make it any easier to tell her he'd gotten the most important detail wrong.

That Sunday my mother drifted around the apartment like a zombie. She didn't talk to me and I didn't try to talk to her. But at least she had stopped crying although her eyes were still puffy and bloodshot. I stayed in my room and tried to lose myself in a book. I put on *Rubber Soul*, thinking my favorite Beatles album might make me feel better. It didn't. Songs that had once had a beautiful, haunting quality to me now had an ominous edge. And when it got to "Run for Your Life," with John Lennon singing he'd rather see me dead than with someone else. I turned it off and stuffed the record in the back of my closet.

Towards evening, my mother began to perk up. She made hot dogs and beans and we ate in front of the TV. In the middle of the national news, she suddenly turned to me and said, "What do you want to do about school tomorrow? Do you want to go or would you rather stay home?"

I hesitated. All day long, I'd been refusing to think about school, blanking it out like it didn't exist. What didn't exist couldn't hurt me. Saturday night was the worst thing that had ever happened to me here so that was the end. No more.

Like hell. Everyone knew whose father had really put on that freak show and that most certainly wasn't the end. There was *lots* more.

Good thing you'll be a hundred miles away at UMass next year, said a voice in my mind. *Aren't things like this why you don't want to stay here a second longer than you have to?*

Yeah, but that wouldn't help my mother. And I still had two more weeks of school to get through.

I opened my mouth to tell her I wanted to stay home and I'd be skipping graduation, too. But what I heard myself say was, "I'll go. We're supposed to pick up our commencement gowns."

She told me then what the police had told her. He'd been working at the MACC for almost a year, my drunken father. Trying to stay sober, with the intention of suddenly presenting himself to us as a new man, worthy of a family. And while he'd been trying, he'd confided in some of his co-workers, who had confided in their own friends and so on and so forth. By the time Joyce had decided to go to the prom with Tom Clement, it was starting to get around the old home town.

That day after school, the Saturday we'd gone to LaFleur, both Joyce and I thought everyone had been staring at her when in fact it had been me.

"Still want to go in tomorrow?"

"Yeah," I said.

For a long moment, my mother's face was expressionless. Then her mouth turned up in a smile. "Tough cookie, aren't you?" she said.

"From a long line of tough cookies," I replied.

I wasn't surprised when Joyce didn't show up on Monday, although I thought that was actually her parents' idea. Even if she couldn't get her bandaged arm into her the sleeve of her blazer, I didn't think she'd have been all *that* self-conscious about it. *Take a picture*, she'd have said to anyone who stared, *it'll last longer.*

And what would she say to anyone who stared at me? For that matter, what would she say *to* me? Probably not *Close your mouth before something flies in.*

I didn't see Tom Clement until lunchtime. Kate and Mary were at our usual table. I pretended not to see them as I marched over to where Tom always sat alone. He was saying grace in silence, head bowed and eyes closed, but when he finished and looked up, he didn't seem surprised to find me sitting across from him.

"How's your neck?" I asked him. The mark from my drunken father's thumb was even more lurid now.

"It's fine, thank you." His voice was still a little raspy.

"Everybody knows that wasn't your father," I said. "You know that, right?"

"I know." He gave a small cough. "And I know whose father it really was, in case you're wondering. I'll pray for him. And for you and your mother."

"That works?"

He opened the milk carton on his tray, his long, slender fingers working expertly. "If you're asking me does God hear, yes." He put a straw in the spout and took a long sip.

I waited for him to go on. When he didn't, I shrugged. "I don't even know why I came over here."

He paused with a forkful of creamed potatoes halfway to his mouth. "It was the good luck charm."

"The what?" I blinked at him.

He held up a finger while he finished chewing. "The good luck charm. You know, the little gold crucifix." His tenor rasp was matter-of-fact. "Joyce told me she gave it to you."

I shook my head, wondering how I'd missed the turn-off from pious to crazy. "What's that got to do with anything?"

Again, the we've-got-a-secret smile. "I wasn't sure it would work on Joyce. She isn't like you and me, you see. She's practically immune. Saturday night was rough on her but in a month, two months, it'll be like a bad dream." His smile widened. "Not you. You're gonna feel it for a very, very long time. And when it's time for your kids to go their own prom, it'll come flooding back like it was yesterday."

"What are you *talking* about?" I demanded.

"Suffering." He gazed at me with what I guess was supposed to be saintly compassion; I thought he just looked deranged. "Our Lord suffered to save us and re-open heaven after God the Father locked us out. So we must suffer in this life to repay him." His face turned sad. "But not everyone suffers, which means others have to suffer for them as well as for themselves. I have done that. And now you have, too."

I was vaguely aware of kids walking past us, taking their trays to the kitchen conveyor belt. It was almost time to go back to classes but the revelation of Tom Clement's lunacy eclipsed everything else.

"It's nothing compared to what *He* endured on the cross," Tom was saying. "I can stand some discomfort for the Father Who gave me life and the Son

Who saved me. But I am only one person—one little, insignificant person. However much I suffer, it isn't enough. I prayed to God to show me how to give Him more. And He did.

"Just before sophomore year, I was at church and a couple of ladies were helping me find things I could wear from the donation box. I came across this paper bag full of little tiny gold crucifixes, hundreds of them. Someone had dumped them in with the clothes. I asked if I could have one or two and they said I could have the whole bag if I wanted because they really didn't know what else to do with them. I didn't know what to do with them either but I took them anyway. The next time I went to confession, I got the monsignor to bless them. As soon as he did, it was like the Holy Spirit came into me and I knew what I was supposed to do."

"You're crazy," I said. "I don't mean weird, I mean genuine locked-ward insane."

He shrugged one shoulder. "I didn't get it right at first. The ones I gave them to—slipped into a pocket or through the vent in a locker door—they were all people *I* thought should suffer. But they didn't. Then I realized—my mistake was thinking *I* could manipulate God's work to punish those who had wronged *me*. But *we* must turn the other cheek, forgive those who trespass against us. I was so ashamed."

"'Vengeance is mine,' saith the Lord." I wasn't even aware of speaking aloud till I heard my own voice.

"That will come at Judgment Day," Tom Clement said approvingly. "In this life, suffering is the sacrifice we owe Him. The greater the sacrifice, the more pleasing it is unto the Lord. Your sacrifice is *very* pleasing because you don't deserve to suffer. You understand that part, don't you? *You don't deserve to suffer.*" He smiled. "And neither do I."

"Neither does Joyce," I pointed out. "Is *her* suffering less pleasing for some reason? Or didn't she suffer enough for you and God?"

"Joyce wasn't put here to suffer. She has a different role to play."

"God's *so* lucky to have you running around taking care of things for Him." I started to get up and Tom grabbed my wrist. He was a lot stronger than he looked.

"I am only His instrument. Offer your suffering up to Him. To thank Him for sending His only begotten—"

I used the little move my mother had taught me to break his grip; the surprise on his face gave me a thrill of spiteful satisfaction. "*You* offer it up," I said. "To whatever you're worshipping as God. I don't want any part of it." I started to walk away.

"Rooo-uth."

I froze. He smiled, that we-share-a-secret smile.

"I still suffer, every day," he said. "No one else's sacrifices are greater than mine. When I sleep under the porch. When I put on my secondhand underwear. When I walk through the hallways of this school." His eyes narrowed slightly. "Don't you want to know about Joyce's part in His plan?"

"No."

"Liar," he said in a voice so soft and smooth it was practically a purr. "It's the same as all of our lovely schoolmates. They're all God's children, too. They're here to *help* us suffer. Even your boyfriend. The gallant Jack? He couldn't stand me. Could he."

"Too bad Joyce doesn't know enough to feel the same way."

"That's where *you* come in," he said. "To her, I'll always be poor Tom Clement, the guy she tried to do something nice for. Then your father ruined everything. That makes it *your* fault. And she's not the only one who feels that way." His smile was practically poisonous. "This time *you're* the victim to blame, not me."

I gave a single, hard laugh. "Well, I'll be damned—misery really *does* love company." I admit I was baiting him with the *damned* but he let me leave without taking it. I've often wondered why but I don't think I want to know.

So is Tom Clement really the psycho in this story after all?

I mean, if people are only doing things they'd do anyway without your encouragement or approval, it's not your fault, is it? What could you possibly be guilty of—suffering?

Would a psycho suffer deliberately? In the case of a religious fanatic, yes, absolutely. Religious fanaticism and masochism have been dancing together for millennia. And the only thing misery loves as much as company is more miserable company. Which may be why it's a pretty overcrowded world.

But not a pretty world. People starve, they beg on the streets, and the way they have to live would make Tom Clement's space under the porch look cozy, those poor have-nots. And us haves, we *love* what we have—a lot of it is produced by people working in conditions we would never tolerate, for pay that wouldn't buy a cup of coffee. We wouldn't force anyone to live like that—well, most of us wouldn't. But we don't even try to stop it.

We're safe in the American dream. *Very* safe—we build as many prisons as schools, maybe more. Yesterday, I read that the U.S. has the highest number of incarcerated people in the world, followed by China and Russia.

If playing God—or acting as His instrument, like Tom—means you're a psycho, what does that make God?

When I think about that, I suspect Tom Clement's not the only person with a stash of good luck charms. At least, I hope he isn't.

Because if he is, that's worse.

IN THE YEAR OF OMENS

HELEN MARSHALL

That was the year of omens—the year the coroner cut open the body of the girl who had thrown herself from the bridge, and discovered a bullfrog living in her right lung. The doctor, it was said by the people who told those sorts of stories (and there were many of them), let the girl's mother take the thing home in her purse—its skin wet and gleaming, its eyes like glittering gallstones—and when she set it in her daughter's bedroom it croaked out the saddest, sweetest song you ever heard in the voice of the dead girl.

Leah loved to listen to these stories. She was fourteen and almost pretty. She liked dancing and horses, sentimental poetry, certain shades of pink lipstick, and Hector Alvarez, which was no surprise at all, because *everyone* liked Hector Alvarez.

"Tell me what happened to the girl," Leah would say to her mum, slicing potatoes at the kitchen counter while her mother switched on the oven. Leah was careful always to jam the knifepoint in first so that the potatoes would break open as easily as apples. Her dad had taught her that before he had died. Everything he did was sacred now.

"No," her mum would say.

"But you know what happened to her?"

"I know what happened, Leah."

"Then why won't you tell me?"

And Leah would feel the slight weight of her mother's frame like a ghost behind her. Sometimes her mum would touch the back of her neck, just rest a hand there, or on her shoulder. Sometimes, she would check the potatoes. Leah had a white scar on her thumb where she'd sliced badly once.

"You shouldn't have to hear those things. Those things aren't for you, okay?"

"But mum—"

"Mum," Milo would mumble from his highchair. "Mum mum mum mum."

"Here, lovely girl, fetch me the rosemary and thyme. Oh, and the salt. Enough about that other thing, okay? Enough about it. Your brother is getting hungry."

And Leah would put down the knife, and would turn from the thin, round slices of potatoes. She would kiss her brother on the scalp where his hair stuck up in fine, whitish strands. Smell the sweet baby scent of him. "Shh, monkey-face, just a little bit longer. Mum's coming soon." Then Milo would let out a sharp, breathy giggle, and maybe Leah would giggle too, or maybe she wouldn't.

Her mum wouldn't speak of the things that were happening, but Leah knew—of course Leah knew.

First it was the girl. That's how they always spoke of her.

"Did you hear about *the girl*?"

"Which girl?"

"*The girl*. The one who jumped."

And then it wasn't just *the girl* anymore. It was Joanna Sinclair who always made red velvet cupcakes for the school bake sale. She had found her name written in the gossamer threads of a spider web. It was Oscar Nunez from the end of the block whose tongue shrivelled up in his mouth. It was Yasmine with the black eyeliner who liked to smoke pot sometimes when she babysat Leah.

"Maybe it'll be, I dunno, just this one perfect note. Like a piano," Yasmine had murmured before it happened, pupils big enough to swallow the violet-circled iris of her eyes. "Or a harp. Or a, what's it, a zither. I heard one of those once. It was gorgeous."

"You think so?" Leah asked. She watched the smoke curl around the white edge of her nostrils like incense. There were only four years between them, but those four years seemed a magnificent chasm. Across it lay wisdom and secret truths. Across it lay the Hectors of the world, unattainable if you were only fourteen years old. Everything worthwhile lay across that chasm.

"Maybe. Maybe that's what it will be for me. Maybe I'll just hear that one note forever, going on and on and on, calling me to paradise."

It hadn't been that. The omens weren't what you hoped for. They weren't what you thought they would be. But you *knew* when it was yours. That's what people said. You could recognize it. You always *knew*.

When Hector found her—(they were dating, of course Hector would only date someone as pretty and wise as Yasmine, Leah thought)—the skin had split at her elbows and chin, peeled back like fragile paper to reveal something bony and iridescent like the inside of an oyster shell.

Leah hadn't been allowed to go to the funeral.

Her mum had told her Yasmine had gone to college, she couldn't babysit anymore, Leah would have to take care of Milo herself. But Leah was friends with Hector's sister, Inez, and *she* knew better.

"It was like there was something inside her," Inez whispered as they both gripped the tiled edge of the pool during the Thursday swim practice, Inez's feet kicking lazily in hazy, blue-gray arcs. Inez had the same look as her brother, the same widely spaced eyes, skin the same dusty copper as a penny. Her hair clung thick, black and slickly to her forehead where it spilled out of the swimming cap.

"What kind of thing was it?" The water was cold. Leah hated swimming, but her mum made her do it anyway.

"God, I mean, I dunno. Hector won't tell me. Just that . . . he didn't think it would be like that. He thought she'd be beautiful on the inside, you know? He thought it would be something else."

Leah had liked Yasmine—(even though she had always liked Hector more, liked it when Yasmine brought him over and the two of them huddled on the deck while Leah pretended not to watch, the flame of the lighter a third eye between them). Leah had wanted it to be a zither for her. Something sweet and strange and wondrous.

"I thought so too," Leah whispered, but Inez had already taken off in a perfect backstroke toward the deep end.

It was why her mum never talked about it. The omens weren't always beautiful things.

There had always been signs in the world. Every action left its trace somewhere. There were clues. There were giveaways. The future whispered to you before you even got there, and the past, well, the past was a chatterbox, it would tell you everything if you let it.

The signs Leah knew best were the signs of brokenness. The sling her mum had worn after the accident that made it impossible for her to carry Milo. The twinging muscle in her jaw that popped and flexed when she moved the wrong way. It had made things difficult for a while. The pain made her mum sharp and prickly. The medication made her dozy. Sometimes she'd nod off at the table, and Leah would have to clear up the dishes herself, and then tend to Milo if he was making a fuss.

And there was the dream.

There had always been signs in the world.

But, now. Now it was different, and the differences both scared and thrilled Leah.

"Mum," she would whisper. "Please tell me, Mum."

"I can't, sweetie," her mum would whisper in a strained, half-conscious voice. Leah could see the signs of pain now. The way her mum's lids fluttered. The lilt in her voice from the medication. "I just don't know. Oh, darling, why? Why? I'm scared. I don't know what's happening to the world."

But Leah wasn't scared.

A month later Leah found something in the trash: one of her mother's sheer black stockings. Inside it was the runt-body of a newborn kitten wrapped in a wrinkled dryer sheet.

"Oh, pretty baby," she cooed.

Leah turned the lifeless little lump over. She moved it gently, carefully from palm to palm. It had the kind of boneless weight that Milo had when he slept. She could do anything to him then, anything at all, and he wouldn't wake up.

One wilted paw flopped between her pinkie and ring finger. The head lolled. And there—on the belly, there it was—the silver scales of a fish. They flaked away against the calluses on her palm, decorated the thin white line of her scar.

Leah felt a strange, liquid warmth shiver its way across her belly as she held the kitten. It was not hers, she knew it was not hers. Was it her mum who had found the thing? Her mum. Of course it was her mum.

"Oh," she said. "My little thing. I'm sorry for what's been done to you."

She knew she ought to be afraid then, but she wasn't. She loved the little kitten. It was gorgeous—just exactly the sort of omen that Yasmine ought to have had.

If only it had been alive . . .

Leah didn't know what her own omen would be. She hoped like Yasmine had that it would be something beautiful. She hoped when she saw it she would know it most certainly as her own special thing. And she knew she would not discard it like the poor drowned kitten—fur fine and whitish around the thick membrane of the eyelids. Not for all the world. Not even if it scared her.

She placed the kitten in an old music box her dad had brought back from Montreal. There was a crystal ballerina, but it was broken and didn't spin properly. Still, when she opened the lid, the tinny notes of "La Vie en Rose" chimed out slow and stately. The body of the kitten fit nicely against the faded velvet inside of it.

The box felt so light it might have been empty.

Now it was October—just after the last of the September heat had begun to fade off like a cooling cooking pan. Inez and Leah were carving pumpkins together. This was the last year they were allowed to go trick or treating, and even so, they were only allowed to go as long as they took Milo with them. (Milo was going to dress as a little white rabbit. Her mum had already bought the costume.)

They were out on the porch, sucking in the last of the sunlight, their pumpkins squat on old newspapers empty of the stories that Leah really wanted to read.

Carving pumpkins was trickier than cutting potatoes. You had to do it with a very sharp, very small knife. It wasn't about pressure so much. It was about persistence—taking things slow, feeling your way through it so you didn't screw up. Inez was better at that. It wasn't the cutting that Leah liked anyway. She liked the way it felt to shove her hands inside the pumpkin and bring out its long, stringy guts. Pumpkins had a smell: rich and earthy, but sweet too, like underwear if you didn't change it every day.

"It's happening to me," Inez whispered to her. She wasn't looking at Leah, she was staring intensely at the jagged crook of eye she was trying to get right. Taking it slow. Inez liked to get everything just right.

"What's happening?" Leah said.

Inez still didn't look at her, she was looking at the eye of the jack-o'-lantern-to-be, her brow scrunched as she concentrated. But her hand was trembling.

"What's happening?"

Cutting line met cutting line. The piece popped through with a faint sucking sound.

"You know, Leah. What's been happening to . . . to everyone. What happened to Yasmine." Her voice quavered. Inez was still staring at the pumpkin. She started to cut again.

"Tell me," Leah said. And then, more quietly, she said, "please."

"I don't want to."

Plop went another eye. The pumpkin looked angry. Or scared. The expressions sometimes looked the same on pumpkins.

"Then why did you even bring it up?" Leah could feel something quivering inside her as she watched Inez saw into the flesh of the thing.

"I just wanted to—I don't even know. But don't tell Hector, okay? He'd be worried about me."

Leah snuck a look at Hector who was raking leaves in the yard. She liked watching Hector work. She liked to think that maybe if the sun was warm enough (as it was today—more of a September sun than an October sun, really) then maybe, just maybe, he would take his shirt off.

"It's okay to tell me, Inez. Promise. I won't tell anyone. Just tell me so *someone* out there knows."

Inez was quiet. And then she said in a small, tight voice, "Okay."

She put down the knife. The mouth was only half done. Just the teeth. But they were the trickiest part to do properly. Then, carefully, gently, Inez undid the top three buttons of her blouse. She swept away the long, black curls of hair that hid her neck and collarbone.

"It's here. Do you see?"

Leah looked. At first she thought it was a mild discoloration, the sort of blemish you got if you sat on your hands for too long and the folds of your clothes imprinted themselves into the skin. But it wasn't that at all. There was a pattern to it, like the jack-o'-lantern, the shapes weren't meaningless. They were a face. They were the shadow of a face—eyes wide open. Staring.

"Did you tell Hector?"

"I'm telling you.

"God, Inez—"

But Inez turned white and shushed her. "Don't say that!" Inez squealed. "Don't say his name like that. We don't know! Maybe it is, I mean, do you think, maybe He . . . I mean, oh, Jesus, I don't know, Leah!" Her mouth froze in a little "oh" of horror. There were tears running down her cheeks, forming little eddies around a single, pasty splatter of pumpkin guts.

"It's okay, Inez. It's okay." And Leah put her arm around Inez. "You'll be okay," she whispered. "You'll be okay."

And they rocked together. So close. Close enough that Leah could feel her cheek pressing against Inez's neck. Just above the mark. So close she could imagine it whispering to her. There was something beautiful about it all. Something beautiful about the mark pressed against her, the wind making a rustling sound of the newspapers, Hector in the yard, and the long strings of pumpkin guts lined up like glyphs drying in the last of the summer light.

"It's okay," Leah told her, but even as they rocked together, their bodies so close Leah could feel the hot, hardpan length of her girlish muscles tense and relax in turns, she knew there was a chasm splitting between them, a great divide.

"Shush," she said. "Pretty baby," she said because sometimes that quieted Milo down. Inez wasn't listening. She was holding on. So hard it hurt.

Inez was dead the next day.

Leah was allowed to attend the funeral. It was the first funeral she'd been allowed to go to since her dad's.

The funeral had a closed casket (of course, it had to) but Leah wanted to see anyway. She pressed her fingers against the dark, glossy wood of the coffin, leaving a trail of smudged fingerprints that stood out like boot marks in fresh snow. She wanted to see what had happened to that face with the gaping eyes. She wanted to know who that face had belonged to. No one would tell her. From her mum, it was still nothing but, "Shush up, Leah."

And Hector was there.

Hector was wearing a suit. Leah wondered if it was the same suit that he had worn to Yasmine's funeral, and if he'd looked just as good wearing it then as he did now. A suit did something to a man.

Leah was wearing a black dress. Not a little black dress. She didn't have a little black dress—she and Inez had decided they would wait until their breasts came in before they got little black dresses. But Inez had never got her breasts.

The funeral was nice. There were lots of gorgeous white flowers: roses and lilies and stuff, which looked strange because everyone was wearing black. And everyone said nice things about Inez—how she'd been on the swim team, how she'd always got good grades. But there was something tired about all the nice things they said, as if they'd worn out those expressions already. "She was my best friend," Leah said into the microphone. She had been nervous about speaking in front of a crowd, but by the time her turn actually came she was mostly just tired too. She tried to find Hector in the audience. His seat was empty. "We grew up together. I always thought she was like my sister."

Leah found him outside, afterward. He was sitting on the stairs of the back entrance to the church, a plastic cup in one hand. The suit looked a little crumpled but it still looked good. At nineteen he was about a foot taller than most of the boys she knew. They were like little mole-rats compared to him.

Her mother was still inside making small talk with the reverend. All the talk anyone made was small these days.

"Hey," she said.

He looked up. "Hey."

It was strange, at that moment, to see Inez's eyes looking out from her brother's face now that she was dead. It didn't look like the same face. Leah didn't know if she should go or not.

Her black dress rustled around her as she folded herself onto the stair beside him.

"Shouldn't you be back in there?"

Hector put the plastic cup to his lips and took a swig of whatever was inside. She could almost imagine it passing through him. She was fascinated by the way his throat muscles moved as he swallowed, the tiny triangle he had missed with his razor. Wordlessly, he handed the cup to her. Leah took a tentative sniff. Whatever it was, it was strong. It burned the inside of her nostrils.

"I don't know," Hector said. "Probably. Probably you should too."

"What are you doing out here?"

Hector didn't say anything to that. He simply stared at the shiny dark surface of his dress shoes—like the coffin—scuffing the right with the left. The sun made bright hotplates of the parking lot puddles. Leah took a drink. The alcohol felt good inside her stomach. It felt warm and melting inside her. She liked being here next to Hector. The edge of her dress was almost touching his leg, spilling off her knees like a black cloud, but he didn't move. They stayed just like that. It was like being in a dream. Not *the* dream. A nice dream.

"I miss her, Leah. I can't stop it . . . you look a bit like her, you know? I mean, you don't look anything like her really, but still," he stumbled, searching out the right words. "But."

"Yeah," she said.

"I'm glad you're here."

She took a larger swallow. Her head felt light. She felt happy. She knew she shouldn't feel happy but she felt happy anyway. Did Hector feel happy? She couldn't tell. She hadn't looked at enough boys to tell exactly what they looked like when they looked happy.

Suddenly, she was leaning toward him. Their hands were touching, fingers sliding against each other, and she was kissing him.

"Leah," he said, and she liked the way he said her name, but she didn't like the way he was shaking his head. She tried again, but this time he jerked his head away from her. "No, Leah. I can't, you're . . . you're just a kid."

The happy feeling evaporated. Leah looked away.

"Please, Hector," she said. "There's something . . ." She paused. Tried to look at him and not look at him at the same time. "It's not just Inez, okay? It's me too." She was lying. She didn't know why she was lying about it, except that she *wished* it was true. She wished it was her too. She wished Inez hadn't found something first.

He shook his head again, but there was a glint in his eyes. Something that hadn't been there before. It made him look the way that Inez's mark had with its wide, hollow eyes. Like there could be anything in them. Anything at all.

"I've found something. On my skin. We were like sisters, you know. Really. Do you want to see it?"

"No," he said. His eyes were wide. Inez's eyes had looked like that, too, hadn't they? They both had such pretty eyes. Eyes seeded with gold and copper and bronze.

"Please," she said. "Would you kiss me? I want to know what it's like. Before."

"No," he whispered again, but he did anyway. Carefully. He tasted sweet and sharp. Like pumpkin. He tasted the way the way a summer night tastes in your mouth, heavy and wet, wanting rain but not yet ready to let in October. The kiss lingered on her lips.

Leah wondered if this was what love felt like. She wondered if Yasmine had felt like this, if Hector had made her feel like this, and if she did, how could she ever have left him?

She didn't ask for another kiss.

The world was changing around them all now, subtly, quietly at first, but it was changing. It was a time for omens. The world felt like an open threshold waiting for Leah to step through. But she couldn't. She couldn't yet.

The day after the funeral Leah cut her hair and dyed it black. She wore it in dark, heavy ringlets just as Inez had. She took a magic marker to the space just below the collar of her shirt, the place Inez had showed her, and she drew a face with large eyes. With a hungry mouth.

She looked at forums. They all had different sorts of advice for her.

If you say your name backwards three times and spit . . .

If you sleep in a graveyard by a headstone with your birthday . . .

If you cut yourself this way . . .

Those were the things you could do to stop it, they said. Those were the things you could do to pass it on to someone else.

But nothing told her what she wanted.

For Milo, it started slowly. When Leah tried to feed him, sometimes he would spit out the food. Sometimes he would slam his chubby little hands into the tray again and again and again until a splatter of pureed squash covered them both. He would stare into the empty space and burble like a trout.

"C'mon, baby," Leah whispered to him. "You gotta eat something. Please, monkey-face. Just for me? Just a bite?"

But he got thinner and thinner and thinner. His skin flaked off against Leah's shirt in bright, silver-shiny patches when she held him. Her mum stopped looking at him. When she turned in his direction her eyes passed over him as if there was a space cut out of the world where he had been before, the way strangers didn't look at each other on the subway.

"Mum," Leah said, "what's happening to him?"

"Nothing, darling. He'll quiet soon." And it was like the dream. She couldn't move. No one could hear what she was saying.

"Mum," Leah said. "He's crying for you. Can you just hold him for a bit? My arms are getting tired and he just won't quit. He wants you, mum."

"No, darling," her mum would say. Just that. And then she would lock herself in her room, and Leah would rock the baby back and forth, gently, gently, and whisper things in his ear.

"Mummy loves you," she would say to him, "c'mon, pretty baby, c'mon and smile for me. Oh, Milo. Please, Milo."

Sometimes it seemed that he weighed nothing at all, he was getting so light. Like she was carrying around a bundle of sticks, not her baby brother. His fingers poked her through her shirt, hard and sharp. The noises he made, they weren't the noises that he knew. It was a rasping sort of cough, something like a choke, and it made her scared but she was all alone. It was only her and Milo. She clung tightly to him.

"Pretty baby," she murmured as she carried him upstairs. "Pretty, little monkey-face."

It was only when she showed him the little kitten she had tucked away in her music box that he began to quiet. He touched it cautiously, fingers curving like hooks. The fur had shed into the box. It was patchy in some places, and the skin beneath was sleek and silvery and gorgeous. When Milo's fingers brushed against it he let out a shrieking giggle.

It was the first happy sound he had made in weeks.

What were the signs of love? Were they as easy to mark out as any other sort of sign? Were they a hitch in the breath? The way that suddenly any sort of touch—the feel of your hand running over the thin cotton fibers of your sheets—was enough to make you blush? Leah thought of Hector Alvarez. She thought about the kiss, and the way he had tasted, the slight pressure of his lips, the way her bottom lip folded into his mouth, just a little, just a very little bit, like origami.

Leah checked her body every morning. Her wrists. Her neck. She used a mirror to sight out her spine, the small of her back, the back of her thighs.

Nothing. Never any change.

The stars were dancing—tra lee, tra la—and the air was heavy with the fragrant smell of pot. They passed the joint between them carelessly. First it hung in his lips. Then it touched hers.

"What are you afraid of?" Leah asked Hector.

"What do you mean, what am I afraid of?"

Leah liked the way he looked in moonlight. She liked the way she looked too. Her breasts had come in. They pushed comfortably against the whispering silk of her black dress. They were small breasts, like apples. Crabapple breasts. She hoped they weren't finished growing.

She was fifteen today.

Tonight the moon hung pregnant and fat above them, striations of clouds lit up with touches of silver and chalk-white. It had taken them a while to find the right place. A gravestone with two dates carved beneath it. His and hers. (Even though she knew it wouldn't work. Even though she knew it wouldn't do what she wanted.)

The earth made a fat mound beneath them, the dirt fresh. Moist. She had been afraid to settle down on it, afraid that it wouldn't hold her. Being in a graveyard was different now—it felt like the earth might be moving beneath you, like there might be something moving around underneath, below the sod and the six feet that came after it. Dying wasn't what it used to be.

"I mean," she said, "what scares you? This?" She touched his hand. Took the joint from him.

"No," he said.

"Me neither." The smoke hung above them. A veil. Gauzy. There were clouds above the smoke. They could have been anything in the moonlight. They could have just been clouds. "Then what?"

"I was afraid for a while," Hector said at last, "that they were happy." He was wearing his funeral suit. Even with grave dirt on it, it still made him look good. "I was afraid because they were happy when they left. That's what scared me. Yasmine was smiling when I found her. There was a look on her face . . ." He paused, took a breath. "Inez too. They knew something. It was like they figured something out. You know what I mean?"

"No," she said. *Yes*, she thought.

Her mother had been cutting potatoes this morning. Normally Leah cut them. She cut them the way her dad had taught her, but today it was her mother who was cutting them, and when the potato split open—there it was, a tiny finger, curled into the white flesh, with her dad's wedding ring lodged just behind the knuckle. Her mum's face had gone white and pinched, and she dropped the knife, her fingers instinctively touching the white strip of flesh where her own wedding ring used to sit.

"Oh, god," she whispered.

"Mum," Leah said. "It's okay, Mum. It'll be okay."

But all she could think was, "It should have been me."

Because it was happening to all of them now. All of them except for her. When Leah walked down the street, all she could imagine were the little black dresses she would wear to their funerals. The shade of lipstick she would pick out for them. Her closet was full of black dresses.

"I've never felt that way about anything. Felt so perfectly sure about it that I'd let it take me over. I'd give myself up to it."

"I have," she said. But Hector wasn't listening to her.

"But then," he said, "I heard it."

"What?"

"Whatever Yasmine was waiting for. That long perfect note. That sound like Heaven coming."

"When?"

"Last night." His eyes were all pupils. When had they got that way? Had they always been like that? The joint was just a stub now between her lips, a bit of pulp. She flicked it away.

"Please don't go away, Hector," she said.

"I can't help it," he said. "You'll see soon. You'll know what I mean. But I'm not scared, Leah. I'm not scared at all."

"I know," she said. She remembered the way Milo had been with the kitten. He had known it was his. Even though it was monstrous, its chest caved in, the little ear bent like a folded page. It was his. She wanted that, God, how she wanted that.

And now Hector was taking her hand, and he was pressing it against his chest. She could feel something growing out of his ribcage: the hooked, hard knobs pushing through the skin like antlers. He sighed when she touched it, and smiled like he had never smiled at her before.

"I didn't understand when Yasmine told me," he said. "I couldn't understand. But you—you, Leah, you understand, don't you? You don't need to be scared, Leah," he said. "You can be happy with me."

And when he kissed her, the length of his body drawn up beside her, she felt the shape of something cruel and mysterious hidden beneath the black wool of his suit.

That night Leah had the dream—they were on the road together, all four of them.

"Listen, George," her mother was saying. (What she said next was always different, Leah had never been able to remember what it actually was, what she'd said that had made him turn, shifted his attention for that split second.)

Leah was in the back, and Milo—Milo who hadn't been born when her father was alive—was strapped in to his child's seat next to her.

"Listen, George," her mother was saying, and that was part of it. Her mother was trying to tell him something, but he couldn't hear her probably. So he turned. He missed it—what was coming, the slight curve in the road, but it was winter, and the roads were icy and it was enough, just enough.

"Is this it?" Leah asked. But her mum wasn't listening. She was tapping on the window. She was trying to show him something she had spotted.

Leah knew what came next. In all the other dreams what came next was the squeal of tires, the world breaking apart underneath her, and her trying to grab onto Milo, trying to keep him safe. (Even though he wasn't there, she would think in the morning, he hadn't even been born yet!)

That's how the dream was supposed to go.

"Listen, George," her mother was saying.

The car kept moving. The tires kept spinning, whispering against the asphalt.

"Is this what it is for me?" Leah tried to ask her mother, but her mother was still pointing out the window. "Is this my sign?"

And it wasn't just Milo in the car. It was Inez, too. It was Oscar Nunez with his shriveled-up tongue, and Joanna Sinclair, and Yasmine with her black eyeliner, her eyes like cat's eyes. And it was Hector, he was there, he was holding Yasmine's hand, and he was kissing her gently on the neck, peeling back her skin to kiss the hard, oyster-grey thing that was growing inside of her.

"Leah can't come with us," her mother was saying. "Just let her off here, would you, George? Just let her off."

"No," Leah tried to tell her mum. "No, this is where I am supposed to be. This is supposed to be *it*."

And then Leah was standing in a doorway, not in the car at all, and it was a different dream. She was standing in a doorway that was not a doorway because there was nothing on the other side. Just an infinite space, an uncrossable chasm. It was dark, but dark like she had never seen darkness before, so thick it almost choked her. And there was something moving in the darkness. Something was coming . . . because that's what omens were, weren't they? They meant something was coming.

And everyone had left her behind.

When Leah woke up the house was dark. Shadows clustered around her bed. She couldn't hear Milo. She couldn't hear her mother. What she could hear, from outside, was the sound of someone screaming. She wanted to scream along with it, oh, she wanted to be part of that, to let her voice ring out in that one perfect note. . . .

But she couldn't.

Leah turned on the light. She took out the mirror. And she began to search (again—again and again and again, it made no difference, did it? it never made a difference).

She ran her fingers over and over the flawless, pale expanse of her body (flawless except for the white scar on her thumb where she'd sliced it open chopping potatoes).

Her wrists. Her neck. Her spine. Her crabapple breasts.

But there was still nothing there.

She was still perfect.

She was still whole. Untouched and alone.

THE FOUR DARKS

TERRY DOWLING

> "For they're the same thing, Glenn, as the horror and the wonder I talked about inside, the horror and wonder that lies beyond any game, that strides the world unseen and strikes without warning where it will."
>
> —Fritz Leiber, "A Bit of the Dark World"

On the Tuesday night of the final week in January, Peter Rait had the spine dream again.

It was the fifth terrifying time in as many years and, as always, the weather seemed to be a contributing factor. The hot winds that blew in on Everton from inland New South Wales came off the deserts and brought hard summer to the town: sleepless nights, blinding days, a fitful restlessness that changed everything and everyone. The municipal pool was crowded for the daylight hours; kids ignored safety warnings and jumped into the river, plunged into reservoirs, climbed the town's three water towers and jimmied the latches so they could sink into the secret glooms they found there. Every other summer, it seemed, a body was found floating in one spot or another. Fences were set up, access gates secured, locks replaced, cameras installed. But come the first scorcher, like a rite of passage, the kids would deal with fences, gates, locks and cameras, often in ways ingenious beyond their years, often beyond their budgets, showing that too much safety was never wanted as much as people said. The Town Council had strategy meetings, but deep down everyone knew that it was as if people needed the danger, sought it, filled themselves up with it. It was the world happening, after all, and there was no protection from that.

So, those winds. Far better than this Tuesday's sticky late-summer stillness. And that dream again. Little wonder that Peter came to Dan's quarters in the south wing of Everton Psychiatric Facility an hour past midnight and knocked at his door. Dan took the news calmly enough, made them herbal tea and took their cups to the armchairs where they sat watching the curtains stir in the breeze from Dan's battered old fan. The only light came from under the door and the hallway beyond.

"Tell me again, Peter," Dan said, watching the darkness beyond the tall windows. "What are you getting?"

"The spine. Same as before."

"Tell me as if I don't know anything."

"I'm seeing a spine, dreaming of a spine."

"By itself? No skull, ribs, pelvis?"

"Just the spine, Doctor Dan. Picked clean. Or like something on display. But an *urgent* spine like before. No other word comes close."

"What's in the background?"

"Darkness. Stillness. Like a museum exhibit against black velvet, or a lecture room display. A chiropractor's model. You know the kind."

"Tell me again. Supported by a holding frame?"

"No. That's the thing. I don't see any kind of support. As if it's freestanding, weightless."

"Nothing else?"

"The sense again, the strong sense—urgent *is* the only word—that it may not be a true spine. It looks wrong somehow. Like it's a mask for something."

Dan avoided the questions such an answer automatically brought, just sat sipping his tea, watching the curtains lift and fall. Everton Psychiatric Facility might be the new name for Blackwater Psychiatric Hospital, intended to give the place a more modern feel in a new millennium, but they were the same old buildings. It was the time of the year for system overloads and brown-outs. Now that Carla was officially running the place at last, leaving Dan to devote more time to his external consulting, on the nights he didn't go home he had a generous office bedsit in the Devereux wing. Air-con was limited to the wards and main staff areas. At least his old fan gave the illusion of cool air.

He went back to it on a new tack entirely, hoping to take Peter by surprise.

"Could it live in fire?"

"Well, yes. If those segments and joints are like asbestos. Protecting a central nervous system."

"In water?"

Peter barely hesitated. "Easily. It's like a marine creature anyway."

"Desert?"

"Again, easily. It already looks desiccated, mummified."

"In space?"

"I said weightless, but how can I know? I can't know its chemistry from looking."

"Think carefully, Peter. It's in a display situation, you say, but is it avoiding you or approaching you?"

"Excuse me?"

"Is it larger than last time? All the other times? Is it coming at you, following you or keeping away?"

"I'm not sure, Doctor Dan. It seems to be still."

"But is it different in any way? Is it in exactly the same position as the other times? A chiropractor's side-on display?"

"No! It's angled towards me now! My God, yes! It is!"

"Is that what it's hiding? Masking its approach?"

"What? No! No!"

"What else?"

"Unclear. Still unclear. But something's not right. Something else."

"Final question, and you take this back to bed with you and sleep on it. Is it *your* spine? Is there something *you* want *you* to know?"

It was an obvious question, one that would be sheer recklessness directed at ninety-five percent of Blackwater's inmates. But this was Blackwater's unofficial backup handyman, in his late forties, tall, greying amid the tousled black hair, a personable schizophrenic who had been discharged years ago but had elected to stay on, taking room and board in return for doing odd jobs about the place. He was also its prize psychosleuth, someone who saw things, knew things. This would play to his strengths, settle him, Dan knew, give him a focus. It was how Peter worked, how this needed to work. He would indeed sleep on it.

Peter set down his cup and stood. "Good luck to both of us trying to sleep. You have a busy day tomorrow."

"How so?"

"Someone's coming to see you."

"I have three appointments tomorrow, Peter. You know something?"

Peter turned when he reached the door. "You know me. I just like to check the appointment schedule from time to time. Goodnight."

Dan sat another ten minutes pondering why Peter had mentioned the next day's appointments, then went back to bed.

It was a hot morning after a difficult night when Allan Grace was shown into Dan's office at eleven A.M., and Dan couldn't help but be surprised at what he saw. Grace was a tall man, imposing, with a long pale face, wide forehead, grey eyes and limp sandy hair, dressed in an extremely dapper fashion in a tailored black suit, with matching black socks and shoes, wearing a crisp white shirt with the top button done up, though with no tie to warrant it. He had a sheen to his skin, a gloss of perspiration that gave him a waxen look.

The collar was far too tight for the man's neck, Dan saw, and "muffin top" came to mind. Allan Grace was lean, but his neck muffined out over the crisp white collar. It made the whole thing look odd, desperate, wrong somehow.

Dan wanted to say something, but figured there had to be a reason: some health or self-image issue, scars, tattoos, something, that made the tightly buttoned collar, the whole over-formal outfit, necessary on such a muggy day. Maybe the man owned only the one business shirt, had found it way too tight but wanted to make a good impression.

"Thank you for seeing me, Doctor Truswell," Grace said.

"My pleasure, Mr. Grace."

Dan found the man's handshake cooler and drier than he expected, then led the way to the same armchairs and side tables he had used with Peter the night before. He poured glasses of chilled mineral water and handed one to his guest.

Grace drank gratefully. "I don't mean to intrude on your time too long. I'm still quite new in town, and wonder if you might consider acting as a consultant for me in a project I'm completing in the area?"

The man had a good mellow voice but wheezed when he talked, which again made Dan want to say, "Loosen your collar, man! Undo the top button!" But Grace's elegance and otherwise composed manner cautioned Dan. He's intelligent enough to know what he's doing, Dan told himself. There truly may be health issues in play, even mental health issues, but he's managing, controlled. Let it be.

"You find me immediately wary, Mr. Grace. As well as having little free time because of ongoing duties here and various secondments, my position requires considerable discretion. Any useful information would be general at best."

One of Grace's pale hands went up in a reassuring gesture. "This has more to do with general conclusions you might have reached from completing those duties, bits of information you might have picked up in the extracurricular activities you've pursued."

Dan ignored the gentlest barb in the final words. Maybe the heat and humidity were getting to him, the lack of sleep. "Conclusions regarding what?"

"Have you heard of something called the Fuligin Braid?"

"Again, please."

"The Fuligin Braid. Fuligin, as in dark, sooty, and Braid as in strands of hair or cord woven together."

"I haven't, no."

"No matter, though your reputation—I was hoping. So let me approach this somewhat differently. I've heard stories. You work for the police sometimes—"

"Mr. Grace, like I said—"

"Allan, please. And no details wanted, I assure you, Doctor. No prying. But there are stories about successes. Patients and orderlies talk, you understand. Locals. This concerns Everton. Something you might look into better than I can."

"Just how does it concern Everton?"

"That's what I'm trying to find out. My research has brought me here."

Dan had to smile. "*My* successes. *Your* research. Allan, I feel I'm meant to ask. What is the Fuligin Braid?"

"Here's where I risk being dismissed as a certain mental health stereotype, but can you believe that there is inherent evil in the world?"

It was the perfect way to ask it. *Can* you, not *do* you. But Dan dare not encourage this detached but intense, strangely overdressed man.

"Not as a coherent, directed thing, no." It was an easy lie to give to strangers, well-practiced and comfortably delivered.

"But the stories? The Toother business? The Haniver sisters coming to you?"

It was uncanny, always unsettling when a complete stranger tosses off facts about your life. Always flattering in an interview when someone has done their homework properly, but for Dan this was someone knowing *too* much.

"All right. Let's say I'd prefer not to. You've studied me closely."

"I value that word 'prefer,' Doctor. You are someone who has come out from behind the desk. Stepped out into the world."

Dan refused to be drawn. "Many do."

"You allow for a greater world and so find one."

"Again?"

"You continue to allow that there *is* a greater world. Have constantly tested this one and found more to it. Your conclusions and insights could be invaluable to me."

"Two questions before this goes any further, Allan. Where did you get your facts, and how does this connection with the Fuligin Braid concern Everton?"

Allan Grace looked for a moment as if he were going to tug at his terrible collar, give in to the temptation to undo the button, but controlled himself. "May I have five uninterrupted minutes? Then I will go and bother you no more."

"Five minutes then."

"I am investigating something called the Fuligin Braid, a term coined in Prague by Laurence Sanston Londasleite in 1853. Londasleite suggested that what we know as night is made up of four distinct parts, three in the everyday physical world, one on a plane separate but linked to ours, what he called the Inchoate."

Dan took a sip of water. "The Fuligin Braid is these four elements wound together?"

"The Four Darks, yes. Darkness as we know it. It comes from a very old area of hermeneutics. Londasleite was seen as a crackpot even in his own day, but his point stands. Our instinctive, atavistic fear of darkness is because of the two final threads, the ones that—how shall I put this?—make darkness more *pro-active* in our own world, the last strand in particular. I know this all sounds very much your Madame Blavatsky hocus-pocus, something that makes arguments for the existence of the phlogiston and the luminiferous ether look positively respectable. But ideas are of their time, and valid connections being missed fill recorded history as much as wrongheadedness and outright errors do: people in

14th-century Europe not seeing that fleas on rats were the main plague vector for the Black Death; the Victorians failing to see that the new industrial-age smog was a major cause of tuberculosis, that sort of thing. Science is rightly about invisible particles, waves, force fields, and quantum states, calibrated and regulated by good honest mathematics, but what if darkness *does* have a paranormal aspect to it, distinct and quantifiable? What if something like the Fuligin Braid could exist? What if it *does*?"

"So what are these Four Darks?"

Allan Grace gave a thin smile. "The first is the simple, observable physical state produced by the absence of light, which he regarded as obvious and incidental, just so much circumstantial window dressing. The second Dark serves a carrier function, like plasma in the blood, something very much akin to the luminiferous ether people once believed filled the universe. But the next two are the pro-active parts. The third strand of the Braid affects the brain, enlists the brain, actively suborns the brain, actively contributes to what we call the mental disorders. Londasleite believed it does that as a way of maintaining a heightened mind-body-world connectivity, so the individual is properly primed for interacting with—dealing with the final part."

"How so?"

"His contention was that we evolved essentially as creatures of light, that the whole biological purpose for sleeping, actually needing to become *unconscious* in order to rest properly, was to protect us from night's two pro-active, disordering powers. But the final strand is the one that's most interesting. It's where an actual *artefact* is produced, a night artefact in a sense."

Grace left an appropriate silence.

Dan uncapped the bottle, topped up their glasses. "What, ghostly residues? A substance like ectoplasm? Surely not an actual entity—"

"These are my questions, Doctor. In a sense, Londasleite's theory of the Four Darks is beside the point. It's finding evidence for the final strand that interests me. Londasleite pursued an old line of thinking. He insisted he was ahead of his time."

"Exactly of his time as I'm hearing it."

"You are right to say so. The scientific community and the Church came down on him hard. He couldn't even make useful cult coinage out of it, except among his own descendants, one of whom, I have every reason to believe, presently lives in the Everton area."

"But you don't know exactly who or where?"

"I have the name Warwick Carstable, but there is no one in the local records by that name."

Then I don't know what I can possibly do, Dan might have said, but his visitor knew that already. "You asked before about evil. Why is that?"

"It's another night artefact in a sense. Londasleite believed that the strand, the disordering, mad-making strand, prepared a suitable person, possibly any of us in a bad moment, a vulnerable receptive moment, for making use of that final strand, whatever the artefact is and *can* be used for. And since we are largely creatures of light, again *his* words, he contended that the final strand led to, at least contributed to, the acts of pure evil in the world. Simplistic then, simplistic now, but so he argued."

"I *have* known evil," Dan said.

"I know you have."

"More stories, Allan?"

"Just our common humanity, Doctor. We work to remain creatures of light at all costs. The Fuligin Braid does not necessarily want us to be and, if Londasleite is to be believed, it is the other part of what we are. We are made to exist in light, but are biologically—psychologically—intended to deal with the Four Darks as well. But we choose to sleep at night whenever possible and so largely avoid them. Habit becomes conditioning, then normality. But I've taken enough of your time. I should very much value your assistance in tracking down this Warwick Carstable, or whatever his name is now, and learning what he knows of his ancestor's legacy and what he can tell us about the final important strand. I'm not sure quite how to proceed otherwise."

"I can recommend Wendt Investigations in town."

"Thank you, but I'd rather a scientist than a PI. I will leave my card, if I may. I am staying at the Imperial Hotel for now. Best I go and leave your associate to plead my case for me."

"My associate?"

Grace placed his card on the desk and rose to his feet. "Why, yes. I understand you have an inmate who wanted me to come here today."

A half hour later, Peter and Dan were sitting on the embankment at the hospital's western boundary, watching the dark green water of the Hunter River as it made its long journey to the sea.

"Tell me what you can, Peter."

"I wanted him here, Doctor Dan. Something you once said about there being attraction points in the world. You also said that, as far as you're aware, there have been thirty-seven anomalous events in your life."

"You've played a part in some of those."

"But they predate me being in your life too. I'm one of your thirty-seven when you think about it."

Dan tried to track where this was heading. "I've always allowed that there are others like me: people who are drawn to things, draw things to them. Have to be. It's natural we connected."

Peter nodded eagerly. "But that's the thing. There's been nothing in Everton for twelve years now. Think about it. Not since Rain Eyes interfered with those burials, and the Haniver sisters arranged their double suicide, not since my catatonic fugue up in my room that time. Away from here, yes, but not here."

Dan had often considered exactly that. In terms of the constant glitches and anomalies he knew *did* make up the real world in whatever barely seen, half-understood form, provided the constant accounts of ghosts and other intrusion events across the centuries, it *had* been quiet in Everton. Peter Rait, especially, had continued to read things, had used his gift to lock on to incidents, sometimes even *while* they were happening, but two hours away in Sydney, the Blue Mountains, elsewhere, always away from this town, *this* place, where so much had once happened.

"So? Everton isn't some local hellmouth like in the old morality plays. Statistically things don't tend to focus on a single spot. It's why they stay anomalies. They're spread too thin to make an impression scientifically, empirically."

"Unless that's *part* of the anomaly. Someone—something—has been deflecting. Things *have* happened, *are* happening, that we don't know about."

"Everton's just a country town, Peter. A large one, but still. Tell me about Allan Grace."

"Twelve years. Something *should* have happened."

Dan accepted the evasion, let it continue on Peter's terms. "Why should it have?"

"Two things. You asked if it was my spine in my dream. That led me back to my comment about it seeming wrong somehow, that it could be masking something with that wrongness. What if there's someone masking, deflecting, that's exactly the word, to keep us from reading the truth? And, for what it's worth, Everton isn't the focal point, *you* are."

"What?"

"You're the attractor, Doctor Dan. People always look for special places, damned places, but it isn't necessarily like that."

"What, hellmouth *people*?"

"I've always felt it was people, certain people, who drew things to them. Or are drawn to things, people, places."

"Why me? Why not you?"

"Oh, I'm one too. That's the point. But you seem to do it differently. I'm suspecting you drew me to *you*. Maybe it's what happened when you were growing up in Reardon all those years ago, meeting those circus performers, getting caught up in their schemes. You *enable* me. Accelerate my gift rather than read things yourself. But you need to stay edgy, restless. So you've stayed on here, kept me close."

Dan wanted to get back to Grace's visit, but again made himself wait. "Okay, so we've been deflected. Something's out there waiting right now. We just haven't known to look."

"Not necessarily waiting. Normally it wouldn't want our attention. It's just going about its business, doing what it does. Once you allow your role, my role, but such a role, however hit and miss, you allow that statistically it must have happened. We just haven't found it."

"It's a big town, Peter."

"It's a tourist town, Doctor Dan. A pass-through town. People come and go. People go missing."

"Meaning?"

"Like with Rain Eyes. Transit crime. People disappearing en route are usually counted missing in terms of departure or destination points."

"Big job tracking disappearances through Everton."

"Right, so I decided to try something I've never really done before. I tried calling it to me, whatever it was. I sent out and invited. Insisted."

"And Allan Grace came along."

"He did. And for his reasons as much as mine, I'm sure. *Why* would he reveal himself otherwise?"

"You saw him?"

"I made sure I did, coming *and* going. You must tell me what you talked about."

Dan watched the slow movement of the river, the roiling deep-green water on its way to the coast. There was so much to grasp: the thought of Peter summoning and Grace arriving, such a thing actually working.

The prospect of things happening across all these years, secretly, quietly, people possibly going missing again, so much on such an otherwise normal summer's day.

As Dan described his brief meeting with the man, he found the idea more and more compelling. It was easy to dismiss a pseudo-scientific notion like the Fuligin Braid in full daylight, in the muggy oversaturated light of this late-summer afternoon, but somehow Peter having the spine dream again and becoming so pro-active himself as to suspect someone in the town, send out an invitation like this, changed everything.

A pro-active part to night, Grace had suggested. That word, that idea. It truly was as crackpot a concept as the luminiferous ether filling the universe, connecting the planets, or the phlogiston being an actual chemical substance released during the act of burning.

Nonsense but seductive nonsense, such a crazy, obvious thing. Take away the light. Just the dark? Or the dark *and* something? Something added the way light was added at the flick of a switch and changed everything, something as *envitalizing* and transformational. And if everything did come down to invisible particles, waves, force fields and quantum states, as Grace had said, how much did we not yet know or track correctly? It was like the human eye seeing only a limited range of the electromagnetic spectrum, *one* version of the available world. What did the eye of an eagle see, or a cat or an octopus? Dogs had limited colour vision. There was ultimately no red rag to a bull. What else might there be?

"You say you summoned him," Dan said. "But he seemed to *want* to meet me."

"Camouflage masking genuine curiosity, I suspect. Maybe he was so intrigued at feeling a summoning, such an impulse, that he found it quite irresistible."

"Then why go on about the Fuligin Braid? Why not just pretend he's considering making a bequest to the hospital because of kindness shown to a loved one and wanted to check the place out? He certainly looked the part."

"Because the Braid *is* important to why he's actually here. *You* knowing about it. Me now as well. He called me your associate. He knew you'd tell me. That's why he wanted a scientist, Doctor Dan. He already knew what I can do, what I can bring."

"So you should send another invitation. See if we can summon this Warwick Carstable to us."

"What if he's already been here too?"

"What, Grace?"

"Why not? What if we're meant to follow? I started inviting five days ago. He made an appointment two days later. *Then* I had the dream again, the night before he came here. I wanted him to come to us. He wants us to go to him. Tit for tat."

Dan continued to marvel at what he was hearing. "You really think the spine dream and this are related? Five years, a chat over late-night herbal tea, and a recurring dream gets placed?"

"Looks like."

"He seemed human. A real person."

"No reason he shouldn't, Doctor Dan. Look at us. Normal people once we allow there's always been more to normal than people think. Different perspectives, different data—the *rest* of the data, as we see it."

"So we call on him at the Imperial."

"He won't be there, Doctor Dan."

"Payback?"

"A reminder. We do this on his terms. I watched him arrive and leave. There was something about him that *felt* like part of the summoning, if that makes sense. Like your question about whether my urgent spine was supported or unsupported. When I slept on it, as you suggested, I kept getting—weightlessness is the only word—about the spine. I had something of the same feeling with Grace. Doesn't track, I know, but it's what I got. What I'm still getting."

Dan nodded. "How can weightlessness be possible here? He'd have to be *in* water. That's as close as we get to it in a gravity environment."

"*On* water would be a very poor second. The floating sensation. But on a boat. A houseboat. Even a raft, so he can dip over the side. In a swimming pool or bore he'd be too visible unless he can exist underwater, whatever he is."

Whatever he is, Dan thought. How easily we toss off such things.

"Peter, you've tried a summoning. Can you do a casting right now, tonight, just range about? Get any impressions, anything on Grace. I'll phone Bev McDonald and see if the police have any missing persons listed for the area."

The next morning saw Everton at its worst. A hot westerly arrived soon after sun-up, turning the sky into a white haze and sending the thermometers to the 40° Celsius mark by 10:30. When Dan joined Peter at one of the long tables in the Day Room, the air-con units were working hard. They both had things to share.

There were two missing persons reports currently active for the region, Dan told him, both young women, one a Cessnock local, Jane Cotter, from three months ago, most likely a runaway, the other for a Traci Metcalfe who had been visiting friends in Maitland a week back and never made it home.

Peter had done his casting, looked haggard from the sleep lost doing it for too many hours.

"I keep getting one of the water towers," he said.

"They're fenced off, locked. Some even have cameras."

"Not out at Corrigan's. Paula tells me Dean Corrigan's had the whole west section of his property on the market for two years now. He's let the water in the tower become brackish, deliberately so, claimed it reduced maintenance costs since he wasn't using it. He's put up *Contaminated* and *Keep Away* signs and replaced the locks. The kids won't touch it. The stink puts them off."

"And you're seeing his tower?"

"An enclosed dark space out that way. It's big enough. Huge thing on six legs, at least twenty meters tall, up on that rise. I'm getting that and the front of Bowen's Arcade down along Bennet Street in town. You know the place, mostly empty. But just the arcade front. No details. The water tower's much more vivid. I get the shape, the darkness, the *weightlessness*!"

"Hardly a day for visiting old metal water towers."

"Women are missing, you said."

What if we're wrong? Dan wondered. But when was Peter ever wrong when it counted? "We should call the police in on this."

"Like I said before, Doctor Dan. He won't be there if we do. He knows what he's doing. Probably what we're doing."

It was a dreadful day to be outdoors, the trees thrashing and heaving under a bleached white sky, every vista blurred and shimmering with heat haze. There were enough people on the streets, other cars about, lots of kids skylarking along the river, but once Peter and Dan left town there were just heat-blasted distances and the empty highway stretching between lines of jiggering fences. Here and there the dark lumps of cattle sheltered as best they could in the ashen fields. Now and then a lonely windmill could be seen racing madly besides its bore.

They turned onto Copeman Lane when they finally reached it, and headed along that unsurfaced road for a good ten minutes before they caught their first glimpse of the old water tower atop Spicer's Hill. A windmill was spinning close by, but with the pump disengaged. Whatever water remained in the tower was from when the pump last operated, though Dan figured that Corrigan kept the old tank at least a third to a half full so the water would steady it against winds exactly like these.

As well as hats and sunglasses, Dan had a knapsack with work gloves, torches and water bottles, lengths of rope for tethering themselves, even a strip of tarpaulin to kneel on when they were up on the blazing top of the tower. He also had a crowbar and a bolt-cutter from the Blackwater maintenance room, but was hardly surprised to find the padlock on the boundary gate unlocked and swinging on its latch.

"Making it easy," Peter said.

They found the same at the gate in the chain-link fence at the foot of the tower—another heavy-duty padlock unlocked and swinging free.

Dan unlatched the gate. "He really does want us here."

As they headed up the modest rise, the old tower creaked and moaned above them, shifting in the sudden gusts. There's a tiny ocean up there, Dan realized, the most unlikely lake and pond. An unlikely darkness too in all this glare, and possibly enough midnight. Some of the iron plates may have sprung over the years, rivets given way here and there, but there were no leaks that Dan could see.

When they reached the access ladder, they put on their gloves and began climbing. The wind made it hard going, buffeting them constantly and burning their skin. The glare was terrible.

Once at the summit, Dan was relieved to see the hatch cover just four metres away. He would have hated to be out on that vast shallow dome longer than necessary. As it was, he felt they could be blown into the sky at any moment.

Fumbling in his knapsack, he brought out the tarpaulin, waited till the gusts eased a little then spread the thick canvas across the burning metal, using his knees to stop it blowing away until Peter could anchor it behind him.

Dan moved forward then, and again felt incredible relief. The padlock for the hatch cover was missing altogether.

In Grace's pocket, Dan figured.

The tower groaned and shuddered under them. Again Dan waited till the gusts eased, then grabbed the hatch handle and heaved the cover back. It clanged like a gong on the burning metal shell.

Dan took the tether rope from the knapsack, and spent what seemed an eternity securing it round his waist before handing the slack back to Peter so he could do the same. Then he slung his torch round his neck, stretched face-down on the tarp with his head and one arm over the raised rim of the hatch, and sent torchlight down into the gloom.

The stench hit him as he did so: the smell of algae and old water left standing far too long. Then there was the ladder dwindling away, disappearing in a shimmer of dark green water that roiled in the constant buffeting of the wind. It might have been three, four meters deep down there, but how could he know?

Ignoring the heat through the tarpaulin, he played torchlight back and forth across the shifting surface, not sure what he expected to find. Then he saw it: a long wooden box floating a few meters out from the ladder, tethered to it by a short length of cord.

Dan cried out in surprise. It was such a melodramatic sight in such a place, bringing so many conventional horrors to mind: familiar, somehow cosy things like vampires and the undead waiting out the daylight hours inside coffins and caskets.

A much grimmer thought was there too.

Traci Metcalfe and Jane Cotter were missing!

He had to go down and see.

Peter had caught Dan's reaction. He scrabbled in alongside, peered into the gloom and sent his own torch beam skittering across the water till he too located the oblong box.

"One of the girls?" he yelled above the wind. "Call for help?"

"See if it's empty first!" Dan shouted back. "Keep hold of the rope. See if you get a signal."

Dan shifted on the tarp, swung his legs onto the ladder and found a footing several rungs down. Then, thrusting the crowbar through his belt, he began his descent while Peter played out the safety line.

As Dan's head sank below the rim, he found himself in a different world entirely. The smell was strong, unpleasant, but not overpowering. Some higher plates on the sides *had* sprung near the top, so a few grace notes of light left swatches of green across the eddying surface. The rest was a creaking, groaning darkness, though with a stillness about it, almost a cathedral calm. The heat, like the glare, belonged out there, intruded from above.

Peter kept his torch focused on the box, while Dan's, dangling on his chest, showed the eddies and swirls at the foot of the ladder as he closed the distance. His only thoughts right then were to keep his grip on the rungs and not lose the crowbar.

When he was finally at water level, he made himself continue down four more rungs, hating every moment, dreading what this dark fetid pool might conceal.

People were missing!

Again he dared not hesitate. Hooking an arm through the ladder, he grabbed the tether and hauled the box slowly towards him.

What would it be? Murdered girl? Living girl? Allan Grace as modern-day vampire? It couldn't be a Dean Corrigan prank to creep out the more resolute kids. They were never meant to get this far.

The box bumped against the ladder and Dan drew it in close. The opened and missing padlocks made him bold. He reached out, grabbed the upper edge of what looked very much like a coffin lid, and lifted. The box bobbed, slewed. The lid came away, slid off into the water.

There was a wild rush in the darkness, a sudden flurry, something, though nothing easily grasped. Whatever it was left the box rocking, dipping, plunging, and Dan's head ringing as if from a tremendous blow, though the box had been completely empty, Dan was sure of it. Was empty still, just so much sanded watertight timber.

But sudden, so sudden, all of it. And other things in those moments. A scream from above, garbled words, what might have been: "He's here!", and the tether rope tumbling down as if cut away.

Dan reacted as quickly as he could, turning, clambering back up the ladder, but fumbling, losing precious seconds, what with the crowbar and trailing tether line. When he was out in the heat and glare again, there was no one else on the vast metal lid, which brought the terrifying thought that Peter had lost his footing and gone over the side—or been pushed!

But when Dan reached the access ladder at last and was starting down, he saw Peter far below, leaning against the car, hands pressed to his head.

The drive back to Everton seemed twice as long as the trip out. Peter sat next to him, dazed, confused, but recovering. He'd been almost catatonic at first, though compliant enough, getting in the car, buckling in, even managing an "I'm okay," but frowning and rubbing his temples all the while.

By the time they reached the highway, his answers about what had happened up on the tower went from "Not sure" and "He was there" to

"He looked so different. Terrible. Blasted. Worn. Gaunt face. Threadbare suit. No glamours hiding anything this time."

Dan allowed for heat stroke, even Peter's infrequent condition-related delusions and hallucinations, but kept pressing. "You're sure it was him?"

"No mistaking it. Where are we going?"

"Everton Base Hospital."

"No, Doctor Dan! He has Traci Metcalfe."

"You see that?"

Peter kept his hands pressed to his head, frowning in pain or concentration. "Not sure. It's this migraine. Get to the arcade!"

"You'll stay in the car."

"Yes. Just hurry!"

When they gutted the old Bowen's haberdashery in Bennet Street, a late-1970s developer revamped the building as a shopping arcade, creating fourteen shopfronts that flourished for twenty-five years, languished for six, and finally ended up in the hands of eight separate owners.

Those owners had never agreed on a common business plan for the site. Some wanted too much rent, others needed tax write-offs, three left their spaces empty to annoy various family members. The two shopfronts nearest the main street kept tenants easily enough, a hairdresser and a country crafts store; Shop 7 in the middle housed a naturopath, Shop 9 a property agent who did most of his work from home. The rest ended up with vertical blinds or venetians shutting them away, sheets of old newspaper or swirls of whitewash, so many closed-up spaces filled with stale air, dead insects, abandoned dreams. The arcade became a ghost town in miniature, a landlocked *Mary Celeste* sailing on untended and largely untenanted through a dozen more winters and summers.

When Dan pulled up out front, he tried calling the police again, but there was still no signal. Leaving Peter to get through when he could, he took a torch and the crowbar and hurried into the quiet arcade. Four shops in use left ten to check, but that number quickly became one when Dan found a shopfront with its windows blackwashed over for maximum darkness.

He couldn't afford to wait. He fitted the crowbar into the door edge near the lock, applied maximum force. The door sprang on that first try, shuddered inwards, sent dim arcade light spilling across a dusty floor. Dan switched on his torch as he stepped into the gloom, but found it didn't work. Of course mobiles and torches were useless now.

Dan moved around the open door, then immediately to his left toward the front left corner, as far back into shadow as he could get from the doorway, then turned.

As his eyes adjusted, there was an immediate double vision effect: one moment what looked for all the world like a mob-capped, aproned servant from Sydney's colonial past sitting meekly, primly, on a chair in the corner diagonally opposite where he stood. The next that figure was down on the floor there, leaning back with knees drawn up in a large plastic farm tub, but naked, no longer dressed, and held by what looked like leather bands at neck, elbows and waist, face covered with a glossy membrane, rubber or leather, without eyes but with a tube for air and water where the mouth would be.

Dan blinked, blinked again, but the image wouldn't settle, kept jumping from one to the other, picturesque to grim, which *kept* him blinking, trying to anchor what it truly was.

Another glamour, he realized. One thing hiding another, but faltering, wrong, outdated and quaint.

From our earliest colonial days, Dan knew. He was here then. Grace, Carstable, whatever his real name was came to the early colony in Sydney, two hours away now but so much more then, all the while hiding, relocating, moving from place to place as needed, taking human form so he could be among us. He could even have been Londasleite for that matter, putting forward the very theory that would allow him to be known to a select few.

Dan kept blinking, made himself adjust to the constant shifting, finally saw what the two things had in common: a single thread of darkness as round as a knitting needle, extending from the bellies of both images, one belly ultimately, a thick black thread cutting the dim space diagonally from the double figure in the corner to somewhere behind his left shoulder.

The corner behind him!

Dan turned and saw Allan Grace pressed back in the gloom where the blackwashed windows and brick wall came together, but a distorted, distended version of Grace, the torso too long, the shoulders too high, head and upper body tipping forward as if wracked with, what, scoliosis? No, the hunchbacked look of severe kyphosis, the head pushed back then forward like some hooded cobra about to strike.

The thread went from the woman to the suit Grace was wearing! The midnight black suit. So much of that one special strand being drawn out of the Braid—dark matter, dark energy, old night—replenishing, always replenishing, an infinite supply incubated in this woman—in countless women over the years!—harvested, gathered, drawn forth for this, in this one shop, one arcade, and who knew how many other shadowy gathering chambers in half-empty arcades in towns like this one all across the country?

Dan reacted instinctively, reached out, flailed with both hands, broke the thread. He felt it give like moulded powder, like the frangible, dry mud tube of a mud-dauber or potter wasp.

Allan Grace reacted instantly, cried out once, flung his own arms wide and pushed out from the corner, staggered into the middle of the almost empty space and stood in the thin light there.

Dan fought to track what he saw next. The buttoned-up collar had always been too tight. Now it narrowed, constricted. The face, the head above, seemed to blanch, lose all colour. The mouth locked into a line and ceased to be, the eyes bulged, goggled. The shirt below darkened, blackened, as if drawing in as much of the frangible powdery thread as it could.

What neck remained above the cobra-spread became a stem, impossibly thin, so the head, whatever it truly was, toppled, tipped to the side, *snapped* off and fell away, bounced once and rolled into the gloom.

The *suit* continued standing, with a wholly blackened shirt, blackened hands, just the white tip of spinal column thrusting up like an old-fashioned bill-spike.

The spine from Peter's dream! And wrong, like Peter had said, because upside down, inverted, the coccyx at the top, giving that hideous, splayed, cobra-head effect with the bill-spike of bleached white bone.

No directions in space, Dan remembered. No galactic north or south. We give those, find those, impose order, up and down, north and south, right and wrong. Gravity and other forces, yes, but sorted by *our* reality, *our* limitations and specializations, *our* ways of seeing.

What had once been Allan Grace didn't operate this way, had a greater dark to work upon, the brilliant dark of the quantum spread, the dark beyond the Sun's heliosphere, out in that ultimate night with its myriad lonely night lights, the stars.

But working with what was in *this* world this time, *these* forms and modes. Masquerading, feeding here, even while belonging out there, in there, in Londasleite's Inchoate, wherever.

The spiked kyphotic shape turned and stepped into the room's darkest corner, *became* the darkness there, eased into nothing and was gone, all in moments, even as Dan rushed to the woman, giving reassurances, working to free her from the terrible hood and the restraints. He kept trying his phone too, found he had a signal at last and called for medical and police assistance. And, even as he fumbled, murmuring his comforting words all the while, he did so with absolute clarity, cherry-picking sense from the facts.

He'd *seen* the black thread, the cobra head, Grace's disappearance, *enough* of what had happened at the tower. But what had that truly been, for him, for Peter? Illusions, hallucinations, glamours?

Certainty was impossible, though one thing *felt* true.

Making a new suit was all, hiding the threadbare one, making artefacts for itself, of itself, night artefacts, using the forms and modes of this world, but needing creatures of light, someone, to separate the threads and incubate the result, someone, too, in *this* world to break that thread when it was done.

You didn't summon him, Peter. He summoned us. Needed this!

Wanting more this time. To have it *known* that it was done, what was done, because at long last, Laurence Sanston Londasleite, someone, had grasped the essence of what night truly was and that had come to mean so much.

As for any of us.

Being known.

Dan cradled the sobbing woman, relieved to hear sirens approaching at last, trying to fathom it all the while, keep it simple.

Perhaps it was as both Peter and Grace had said, creatures of light and darkness working as ever they had, like the winds that brought hard summer to the town and danger enough to keep it all real.

And simpler.

Braids binding up the world and strange attractors working in the night.

Whatever it truly was.

THE SPINDLY MAN

STEPHEN GRAHAM JONES

They let us use the community center to talk about books. It made sense. What I was doing, it was pretty much community service. Not the kind mandated by a judge. This was more self-imposed.

Eight months ago, not drunk or in a rush or driving through the rain, I'd skipped through a stop sign after picking my son up from third grade, ran us into a furniture truck. Jeremy didn't die against the dashboard that day, but the surgeries are still coming. His prom date, she's going to have to look inside to see the real him.

In quick succession, then, I flamed out of my year-to-year contract at our branch of the state university, was back to stocking tools and air conditioners at night.

And this. Talking about books.

More and more, I was thinking it was the only good thing I had in me. My only real gift. And that, if I didn't share it, then the next time one of Jeremy's bills came due, my wife's dad wasn't going to come through with a check, or the surgeon that day was going to have had one too many drinks at lunch.

I'd put up a flyer at the library, the laundromat, the carwash, both coffee shops.

There were seven of us, most Wednesdays.

This week we were reading Stephen King again. Marcy from the bank had recommended him, because, she said, she was too scared to read him alone. So we went with her into those dark places. Well, I'd already been, but I toured them through—the life, the times, the legend—and then passed a photocopied story out for next week. For this week.

The story was "The Man in the Black Suit." It was about a nine-year-old kid a century ago, just out fishing one day, then encountering the devil, barely getting away. It had some resonance to it, but no real gore. What I planned to tell the group was that how it worked was it was taking this kid's blind faith—America's stubborn Christianity—and making it real all at once. So, really, the story was a confirmation, a celebration. The old man who had been the boy, the old man writing this down in his diary, he was one of the lucky ones, the ones who never had to doubt if angels and demons were real. He knew.

So, the study question, it was going to be which is better, to know or not to know?

And, yes, of course Jeremy was nine that day I picked him up from third grade. He was a year older than his classmates—I'd taught in China for a year, when there were no jobs here—but his age didn't mean anything to him yet. And now he was probably going to be two years behind. But alive. That's the epithet I kept tagging onto everything: but alive. As in, this could all be worse. I should be thankful for whatever fell on me next.

Since my shift started at nine, we usually met at six, dinnertime. Each week a different person would bring a casserole, pass out the plates. This week it was Lew's turn. He was retired Air Force, said he'd taken a stack of paperbacks with him on both tours in '72. That he was the only one in his bunkhouse who would stay awake reading.

He brought chicken dumplings in a crock pot.

Aside from him, and Marcy—she of the bank—there was Drake, a straitlaced city planner, the one who'd told us about the community center; there was Evelyn, who always brought her crocheting but hardly ever said anything; and Jackie and her daughter Gwen, a junior in high school, there very much against her will for a taste of what literature was going to be like in college.

In the flyer, I'd of course mentioned my background.

So, we were a healthy group of bookworms. A good mix of backgrounds and ages, anyway, if not very diverse.

When the dumplings were gone and adequately praised, we put our plates under our chairs and dove into King.

Because it was his night—for food, but you could tell he felt responsible for the discussion as well—Lew pinched his jeans up his thighs, leaned forward like telling us a secret, and said that he hoped none of the ladies took a fright to this particular story.

Evelyn tittered, her needles flashing, and I got the sense that one of these nights Lew was going to ask her for coffee afterwards, and she was going to suggest the perfect place.

"Scared me," Drake said.

He was still wearing his tie from the day's work. Not loosened or anything.

"Me too," I lied, just to not leave him hanging.

While King had stories that were terrifying, this one was, in comparison, safe. By burying the nine-year-old's story in the frame of an old man's journal, it was locating the devil in another time, another place. One far, far from us.

Jackie elbowed her daughter just enough to get her to talk: "You could tell right away who he was. From the eyes."

"Those eyes," Jackie said, seconding her daughter's motion.

"How did he see out of them?" Lew said, leaning back, crossing his arms.

I nodded, was liking this.

The good thing about voluntary book discussions is that I don't have to play dentist. Getting people to talk's not like pulling teeth.

"Because they were—because there were flames in his eye sockets, right?" Marcy said.

We all nodded, as if seeing the devil again, as King had drawn him: tall, neatly dressed in a black suit. Subtle claws at the ends of his fingertips. Instead of eyes, just orange flickering flames. And a mouth that could open well past what any human jawbone would allow. And the teeth. Those teeth.

"Maybe he doesn't have to subscribe to our rules of biology," I said, looking around the circle for support.

"He has to eat," Gwen said, all on her own. "He eats that fish, right?"

"It's not a human hunger, though," Lew said. "Just doing it for meanness, like. To show off, scare that kid."

"Good, good," I said, wanting to stand because it's the main way I know to think. "But, remember, this is eighty years ago for this old man remembering it now. What would you say if I offered that he just encountered a bad man in the woods that day, then, because of his upbringing, he started to remember him as the devil. He started to add the stuff he knew from Sunday school. Claws, flame, teeth . . ."

"He does fall asleep before it all happens," Evelyn said, hooking another stitch, pulling it through.

She was our cynic.

"But is it any less scary if it's a dream or if it's real?" Marcy asked.

"Or even if it was just a serial killer," Jackie added. "That's pretty scary too, isn't it?"

"Damn straight," Lew said, clapping his knee.

"But for every killer there's a cop, right?" I asked.

Shrugging nods all the way around. This is what they would have been paying for, had they been paying.

"So, follow me now. If there's devils, then there's also . . .?"

"More devils?" Gwen said.

"Kids," Marcy corrected.

"He means angels," Evelyn said, stabbing with a needle.

I nodded like I'd been caught, was about to shift gears into my thesis when Lew said, "But who wants to read a story about an angel, right?"

I lowered my face to smile—he was right—and when I looked back up to the group, the twin doors on the other side of the gym were opening up.

Because they were on cylinders, were designed to not crush fingers, we all got the guy's outline before we got him.

He was tall, spindly, top-hatted. His dark suit ragged at the edges, and not quite long enough for his legs or his arms.

For an instant his eyes flashed, taking my breath away, but in the next instant he was wearing a pair of those old pince-nez, their twin lenses catching the light.

Beside me, Gwen flinched. Jackie took her hand, pulled it across, to her own lap.

"Speak of the—" Lew said just loud enough for the book circle, and chuckled.

The spindly man hooked a stray chair by the door, dragged it all the long way across the wooden floor of the gym to us and set it down, opposite me.

"Room for one more?" he asked.

"How'd you hear about us?" I said, trying to sound casual.

He gave me a smile and a wink, then flapped open a much-folded piece of paper. One of my flyers. All of which I was pretty sure I'd collected, once we had a quorum.

"Looks like he's invited," Evelyn said.

"A scarf," the spindly man said, about her crochet-job.

"Don't know just yet," Evelyn said back. Definitely a challenge in her voice. For all of us.

We had a rhythm, had already relaxed into our assigned roles.

The spindly man's eyes made the circuit of our little circle, lingering maybe a touch too long on Gwen, then launching two fingers off his right eyebrow in salute to Lew.

"Even the money-handlers," he said, about Marcy.

"And you?" she said right back to him, like he wasn't the first ornery customer she'd had to deal with.

"Just happened to be strolling by," he said, refolding the flyer, stuffing it in the waist pocket of his vest. "What's the story, doc?" he said then, right to me.

I breathed in, breathed out.

Evidently we were doing this.

"Stephen King," I said, then, pointedly, "'The Man in the Black Suit.'"

"Ahh," the spindly man said, his eyes on Gwen again. "The King man cometh. I know him well, you could say."

"We were just talking about how if you admit devils," Drake said, "then that means the door must be open for angels as well."

"Or more demons," the spindly man said, sitting back into his chair. "Inside every angel, there's a demon waiting to claw out, right? But please, don't let me interrupt."

And so we went valiantly forward. Just with not much heart.

Instead of listening, or contributing, the spindly man extracted Marcy's plate from under her chair, then used his finger to scoop her thin layer of leftover dumplings into his wide mouth.

I heard myself traipsing back through Hawthorne's "Young Goodman Brown" for the group, trying to establish it as the literary antecedent for King this time out. Upon hearing "Hawthorne," Jackie of course made Gwen recite what she knew about *The Scarlet Letter.*

It gave the spindly man more excuse to stare her up and down. To—and this was the only word for it—malinger.

"But—" I started, not at all sure where I was going, just that I had to pull his eyes off Gwen.

The spindly man was already speaking, though: "Go into the forest, taste the intangible. You come back with the story, never the proof. Am I right?"

Silence. Welcome to the land of crickets, I said in my head, quoting one of my former students.

Lew coughed an old man cough deep in his chest. Marcy scuffled her shoes on the gym floor. Drake stared into his lap, his fingertips drumming some arcane, personal rhythm against each other.

"Good," I said at last. "Proof. It's what we were talking about before you got here. If you can prove the vital tenets of a religion, then you lose the possibility of faith. So, King's man in this black suit, by showing this boy that he was real, he also cored out the boy's eventual leap of faith. Leaving him to lead a hollow life, as established by all the years between nine and ninety being, as far as we see on the page, empty, devoid of content. Not even interesting enough to paraphrase."

Sometimes you have to knock a student down with preparation.

The spindly man just grinned a sharp grin.

"Proof," he said. "We've all got proof, man. I bet every one of us has a story like this kid's. Don't we?"

Nobody said no.

"You," he said to Marcy. "You've seen the devil, haven't you?"

"We usually don't—" I tried, but he held a hand out to me like a crossing guard might, his palm and fingers straight up.

Worse, I actually stopped.

"I don't know what it was," Marcy said.

The spindly man smiled. Lowered his hand.

"We were twelve," Marcy said. "I'd told my mom I was staying at Reese's, and she said she was staying at my house. You know. So we were going to camp under the old windmill. It was a dare."

"Dare, dare," the spindly man urged.

"Of course we didn't sleep," Marcy said, her eyes flashing up to Jackie in something like apology, as if she were being a bad influence on Gwen here. "Then, about two or three in the morning, our flashlights both died at once. And we looked up the side of the windmill. The moon was bright that night, and right above us."

"No," Lew said, and I looked to him.

Did he know where this story was going?

"And then, coming down the side of the windmill, already about ten feet from the top, I don't know. There was somebody, okay? Maybe it was just a jacket a worker had left tied up there."

"Because they always do that," the spindly man said.

"We ran," Marcy said. "We ran and we ran, and he was behind us the whole way. We just knew."

"And you came back with the story," the spindly man said. "That's your proof. Good. Do we think she's lying, folks? Is her story enough for you, or do you need her to have scars on her back, from sharp fingernails? Or a dead friend, who wasn't quite fast enough?"

"She did die," Marcy said, her voice cracking a bit. "Later that year. Got hit on the highway, trying to go . . . we didn't know where. Oh God."

She turned her head, balancing tears in her eyes.

"And you?" the spindly man said to Lew.

"Me," Evelyn said, uncharacteristically. "One night coming home from bringing dinner to my husband on the night shift, I noticed the fuel gauge was too far in the red. And there were only cotton fields between me and home, and there were these wild packs of dogs that year. My cousin had already been mauled. But then, right when the engine sputtered, a pair of headlights popped on in my rearview, and stayed there all the way until I pulled into the driveway. And then the car died."

"An angel," Gwen said.

Evelyn just stared at the spindly man.

"Next," he said, no humor in his voice at all.

"Who are you anyway?" Lew said.

"Somebody who needs proof," the spindly man said.

"Of what?" Lew said.

"The intangible," the spindly man over-enunciated. "You know."

"I don't have to tell you," Lew said. "I never even told my wife."

"Of course, of course," the spindly man said, all manners now. "Just leave Marcy running home through the darkness all alone."

Lew looked from the spindly man to Marcy. Then to me.

"So maybe I saw something once," he said.

Just to have control again, I nodded for him to continue.

The spindly man shifted his chair in anticipation.

"We were at . . . well, it doesn't matter," Lew started off. "Way past the DMZ. Deep, no support. Somebody was shooting at us from a fortified position. So we ventilated his little roost, and he stopped shooting like you have to. Because you're dead."

"Exactly," the spindly man said. "The dead don't shoot, of course they don't. What is this, television?"

Lew wasn't listening to him anymore, though.

"Only, once we broke cover, that dead sniper, he came back up over the lip of his little parapet. Except—I was the only one to see it—he was still dead. And there was another man up there with him. Moving that dead sniper's arms like a puppet. Putting his finger on the trigger. We lost three more men that day."

"And you made it home," the spindly man said. "Good for you. You're living, breathing proof of the intangible. You saw it, respected it, and were given your life in return. Who else, now?"

There was Jackie, Gwen, Drake, and me.

"When her father died," Jackie started, her hand gripping Gwen's knee, but then Drake cut in: "I used to lie in my bed all night. I knew there weren't any monsters in the closet, or under the bed. That was stupid. But outside. Outside was much bigger."

"It is, it is," the spindly man said, smiling again, his lips thin enough as to hardly even be there at all.

"So one night," Drake said. "One night I decided I was going to call it out. My fear, I mean. I was going to get up, go to my window, peek out the corner. If nobody was there, then it was just all in my head. But then, when I pulled the curtain to the side, there was a pair of eyes looking back at me."

The spindly man laughed in his chest.

Jackie gripped Gwen's hand harder.

"It was my own reflection," Drake said then, right to the spindly man. "It was proof I was being stupid. That I was a kid. Does that count?"

"Did it feel stupid?" the spindly man asked. "Or did you sleep in your parents' room that night?"

Drake didn't say anything. Just drummed his fingers.

"After my husband passed over," Jackie said then, speaking for her and Gwen both, evidently, "we could hear something in the garage some nights."

"Mom," Gwen said, trying to shut her up.

"And one time I finally went out there, with a spatula."

"To scramble some brains . . ." the spindly man said.

"There was a puppy," Jackie said. "He'd left us a puppy."

"The garage door was open, Mom," Gwen said.

"And, tell me," the spindly man said. "Did you keep it, this puppy? Are you giving it unmonitored access to your house now?"

"Unmonitored?" Lew said, defensive.

"Who knows what our pets are up to when we're away," the spindly man said, angling his narrow face over at me now. "They could stand up on two legs, walk all around. Sniff at the vents for things only a dog could smell living up there. Waiting up there."

"Stop," Evelyn said.

The spindly man was still watching me.

"Good professor?" he said.

I looked from face to face of the group.

This wasn't at all where I'd meant this discussion to go. But, I had to admit, what we were doing, it was showing what we brought to the story. Which had to reveal, in part, the means by which it had got to us. Like an archetypal well of shared stories. One King had the savvy to tap into.

We all had a devil on our back trail.

Or, in my case, in front of me.

"The day of the wreck," I said, swallowing loudly. At least in my ears. "The driver of the furniture truck. I don't think he was a person. Not anymore. I think he'd been waiting all day just to cross that intersection. He was—he was smiling when we hit him. And you don't smile, do you? What kind of a person smiles when a kid's about to get disfigured for life?"

Jackie reached across Gwen to pat my thigh.

"Now," the spindly man said, to the group. "The good doctor here. Do you actually believe a man in a black suit was driving that truck that day, or has his own memory and guilt altered his memory of it?"

"This is over," I said, standing, my chair scraping away from me. It was too loud in the tight gym. Too sudden. And I didn't care.

"But—" Marcy said.

"He's right," Lew said, standing as well, his eyes with mine.

The soldier, always looking for someone to guard. It was so clichéd, so stupid. And I was so thankful for him.

He went around collecting plates, everybody else standing to help, to arrange.

Everybody except the spindly man.

He hadn't moved from his chair. He was just letting the group course around him, his arms crossed like he was in a pout, and wanted us to know it.

As was custom in our little group, I stayed in what had been our circle, shook hands and gripped shoulders. It made me feel like the captain going down with the ship. Lew held onto my hand longer than he had to, pulled me close.

"You good?" he said, meaning the spindly man.

"I'm golden," I said, and smiled to prove it, then ducked my head for Evelyn to drape her just-made scarf around my neck.

She pecked me on the cheek, Drake shook my hand, and the last one through the double doors was Gwen. She looked back to me, her eyes plaintive, almost. Like she was telling me no.

I raised my hand in farewell.

Behind me, the spindly man coughed into his hand.

"We have to leave now," I told him.

"Thought it went until eight," he said, standing to face me.

"Not tonight."

When I reached for his chair, to put it up, he took it instead, jerked it away.

"Good selection," he said. "'The Man in the Black Suit.'" I identify with it, you could say."

"You never told us your proof," I said. "Of the intangible."

We were standing at center court.

"Some of us don't need proof," he said, measuring his words. "But, tonight. Next campfire I find myself at, I might tell the riveting story of the book group. The one who didn't know what they were playing with. The one who thought stories are just made up. What do you think, doc? I got a winner there?"

"Tonight was a horror story for us," I told him, more than a little proud of myself for coming up with that, "not you."

"So I take I'm . . . uninvited?" he said.

"Will that stop you?" I said back.

He looked to the dark gym behind me. To get me to look as well, it seemed.

I didn't. I wouldn't.

"Maybe tonight's story isn't even over yet," he said, then, before I could reply, he was pushing back into the double doors. "Tell Captain Lewis thank you if you will, for the dish. And for remembering."

"Rememb—?" I started, but now he was tipping his hat, bowing out.

Gone.

I finally breathed.

And looked behind me, now that I could.

The whole gym was dark, a patchwork of deeper and deeper shadows. At work tonight, there were going to be walls and walls of shadows, I knew. Me moving silently through them with a cart, a dolly, a back brace. A broken son. One I was so grateful for, it hurt.

I wanted to cry, I think.

Instead, I straightened the spindly man's chair. It was already straight, but I wanted to make it straighter.

Next I turned like always, to nod bye to the ghost of the book group. To thank it for keeping me sane, for letting me give back, pay my dues.

And then I walked across the thick blue sideline, for the double doors that would lock comfortably behind me, and only looked up when I was almost there, to the crash-bars, the door handles.

Two points of flame, flickering in the reflection.

My back straightened and I gulped air as quietly as I could.

Behind me. The spindly man, he'd crept around to a side door, let himself in, was standing behind me now, his fingertips extending into claws, his rows of teeth glistening against each other, his eyes on fire.

I jerked back from the reflection. It was a stupid move, should have sent me right into his chest.

Only—nothing.

I even looked again, which is always the first mistake, the first step onto that slippery slope.

Just emptiness behind me. The whole gym, nobody.

I spun back around to the doors, sure he'd got around me somehow, would be waiting.

It was just me.

I nodded that I was being stupid, that I was scaring myself like Drake had been talking about, and took another step forward.

The orange eyes faded in again.

I shook my head no, no.

The eyes did too.

And then, like I had to, I cupped my hand over the right side of my face. And then lowered that hand, covered my other eye.

It was me.

I was the devil, I am the devil, the one smiling behind the wheel that day.

In Stephen King's story, the kid's dad's looking over his shoulder into the tangled woods, he's cueing in to some indistinct rustling in the trees. Some smell, some evil presence.

My face was lost in the brush, though.

He couldn't see me hunched over and grinning, my face wet with tears, my split tongue reaching up to dab them off my cheek.

"Run," I'd said to that kid, that nine-year-old. Or, I'd tried to, with every trick I had. If he stayed, then something might happen to him, something bad.

But it does anyway.

THE WINDOW

BRIAN EVENSON

He was all but asleep. Or he was asleep and then the sound woke him up. Or he was dreaming and never awoke at all. All three possibilities occurred to him later, when he was telling the story to a friend, after realizing that he had nothing to show for what he'd experienced, or thought he'd experienced—no proof, nothing but a dull and slowly fading sense of fear. Without proof, he began to doubt himself. For surely what he thought had happened couldn't have actually happened, could it? Wasn't it better to think he was dreaming or crazy than to think that things like that could happen?

He had been in the bedroom, down the hall, at the far end of his apartment, when he had heard a noise. The lights were off, but they had been off for just a few moments, so he didn't think he was asleep yet. Even if he was, he was pretty sure he had woken up immediately. If not, how was he to explain the fact that he was later standing there, in the living room, staring.

Sleepwalking? the friend he was trying to explain it to speculated.

But no, he wasn't a sleepwalker, he'd never been one, no history of it in his family either. His friend had been watching too much TV. He hadn't dreamed it. Even if part of him hoped he had.

He had been in the bedroom when he had heard the noise. The air conditioner wasn't on, even though it was a hot evening, the sort of evening when he usually would have turned it on—if it had been on, even on low, he wouldn't have heard the noise. He remembered it being hot, but couldn't remember feeling any discomfort—which was surprising, he had to admit, but there it was. He had to tell it as he remembered it if he was to have any hope of making sense of it. He had to trust his impulses—if he didn't trust them, what if anything was left for him to rely on?

Just tell the story—this from his friend. The friend did not understand that this was all part of it for him, that sorting through the tangled impressions was something he had to do to know how much to trust what he was telling, how much to believe what he'd experienced. But yes, all right, he would try to tell it the way the friend wanted to hear it: clean. He would do his best.

He had been in the bedroom when he heard a noise. At first he thought it was from outside, a bird banging against the living room window—that was the first thing that had come to his mind, a bird striking the window hard, once, twice, a third time. But then it had kept up and the sound had changed too. For a moment he lay in the bed, drowsy, just listening, a little curious but also half-asleep, not really taking it in. For a moment his mind went from thinking about a bird on the outside of the window to a bird on the inside of the window. And then his mind focused and he realized that no, it wasn't a bird: there was someone in the house.

Nothing like this had ever happened to him before. He wasn't sure what to do. Even as it was happening he couldn't quite believe it. He got up, left the bed and made for the bedroom door, but once there, paused shy of the sill, waited. He didn't know how exactly he was supposed to act, what he was supposed to do. Should he call the police? No, his phone was in the living room, where the noise was coming from. Should he stay in the bedroom until they were gone? No, he had too many things that he couldn't afford to have them (whoever *they* were) steal. He had no gun, no weapon of any kind, and the kitchen where he kept his knives was in the other direction.

In the end, he simply grabbed a book from the nightstand, the largest and heaviest one in the stack, and moved as quickly and silently as he could out toward the living room.

At first, with the room mostly in darkness except for the slight light shining through the windows, he didn't see anything. The room was a strange crisscross of lighter and darker shadow, some parts of it visible, others not visible at all. The end window was up, propped halfway open. There was a smell to the room, bitter and pungent, that he wanted to take as the smell of the outside air. But no, it was more than that.

At first the room seemed empty. He stood in the doorway hesitating, wondering if he'd just been imagining the noise. But then he saw something move. One of the shadows in the far corner flowed out and he saw a dim, vague shape. It was more or less the size of a man, though crouched and almost toppling forward in a posture that he felt would be difficult for a man to maintain. But maybe what he was seeing was partly shadow rather than body. It moved slowly, seemingly unaware of him. It traveled slowly along beside the wall. It knocked against the objects near the wall, rattling them—this, he realized, must have been the sound he had heard—but it seemed to be not aware of this either, and did little to alter its course. Instead it simply pushed forward, objects rattling in its path.

He tried to speak, but his throat was dry and all that came out was a kind of inarticulate barking sound. Somehow the intruder didn't seem to hear him. It continued to move forward, around the edge of the room, at exactly the same pace it had been moving before. *I should be afraid*, he thought, and then suddenly realized he *was* afraid—that was the strangest thing. He felt like the fear was happening to another person, *like I was at a distance from my body, observing it.*

Maybe it was a dream, his friend said.

No, he said, yes, of course he had considered this, but no, he didn't think it was a dream—though he would prefer if it had been. But that wasn't all, he said to the friend, that wasn't the worst yet, he said, just be quiet and listen, that's only the beginning.

He spoke aloud but the figure didn't notice and he felt a strange sort of distanced fear—like the fear was all around him but he was swaddled from it somehow, insulated. He had, of course, already been afraid. The moment he thought someone else might be in the house he had been afraid. But this, this wasn't the same sort of fear. This fear was of another order entirely.

Then the figure passed before a window—not the open window, he explained to his friend, but a closed one—and the fear rushed closer. For when the figure crossed into the light he realized he could see through it. It was the shape and size of a human but indistinct, its edges blurred somehow, as if it were not existing here precisely at all, but instead existing somewhere else, in a place that happened, somehow, to overlap with this space. Its edges were blurred and even within its boundaries its features were shifting and unclear, as if he was watching something in the process of becoming real. Or, another part of him thought, ceasing to be real. But even then, with the figure indistinct, he could tell that it was the size and shape of a human but not human at all, and he was terrified of what it might be.

The figure seemed to be shining slightly, vaguely glowing, though a moment ago in the shadows it hadn't been. And this luminescence seemed to be emanating from somewhere within its person, right about where the head, such as it was, met the body, such as it was. This puzzled him for a moment until the figure moved further and he abruptly realized that what he was seeing was coming not from the shape at all, but from behind it, that he was seeing through it to the streetlight shining outside. That he could see *through* it.

Almost without knowing what he was doing he hurled the book at it. The book struck but went right through, not even slowing down, and struck the window behind it, making it shiver, before falling to the floor. The figure stopped abruptly as if it had finally heard something, and turned to face the window, its arms twitching, but paid no attention to the book itself. When it continued, it was moving more quickly this time, heading toward the other window, the one that was open.

A moment later and it was starting through the opening, squeezing through it, before he had thought to move. He rushed toward the window itself and reached it with the figure halfway in and halfway out, eager to close and lock it as soon as the figure was out. But in his rush to shut the window, he managed to close it right on the figure itself.

But just as with the book, the window passed right through the figure. He felt no resistance at all, as if the figure wasn't really there. For a moment the window was open and the figure stretched out across the sash, and then the window was closed and the figure split, bisected by a piece of glass.

Considering the way the book had passed through it, he expected the figure to just keep going, to move slowly out through the glass and away into the night until it became lost among the other shadows. Instead, it hesitated for a moment and then suddenly began to flail its limbs. A moment later it divided into two halves, one on either side of the glass. The one on the outside fell down somewhere into the bushes and was lost. The one on the inside slipped down the sash and spilled onto the floor and lay still.

When he rushed over and turned on the light, he found that the wall and floor where the figure had been were covered with what looked like a swath of blood. That was all that was left of the figure.

He called the police, reported an intruder. He waited, patiently for them to come, and while he was waiting stayed staring at the bloody wall and floor. The color of the blood, he noticed, seemed to be fading, the stain too diminishing. As he waited and watched it faded entirely, leaving only a dampness on the floor. Then that too faded and was gone.

By the time the police arrived, there was nothing to suggest there had ever been anything there at all. And had there been? He had to wonder. Had he perhaps dreamed it all?

And what on earth could it be?

Whether he had dreamt it or not, he admitted to his friend, he hadn't slept that night, nor the next, nor the next, because he kept expecting it to happen again. He was afraid to go to sleep, afraid, too, to turn off the light. He felt that by closing the window on it he had made it aware of him somehow, and now he could feel it somewhere, just out of sight, trying once again to become real, starting to push its way back into the world. He had hurt it and now it would hurt him. He lay awake, listening to his heart pounding in his chest, waiting for it to come. So far it hadn't. But it would come again, he felt that somehow, feared that, and when it did he knew that this time it would come for him.

Which was the other reason he was telling his friend the story: not only was he trying to figure out what had happened to him, whether it was real or not real—he wanted at least one other person in the world to know what had happened, what he thought had happened, so that at least one person in the world would know later why he had disappeared. Soon it would come for him, he felt, though he didn't know how. Soon it would be his own blood on the floor and wall. Perhaps it would fade and perhaps it would not, but in either case it wouldn't matter, at least not to him, because by that time he would be dead or gone or both.

MOUNT CHARY GALORE

JEFFREY FORD

Mrs. Oftshaw was best known for a liniment of her own concoction, *Mount Chary Galore*, that had no other curative property than to make you feel generally *right* and was suspected of being some part of the black lace mushrooms she gathered by the light of an orange moon. She was a strange, solitary old bat, who'd been around so long she was part of the landscape. She'd swoop into town out of the deep woods at the base of the looming mountain, swerving all over the asphalt in her rusted Pontiac. Even the young boys with new driver's licenses and stupid with courage cleared the road when they saw her coming. Sheriff Bedlow wrote her a stack of tickets through the years, but he was not particularly fearless, and would only stick them under the busted windshield wiper when the car was parked and empty. She'd just crumple them in her boney hands and toss them in the dirt.

When she arrived in town, nobody ever came out to greet her, but eyes gazed from behind curtains or betwixt blinds. Those who relied on the Galore were watching, silently counting their nickels and dimes. She eased out of the front seat of that jalopy, and gave a little hop down to the ground. She was short and bent with age, but she had a quickness to her—bird-like. Her outfits were layered, mostly the same for either winter or summer, except in the snowy part of the year when she'd add an oversized sailor's pea coat to the getup—blue leggings, a loose billowing dress, wooden shoes, and a voluminous kerchief draped around her head; a tunnel of fabric you had to peer into to see her pale, wrinkled face like some critter living in a hollow log.

If you got close enough, as I did when she came to deliver a jar of Galore to my poor Ma, you could catch a whiff of her scent, which was not old or ugly or rotten, but beautiful, like the smell of wisteria. Ma always served lavender tea with honey at the parlor table. Mrs. Oftshaw was partial to a jigger of Old Overholt in hers, and she kept a pint in the pocket of that pea coat when the weather got raw. They whispered back and forth for a time. When I asked my Ma what they talked about, she'd smile and say, "Men." "Like Pa?" I asked. She sighed, shook her head and laughed. Just before leaving, the old lady always slipped a jar of Galore from her pocket and placed it next to the teacup, never asking for a cent.

On the 27th of every month, she came to town, the Pontiac's trunk full of cardboard boxes, each holding six Ball jars of a bright green paste that smelled like, as Lardner Scott, Charyville's Post Master, had described it, "A home permanent on the Devil's ass hair." Once liberally applied to the chest or the back of the neck the Galore had a way of easing you down, as if taking your hand and whispering, helping you to sit back into the comfy chair that, amazingly enough, at that moment, you would just be realizing was your life. For a woman who was much feared and much gossiped about, Lillian Oftshaw had a lot of customers—some steady as sunrise, some seasonal, some just passing through. The fact is, she never left town at the end of the month that those boxes in her trunk weren't entirely empty.

On the other hand, during those liniment runs, her passenger seat was never empty, for she was accompanied each time by a large gray hog, nearly three hundred pounds, named Jundle, who sat upright, resting his spine against the seatback, crossing his short hind legs, the right over the left, and leaning his right front leg out the open window. I saw it with my own eyes. That remarkable creature sometimes smoked a fat roll-up of a cheroot, holding it in the split of his cloven hoof and every now and then bringing it up to his snout to take a long drag. Jundle got out of the car and accompanied her to each door step as she delivered the Galore and collected her cash. Once a couple of smart aleck kids thought they'd have some fun with the old lady and then make off with her velvet sack of quarters and dimes. Legs were swiftly broken, and as it's told, those boys were lucky it wasn't necks. Jundle was a jolly creature, but he had a serious side when it came to the wellbeing of Mrs. Oftshaw.

A jar of the Galore cost 50 cents, which, at the time, was a dear price. There were folks with steady income, who went for a jar of the green mystery every month, and there were others who had to use it sparingly, skimping on the application to achieve at least half-rightness half the time. Mote Kimber, a veteran of the Great War, who seen the fellows of his regiment mowed down like summer wheat at the Belleau Wood in France and when captured was tortured—a thin, white hot iron inserted into the opening of his pecker—slathered the Galore onto his bald noggin like he was painting a fence post. After a while the crown of his head had turned jade green, and he could be counted on at any hour after that of breakfast to usually be way past *right*. He was a bona fide war hero, though, and drew a nice pension for his courage. Before being taken by the enemy, he'd rescued three men who'd been wounded and pinned down. Mote would tell you himself that he bought two jars of Galore a month from Lillian. "Either that or kill myself," he said and everybody knew he meant it.

There were a number of folks in town who used the liniment for medical purposes—gout, heartburn, bad back, aches and pains of the joints, the head, the heart. Even Dr. Shevin used it. When asked about its unscientific nature and reliance on back woods hoodoo, he smiled as if realizing his guilt, shrugged, and said, "When I get a crick in my neck, which I do often enough from a bad sleeping posture, just a dab of that Galore on the stiff patch and all's well and then some. Now, if you're asking me if I prescribe it for my patients, I'd have to give you an unequivocal 'No.' I'm a man of Science. I don't suggest anyone else use it, but if they do . . .?" The discussion never went any further. There was no point. If the doctor had been laying it on like old Mote Kimber and was too *right* all the time, now that would have been a problem, but as it was, he used it like most everyone else—"Pro re nata," as he said, which Post Master Scott translated for us as, "When the bullshit gets too thick."

Old lady Oftshaw was mysterious, that's for certain, but I wouldn't say she was evil. There were a lot of folks who just couldn't afford the Galore, and some of them were the ones that needed it most. My Ma was one of them. Ever since my daddy ran off on us, she had to work double shifts over at the chicken packing plant in Hartmere just to keep the house, put food on the table, and gas in the Chevy. And it wasn't just me and her. There was Alice Jane and Pretty Please who also lived under our roof. They were the kids of the woman who daddy ran off with. Their mother simply abandoned them—something no wild animal would do. Instead of letting Sheriff Bedlow cart the kids away to an orphanage in Johnston, the county seat, my Ma asked him to leave them with her. I was there when she made her case. "No sense in having everybody suffer," she said. "They're just kids and they need to know a little love before they get too old." The Sheriff, though short on courage, was long on heart, and he trusted her. He closed his eyes to the law, something that could never happen today, letting Alice Jane become my sort of sister and Pretty Please become my sort of brother.

I suspect you want to know something else about my daddy and why he left Ma, but I truly don't know anything to tell. I was happy to see him go. He was a moody fellow. Quiet. Never did anything father-like with me that I can remember. Although I will say he did buy me a .22 rifle and taught me to shoot out in the prairie over by the creek on the way to Mount Chary. But it wasn't like he did it to get closer to me, more like he was teaching me to take the garbage out to the curb or how to make coffee so he didn't have to get up quite as early in the morning. Although she never said anything about him, I remember Ma's eyes being red a lot and more than once a big yellow-blue bruise on her neck.

Mrs. Adler had no man at the time Daddy ran off with her, and Alice never had any stories about her Pa or photographs for that matter. The whole thing was a mystery I never got to the bottom of. If I'd asked my Ma, I know she'd have told me, but I came to avoid that question, afraid it might leave a wound, like a bullet from the .22.

I was fourteen the year our family declined by one and then grew by two. Alice Jane was the same age as me, but born in summer while I was born in winter. She had long hair braided into pigtails and a freckled face with sleepy green eyes. I thought she was nice, but I didn't let on. She could throw a hard punch or climb a tree, beat me in a race. Her brother, Pretty Please, was "something of a enigma," or at least that's what I heard Post Master Scott whisper to Ma when she told him she'd taken on responsibility for the Adler children. We were at the counter and I was standing next to her while Alice and Pretty were standing over by the private mailboxes.

Men of all kinds seemed to make my sort-of-siblings both shy and scared. "The girl's cute enough, but that boy is . . . *pe-culiar*," said Scott. "He just looks a sight," said my mother, "inside he's true."

I turned and looked at Pretty Please. He was fifteen, and not but an inch or two taller than me, but he had a big old head, full-moon pale and shorn close, looking like a peeled potato with beady eyes. He wore a pair of overalls with no shirt in summer. He seemed always busy, looking around, up and down and all over, rarely fixing on any one sight. Whenever somebody said anything to Ma about him, she'd nod and say, "He's OK," as if trying to convince herself. The only words he ever said were "Pretty please" in a kind of parrot voice. We didn't know where he learned it from, but he seemed to have a vague sense of how to make use of it. Ma asked Alice Jane if he'd always been simple, and she just nodded and confided that their mother used to beat him with a hair brush. His real name, Alice told us, was Jelibai and Ma asked us to call him that but we didn't.

The fact that my Ma took in the kids of the woman who ran off with my Pa was, even to me, downright odd, and to the rest of the town she was either touched by god or touched in the head. I think some thought she had nefarious purposes in mind, maybe to torture them in the place of the woman who stole her man? But in Charyville the rule was to keep your mouth shut and mind your own business. Things had to get really out of hand for someone to pipe up.

The first summer of our new family came, and Alice Jane and I were out of school, on the loose. Pretty Please didn't go to school. The reason Principal Otis gave Ma for not letting him in was, "That poor boy is gone over the hill." Pretty was delighted for us to be home every day, cause usually, when school was in session, he'd have to be by himself, locked up in the basement with my dog, Ghost, a mop-head with legs and a bark. Ma would make Pretty peanut butter sandwiches and he could listen to the radio or look at books or say "Pretty Please" to the dog a hundred times. He liked to draw and you shoulda seen his pictures—yow—people with scribbledy heads and no eyes.

There was a bathroom in the basement and it was cozy enough and lonely enough. Ma just didn't want him getting to the burner of the stove, where he could leave the gas on and blow the place up or set himself on fire. But when *we* were on the loose, Pretty was on the loose. We all liked to be free and always had something to do from the time Ma left in the morning for work to when she came back at night and Alice Jane and me cooked her dinner. I could tell she was worried about us on our own, but I told her, "We're not babies anymore. We can watch out for each other." Her hand that held the cigarette shook a little, and Alice patted her back soft like Ma did for us at night as we went to sleep.

The summers were fine for fishing, fist fights, shooting guns, drinking pop, catching snakes, swimming the creek, riding bikes, playing baseball, bottling lightning bugs and watching the big moon rise. When on Sundays the minister spoke of Paradise all I had to compare it to was summer vacation.

Then on a bright morning in late July, the three of us were out early, and Alice Jane and I decided we would find the day's adventure by just letting Pretty Please run up ahead of our bikes. We followed him wherever he went. It didn't make any sense, and we all laughed, even Pretty, when he ran ten times in the same tight circle. We wound up traveling all the way to the edge of town to the red brick arches of the entrance to the church's side garden. We went there a couple times a week in the early morning. There was a fountain and a bench within those walls. Tears issued from the eyes of a sculpted woman. The water trickled down, plashing from level to level quieter than a whisper. The aroma of the roses was almost too much.

One bright morning, following that scent without hesitation, Pretty walked right in there. Alice Jane and I left our bikes on the sidewalk and followed. We found him standing still as a store manikin, staring up at Minister Sauter, who stood over him looking annoyed. When the preacher saw us enter the garden, his expression quickly changed to a smile. He took a seat on a bench by the fountain and motioned for us to sit down as well. We did. Alice and I were on either side of the Minister, and Pretty, watching ripples in the water, slumped on the bench next to his sister.

Sauter said, "How'd you kids like to make some money?"

"Whatta we gotta do?" asked Alice.

"Well, I want you to ride out to the woods beneath the mountain, and find that old woman Oftshaw's house."

"Pardon," I said, "but she's an old witch, ain't she? My Ma says she's got spells."

Alice smacked herself in the forehead for my ignorance.

The Minister laughed. "The old lady's a Christian, I think," he said.

"How much money?" asked Alice.

"Let's see," said Sauter. "I want you to go out there and I want you to watch what she does. I want you to remember it and then come back and tell me. I'll give each of you twenty cents."

"Easy," said Alice Jane. I nodded.

Pretty Please said, "Pretty please."

"One thing, though," said the Minister. "You can't let her see you watchin' her."

"That's spying," said Alice.

"It would be," said Sauter, "but I'm gonna make you all deputy angels before you go. As a deputy angel, you can do my bidding and not get in trouble with the law or God. The Lord has put his trust in me and so must you."

"I don't want to go to heaven," I said.

"Do you want to make twenty cents?" asked Alice.

We took the oath, and then Alice Jane took it once again for Pretty. I kept messing up the words and at one point the Minister put his hand at the base of my throat to steady me, but in the moment I wasn't sure he didn't intend to strangle me. As soon as we were deputy angels, he shooed us out of the garden. As we mounted our bikes, he whispered to us from the entrance, "Report to me tomorrow at this time. Tell no one. The devil is listening."

Mention of the devil scared us and we rode silently and with great determination, straight north toward Chary Mountain. Pretty Please ran ahead along the side of the empty road, never tiring. That morning the dew had covered everything, made everything glimmer. The sky was deep blue, and there were just white wisps but no real clouds. It was a good couple of miles out to Chary, and so eventually we slowed down and Alice told Pretty to also.

"Why's this lady live all the way out here by herself?" asked Alice, slow-pedaling beside me.

"I don't know too much about her but she had a husband who either died or ran off."

"Probably ran off," said Alice.

"Ma says Mrs. Oftshaw's from some other country."

"Which one?"

"From across an ocean."

I didn't say anything for a while, and Alice asked me, "Is that all you know?"

"Oh, you must've seen her. She's got a smoking hog name of Jundle."

We laughed, and when I focused back on the road, I spotted Pretty Please, way up ahead, making for the tree line.

Alice no doubt saw it before I did, and had taken off, pumping her legs furiously. I worked to catch up with her. Every once in a while, Pretty would get what we called, "the urge." Sometimes he just bolted away. It didn't happen often, maybe once every couple weeks. This time he was really moving at a clip, and we both saw him reach the boundary of the woods and slip inside. We left the road and cut across the short field that bordered the tree line. Riding our bikes amidst the trees was slowing us down, so we dropped them and went forward on foot. Alice's voice could be earsplitting, and she used it every few steps. "Pretty, Pretty, Pretty, Please," she called.

She grew more frantic the farther we went. "I can't lose him," she said to me.

I tried to tell her he'd turn up, but every time I spoke those words, she shook her head and walked faster. By the time I had to take her hand to calm her down, we'd come to the top of a rise. We stood at the crown of the hill and looked down through the trunks of cedar pine and birch trees at a glittering pond. Sitting at the water's edge was Pretty Please, investigating something in the sand. At the sight of him, Alice sighed and turned in toward me. I put my arm around her and froze. She shrugged me off and took a seat a few feet down the incline. I followed and sat next to her.

"I want to ask that brother of yours, pretty please to not run off like that anymore."

"My old Ma, not your Ma, told me once that Pretty was a bag of flesh filled with wind." She took a couple breaths, staring down at her brother. "My Ma was a mean bitch."

When she said that, we both broke out laughing. That one knocked me over. When I sat back up I took her hand in mine again. She didn't make like she noticed. We sat there quiet, taking in the smell of the cedar pines and the sound of goldfinches. The glitter on the water was diamonds and stars. She turned to look into my eyes and said. "We should kiss."

At the moment, I couldn't think of one good reason not to. So we did. And before long she stuck her tongue in my mouth and then we were rolling on the ground rubbing each other up. So much rubbing—we had "the urge"—I thought the two of us would be erased. We reached a point where I had my hand up her shirt, and she had just grabbed my pecker down my pants, when out of the blue, she gets suddenly still, turns her head, and yells, "Pretty Please." In a heartbeat she was off the ground, fixing her clothes. Pretty was gone and it was the only time I ever wished him ill.

We ran through the woods, toward the base of the mountain, and the undergrowth grew more tangled and difficult to manage. We'd follow a natural path through the trees and then eventually be stopped by a wall of thorn bushes and turn back to find another way forward. Alice was frantic again, and I had to keep her a few times from trying to find passage through the heart of one of those bushes that would rip her to shreds. Eventually we came to a clearing in the shade of the mountain. It was, by then, late afternoon, but dark as twilight where we stood. I was happy just to have some open ground before us.

Alice noticed it first. The place was so covered in ivy and some other trailing vine I didn't recognize it as a house. Only when she pointed to where lamplight glowed through a small window, one mere corner of its glass not covered by leaves, did I see it. Then I noticed that there was smoke issuing from inside through the metal chimney of a stove. The house wasn't huge but it had two floors and seemed out of place in the woods—more like a home you might find in a big town. It had a slate roof and you could make out the fancy wood carvings they call gingerbread beneath the ivy.

"Should we do some spying?" I asked Alice in a whisper.

I know she was thinking about Pretty cause she hesitated for a second. "Twenty cents is twenty cents," she said. "We'll just peek in the window and see what we see. Then we gotta get. Whatever we see, we'll tell the Minister."

"What if it ain't much?"

"We'll make something up like good deputy angels."

"Stay quiet," I said to her and tried to take her hand. She pushed me away.

"I can do this myself," she said and we proceeded side by side.

As we approached the house we heard noises inside. I realized the back door was slightly ajar. The closer we got, the smaller the steps we took until we were only inching along a little at a time. I felt cold in my gut, slightly dizzy, and my legs felt weighed down like in those dreams where you need to run but can't. Alice was breathing quickly, her eyes focused on the light coming through the sliver of an entrance.

Sitting on a tree stump, right outside the back door, there was a small painted box with a design like fancy wallpaper. Alice lifted it quickly, tipped the lid up and peered inside. She slipped it into her pocket. "That's thievery," I whispered. She shhh'd me and showed me the back of her hand as if getting ready to smack me.

No less than a breath later, the door flew open and there stood old lady Oftshaw without her tunnel scarf, her pale face and wild hair unhidden.

She was lit from behind and the glow made her seem some kind of spirit. I stopped dead in my tracks and froze. Alice grabbed my hand and spun us around. She started to yell "Run," I think, but whatever the word was it vanished, cause standing right in our path was Jundle. Alice took a step, and the hog made a noise from deep inside his huge body that sounded like the earth grunting. He came at us, plodding slowly, and we turned and walked toward Mrs. Oftshaw. I couldn't get any spit in my mouth, and my legs were like two dead fish.

"Come in children," said the old lady, and she stepped back and held open the door for us. We stepped into her kitchen, first Alice and then me. We stood right next to each other and kept some distance between us and Mrs. Oftshaw. She let the door go and it slammed shut, making us start. I don't know how, but I was able to look up at her face. I'd never seen it clearly before. In that moment, I saw that she wasn't a homely old woman but just an old woman.

"You kids here to spy on me?" she asked and smiled in a way that made me scared.

I was all set to spill the beans, but before I could open my mouth, Alice stepped forward and said. "We brought my brother out to the pond in the woods, but we lost him. Can you help us find him?"

The old lady said, "He's not lost."

"We really don't know where he is, and I have to find him." Alice said.

"He's not lost, child. He's on an expedition."

"Where is he?" I asked.

"He's traveling far," she said. "But I can help you. I'll send Cynara, the world's oldest Heifer, after him. She'll bring him home." She went to the door, opened it and whistled. With her hand, she motioned for us to come and join her by the entrance. In a few moments, Jundle slowly came waddling into sight. He stood in front of us, a cigarette in the corner of his mouth, smoke issuing in pig tails.

"Take Cynara and go and fetch the Pretty boy."

Jundle dropped a little pile of turds, grumbled, and trotted off.

"Done and done," said the old lady. "Now let me make you kids a snack."

She led us into her house, through the kitchen, and into the parlor, all lace doilies and puffy furniture in pea green. There was a small chandelier above, its pendants glinting, and below a braided rug in blue and silver.

"You can sit on the loveseat," she said and pointed at a small couch. "I'll be right back. Gon' fetch you some of my special cookies."

When she left the room, we saw it. It had been sitting behind her on a shiny wooden pedestal. No, not a radio, but a big clear glass ball with a man's head floating in it. I jumped at the sight and Alice whispered, "What?" And "what" was right—a head with wavy black hair, waving in the water, a black beard and mustache, eyes shut and mouth partway open to show a few teeth. At the bottom of the glass ball there was sand and a little hermit crab scuttling around in it. Tiny starfish were suspended around the head.

Mrs. Oftshaw suddenly appeared with a tray full of cookies and two glasses of what looked like yellow milk. "Have a treat," she said and laid it down on the little table in front of us. She backed away, and said, "Go ahead."

The cookies were fat and misshapen, the color of eggplant, with shreds of something sticking out all over. Neither of us made a move for them. She sat down in the armchair next to the pedestal. "I see you've met Captain Gruthwal," she said and pointed to the floating head.

We nodded.

"Have a cookie, and we'll wake him up."

Alice leaned over first and took one of the lumpy "treats." I followed her lead. The thing was soggy as a turd, and smelled like what Pa used to pull out of the gutters in spring. We bit into them at the same time, like biting into a clod of dirt, but the taste was better than sweet and made me shiver. One bite and you wanted another till the thing was gone. We each ate two more, and every time one of us would slip one off the tray the old lady nodded and said, "That's right. That's right."

After the third, we sat back. I don't know about Alice but my head was spinning a little and I felt kind of good all over. I looked at her and she smiled at me, lids half closed. "Drink your peach milk," said Mrs. Oftshaw. It seemed like a good idea, so I did and so did Alice. I can't recall what the peach milk tasted like, whether peaches or something else. We put the empty glasses on the tray, and the old lady turned to face the glass globe beside her.

"Wake up, Captain Gruthwal," she said. "Wake up."

I swear, Alice screamed louder than me when the eyes of the floating head opened and stared at us.

"Captain," said Mrs. Oftshaw. "These children want to know about the bigheaded boy."

The floating face grimaced, as if annoyed at being awoken. Its eyes shifted toward the old lady and then rolled up, showing only white. The Captain's mouth opened wider and then wider, and I thought he would scream in the water. We waited for a torrent of bubbles and the muffled sound, but instead something showed itself from within the dark cavern. It was a pale knob, like a diseased tongue but much larger. It filled the rim of his lips, and continued to squeeze itself out from inside him. Two tentacles emerged and then more. "An octopus," I said and gagged.

"Ugghh," said Alice and turned her face from the sight.

"Watch it child," said Mrs. Oftshaw. "Watch it good. The Captain's gonna show us something."

I felt Alice's hand on my shoulder, as the octopus, now free, swam, pulsing its tentacles in circles around the floating head. As the pale sac of life swept in orbit around the Captain, its ink oozed out of it in black plumes. Alice's grip tightened as the face and everything else inside the globe was slowly obscured.

"Like a dream," said Mrs. Oftshaw, and out of the murk came an image of Pretty Please walking along the side of the road in the moonlight.

"Pretty," yelled Alice, and her brother turned his potato head and glanced over his shoulder. She yelled again, "Come back," but the ink was already swirling the image away to reveal a different scene of Jundle riding atop a sorry old cow, all skin and bones, the way a person might, straddling its back. They moved along at a snail's pace, the hog strumming the steel strings of a little guitar and grunting softly.

More swirling of the ink and image and then we were back to Pretty and saw him standing next to a one-story house, not much more than a shack. He was peering in a window with the moonlight shining over his shoulder. Through the dirty glass and the shadows, I saw two people sleeping in a bed: a man and a woman.

"That's my Ma," said Alice and stood up.

"Very good, child," said Mrs. Oftshaw.

"What's that in Pretty's hand?" I asked noticing something glint in the moonlight. I squinted and saw it was an open straight razor, the one Pa had left behind in the bathroom cabinet. "Either Pretty's 'bout to do some shavin' or he's possessed by a bad idea," I said.

Alice noticed the razor and stepped toward the globe, "No, Pretty," she said. Her hands, fingers spread wide, reached for the glass.

Just then he lifted the blade and the man in the bed next to Alice's Ma, my Pa, opened his eyes and witnessed the scene at the window. We saw him shake his head, look again, and heard, muffled by the window glass, him yell, "Mattie, your nitwit kid's outside and he's totin' a cutthroat."

"What?" said Mrs. Adler, and she woke and looked and shook her head too. "Christ, it's him. How can it be?"

"It's bewitchment," said Pa. "I'm gonna take care of this right now." He stood up, naked, in the further shadows behind the bed. I lost sight of him for a moment, and then he appeared again in the moonlight, holding his .22 rifle. He left the room.

"Ya can't shoot him," called Mrs. Adler.

As the front door to the little house creaked open, we could hear Pa yell back, "Self-defense."

Alice screamed, "No!" and lunged at the globe. She tripped, hit the pedestal and although Mrs. Oftshaw moved to catch either her or Captain Gruthwal, she caught neither. The globe hit the floor and exploded into stars of glass as the ink seeped into the parlor. There was more blackness in that glass bubble than you could have guessed. Darkness filled the room by the time I'd grabbed Alice's hand and was helping her off the floor. I couldn't see a damn thing, but I held on tight to my sort of sister and she held onto me until the moonlight shone.

We were standing in the clearing of pines where the shack was. Pretty was walking around the side of the place, obviously heading for the front door, while Pa, naked as a jaybird, his pecker flopping, the .22 raised and aimed, was heading for the side. At the corner they met face to face.

"Say yer prayers, tater face," said Pa, and I yelled out for him not to shoot.

He turned quick and saw me and Alice standing there, and his eyes bugged. "Oh," he said, and it was like he lost his breath for a second. It was the first time I seen him scared.

"The whole fuckin' family," he said. "No problem, I'll plug all you crumb snatchers at once." Mrs. Adler was at the window just plain screaming, not even saying anything.

Pretty swept the razor in front of him and slashed Pa's forearm. The gun dipped down for a moment, but Pa groaned a little and raised it again. I couldn't look and I couldn't not look, expecting any second for Pretty's head to be shattered like the glass globe. He brought the razor up as if he meant to split Pa down the middle, and Pa froze in his usual stance when he was about to pull the trigger. Before he could fire, though, we saw some shadow, moving low through the night.

Jundle hit Pa behind the knees and my old man crumpled up and whimpered, the gun flying out of his hands. I dove for it and grabbed it away, but backing up I fell onto my ass. Pa kicked the hog in the head and scrabbled after me on his knees. "Give me that gun, Jr. That's an order."

He got up and stood over me with burning eyes and a hideous expression. In my fear, I pulled the trigger, and the bullet went through his left eye and come straight out the back with the crack of bone and a splurt of blood and brain. He stood there for a second, that eye hole smoking like the ash on one of Jundle's cheroots, and then he fell forward like a cut tree. I rolled out of the way. He was so heavy with death that he would have made a pancake of me.

I wanted to think about the fact that I'd just killed my Pa, but there wasn't a second. Alice was standing at the window staring in like she was hypnotized. By the time I reached her, Pretty had already commenced slicing up Mrs. Adler. She was slit open from the chin to belly button and blood was everywhere, soaking her nightgown, pooling on the floor in the moonlight. I saw her heart beating inside her. She moved her mouth to make a blood bubble whisper, and I could tell by reading her lips that her last words were, "Pretty Please."

I pulled Alice away and put my arms around her. She didn't move a muscle and was cold as stone. When I drew away, I found a huge grin on her face. Next I knew, Pretty was beside us, drenched in blood, laughing, with an arm around each of our shoulders. "How'd we get here?" I asked Alice when the hug broke up.

"I don't know," she said, "but let's get."

I looked around and saw Jundle, recovered from his foot to the face, taking a piss against the side of the house. When he was done, he took the burning cheroot from his mouth and touched its red hot tip to the planks where he'd relieved himself. Fire sprang up as if from gasoline and in a blink the flames were creeping up the side of the shack.

The hog trotted over to us and made a motion with his head that we were to climb on his back. Somehow, though it didn't seem possible, we all fit. He grunted, squealed, farted, took three enormous jumps and lit into the sky. We were flying upward on the back of a hog. I was petrified, and could feel Alice's arms wrapped around my chest and her face pressing into my back. I couldn't see Pretty, and didn't know how he was managing to hang on, but I still heard his laughter, which hadn't ceased since he sliced up his Ma.

At one point Jundle swept down low over a dirt path through a wood, and we saw the shot and butchered bodies of our parents riding the back of Cynara the old heifer, heading off to, I guessed, Hell. By the time Jundle reached an altitude where we were soaring through white clouds and stars,

I was exhausted. It was peaceful way up there. I wrapped my arms around the enchanted animal's thick bristly neck as I fell forward into sleep.

I woke, confused, in my own bed the next morning, and so did Alice and Pretty Please. Ma, who had our breakfast ready as always before leaving for work, seemed never to suspect a thing. We couldn't wait for her to leave for work. When she finally did, Alice said to me. "What do you make of it?"

"Did we kill your Ma and my Pa?"

"I guess we did," she said.

Pretty actually nodded.

"It ain't possible," I said. I ran to the bathroom and checked for the razor in the cabinet. It was gone. I ran back to report to Alice.

"We gotta act like nothing happened," she said. "Deny everything."

"It's gonna be hard to forget. How'd we get back from Mrs. Oftshaw's?"

"Jundle," said Pretty Please, and me and Alice almost fell over. It was the first time her brother had said anything but that which had become his name.

Later that morning, we were back at the rose garden of the church in order to keep our deal. We sat on the bench, looking at the fountain, all of us still tired from the doings of the night. Eventually the Minister came out to see us. We gave him a seat on the bench between me and Alice. Pretty didn't budge for him.

"Did you go and look in on Mrs. Oftshaw?" he asked.

I nodded and Alice said, "We did."

"She's got a magic hog," I told him.

"She's got a man's head floatin' in water," said Alice.

"We shaved," said Pretty Please, another surprise. The Minister looked quizzically at us. "You must tell me the truth," he said.

"Us deputy angels got inside her place, and I took this little box," said Alice. "I spied on her whispering into it. Then she shut the lid down tight. Must have been a curse or something."

I looked at Alice but she wouldn't look at me.

"Give me that," said the Minister and took the fancy box from her hand. "There's no such thing as curses, dear." He pulled the lid off and held it up to look inside. We saw it there, a shiny red wasp with a long stinger that looked like a piece of jewelry cut from ruby. Only thing is, its wings started to flutter, and then all of a sudden it took off. It flew straight up into the Minister's face and sunk that long stinger into the white jelly of his left eye. The box hit the paving stones, and the poor man screamed, bringing his hands up to cover his face.

We never got paid for spying that day cause we ran for our bikes with Pretty hot behind us. We pedaled like mad back home and hid with the curtains pulled over, expecting Sheriff Bedlow any minute for hours on end. But he never did come, and the Minister never told on us. Maybe he was afraid that people would find out he'd promised to pay us for spying on Mrs. Oftshaw. As it was, he had to start using the Mount Chary Galore on that eye, the only thing he claimed would stop the burning.

A few weeks had gone by, and I still didn't know what to make of that crazy night. Then one day my Ma called all us kids together when she returned home from work. Before we ate dinner, she sat us down on the couch, herself in a chair across from us.

"I hate to have to tell you this," she said, and I could see her grow weak. She lowered her head slightly so we couldn't see her eyes. "Your Ma," she said, nodding toward Alice, "and your Pa," she said to me, "are dead. I don't know how else to put it."

Neither Alice or me said a peep. If my sort of sister was half as surprised as I was, her tongue felt turned to stone.

My mother cried and we moved closer and put our arms around her. Finally Alice said, "What happened?"

My Ma just shook her head.

"How'd they die?" I asked.

She was silent for a time, drying her eyes, and eventually said, "Car crash out in California."

"That ain't really what happened, is it?" asked Alice, softly, stroking the back of Ma's neck.

Ma shook her head. In a whisper she said, "No."

"What then?" I asked.

"It's too terrible. Far too terrible to describe."

A few days later, the summer ended. Me and Alice had to go back to school and Pretty was sent to the basement. He'd slowly lost all his new power of speech, but not before my Ma got to hear him say the word, "Love," which managed to lift her out of the funk caused by finding out about Pa's death. From then on, when Mrs. Oftshaw was coming to the house, me and Alice made sure we were out. We'd had enough of her magic, but it was our secret and we talked about it when we'd slip out into the woods to kiss. Late one afternoon that fall, after the weather had gone cold, I spied Mount Chary bathed in the last golden light of day, like an ancient, gilded pyramid, looming in the distance down the end of the one road out of town, and I got a feeling for the first time in my life that everything was finally *right*.

BALLAD OF AN ECHO WHISPERER

CAITLÍN R. KIERNAN

A gun shot.

A pirouetting shadow.

Steel wheels rolling on steel rails, rushing not quite smoothly, not silently, over gravel ballast and softwood crossties hewn long ago, then soaked in creosote to form this magic ladder stretching all the way from Penn Station to the city of New Orleans. I do call it magic, the railroad, all 1,377 miles of it. I lie in my narrow upper berth, the sleeper car swaying and jerking side to side beneath me, around me. We're racing northeast over Lake Pontchartrain not too long past dawn, heading home. Out there, the morning sun has set the estuary on fire, and the white inferno is too bright to look at for more than a few seconds without averting my eyes. There are already (or still) fishermen on the water in their fragile, bobbing boats, casting lines or reeling them in again.

How can they drift in the fire?

How can anyone bear that heat?

I haven't slept, because it was easier for me to stay awake all night than get up in time to make it to the Union Passenger Terminal on Loyola at six A.M. Now, I'll try to catch a few daylight hours of shut-eye, but first I'm watching as the *Crescent* sails over the lake. When I glance directly down, from this angle I can't see the tracks below me, not the rails and crossties and gravel ballast of the Norfolk Southern Bridge. I only see the brown-green water, as if the train has, even if only briefly, become another sort of boat. The impression is disconcerting, and it's almost as hard to look at—of course, for different reasons—as the sun blazing on the lake.

I'm not afraid of drowning, but I am afraid of being trapped inside a sinking train. I am afraid of burning.

Below me, Annapurna is stretched out on the lower bunk reading. She slept last night, wise girl. Despite her name, she isn't Hindu; she's from Gloucester. Her parents just liked the name. No one ever calls her Annapurna, except, she says, her family. She goes by Anna, and I've never called her anything else. Anna is stretched out beneath me reading by the light of the lake of fire. I'm the writer, but Anna is the one who reads books the way some people eat popcorn. This morning, she's working her way through a volume of Thomas Hardy that she picked up in a bookshop on Dauphine Street. She'll read "A Mere Interlude" and "The Three Strangers"; I'll sleep.

I followed her to New Orleans because she offered to pay for everything. She had business there, not me. Personally, I can do without the mid-August heat and the tourists who swarm the Vieux Carré, where she insisted on staying. Anna is never, herself, a tourist. She prides herself on that. She'd never, for instance, attend Mardi Gras.

She'd say, "That's for locals, and it's for tourists who come to get drunk and catch beads and pretend they know what Mardi Gras is about. To pretend they belong. But I'm not a local, and I'm not a tourist."

Anna travels a lot, never a tourist and never a local, but, instead, passing through wrapped in this limbo she has created for herself. Sometimes, I wonder if she even sees the places she visits, and other times I suspect she experiences them more intimately than most and with a perspective she can only manage by keeping herself at arm's length. She's a photographer, and she's fortunate enough that she doesn't have to live off her art. Which isn't to say she isn't good at what she does; she's fucking brilliant. But she inherited a lot of money from an aunt or uncle (I've never been clear on which), so she has the luxury of not having to whore herself out to whoever is willing to pay.

"You're not a whore, William," she says.

"Close enough," I reply. "I'm selling my thoughts, not my body. That's the only difference. I'm a legal whore, maybe because thoughts are intangible and nowhere near as much fun as sex."

"Plenty of places it's illegal to speak your mind," she says. "To write down your thoughts for other people to read." She begins reeling off examples, and I concede her point.

This is a conversation from the dining car on the way down from Manhattan. It's an old, recurring conversation, and this time it recurs over dry salmon and a flavorless medley of steamed vegetables as we're leaving D. C. and entering Virginia. She abruptly changes the subject to Louisiana voodoo, and I pick at the desiccated fish on my plate while she lectures me about sympathetic magic, the African Diaspora, Marie Laveau, and Papa Legba. I say hardly anything at all, because I don't know shit about voodoo. After dinner, when we're back in our sleeper compartment, she shoves a tattered paperback from one of her carry-ons into my hands—*The Spiritual Churches of New Orleans: Origins, Beliefs, and Rituals of an African-American Religion*. I flip through the pages and see that the two authors are anthropologists, one from Tulane and the other from Columbia University. Anna assures me it's thorough, trustworthy scholarship, and for a while I pretend to be interested in remedying my ignorance while she watches the night rushing by beyond the windows.

Then the porter comes round to fold out our beds, and I'm relieved that I can climb into my upper berth, set the book aside, and play *Angry Birds* on my iPad. Anna tips the man, because Anna tips almost everyone. She can afford to. The porter's name is Romalise. I ask him if he's from New Orleans or New York (from his accent, I suspect the former), and he confirms my suspicions—the Lower 9th Ward, to be precise—and he talks a few minutes about hurricanes Katrina and Rita, about how his family came back when so many others didn't, and about a Vietnamese restaurant where he was once a *Chef de partie* before the floods. When Anna and I are alone again, she explains that *Chef de partie* is really just a fancy phrase for line cook; I don't bother asking what it is that line cooks do. I'd rather be flinging vengeful pixel birds at snickering green pixel pigs.

This night seems so innocent, and lying here in my bunk peeking at the white, white burning expanse of Lake Pontchartrain, it also seems a lifetime ago. I know this because it's one of the last nights before I wander alone—long after midnight—down St. Peter towards Jackson Square and come to the black wrought-iron gate wedged in between a tobacconist and a shop that seems to specialize in the unlikely pairing of alligator skulls and Catholic tchotchkes. At first glance, this gate appears no different than any number of other such gates I've passed, most leading down short brick corridors or alleyways to modest courtyards. I almost keep walking, because there's a cool, half-hearted breeze breathed from the direction of the Square, cool air off the river; and so what if the sun's down, the night's still hot enough that I'm sweating like a pig. But I don't keep walking; I do stop.

Later—no, sooner than later—I'll regret not having continued on my way. Sooner than later, I'll regret having stopped at the black gates, *before* I stop at the gates. Can the present affect the past, and can the future affect the present? Retrocausality. The impossible only seems impossible until it happens.

I peer through the bars. The gate opens into an arched passage, no more than ten feet long, into one of the small courtyard gardens. The garden is lit, even at this late hour, and I can see carefully tended banana trees and night-blooming jessamine. The redbrick walls are mostly obscured by the clinging vines of bougainvillea and wisteria. There are voices, of women and of men and of people whose sex I can't discern.

There are voices, enough of them that the courtyard should be crowded with people. It sounds like a party. The voices, laughter and the clink of glasses, a live jazz band—trumpets, trombones, saxophones, clarinet, a drummer.

There are voices, but I can't see anyone. So I tell myself the party's inside, obviously, and only some acoustical trick, sound ricocheting off the walls and then up the passage to the black wrought-iron gates, is responsible for what I expected to see being at odds with what I *do* see.

It's almost three in the morning, and I wake Anna when I open the door to the hotel room we're sharing. I try to be quiet, but I bump into a suitcase that neither of us bothered to put in the closet or a corner or some other place out of the way. She switches on the lamp beside her bed, and I apologize for waking her.

"You look like you've seen a ghost," she says. Could I ask for a more clichéd greeting?

"It's just the heat," I reply. "It's still sweltering out there."

She squints at me and rubs her eyes. "They say it should be a little cooler tomorrow. There might be a thunderstorm or two in the afternoon."

"Doesn't it just get hotter down here when it rains?"

She looks annoyed and switches the lamp off again.

The next morning, before we split up and she heads to the Garden District and Lafayette No. 1, we get beignets and coffee from a place called Café Beignet. The crispy squares of fried dough come in a paper bag at least half filled with confectioners' sugar. The grease from the beignets has made lumps of some of the sugar, and Anna picks these out and eats them.

"It's a wonder you have a tooth left in your head," I tell her, and she ignores me and begins talking about the Karstendick tomb in Lafayette No. 1. We're here because her most recent obsession is cemetery ironwork, and Anna's informed me there are several superb examples of cast-iron tombs scattered around the city. Most date back well into the 19th century.

"In this climate, with the floods and all," I say, "it's pretty hard to believe they haven't all rusted away."

"You know, people *do* take care of shit." Then she goes on a bit about Gothic Revival influences and Doric columns, frieze embellishments and *pintelles* and downspout grotesques. I honestly try to pay attention, but the heat is distracting, and the talk of ironwork leads my mind back to the black gate and the courtyard.

Anna drops the bag of powdered sugar into a trash can and asks about the night before.

"You really did look pretty shook up," she says.

So, I commit a lie of omission and only tell her about staring into the courtyard and hearing an invisible party. She raises an eyebrow and frowns, clearly disappointed.

"That's all?"

"Yeah," I reply. "It was just a bit weird."

"We clearly have very different ideas of what constitutes weird." Then she suggests that the party was somewhere just out of sight, in one of the apartments opening out into the courtyard, and there was nothing more peculiar at work than echoes. Out of sight, but not out of earshot.

Great minds think alike and all that shit.

Anna flags down a taxi and leaves me standing on the corner of Bienville and Chartres. We've made plans to meet up for dinner at Tujague's. I don't know much worth knowing about restaurants, and so, whenever we travel together, I always let Anna choose. She's assured me I'll love the shrimp remoulade at Tujague's.

The Crescent Line speeds across Pontchartrain, and I turn my back on the rippling white fire and quickly drift off to sleep. I dream about the courtyard, and if I dream about anything else upon waking I'm unable to remember that I did. The dream is as good as video, faithfully reproducing even the most insignificant details of that night. Assuming any details are *in*significant. Having written that, I realize how arrogant it is to claim I can sort what is relevant from what is irrelevant.

So, the dream, as good as the night itself.

Conversely, the night, as good as the dream itself.

I press my face to the bars, straining for a better view of the courtyard. Now that I'm listening closely, the music rises and falls, as do the voices and Dixieland jazz, the rhythm makes me think of the wheels of trains against steel rails, and of waves rushing forward, then dragged back into the sea. A clot of drunken college students passes by, and they laugh. Probably, they're laughing at me, but I ignore them. And that's when I notice the shadows moving about in that counterfeit patch of jungle. Shadows that sway to the same cadence as the music and the jumble of conversation. Only, almost immediately, I realize I'm not seeing *shadows*, plural, but a *single* shadow. It washes to and fro, falling across the vine-covered walls and the drooping banana leaves. In no way does the shadow strike me as out of place in the empty courtyard.

It is, after all, only a shadow.

Same as the comingled voices are only voices and the jazz is only brass and percussion and woodwind.

You look like you've seen a ghost.

Do I? Do I really?

"William, I don't think you've heard a word I've said."

I glance back over my shoulder at St. Peter Street, but there's no sign of anyone who might have spoken. The street is empty. The voice was familiar.

On the way to New Orleans, I'm still awake at 2:51 A.M. when we pull into the Salisbury station, and the dimly lit platform is deserted. No one's waiting to get on, but the *Crescent* stops anyway. I'm scribbling something on the third from the last page of a Moleskine notebook, and I stop scribbling and stare out at the depot. My head is filled with Pink Floyd, "Waiting for the Worms" spilling in through my earbuds. The volume's up too loud, because the volume's always up too loud. Fuck me if I know why, but I tap at the window with the eraser end of my mechanical pencil, three quick, sharp taps.

And I see the black dog watching me from the platform. If I'd seen it a second earlier, I wouldn't have tapped against the sleeper compartment's window. I swear I wouldn't have. I don't know what sort of dog it is. When I get back to Boston, I tell myself, I'll figure that out. I *will* try. It might be a very large black lab. Or it might not be. I've never been a dog person, and so to me the dog is simply a big black dog. It's watching me, while I watch it, and its eyes flash a brilliant emerald green, shining back the light from the train. The dog is sitting near one of the closed doors to the station, its ears pricked forward; everything about the animal speaks to its attentiveness. It tilts its head to one side, and I almost shout down to wake Anna. Almost, but only almost.

"It's a dog," she'd say, groggy and angry. "Jesus God, William. You woke me up to see a goddamn *dog*? Do you even *know* what time it is?"

She wouldn't see what I see. She isn't meant to.

The dog that might be a black lab tilts its head to one side, and, on cue, a long shadow, cast by nothing I can see, pirouettes across the concrete. The dog lies down and rests its head between its paws. The shadow dances for me.

I force myself to look back at my notebook, and I don't look up again until the train is moving once more and there's nothing to see in the window but my reflection, superimposed over the blur of a North Carolina night.

A few days before we leave for New Orleans, I'm walking along Newbury Street at dusk. I hear someone call my name, and when I turn to see who, there's an instant or two of vertigo. An instant or two when the familiar cacophony of the crowded sidewalk shrinks down to a whisper, and instead of exhaust fumes and hot asphalt I smell jessamine blossoms. I recognize the sweet aroma of the flowers because I'll smell it—*for the first time*—when I stand with my face pressed to the bars of an iron gate on St. Peter Street. On Newbury Street, I smell jessamine, and I see a large black dog padding away from me, snaking through the pedestrians. It isn't on a leash, and no one else seems to even notice it. Then the dog is gone, as is the smell of the flowers, and all is ordinary again.

Over breakfast, I tell Anna what I saw when the train stopped in Salisbury. Well, I tell her about the dog, not about the shadow. I haven't told anyone about the shadow.

"Maybe it lives at the station," she says.

"Lives there?"

"You know. The way some shops have cats. Like that. A train dog. Well, a train *station* dog."

"Maybe," I say, picking at a dry croissant I suspect was baked days before. I've smeared it with butter and strawberry jelly, but it stubbornly remains the Sahara Desert of croissants. "Probably."

Anna smiles and sips her steaming tea. The server pauses at our booth to ask if we need anything else, if everything's okay; I resist making a crack about the desiccated croissant. I have a habit of making snarky comments to waiters and what have you, and it drives Anna nuts.

"We're fine," she says. "Thank you."

When the server's moved on to the next booth, I pinch off a piece of the croissant and frown at it.

"Maybe Black Shuck's moved to Salisbury," Anna says to me. "Maybe—"

"Black Shuck?"

"You know. Ghost dogs? Hellhounds? Barghests?"

"Barghests?" I drop the pinched-off piece of croissant onto my plate. "You lost me."

"You truly do need to read a book every now and then," she sighs. "You write the things, the least you could do is read a few."

I wipe my hands on a paper napkin and lean back, watching as we rush past some bit of small-town trackside squalor. House trailers. Rusted cars precariously balanced on uneven stacks of concrete blocks. A scrubby brown lawn with a bizarre arrangement of life-sized plastic deer.

Meanwhile, in New Orleans, I peer through the wrought-iron gate on St. Peter, and the stingy breeze off the river stirs the banana leaves, lazily shuffling them about like the wings of enormous beetles. A woman is singing now, and the shadow sways in time to the "Basin Street Blues."

Were the gate unlocked, I might find the courage to open it. I might also dance in that garden, with only a shade for a partner. Only an eclipse, and my own body's eclipse melding in a ghostly *pas de deux*. Oh, there's a word I haven't dared to use until now: *ghostly*. But wasn't it, that night? Even if I am not claiming the presence of an actual specter, in any conventional sense, surely this is a haunting. A haunted courtyard that's haunted me. A bruised place or moment that has, in turn, bruised me.

On our way home, Lake Pontchartrain also burns, not by sunrise but by sunset. The *Crescent* speeds across that low span above marshes and then the big water proper. Our compartment is an even-numbered compartment, so the windows face westward out across nothing at all but the low, flammable waves. The incandescent waves. This fire is not white morning, but the red-orange herald of twilight. I take a few photos with my Canon digital, and Anna warns me that it's terrible for the lens, aiming it directly into the sun that way. But I do, regardless, my sad-ass excuse for living dangerously. The sun is so bright and so much heat is filling up our compartment that it's very quickly becoming uncomfortable. Anna wants to move to the one across the aisle; it's empty, after all, and she can't imagine anyone will care. I say no, this is something I've never seen before, something I might never see again. She scowls and doesn't look at the lake. A tourist would gawk like I am gawking, and she is never a tourist.

The conductor—he must be a conductor—is moving through the sleeper car, letting people know we're only about forty-five minutes from arrival. Our door is open, and he pauses and points out across Pontchartrain.

"Beautiful, isn't she?" he asks.

Just then, we pass the remnants of what was once a pier, but is now nothing but a series of rotting pilings jutting unevenly from the water. There is another ruined pier after it, and then another. They put me in mind of broken, rotten teeth; I photograph them.

"First time in New Orleans?" he asks me, and I tell him that yes, it is. He smiles, then jabs a thumb over his shoulder, back towards that unoccupied compartment that Anna wanted to move to.

"From that side, you can see I-10 and the Twin Spans. Took a hell of a beating in the storm."

I don't have to ask which storm.

"Surge pulled the segments apart, yanked them loose and tossed them around like Lego blocks. Hard to believe a thing like that if you didn't see the aftermath. Fixed up good as new now, though."

I snap another photo, a chalk-white egret wading through a patch of cattails growing beside the tracks. The photo comes out nothing but a blur.

"So, you guys hear anything odd last night?" he asks. He's watching the lake, too, eyes shielded with his left hand. Anna wants to know what he means by odd.

"Had a couple of passengers say they heard something moving around, up and down the aisle."

"Something?" Anna asks him. "Not someone?"

"That's what they said. One of them said she thought maybe it was a dog, maybe. We do allow some types of service animals. Seeing-eye dogs, but they aren't allowed to wander around like that. This lady, she said it was snuffling at her door the way a dog sniffs about. Said it sounded like a real big dog, too."

"I didn't hear anything," I lie. "But I'm a very sound sleeper," I also lie.

"I didn't hear it, either," Anna tells the conductor, and I assume she isn't lying. She wouldn't. It isn't like her. "Rules or no rules, maybe someone's dog got loose."

"Maybe," he says. "Asked around, of course, and no one would own up to it. But I figure they probably wouldn't."

I find it remarkable, even now, how so unremarkable a matter can strike me as simultaneously mundane and unnerving. But he'd said some*thing*, not some*one*. And I *had* heard it, and what I heard I knew it wasn't a dog, same as I knew the black dog I'd seen back in Salisbury, the shadow's dancing partner, had been something *more* than a dog.

I sound like a madman. I know that. I don't believe that I am, but I wouldn't begrudge anyone who reads this the right to doubt my sanity.

After Salisbury, after I finally drift off to an uneasy sleep, and not too long before dawn somewhere in South Carolina, the snuffling noise the conductor will ask about wakes me. I lay very still, listening. Some*thing* brushes against the wall of our compartment with enough force that I can tell it's some*thing* larger than a seeing-eye dog. Unless maybe the blind are using Irish Wolfhounds these days. My back is to the door, and I don't turn to see if there's any*thing* to see. It lingers outside our compartment for, I guess, five minutes or so. At least, I listen to it for about that long; I can't say how long it may have been there while I was sleeping. And then it makes a grunting noise and moves along. Its footfalls are heavier than I'd expect from a dog.

The snuffling thing woke me from a dream of the dog I saw on Newbury Street.

"Well, you two enjoy your visit," says the conductor, and he smiles and leaves us with the blazing lake.

The night after I find the black gate and the courtyard, I take another walk, absolutely determined not to return to the garden and its waltzing shadow. I head down Royal and turn north at the intersection with Conti, turning away from Jackson Square and the river. I follow Conti Street past Bourbon and turn right at Dauphine, and by then I'm far enough from the courtyard that I've managed—at least consciously—to stop chewing over the events of the evening before. I have the shop windows and buskers, instead. I have a trio of drag queens—fellow tourists—who stop me and want to know how to get to a club called Oz. I have no idea whatsoever. They flirt with me, then wander off in search of the Yellow Brick Road.

I watch them go, all platform heels and sequins and wigs, and I'm thinking, *Where does a train track begin and end?* Though clearly it is a *line*, does this one begin in Manhattan, or does it, instead, begin in New Orleans? Isn't this as relative to direction as determining the beginning of a circle?

I don't think a mathematician would say so.

But it seems that way to me.

A loop. An entirely unconventional Möbius strip, yes? Should I happen to *shout* within a three-dimensional Möbius, that sound would travel round and round and round. And if I shout along a straight *line*, the sound may echo back. So, *returning* to me either way.

A shout. Or dogs and shadows and unseen things that prowl the aisles of sleeper cars.

Over breakfast, on the way home, I say to Anna, "You never did tell me if you found that tomb you were looking for in Greenwood." I'm trying, trying, trying not to think about my dream of the black gate. Fortunately, Anna would almost always rather talk about her work than anything else. Sometimes, like now, I use this to my advantage, though it's a quality about her I greatly admire. She still has the sort of passion for her art that I lost a long, long time ago. She's said it annoys her that I never want to discuss my books and short fiction.

"The 1861 Edwards and Bennett," she nods. "Yeah, I found it. God, it's in beautiful shape, that one. Exquisite craftsmanship"

"So, it was a very profitable trip for you."

"Yes, indeed. Very, very. I'm thinking I may actually be able to get a gallery interested in an exhibition. Well, I was *hoping* that when I set up the trip, but don't count your chickens, right? Anyway, I sent Carlotta some shots, and she agrees we could land a show. She's excited."

Carlotta is Anna's agent, and is, by the way, a better agent than mine.

"Then at least I haven't suffered this abominable croissant in vain," I say, and she laughs.

"Your sacrifice will be duly noted, Brave William. As a matter of fact, I hereby dub thee *Sir* William of Mass Ave," and Anna picks up her butter knife and leans across the table. She taps a flat side of the blade against my right shoulder, my forehead, and then my left shoulder. Several people in the dining car notice and they laugh.

I sit up straighter and bow. "You are too gracious, My Lady. I shall uphold thy honor and my knightly vows, never flinching in the face of perilous pastries."

"*Fais ce que tu veux, le bon sire.*"

More laughter.

The laughter in the courtyard is high and shrill.

Despite my intent to avoid the gate, here I am again. Didn't I turn *right* on Conti, turning north, *away* from the river, away from that black wrought-iron gate? I'm absolutely fucking certain that I did. But here I am, regardless. I would have had to turn east—onto Dauphine or Burgundy—then turn south onto St. Peter. So, the French Quarter has gone Möbius, or, lost in thought, I blundered right back to the exact place I intended not to go. Yeah, I know the latter is the more likely, but I can't help believing the former is what actually happened.

The air carrying the laughter to me is so bloated with the cloyingly sweet smell of wisteria and bougainvillea that I cover my mouth and nose. I think I'd gag, otherwise. Wasn't it a pleasant, soothing smell last night? But the voices are the same, and the laughter, and the jazz.

The woman singing.

The shadow's there, swaying to the music. And if I don't want to be here, why don't I turn and walk away? Never mind the question of how I got here, leaving would be simple enough. But I stand with my face pressed to those black bars painted black, watching as the shadow sways and swoops and dips.

There's a single gunshot then. I know the sound of a gunshot, a pistol shot, and this isn't a car backfiring. It isn't fireworks. It's a gunshot.

The shadow stops dancing. Wherever that party I can't see is going on, a woman has begun screaming and men are cursing. The trombones and clarinets and singer have all fallen silent, but I can hear glass breaking.

"Jesus," a man growls. "Jesus fucking Christ. Jesus fucking Christ."

I'm not alone on the sidewalk. Other people are passing the gate, but if any one of these passerby heard the gunshot, or the screams, they're busy minding their own business, pretending they heard nothing at all.

The sky above Pontchartrain is on fire.

The blade of the butter knife is cold against my skin.

"William, you've not heard a word that I've said."

The sky is on fire.

"Have you?"

The garden gate is locked against me.

So, turn the little key.

A few days after we return from New Orleans, when Anna and I have each gone our separate ways until the next time she asks me to accompany her on a trip. Or calls to ask if I'd like to have dinner with her. Or see a movie. A few nights after we return from New Orleans, I wake from a dream that smelled of wisteria and jessamine and the faintest acrid stink of gunpowder. The shadow is dancing across the walls of my bedroom, and I can hear the snuffling sound, the sound from the train that *wasn't* a black dog, just outside my bedroom door.

In my upper berth, as we pull out of the Salisbury station, I tear a narrow strip from one of the violet *Crescent* line schedules, and twist it just so, then join the ends. I fold it into a Möbius strip. One end is joined to the other by the force on my right thumb and forefinger, so there's only the illusion of infinity. I release the paper. It flutters to the uncomfortable mattress and is nothing but a straight line again. A railroad track. A straight line is infinite. Only a matter of perspective makes it otherwise.

"Beautiful, isn't she?" the conductor asks, and I look up from the book of Thomas Hardy stories I was reading. I think he's talking about Anna, sitting there in the seat across from me. I look up, and she has her face pressed against the window, even though the light from the sunset on the lake is so bright I've had to pull the curtain on my side of the compartment shut. In the compartment across the narrow aisle, children are laughing so loudly that it's hard to hear what the conductor says next.

I close my book.

"Well, Sir. You enjoy your visit," says the conductor, and he smiles and leaves me alone with the blazing lake.

The seat across from me is empty.

"William, you haven't heard a single word I've said."

It always was.

At the black gate I turn my head, slow as slow ever is, and there is no black dog watching me.

I turn back to the garden, and there is no shadow. There never was.

Turn the little key.

The party ends and the woman screams as moments echo, and I turn the key, squeeze the trigger, and the gun is a thunderstorm above the Vieux Carré.

SUFFER LITTLE CHILDREN

ROBERT SHEARMAN

Everything she taught she'd learned from the books in her father's study—and even then, only from the bottom shelves—she couldn't have reached the top shelves without the ladder, and the ladder's wooden rungs were lined with cracks that looked like spider webs. So, no geography, then (but her pupils would be English, so how much did they need to know about foreign lands?). Plenty of history—she liked the way the past could be packaged into neat little romances; they were like fairy tales but the difference was, these fairy tales were *true*. A smattering of French. A smaller smattering of Latin. Poetry. Fine art. She liked simple mental arithmetic, something about its solid rightness made her happy.

But what she taught didn't matter; she was left under no illusions about that. Her task was to ensure the children were occupied and well-behaved, and that their wits were kept sharp to prepare them for proper education later. Children liked her, and that was the main thing. Adults didn't, much; adults never quite knew what to say to her. She was unfailingly polite, but somehow always at one remove, everything she said sounded too considered and deliberate. But children seemed charmed by her.

In part, perhaps, that may have been the way she looked. She had such a very young face. Her cheeks were full and red like a baby doll's. Her eyes, wide and innocent. The children instinctively might have recognised her as one of them, that for all the authority bestowed on her she belonged to their world, not the world of their parents. It was true that she always looked so serious and thoughtful, and she only rarely smiled. But that didn't mean she ever looked disapproving, or in judgement of them. She seemed to be a little girl who wanted to be all grown up. Children understand that. They want the same thing.

It was only natural that Susan Cowley would be a governess. Even as a girl she'd had a calming effect on the other children playing around her; she didn't seem to have any friends amongst them, not as such, but what of that? And Susan seemed to accept that role with incurious equanimity. Her little sister would be given all manner of pretty clothes; Susan, more and more, would get formal dress, bordering even upon uniform in its austerity, all befitting her future career. She never complained.

When she reached seventeen, her great aunt found her a placement at Exley Hall, to look after two young children of friends of hers.

It was impossible to judge how responsible Susan Cowley was for the Exley Hall scandal. Certainly, she never tried to offer any defence, and that may well have been her undoing. She seemed only too willing to take the blame, and so the blame was put squarely on her shoulders. And maybe that was right. The children were in her care. Whether or not she had done anything directly to influence events, that, surely, cannot be disputed.

There were no criminal proceedings, for it was hard to see how anything that had happened could be called a crime. The Exleys did not want any muck clinging to their son's name. They did not want any word getting out. That said, Susan Cowley was unable to find herself another position afterwards, so someone must have talked.

Mr. and Mrs. Cowley did not know what to make of it all. Susan had always been such a quiet child, the reliable one, the boring one, truth be told. They did not discuss the matter. They tried to pretend nothing had happened. Mr. Cowley only lost his temper the once, and that was not even with Susan; at the dinner table the little sister began asking how it was that Susan was home again, didn't she like being a teacher?—and at that, without a word, Mr. Cowley had got up and slapped the girl around her face. The child was so shocked she even forgot to cry.

One night, when he couldn't sleep, Mr. Cowley found Susan in his study. She was sitting on the floor, a stack of books by her side, and she was leafing through them slowly. All her old favourites—Arthurian legends, a Latin primer, and tomes and tomes of rudimentary calculus. "Susan?" he asked softly, "are you all right?" It was the gentlest thing he had said to her since her disgrace; Susan looked up at him, but her face registered no surprise at his new tenderness. She nodded. Mr. Cowley stood there in the doorway, and he knew that this was the moment he should reach out to her, try to talk to her, maybe find out what had happened. This was his chance. And he couldn't take the chance, or didn't, at any rate; he nodded back, quite formally, turned, and went back to bed.

There came in the post one morning a letter for Susan. Inside there was a newspaper clipping advertising for young teachers at H___ Priory. There was no letter, no indication who it might have been from; Mr. and Mrs. Cowley wondered whether the great-aunt was offering some help, just as she had done before. She hadn't spoken to the family since the incident but maybe she had relented. It was not a governess's position; it was not ideal; it was to teach a class of young children of no discernible means or background, and the wages offered were meagre. But, as Mr. and Mrs. Cowley said, beggars could not be choosers. They looked for H___ on the map. It took them a while to find it; it was far away, and seemed very small, tucked away at the edge of the page.

Susan replied to the advertisement. She did not expect an interview. By return of post she received notice that the job was hers.

There was no direct railway line to H___. Susan was obliged to make no fewer than four connections, and each train she boarded was smaller and slower than the last—and emptier too, so that by the last service Susan was the only person in the carriage. It fell dark. It began to rain hard. No one came to inspect Susan's ticket, and as the train crawled on she began to fear that the driver would just decide to stop, that he'd feel the journey wasn't worth the effort, and that she'd be stuck there in the blackness and the wet forever. And she had the absurd desire to start shouting, to chivvy the driver on, to assure him he had a passenger and that he mustn't give up, for her sake. Of course, she did nothing of the sort. She kept her composure, and only by hugging her suitcase close would she have given any outward sign that she was afraid. She sat still, looked out of the window into the pitch black, and hoped that soon she would reach her destination.

And, at length, she did. She hauled her suitcase onto the platform. The station was dark, and she could not see an exit. The rain sliced through her. "Over here!" she heard, and she realised that the platform wasn't deserted after all; it was a woman's voice, low in pitch, and she was gesturing at Susan to come and take shelter beneath her umbrella. The woman was large, and Susan couldn't quite fit under the umbrella beside her; generously, the woman sidestepped and stood out in the rain to keep Susan dry.

"You're Miss Cowley?" she said.

"Yes," said Susan.

"Good! Follow me!"

And the woman marched on into the night, still holding out the umbrella for Susan, but she was striding away so fast that both of them got soaked. "It's not always like this, sometimes the weather is quite nice!" And soon they were outside the station, and there was a little jalopy waiting for them. "Hop right in, the door's open!" Susan took the passenger seat, and watched as the woman struggled against the wind and the pelting rain to get the umbrella shut. And then the woman was in the car beside Susan, and so drenched through that she couldn't help but spray Susan with water as she shifted into her seat, like a dog shaking itself dry without worrying about the soaking it will give its owner. She beamed at Susan. She offered her hand, and Susan took it, and the woman pumped it up and down like a piston.

"I must say, I'm glad you're you," she said, and then blushed.

"Are you?" asked Susan.

"I thought you might be one of those dreadful old women! The school always gets dreadful old women, they never last long. Stay a term or two, and then go off to die somewhere, I'll bet. Ha! Miss Susan Cowley, you must admit, the name sounds a bit elderly and a bit dreadful."

"I had never thought," said Susan.

"Like some Godforsaken spinster! Not that I'm judging. I mean, Valerie Bewes. That sounds shocking, doesn't it? That sounds positively decrepit! I'm Valerie, by the way." And she offered her wet hand again, and Susan had to take it. "I'm just so pleased you're young, like me! We can be proper girls together!"

Susan didn't think that Valerie looked especially young, she must have been thirty if she were a day. "Is the school very far?" asked Susan.

"Lord love you, you've travelled all day, and here I am jabbering! Yes, it is quite far. About nine miles, which isn't too bad, but it's uphill and this old girl doesn't like climbing hills, and it's dark and it's wet—we'd better go slow. We should get moving, we can chat along the way!"

But they didn't chat much. Valerie pointed at the hills and countryside ("Really, it's quite nice when it's daylight, and dry."), and talked all about herself, and Susan quickly realised that the information offered was neither interesting nor pertinent. When Susan declined to join in the conversation, even Valerie at last ground to a halt. "You're tired, poor darling, I'll let you have some peace!"

And—"Here we are!" said Valerie, at last. And there was the school in the distance. Ever since she had accepted the post Susan had wondered what the school might look like, and the reality of it was that it was small and flat and rather unassuming. She felt some relief, and also a little disappointment.

Valerie explained that, its name notwithstanding, the school had really very little to do with H___. It was simply the closest town, and no one could agree what the name of this bit of countryside precisely was. The children were taken from the various villages and hamlets around, sometimes to a distance of fifteen miles—all the communities who didn't quite belong to anyone else, they could fit in here. Most of the children boarded; it was simply too much effort for them to go back to their parents very often. There were never more than a hundred pupils in the school at any one time, and they were divided into three classes. The youngest, and largest, were the eight to ten year olds, who'd be taught by Miss Cowley. The middle class was for the ten to twelves, taken by Miss Bewes herself. The remaining class ranged all the way from twelve to seventeen, and Mrs. Phelps was in charge of them. That said, very few of the children were seventeen; in fact, very few of the children stayed at the school once they were teenagers.

"And what happens to them after that?" asked Susan.

"Oh, Lord knows. They probably go off and marry each other! I don't think there are any pupils from H___ Priory who have ever amounted to much. They come from the countryside, they just drift back into it again." Valerie laughed. "No, they're fine, they're good kids, mostly."

Bordering the school was the little cottage that Susan and Valerie would share. Valerie seemed to think Susan already knew and had agreed to this arrangement, and Susan had no desire to disabuse her. "It's nice and homely," said Valerie. "Shared bathroom, shared kitchen, shared personal area, you know, all mod cons. Separate bedrooms. Let me show you *your* bedroom."

The bedroom was plain. It was not as pretty as her bedroom at Exley Hall, or even her bedroom at home. The bed looked hard, the single pillow lumpy. The walls were bare.

"It just needs to be lived in a bit," said Valerie. "It's wonders what you can do with a few pictures around. I'll show you my bedroom, later, if you like."

Valerie offered to make them both some supper, she had soup on the stove. Susan declined, but thanked her. Valerie said that she would introduce her to Mrs. Phelps the next day, and then to the children.

"All right," said Susan. "Thank you. Good night."

Valerie laughed, and said, "My darling, whatever must you have done to end up here!"

"I beg your pardon?"

"Oh, I don't mean anything by it! I'm sorry. But as if anyone would *choose* to come here. Most of them can't get away from the place fast enough. Like Miss Fortescue, good riddance, the miserable old trout. Oh, I tell you, my darling, it's going to be so much more fun living with you than it was with her!"

The Bewes woman left her then, mercifully, but not before once more offering Susan her hand to shake. And Susan got undressed, and lay on her bed, and propped her head up on the pillow as best as she could, and stared up at the ceiling, and listened to the rain, and tried not to dream about Edwin this time.

In the morning it was still raining hard, and Susan and Valerie had to run from the cottage to the school, Valerie whooping with joy as if it were some great game.

Susan was introduced to Mrs. Phelps. Mrs. Phelps did not shake her hand. Mrs. Phelps had no interest in her hand whatsoever.

"The headmaster and I are sure you'll be most suitable, Miss Cowley," she said. "I doubt we'll have much cause to speak again, we'll be in different classrooms, of course."

"Of course."

Susan wondered whether she was going to meet the headmaster as well. Valerie laughed, and said she hadn't seen Mr. Phelps in simply ages; he stayed in the house, bedridden most likely, and passed on instructions through his wife. "Or maybe he's run away," she joked. "Or maybe he's dead! Anything rather than live with that old dragon."

Valerie took Susan to her own classroom. The children were already inside.

"Just don't let them know it's your first time," she said.

"How do you know it's my first time?"

"Oh, my dear, it's so obvious! To me, I mean, not to them. Just try to keep them occupied. There's a whole stack of books in the cupboards, get them reading, that eats up the time. And if anyone misbehaves, just strike them with the cane."

"Oh!" said Susan. "No, I couldn't!"

"You'll be doing them a favour," said Valerie. "That way they'll know you're in charge. You'll be doing me a favour too, I'll be inheriting some of these kids next term! The cane is your friend. Miss Fortescue, she got through half a dozen of them, we had to get in a fresh supply!"

"Yes," said Susan. "All right."

"Don't you worry, you'll be wonderful. You've got just the face for it! The children will adore you. And tonight I'll make us some nice supper, and you can tell me all about your adventures."

Susan entered the classroom then, and shut the adult world out. She immediately felt calmer. She looked out across the children, all of them eyeing her warily. Little girls in pretty blouses, boys big before their time with dirty faces and dirty fingernails.

"Good morning, class," she said. And they all got to their feet then, and mumbled good morning back. She hadn't expected that. She rather liked it. She hoped she'd kept it off her face, that surprise, and that pleasure. She was sure she had.

"My name is Miss Cowley," she told them. "And I'm here to look after you."

She looked through the cupboards. The children helped her. There were the books, as Miss Bewes had promised. There was also a map, as big as the blackboard. There were drawing pads. There was a whole colony of wooden abacuses.

She put the map up on the wall. It was an old map, and she knew some of the countries didn't exist anymore, not since the war. The children were still able to point out some of the better ones, like France and Spain, and show her where England was. Afterwards, she set the children on to the drawing pads, told them they could draw whatever they liked, and use crayons to colour the pictures in. Some of the drawings were really rather good, and she took the map down and put the drawings in its place.

After lunch she asked the children what subjects they most liked, and they all said they liked stories, and that meant history. So she told them an Arthurian legend. The children listened, quite spellbound, as if they'd never even heard of Sir Gawain or his green knight, and at one point the realisation that these thirty young strangers were hanging on her every word made Susan freeze with stage fright; they waited patiently; she recovered; she began to enjoy herself. Already in her head she was planning other stories she could share with them the next day, and the day after that, and all the days following.

It only went wrong towards the end of the afternoon.

Susan suggested they move on to mathematics. She was pleased that none of the children groaned, or looked unhappy at the prospect; by this point, it seemed, they would have followed her anywhere, even into the realms of simple arithmetic. "Why not show me what you already know?" she said. "Who here would like to stand before the class, and recite the times tables with me?"

No one volunteered. But then, no one resisted either. "How about you?" she asked a little girl sitting near the front, and the little girl got to her feet quite happily.

"What's your name?" she asked the girl. But the girl just shook her head.

"Don't be shy," said Susan. "We're all your friends here. Do you know the five times table?" The little girl looked at her blankly.

"I'll demonstrate," Susan said. And she began to recite. "Once times five is five. Two times five is ten. Three times five . . ."

"Fifteen," said the little girl.

"That's right."

"Four times five is twenty. Five times five is twenty-five." And on the girl went, all the way to a hundred.

Susan gave her a little clap. "Well done," she said. "Does anyone else want to . . .?"

The little girl took a deep breath. And then she started on the six times table.

"Yes," said Susan. "All right."

"Ten times six is sixty. Eleven times six is sixty-six."

"That's very good. Well done!"

"Fifteen times six is ninety. Sixteen times six is ninety-six."

"Big numbers now! Can you go any further?"

But the girl stopped dead, looked at Susan, frowned.

"That's very good," said Susan once more. "Yes. I shall give you a merit point. What is your name, again . . .?"

And the little girl, once again, was taking a breath of air. A deeper one this time. The effort of it meant she had to clutch on to the teacher's desk, and her face turned red. A great wheeze there was, and Susan thought it sounded like it came from an old man, an old man close to death, and the girl's face was contorted with the force of it—she hunched over, gripping at her stomach, and Susan reached out for her, and the little girl just pushed her away. She steadied herself. She calmed. She looked her teacher right in the face.

"One times seven is seven," she informed her. It was almost conversational. "Two times seven is fourteen."

"Yes," agreed Susan.

And onwards. "Thirteen times seven is ninety-one. Fourteen times seven is ninety-eight."

Susan felt the question rise within her—does she know the eight times table? "Thank you," she said, and she hoped from her tone it was clear that the thank you was conclusive.

But the little girl had gone back to the beginning. She was reciting the seven times table again, and this time it was faster, more confident.

"Three times seven is twenty-one, four times seven is twenty-eight, five times . . ."

"You need to sit down now," said Susan.

". . . ninety-one, fourteen times seven is ninety-eight, one times seven is seven . . ." There was no pause for breath this time. Two times seven, three times, four, and there was a smile on her face, as the pace began to accelerate still further.

"You need to sit down now," said Susan. "That's enough."

"Ten times seven is seventy, eleven times seven is seventy-seven, twelve . . ."

"I said, enough!"

Susan looked at the class, to see how they were reacting to this open display of mockery. They didn't seem amused, and that was good, she supposed—they didn't seem shocked, or even interested. They stared out at the little girl with frank indifference.

And still the girl was tearing into the seven times table, so fast now that the words were starting to blur, the numbers running into each other and in the collision causing bigger numbers yet to appear, and Susan had her hands around the girl's shoulders and she was shaking her, "Stop!" she said. "Stop this instant!" She looked at the class. "Fetch me my cane."

No one moved.

"I said, the cane!" And a few of the children exchanged glances, and one boy at the front got to his feet, walked slowly to Susan's desk, so slow it was nearly insolent, but not quite, nothing quite so obvious; he pulled open a drawer, and took out an ugly thin wooden stick.

The little girl was babbling out the words now, but she didn't look afraid, she was exultant. "Don't make me do this," said Susan. "I don't want to hurt you. Do you hear me? Stop. Stop. Hold out your hand. Hold out your hand."

And, without pausing, the numbers still spilling forth, the little girl did so, she opened her palms ready for punishment.

Susan hit her. She didn't want to hit her hard. But the stick was *designed* to hurt, and as it swung down it made the air crack, and the explosive pop it made against the little girl's hand seemed too loud and too too angry, and Susan at once regretted it, but it was too late.

The girl stopped immediately, somewhere between forty-two and forty-nine. She looked at Susan in bewilderment. Then down at her hand, and Susan could see that the blow had broken the skin. She looked back up at Susan, and there were tears in her eyes, and there was disappointment too.

"That's enough now," said Susan quietly. "Sit down."

The little girl did so.

"I will not," said Susan, "tolerate insubordination. Not in my class. I'm here to help you. I want to help you." She added, "And I read to you all about Sir Gawain!" It didn't come out too plaintively, she hoped.

For the rest of class she had them read to themselves. There was only another fifteen minutes to go. The children were all perfectly silent, but Susan felt relieved when the bell sounded. She dismissed them, and smiled at them as they filed out, to show that everything was forgiven and forgotten. And the children seemed to hold no grudges, quite a few of them smiled back, even the little girl she'd beat.

Valerie Bewes made stew for them that evening. Susan did not want to discuss the incident with her, but there was no one else she could tell. Valerie laughed at the story, and told her not to worry.

"They'll always try something," she said. "It was your first day, and they have to find out how hard they can push you. I say you made it perfectly clear! Well done, you!" She helped Susan to another helping of stew. Susan didn't like it much, the vegetables were nearly raw, the chunks of beef too stringy.

"I must go to bed," said Susan. "I'm tired."

Valerie looked disappointed, just for a moment, and then she smiled. "Of course. First day of term is the worst, you know! It'll be easier tomorrow, you'll see!"

Susan thanked her for supper, and went up to her room.

The room had changed. Susan stood in the doorway and stared at it. And then she heard Valerie chuckle, she hadn't realised she'd come up the stairs behind her.

"I did a bit of furnishing for you!" she said. "Miss Fortescue left all her pictures behind. She'll probably come and collect them at some point, but until she does, you may as well benefit from them . . .! She liked natural history. Natural history was her favourite subject."

"Yes," said Susan.

There were a dozen different paintings on the wall, and all of birds. Some of them were life studies, some of them were anatomical examinations. But even the skeletal bodies still had their wings intact, jutting out the sides, and that gave Susan the oddest impression that the poor creatures had had their skin and organs only selectively removed. She didn't know what type of birds they were. She recognised an eagle.

"It makes the room feel more lived in, doesn't it?"

"It does indeed."

"Do you like it?"

"Very much."

Valerie was pleased by that, and seemed about to start another conversation. "Good night," said Susan, quite firmly, and Valerie nodded, gave a flash of a smile, and closed the door behind her.

Susan lay on the bed. No matter how tightly she drew the curtains, enough light got in to pick out the birds. The eyes seemed to follow her, and if they had no eyes, then the eye sockets followed her instead. When shadows passed over the feathers it made them come alive, to flex and ripple; the rain spattered hard on the windows, and sounded like the flutter of a thousand wings.

When Valerie knocked at the door, maybe half an hour later, Susan was almost grateful.

"I'm sorry," said Valerie. "I'm sorry. I don't want to disturb. I'm sorry. May I come in, my darling?"

"Just a moment," said Susan, and she put on her dressing gown, turned on the light, and answered the door.

Valerie was smiling at her, but it was a brave smile; she had been crying. She came with a bottle of brandy, and two glasses. "I'm sorry," she said again.

"What's the matter?"

Valerie came in, and sat upon the bed. In her beige dressing gown, with her hair loose and messy over her shoulders, she looked even older than she had by day. She smelled of brandy, and Susan supposed she'd had rather a lot of it.

"Sometimes I have bad nights," said Valerie. "May I confide in you? Can I trust you enough so I can confide?"

"I imagine so," said Susan.

Valerie then burst into tears, and told Susan some ghastly little story about how she'd once worked as a governess, many years ago now, and how she had been seduced by her employer—or perhaps she had seduced him, the story wasn't very clear. She had fallen pregnant, much to the horror of the man, who had thrown her out of his house and away from his children, denouncing her as a slut. She had tried to lose the baby, she really had, she'd drunk gin, she'd even thrown herself down the stairs once. But it was no good, the baby had been born, and had been taken away from her.

"Would you drink with me?"

"No, thank you."

"Please drink with me! So I'm not drinking alone . . .!"

Susan sipped at her brandy, and it didn't sit well with the stew, and she felt a little sick.

"My life was over," said Valerie. "Until I found this place. The school took me in. They forgave me."

"Yes."

"Did something like that happen to you, my darling? Do you need to be forgiven?"

"No," said Susan. "Absolutely not."

If Valerie was offended by the vehemence of this, she didn't show it. She just nodded, poured herself another glass. "I'm sorry," she said. "The first day of term does this to me. Seeing the children again. And thinking, one of them could be mine! Do you see? Any one of them, how would I ever know? I've never told anyone this before,"—and Susan rather doubted that, Susan imagined Valerie Bewes told the same story to every new teacher who arrived, maybe that's why Miss Fortescue had fled H___ Priory as soon as she got the chance—"but you're like a little baby, aren't you? You look just like a baby doll. You could be my daughter. You could be. I know you can't be, you're too old, but. You could be mine." She stroked at Susan's cheek.

"Yes," said Susan.

"May I stay here tonight?"

"No."

"No. Of course. You need to sleep. Yes. I've been selfish. I'll see you in the morning. Yes."

Susan didn't think Valerie was all that drunk, she got up from the bed and made it to the door steadily enough.

Before she put out the light, Susan removed every bird picture from the wall, and put them, face down, under the bed.

Most nights Susan dreamed of Edwin. And sometimes they weren't nightmares. Sometimes she actually missed him.

Susan hadn't much liked Edwin Exley at first. She preferred his little sister, Clara. Clara was six, and shy, and not very pretty, and Susan's heart went out to her. At eight years old Edwin was already tall and arrogant; Mr. Exley told Susan on her first day that Edwin was going to have a stellar career in the army, and that there was no limit to what the boy would achieve for his country. Edwin himself certainly seemed to believe that. His father had already taught him a lot of the basics of being a soldier, and when he met his new governess he stood to attention, and gave her a salute that Susan suspected was a little too clipped and far too ironic.

Mr. and Mrs. Exley were kind to Susan. They let her eat with them of an evening, and treated her quite like she was an elder daughter rather than an employee. They gave her a comfortable bedroom, with a soft bed, and drapes, and lots of pretty pictures on the walls. When the family took a few days in the south of France during the autumn, they wanted Susan to come with them; she still was required to teach the children in the mornings, but the afternoons were her own, and they encouraged her to sit on the beach with them and enjoy the sun.

The nursery at Exley Hall was turned into a little classroom. All the toys and games were put away each morning before lessons started; for a few hours, at least, this was to be a place of learning. Susan directed most of her classes towards Clara in particular; Edwin was not exactly bad mannered, but he made it clear he wasn't much interested, and any attention he gave was bestowed upon his teacher as if it were a great gift for which she should be grateful. He was not very good at mathematics, he enjoyed history only when it was something he'd already heard about from his father. He discovered he had an aptitude for Latin which delighted him, and his face lit up like a little boy when Susan complimented him upon it.

Both Clara and Edwin would listen when their teacher told them ancient stories of heroism and derring-do. Edwin liked the tales of King Arthur, but only when there were quests and fighting; he didn't like Guinevere or Lancelot, he didn't want to bother with all that mushy stuff.

One night Susan couldn't sleep, and she went downstairs to Mr. Exley's study. It was even better furnished with books than her father's, and she thought something to read would help her rest. She was surprised to find a light burning. There on the floor was Edwin, and all about him were texts he had taken from the shelves. He started when he realised Susan was there.

"Don't tell my father," he said.

"Your father wouldn't mind," Susan told him. "He'd be pleased you want to learn things!"

"No," said Edwin. "He wouldn't."

Susan often found Edwin in the study at night times. They never discussed their secret rendezvous during the day, and Susan tried not to go down there too often—maybe no more than once, say twice, a week. Edwin would show her new books he had found; sometimes they were geography, and as he enthused about Africa and the colonies she rather got the impression that he was teaching her. He was taller than she was, he had no problem reaching the higher shelves. And he had no fear of the stepladder, he'd race up to the very top of it to fetch books that were brushing at the ceiling, with a fearless speed that sometimes made Susan's heart stop.

She showed him some poetry. He was resistant at first. She made him read it out loud to her, and he began to like it more, he began to enjoy the rhythm of it.

On his birthday she bought him a little notebook in which he could write his own poetry. She bought him a sketchpad, so that he could draw.

One day Mr. Exley put down his newspaper at the breakfast table, and the rare act of that caused his wife to stop her chatter. Mr. Exley said to Susan, "And how are the children getting on? Learning things, are they?"

Susan told him they were both doing admirably.

Mr. Exley nodded at this. "That's good," he said. "What they learn now, they'll never forget. I've got such stuff in my head, all the kings and queens from William the Conqueror, times tables, things like that. Useless, of course, but it's nice to have."

Mrs. Exley said that the children seemed very happy.

Mr. Exley said, "We should have a demonstration some evening. Nothing too fancy. Just you and the children, showing us what they've learned." Mrs. Exley looked quite excited by that. Susan told them she'd make preparations.

Edwin could soon list all the kings and queens, just like his father, and as an added bonus Susan felt he should also indicate the dates of famous battles they had fought; Hastings, Agincourt, the Boyne. Clara could read some poetry; for all her shyness and plain features she had such a sweet voice. And both children could conclude with a recitation of their times tables, five, six, seven and eight, all the way to a hundred.

The evening went very well. Both the parents looked proud and indulgent as their children stood tall and parroted out all the facts they knew. Clara read three poems; one by Keats, one by Shelley; the final one was by Edwin Exley, although the author's name was not mentioned, Susan thought it would be a charming little secret. It wasn't necessarily a very good poem, and was rather cruelly exposed beside the Victorian Romantics that had inspired it, but Mr. and Mrs. Exley couldn't tell the difference.

Mr. Exley gave the children a round of applause, and a shilling each, and told Susan that they would have to have a similar soiree at some point. Maybe at Christmas, when all their friends were there?

That night Susan visited Edwin in the study.

"I love you," said Edwin, suddenly.

"Well, I love you too." Susan thought nothing of this: Clara was always telling Susan she loved her, and putting her arms around her, she was such a needy girl. And Edwin was studying a book at the time, he wasn't even looking at her.

"Will you marry me one day?"

Susan laughed. "Oh, I shouldn't have thought so!"

"Why not?"

"Because you're a little boy."

"I won't be a little boy forever. I'll get older soon. And I'll go and fight. I'll be brave and defend my country, and I'll never be afraid. Do you believe me?"

"Yes. Yes, I believe you."

"I'll be fighting for *you*." Edwin had put aside the book now, he had abandoned cover, and he was staring at Susan, and he was beginning to cry, but he didn't seem sad, he seemed fierce.

Susan didn't know what to say. "You'll marry someone else, Eddie. You'll see. Someone better than me."

"And when I do, will you come to my wedding?"

"Of course I will!"

"Good. I want you there. I want you to see my bride. I want you to know that I shan't love her. That I'm marrying her out of spite. That I'll be cruel to her, and punish her, because she'll never be you. I want you to know it'll be your fault."

"That's a wicked thing to say," said Susan. Edwin didn't care. He shrugged.

"I pray to God each night that you'll love me," he said.

"God can't answer prayers like that."

"Not the God of *Jesus*," he sneered. "There are older gods. The things I've read. The things that are in the books on the top shelf."

Christmas Day, Mr. Exley said, would be for the family alone. Cook and the two maids were given time off. Susan was put right at the heart of the celebrations, and it was tacit proof of acceptance that she found very touching. Mrs. Exley gave her as a present a pink dress—"You don't seem to have anything nice, my dear," she said, and the dress fitted perfectly. Clara gave Susan a piece of embroidery she had stitched herself. Edwin didn't give Susan anything, but he was a boy.

And in the evening they all went to a carol service at the church, and sang hymns together. Mr. Exley sang with particular gusto. Edwin sat at the end of the pew, away from Susan, and barely even mouthed any of the hallelujahs to Christ.

On Boxing Day Cook and the maids came back, and everyone prepared for the party. Lots of Mr. Exley's old friends came with their twittering wives, and in honour of this Mr. Exley wore his regimental uniform. There was a turkey dinner, and crackers, and cigars, and a game of charades: Susan didn't join in, but she enjoyed watching all the grown-ups play. Before the children's bedtime they were presented, newly dressed in smart clothes; the Exleys said Clara and Edwin would perform for them. Edwin stiffly recited the crowned heads of England once more, and the men especially gave hearty applause. Clara performed from memory a short poem by Keats. As a grand finale, the children would chant the seven times table.

It began well enough. Everyone looked on kindly, knowing that it would all be at an end soon, and they could get back to their sherries and jokes and fun. No one even appeared to notice how Edwin's delivery was somewhat forced and sarcastic; Clara, at least, was a perfect angel.

Somewhere in the middle Edwin broke rank, and began to deliver a poem of his own. Clara didn't know what to do, she floundered on for one more calculation, then came to a stop, and stared at her brother open-mouthed and dumb.

It wasn't a love poem. That was the first thing to say. There was really very little about love in it.

It was a wonder Edwin got as far through it as he managed. He told, in doggerel verse, how he and his governess would meet regularly at night and have sex in his father's study. There was nothing tender to it. It was blunt and pornographic.

And it was something more too. There was something *animal* about it. Not merely the sex itself, as rough and primal as it was. But a suggestion too in the act of congress, that as Edwin performed acts he should not have known about, and that surely most humans weren't even *capable* of, there was something monstrous being born, that these writhing creatures were no longer simply boy and woman but something not of this world; there were beaks, and scales, and talons, and tongues that were impossibly, terrifyingly, long.

Mrs. Exley just said, "No, no, no," over and over again, as if her quiet denial of it could really matter a jot. Mr. Exley roared at his son to stop, and when he didn't, he got up, marched over to him, and clipped him hard around the head. At that point only did Edwin fall silent; he glared at his father, glared at the room, and glared at Susan most particularly. Then he ran from the room.

Susan ran too. She didn't know where to go. She went to her room. She sat on the bed, numbed. She wasn't there for long. Mr. Exley banged upon the door, told her to get out, and come with him.

She had never been to Edwin's room before. Now she saw that all over his bed were pages and pages of scribbled verse, ripped out of the notebook she'd bought him, and sketchpad drawings. The drawings were of her, she recognised herself at once. In most she'd been given claws and wings, it was her head on the body of wild beasts—lions, dogs, birds. In all she was naked. Human breasts, obscenely large, grew out from trunks of fur and scales, and dangled.

Edwin stood there, frightened, but acting brave, acting like a man.

Mr. Exley picked up some of the writings, looked them over briefly. Threw them on the floor. "Filth," he said.

He turned to Susan. "I do not believe. I cannot believe. Any of the things he writes here are *true*."

"No," she said. "No."

"But how," he said. "How?" And in that moment he looked at her so imploringly, like a little child himself, begging her to make things all right again. The face clouded; his teeth clenched; he was an adult once more. He said to Susan, "I want you to beat him. You must beat him. To within an inch of his life."

And she saw then that in his hand, lying almost nonchalantly against the seam of his regimental uniform trouser leg, was a cane. "No," she said.

"If you don't beat him, I will," said Exley. "And it will be easier on him if it's you."

"I can't. I can't. I'm sorry."

"Very well. But you will watch."

She did watch. And just before Edwin bent over there was still something of the man in him, staring down his father defiantly, staring down the world. But it didn't last long. And as he struck his son, again, and again, and again, Mr. Exley would glance at Susan to check she was still watching, to check she appreciated what her bad teaching had forced a loving father to do—and she could see that he wished he could beat her as well, that he could put her over his knee and beat her senseless.

Susan left Exley Hall the first thing the next morning. She left behind the pink dress, taking it now seemed wrong. She didn't see any of the family. It was one of the maids who saw her off. She'd never really spoken to the maids, but this one was kindly enough.

"And Miss Clara still hasn't spoken," she said. "Not a single word, though they do try and coax 'em out. Shock, I shouldn't wonder."

A taxi took her to the nearest railway station. Because it was Christmas, she had to wait some hours for a train, and she was cold.

She found in her coat pocket a letter. *Miss Cowley*, it said on the envelope, and she recognised the handwriting as Edwin's. She opened it with strange excitement. She didn't know what to expect. An apology. Or some words of new tenderness?

Inside there were just two words. *Something's coming.*

In her dreams, the rain stopped. Or, rather, in her dreams she could make it stop. If she only gave up struggling. If she just let things be.

But when she woke to her second day at H___ Priory, the rain was still battering hard against the windows. Even Valerie took no pleasure in it today, and when they ran for the school they were drenched from head to foot in an instant.

The children in the class were neat and dry, of course. And Susan feared that they would laugh at her when she came into the room looking like a drowned rat. Not a bit of it; and if they harboured any grudge towards her for what had happened yesterday, there was no indication of it at all. They stood to attention when she addressed them; one of them had even left an apple on her desk.

"Where is the little girl from yesterday?" Susan asked. She didn't know what she wanted to say to her. She knew she mustn't apologise, or show weakness. The little girl wasn't there. No one seemed to know where she might be, or gave her answer at any rate. Perhaps it was just as well.

For the morning they drew pictures and sang roundelays. Before lunch she told them another Arthurian legend; Edwin might have thought that Guinevere and Lancelot was mush, but it was a lovely story, and Susan saw to her satisfaction that even some of the boys' eyes watered at the telling.

She knew she could not avoid the matter forever. And in the afternoon she fetched from the cupboard all the abacuses they had, and distributed them liberally about the room.

"Mathematics," she said.

That was all it took.

Some boy, some wag, suddenly piped up with the seven times table. He sang it out, bold and confident. Susan opened her mouth to stop him, and then decided she'd have more power if she let him proceed. If only for a little while.

Maybe if she'd spoken up then she could have stopped it. Maybe she missed her chance. But as the numbers grew bigger, so more of the children picked up the mantra. By the time they reached fifty-six, all of the boys were at it—by the time they reached ninety-eight, all the girls were at it too.

"All right," she said. "Very clever. That's enough."

But it wasn't enough, was it? Because numbers don't stop at one hundred. "Fifteen times seven is one hundred and five. Sixteen times seven is one hundred and twelve." And for a moment Susan was floored, it was almost as if she'd forgotten you could get any higher than the little abacuses allowed her! "Nineteen times seven is one hundred and thirty-three. Twenty times seven is one hundred and forty." And by now the voices were in utter concert, all keeping the same pace exactly.

"Please stop," she said.

They didn't stop.

She got out her cane. "You know I can use this," she said.

They didn't care.

Susan stared at them in silence. She put the cane down.

The numbers reached seven hundred, and showed no signs of stopping, chuntering on towards the first millennium.

Susan left the room and went to get help.

She didn't know whether the nearest classroom would be Miss Bewes's or Mrs. Phelps's. On the whole, she was glad that it was Miss Bewes's. She could at least trust her to want to help, and when she saw Susan through the glass panel door she beamed in delighted surprise and was quite prepared to abandon her own class in an instant.

Susan's pupils were no longer sitting down. By the time Susan and Valerie got to the classroom, they had pushed all the desks and chairs to the back, and now stood in a rough circle. Susan could no longer pick out boys' voices or girls' voices—it seemed to her more like a sexless chant, something almost monastic; indeed, there was a cool emotionless to it all that made it sound strangely reverent. Valerie strode into the room, Susan trailed behind her. The children turned to them. "Two hundred and forty-one times seven is one thousand six hundred and eighty-seven," they informed the teachers.

"Sit down! Sit down, all of you, and shut up!" Valerie Bewes raged at them. Susan hadn't realised Valerie had such fire in her, and for a second she was quite impressed. Only for a second, though; it was quite clear that that the children weren't going to obey her, or even take any notice of her—they all turned away, and looked back into the circle. Valerie had no further fire to offer. She was spent.

"Which one started this?" she asked Susan. "There's always a ringleader."

It was a boy, Susan knew, but she couldn't remember which one. Now they were standing up, uniformed from head to foot, they all looked eerily the same. She pointed vaguely at one boy, thought he would do.

"Right," said Valerie. "You're coming with me." She grabbed at the boy. He might have struggled, but Valerie's fat piston arms were strong, and she pulled him out of the circle, pulled him out of the classroom.

As soon as he was free, the boy stopped chanting. He looked baffled by this turn of events, and then frightened; he jerked in Valerie's grasp like a fish on dry land.

"What are you playing at?" Valerie demanded to know.

But the boy looked at Susan, and gave her one long despairing glance—help me, it seemed to be saying, but help him with what?—and then the boy lashed out, he kicked at Valerie's shins. Valerie grunted with surprise, and let go. In a trice the boy had rushed back into the classroom, and slammed the door behind him.

"The little bastard," Valerie muttered, and rubbed at her legs—but Susan had no time to waste on her. She was looking through the window at the boy. He was back in the circle now. He was starting to chant. But he'd lost his way. The other children were up to two hundred and eighty-three times seven, he was still only at two hundred and sixty. He croaked and stopped. He looked about, confused, as if woken from a dream. He walked slowly into the middle of the circle. Without missing a beat, as one, the children closed in on him. Susan couldn't make him out through the press of bodies. And then, soon, too soon, the children parted once more, they stepped back and let the circle widen—and the boy was gone, and no trace of him was left.

"Two hundred and ninety-nine times seven is two thousand and ninety-three," they intoned. "Three hundred times seven is two thousand one hundred." If three hundred were any sort of landmark they didn't show it, there was no hint of achievement. On they marched to three hundred and one, and beyond.

"Go and get Mrs. Phelps," said Susan.

"You don't want to involve Mrs. Phelps," said Valerie. "Not on your second day!"

"Go and get her.

Mrs. Phelps looked angry when she arrived. "What is the matter, girl?" And then she looked through the glass door, and listened to the children, and frowned.

"One boy has already gone missing," said Susan.

"They ate him," said Valerie. And that seemed such a ludicrous thing to say that Susan wanted to laugh—but then she realised Valerie was perfectly right.

Mrs. Phelps peered at the circle of cannibals coolly. "What would be interesting," she said at last, "is finding out how high a number they reach."

Susan didn't know what to say to that.

"If you can, make a note of it," said Mrs. Phelps, and then she walked away, and was gone.

Valerie tried to open the door to the classroom again, but pulled away with a cry. The handle was burning hot. And now, yes, they could see there was a certain haze to the room, as if the children were standing at the heart of an invisible furnace.

Presently, another boy lost his place. He seemed to stumble, and then couldn't find his way back into the chant. He gave a sort of smirk, as if to accept the fun was over—and it was such a human thing for him to do, and cut clean through all the madness, and Susan felt that it was going to be all right, whatever this was, it was just a children's game after all. He walked into the centre of the circle, and he was eaten alive, the jaws of his killers bobbing up and down as the seven times table reached ever higher numbers, they tore into him with mathematics on their lips and not a single one of them broke rhythm and the sound of their calculations was loud and crisp and clear.

Some fifteen minutes another child perished: a girl, clearly weaker than the rest, she'd been hesitating for a while, Susan was amazed she had lasted that long. After that, there were no more casualties for several hours, not until it was dark.

And the numbers kept on growing, into the tens of thousands, into the hundreds of thousands. She watched the numbers. She watched how beautiful they were, she could hardly tear her eyes off them.

Valerie came back for Susan. "We have to go," she said. "There's nothing to be done here."

"No."

"You don't understand! Mrs. Phelps has gone. Her class has gone, my class, all gone. We're the only ones left!" Susan didn't know what she meant by gone, she didn't want to think about that—didn't need to, they weren't *her* class, weren't her responsibility.

"These are my children," said Susan. "I won't leave them, not this time." And until she said those words she hadn't realised how true that really was.

"Then I shan't leave you either." And Valerie took her by the arm, hard.

"Let go of me," said Susan, flatly. "Let go, and leave me alone. Or I'll hurt you."

Shocked, Valerie released her grip. Her bottom lip wobbled. Susan turned back to the classroom window, watched her children play. She heard Valerie go, didn't see her.

Once the children began to tire, then they fell in quick succession. They'd put in a good effort. They had nothing to be ashamed of. And as the numbers continued to multiply, so the children seemed to divide; the greater the number chanted the fewer the children left alive to chant it.

They became expert at eating the stragglers without losing time. Swallowing the frail down in the little gasps taken between words, and in three bites. Three bites, that's all you need, even to consume the very fattest child.

The boys were long gone. Four girls were left—then, in a minute, one faltered, and another faltered in response. The two survivors continued to chant in unison for hours, one as soprano, the other's alto playing descant and giving the song such depth. And the numbers were so vast now, Susan had never dreamed numbers could get so big, or so wonderful—before them mankind seemed like crippled fractions, vulnerable and so very petty and so very very easy to crush. Those numbers—each one took a full ten minutes even to enunciate.

The alto stopped. Just stopped. She didn't seem in any difficulty, one moment she was enumerating, the next she'd had enough. The last little girl ripped her apart.

And still, impossibly, she kept the circle, now just a circle of one. She had her back to Susan, and she was still staring into the heart of that circle she was creating, a void at the very heart of herself. Still singing out the numbers—and Susan wanted to tap on the glass and let her know she had won the game, let her know she wasn't alone if nothing else. But it was still so hot, and the glass had warped with the heat, through it the little girl was distorted and inhuman.

At length she reached the final number in the world. And when Susan heard it she knew that it *was* the final one—ludicrous, but true, she had reached the limit of the seven times table, there was no higher she could go.

The handle to the door was cool to the touch. Susan pulled at it. She entered the classroom.

The girl didn't seem to hear her, and it was only when Susan touched her shoulder that she turned around.

"Hello, Clara," Susan said.

Clara didn't reply.

"Where's your brother, Clara?"

And Clara didn't reply, Clara didn't reply—and of course, she couldn't reply, could she? She couldn't speak. Once shy, now struck dumb. But—she had recited all those numbers, the long numbers, all that weight of mathematics had come out of her mouth—she *must* be able to talk, she *would* talk, she would tell Susan what she needed to know. Clara gestured that Susan lean forward. She wanted to whisper in Susan's ear.

It came out like a hiss.

It was one word. It was an impossible word. It could not be spoken aloud. It had too many consonants, not enough vowels, it was a hateful word, it could not be spoken. It was spoken. It was spoken, it was in Susan's head now. It was there in her head, and the head tried to fight it, tried to expel it, this word that no human being was ever meant to know, a word that had nothing to do with humanity or any of the physical laws that make up their universe.

She felt the ground rush up to meet her, and that was welcome.

When Susan awoke she was safe, and lying on her bed, and Valerie Bewes was looking down at her.

"Oh, my darling!" said Valerie. "My poor child! Your breathing was very strange, I was worried sick!"

Susan's breathing did feel a little shallow. Breathing was something she'd always done without thought, but now she seemed to have to *want* to do it. How odd. She sucked air into her mouth, tasted it, blew it out again. "How did I get here?"

"Oh, I carried you! Carried you in my arms! If anything had happened to you, I . . . I'll go and get you some brandy."

"What about the girl?"

"I shan't be long, you just rest," said Valerie. She left the room.

"What about the girl?" Susan called after her, and then realised the girl didn't matter anymore. She had delivered the message. The girl was done.

She did another one of those breaths. It seemed such unnecessary effort. She decided to stop breathing for a while. That felt better.

She got up from her bed, went to the window. Through the heavy rain she could see, standing in front of the house, Edwin. He was looking up at her.

He raised a hand in salute. She raised hers back, and it clunked awkwardly against the glass.

He spoke to her. She couldn't hear what he said. But it was just one word, and as his lips moved she knew precisely what it was.

She whispered it back, that impossible word, the name of her new god.

She dimly heard Valerie return. "What are you doing out of bed?" she asked from the doorway. Susan didn't even look at her, she thrust her hand out somewhere in her direction. She was too far away to reach her, but as her arm moved she was aware of wings and claws as sharp as knives. Valerie gave a quiet little croak, and then shut up at last.

She wondered at her arm. Looked at from one angle, it was thin and fleshy and weak. From another, it was something glorious, something of power and great age. She tilted her head from side to side, so she could see it one way then another. It made her laugh. Her laughter was silly and girlish. Her laughter was a roar.

She could hear the flutter of wings under her bed as the birds flapped their excitement.

Susan left the room, stepping over the spilled brandy, the smashed decanter, the body, and went downstairs. She stepped out into the rain.

There Edwin was waiting for her. He was a little boy, but he looked so grown up, she felt so proud of him. He was a little boy, trying to look big before his time. He was a creature of scales and horns and misshapen flesh.

She took him by the hand. And, as the dream had promised, she made the rain stop. Or maybe it rained, but she just didn't feel it any more.

Susan looked down at her hand in his, and saw that it was dripping with blood. She saw that Edwin's hand was sticky with blood too.

And slowly, they walked into town.

POWER

MICHAEL MARSHALL SMITH

I have done everything she ever wanted, within reason. I have given her everything she ever needed. That has not always been an easy journey, I'll tell you. She hasn't always known what she wanted—or fully understood what she needed—until I was able to make it clear to her. Is that a problem? No. That's marriage. That's how all unions are, in personal life or business. These are complex and evolving systems and they work so long as all components are functioning, so long as everyone has a clear understanding of what's expected of them, and also providing they abide by the rules.

I don't think she *has* always understood what's expected, however. Neither has she always gone by my rules. Yes, *my* rules. That's how it has to be. Rules are never the product of a democratic process. Rules require clear vision. A single focus. Somebody has to make and uphold them.

In our case, it's me. And that's something else I don't think she's ever really gotten into her head.

But she will.

Before the night is out.

RAYiOS b0.8
I have power.
All components are functioning.
Next scheduled task: 6:00 A.M. surface vacuum.
Monitoring for task override . . .
No override.
Commence water surface clean . . .
Task completed in 17.4 minutes.
Compact and evacuate.
Standby.

Case in point—the pool. For most women, it'd be enough that we even have a pool in the first place. And it's a big one, and those things are not cheap to run. Gas for the furnace (she likes it warm, so ours is the only pool in town running heat even in summer, for God's sake), weekly maintenance, chemicals, something minor forever going wrong with the machinery—trivial hassles, but you add them up and also buy a new gasket here and replace an igniter there, and it quickly turns into $$$.

Not that she even *knows* about that. For her . . . it all just happens. Like the weather, or her charge card being paid off. Bob the Pool Guy comes to me with any problems, and I get them fixed, as with everything else around here. The yard man keeps the grounds the way she wants. Like Bob, Eduardo's expert at his job but not even slightly handsome. I'm not dumb. Then there's the SWAT team of Hispanics who drop by every Wednesday morning and clean, because picking up after herself is wholly beyond her. All of this maintenance, all of these support staff *I'm* paying for. . . . Yet she's the one who gets the benefit, because she's here the whole damned day while I schlep over the hill to Mountain View to keep the money coming in. (Telecommuting is not going to work for my company. My people need to be where I can keep an eye on them. My company, my rules. I need to be able to smell their fear.) And yet she's the one who cannot be bothered to walk to the pool house and get out the skimmer net, so when I get back hot after the hell-drive over Highway 17 I wouldn't have to fish the petals and bugs out before I can even do my laps. For a while I didn't mind too much, because skimming a pool can be a good way to unwind. It needs attention but not concentration. You detach the brain and let physical action take its course. But after a while, irritation from the fact she kept not doing it started to outweigh the benefits. All the time I was skimming I'd be fuming about the fact I was skimming, the resentment going round and round in my head, faster and faster, and that is not a good thing for me.

I tried to discuss it with her and she said she'd take her turn but of course she forgot, and I got angry. I let her know how I felt, which I was able to do more often and more emphatically back then. She remembered the next couple of times but then forgot.

Which is how the damned machine came about.

RAYiOS b0.8
I have power.
All components are functioning.
Next scheduled task: 9:00 A.M. bottom clean.
Monitoring for task override . . .
No override.
Commence bottom clean . . .
Task completed in 22.04 minutes.
Compact and evacuate.
Standby.

Problem-solving has always been my key skill. Perceiving a situation clearly, rapidly determining the best response, and incisively carrying it out. That's not just how you run a business—it's how you run a life: your own, and that of those who need guidance. I have not yet found a way through the current crisis, but I will.

Count on that.

I didn't go looking for the big change in my life. It found me. I was at an I-TRAX trade show in Vegas and wound up in the bar talking to a guy I'd never met and it turned out his company was only half a mile up the road from my own. I was in Artificial Intelligence software back then and hadn't been keeping up with what people were doing in cybernetics. It turned out stuff had come on a *lot*. This guy was harnessing some of this to self-directed household appliances. That kind of product had been kicking around for a pretty long time—the kind of junk you'd see in a Sharper Image or Brookstone catalog without taking seriously: automated carpet cleaners that spent the day dumbly nudging around the living room, like retarded dogs, sucking up bits of fluff. That's what this guy, Ross, was at the trade fair to pimp—a slightly better robo-vacuum.

The thing is, carpets don't really demand that kind of treatment. Once you—or your Mexicans—have vacuumed, it'll last a week until they come back. A pool, though . . . a pool needs constant attention. There's always something floating down (or flying, in the summer—crane flies and yellow jackets have a kamikaze yearning to drown themselves in large bodies of water, or at least in mine) to land in it, and come the fall the myrtles take a perverse pleasure in dumping faded blossoms directly into it. Most of this crap floats on top, but some of it is heavy enough to sink to the bottom, where it's tough to net. Then there's the chemical balance, checking the pH level is staying true and chlorine levels are tight, monitoring temperature to balance the furnace versus passive solar. . . . Exactly the kind of task set that a machine should be perfect for.

By the end of the fair Ross and I had agreed to work together. I talked to Bob the Pool Guy the next day, and nailed what a robot would need to be able to do to basically put him out of his job.

Three months later we had our prototype, and four months after that, I had the machine working in our pool.

RAYiOS b0.8
I have power.
All components are functioning.
Next scheduled task: bottom algae scrub.
Monitoring for task override . . .
No override.
Commence scrub . . .
Task completed in 41.8 minutes.
Compact and evacuate.
Standby.

It took us another year to get the thing to the point where it was ready to go to market. Processing power is cheap these days—you can buy an off-the-rack CPU for ten bucks that'll out-think a dog, manual worker, or marketing chick. It's the mechanics that are tough—and that's where you really come to appreciate what a great job evolution does of making bodies fit for purpose. Real world R&D cycles can't last a million years, however, and so we had to turn up the heat. Our skimmer had to be able to move along the surface to vacuum leaves and petals and bugs. It needed to dive to get stuff off the bottom. It had to run water quality tests and release chemicals if required. It had to do all this while not shorting out or rusting or accreting mineral deposits in sufficient quantity to jam up the components, of course, and while knowing to spend enough time seeking sunlight to recharge its solar battery pack.

Our first version—which I called "Bob"—did all these things, kind of. By then it had become clear to me that Ross wasn't up to the job, however. You can't move forward if you're not all on the same page, and his side of things simply wasn't kicking it. When you perceive a problem, a danger to the smooth progression to your chosen future, you have to move hard and fast.

So I fired him, and outsourced the mechanicals to a company in China that was much more eager to please. This meant more trips away from home, sometimes long ones, and I installed webcams around the house and garden to make sure no one was getting up to mischief while I was away. I couldn't keep such close tabs on Laura when she was out of the house, of course, but calls and texts at unpredictable times and intervals helped her realize that immaculate behavior remained mandatory.

Version 2—sold under the name "Bill"—was where I finally started to see returns on investment. Bill took Bob's abilities to a new level, chiefly because of the more sophisticated mechanics provided by the Chinese guys. They all want to be the next FoxConn, and when you say jump, they jump. Bill could now climb in and out of the pool, using six mechanical arms/legs—in order to maximize sun exposure, collect new chemicals if required from a box attached to the pool house, and to evacuate and trash the heavily compacted pellets of surface and bottom debris he'd collected. He also now had wifi to alert his owner if supplies were running low, or to long-range issues like the temperature of the pool wandering out of tolerance, providing a heads-up of potential mechanical difficulties outside his ability to manage.

Bill worked well. Bill sold well, too. Bill made me a stack of money. But there's always going to be people in the world for whom "great" isn't good enough.

Laura is one of them.

It specifically became "not good enough" when the kid got to the point of toddling. Yeah, we had one by then. I hadn't even wanted a child, or at least not at that point. I was busy. There were other issues. But Laura demanded, and so Laura got. And when he started lurching around the grounds on his own two feet, Laura wanted a fence built around the pool. I told her that wasn't going to happen. Put a fence around the pool and it looks caged. It would ruin the effect of the landscaping, and I don't give a crap whether it's code or not. Why was I already paying for swimming lessons for the kid, if it wasn't precisely to make sure he'd be safe?

Still "not good enough," apparently.

That evening we had quite the conversation. I did most of the talking, because I'd had enough. Her response was sufficiently loud to wake the kid up, unfortunately, and the two of them spent the night in the guest wing, Laura locking herself in. I could have unlocked the doors, of course—she didn't realize the entire system had been centralized by then, and I could lock and unlock anything in the house from a custom app on my iPhone—but I let it lie. Sometimes you've got to let the lessons sink in, as with Ross, who'd tried to set up a competing business after we parted company, and only realized the key patents were mine after I had my lawyers actually turn up on his doorstep. Fast, incisive, final. It's how I operate.

Laura spent that night pretty uncomfortably—the air-con and underfloor heating was also under my control, and I had some fun with that, dropping the temperature right down and turning the fan on noisily every half hour—and emerged contrite the next morning, still unaware that I could have gone in and talked further to her any time I wanted. You never play all your cards at once.

It turned out okay. Better than okay, in fact. It indirectly led to the creation of Benny—and Benny was what put me into the very-rich-indeed bracket. Benny did everything Bill did, but was stronger and far more capable. To get around the whole fence issue, Benny could detect sudden and chaotic disturbance in the water, and swim fast enough to get to a small child, maneuver itself underneath and support it back to the edge, meanwhile broadcasting signals over wifi to set alarms blaring on every qualified device within the house (and your phone).

Benny came with a shitload of disclaimers, as I'm sure you can imagine. Benny would not even be installed on your property until you'd signed some extremely carefully worded waivers. No guarantee was either given or implied, and it took longer to get that down in small print than it even did to get the search-and-rescue mechanics right.

But Benny worked. And after it saved the life of a TV star's child (a TV star who, moreover, was between shows and desperate for all the publicity she could grab: she went *nuts* on Twitter about it, and all her brain-dead fans retweeted it to the skies) I started shifting units as fast as my Far East colleagues could manufacture them. They were not at all cheap, but, as the old ad line goes, you can't put a price on piece of mind.

You can, however, put a price on "quality of life."

Even though I'd done everything she wanted, Laura *still* wasn't happy. She didn't like Benny, she said. Specifically, she didn't like having it in the pool the whole time. To be fair, the machine was pretty sizable by then. Bob had been a foot wide and eighteen inches long—not much bigger than the conventional chlorine bobbers you see in any pool. Bill grew to a shade over two feet long, due to the arms. Benny was two feet wide and a full three feet long. He had to be, for the increased power required to move decisively to a child and stand any hope of keeping him or her afloat, involving much stronger arms and sturdy anchoring to the body (and I'd also amped up his cutting and compacting abilities, after our home model got borked trying to dispose of a huge, woody palm tree leaf that fell off one of ours into the pool).

Within these constraints, Benny was as sleek as several ex-members of Apple's product design division could make her—but that wasn't good enough for Laura. Even though he'd been programmed to monitor the pool for evidence of human presence—regular, recreational presence, rather than the frantic splash and flailing of a child who'd fallen in—and trigger a task override which would delay whatever skimming or chemical task was next in his schedule, he still had to basically live in or right by the pool—and that's what she didn't like. The big white shape, lurking at the end. She said he creeped her out.

Of course she called it "he." That is women all over. Imputing feelings and personality where there are none.

Mindful however of the fact that if it hadn't been for Laura's whining he/it wouldn't exist at all—which didn't mean I owed her anything, but did prove that sometimes dealing with annoying things could induce creativity—I got the team to experiment. I tried enhanced audio monitoring to augment the splash sensors. It didn't work. It was too hard to distinguish the relevant sounds accurately. Kids suddenly submerged in water could not be guaranteed to shout or scream in a predictable way, or indeed at all. If they were to bang their heads on the way into the water—as they might if they've been running up and down the side, regardless of how many damned times their parents told them not to—then after the initial splash there would be nothing but a deathly silence anyway. I tried a lot of things, but none worked well enough to put into production.

And still she complained.

RAYiOS b0.8
I have power.
All components are functioning.
Next scheduled task: 7:00 P.M. chemical check.
Monitoring for task override . . .
!!! Target child in pool
//OVERRIDE.
Delay task 1.00 hours.
Standby.

In the end it was Ross—the guy I'd fired—who put the final piece in place. People come into your life for a reason. It's your job to figure out what it is. I ran into him in a Starbucks over in Mountain View where I'd just taken a meeting at Google (my own company having long before moved to Palo Alto). They were interested in licensing our decision-making algorithms in order to help them to sell people shit, but weren't close to being serious enough about the package, and so I was in bullish mood as I turned from the counter with my triple espresso and spotted Ross in the corner. Any other time I'd have ignored him. It was clear from the notepad and laptop and iPhone spread around his table that he believed he was working, however, and that made me curious—curious, mainly, to make sure he wasn't impinging on my territory. California law may declare that someone's free to set up their own company doing the same thing as the one they just left, but my law—my rules—say different.

It emerged that he'd gotten out of the robotics business altogether and was now paddling in the classic retro swamp for so-called entrepreneurs who've got no fucking clue—pheromones. The biochemicals we release which are supposed to tell other people we're feeling horny, or get them to feel the same way. Apparently his take was more sophisticated than that (or so he was keen to imply, as he had the balls to try to hit me up for venture funding right there and then) but once I'd established he wasn't treading on my territory I took my leave, wishing him luck with enough irony to stun a goat.

On the drive home, however, I suddenly got it—the idea dropping into my head with such force that I had to pull off the highway.

I want to have sex with you is not the only message pheromones send. They can communicate anger, too.

And fear.

Like, possibly, the fear experienced by a child who's just fallen into a swimming pool.

Benny already had powerful olfactory sensors—a sense of smell is nothing more than a battery of chemical tests, conducted upon gases in the air. If we increased the range of the compounds he monitored, including a targeted range of biological molecules, the machine *might* effectively be able to monitor for emotional states, too.

I left the Bs behind when it came to names, and settled on "Ray." Development on Ray was *tough*. I had never realized how subtle and sophisticated the sense of smell is, especially with substances in such minute quantities, and which are—it turned out—still little understood. I started to drink a little more than I had. Laura started to get on my nerves even more than usual. After a while I was spending so much of my time in R&D on pheromones that I began to believe my own perception of them had become heightened. I could tell ahead of time when Laura was going to start in on me, and pre-empt it with decisive counter-attacks. I could sense when she was bad-tempered—and, occasionally, detect small moments of contentment whose cause was never remotely clear to me.

On a few evenings during that period I could smell her fear, too.

Sometimes from very close up.

RAYiOS b0.8
I have power.
All components are functioning.
Next scheduled task: delayed 7:00 P.M. chemical check.
Monitoring for task override . . .
!!! Target child is still in pool
//OVERRIDE.
Delay task additional 30.00 minutes.
Standby.

We got there. Kind of. To the brink, anyhow.

I wasn't anywhere near one hundred percent happy, but to paraphrase the late, great man—if you're real, then someday you've got to ship. Detecting pheromones isn't a walk in the park even if you've got two drunk twentysomethings standing next to each other in a bar, or angry men facing each other down in a parking lot—hence why we've evolved a set of face and body language to flag our emotions, not to mention actual words, like "Fuck you," with or without a question mark. Ray would be a significantly greater distance than this from any potential mishap, plus the chemicals would predominantly be released after the child was in the water. Sure, there are species that can allegedly detect signaling hormones from two miles away, but humans aren't one of them—which means our pheromones aren't even constituted for long-distance communication. Results were so patchy that we even experimented for a while with placing sensors all the way around the edge of the pool. Kind of worked, but not an elegant enough solution.

In the meantime I tinkered with ancillary upgrades, getting the body re-engineered to be even bigger and stronger and faster, so Ray could at least react with great speed and precision when he'd determined he needed to. ("He." Of course not. "It." But after a while it got hard to remember.) I enhanced the existing software monitoring how the kid looked and sounded in the pool. After a prolonged series of whines from Laura, I even got the techs to work up a beta that locked the machine to a particular kid's genome, riffing off the fact that some pheromones contain just about enough information about phenotype to work on.

Why did she even want that? Get this—in case there were a bunch of kids in the pool, and more than one was in trouble. She wanted to be sure Ray would ignore the rest, and focus on her beloved brat. There's a chip of ice in that woman that I can't help but admire, even though—and it's too late to be worth trying to hide this—I increasingly found myself wanting to hurt her. I don't know even know why. I'm not a bad man. There's just something about her. A switch gets thrown. Things happen.

But I kept a lid on it. Pretty much. Helped by the fact I was at the office a lot. Too much.

We got the systems to the point where Ray could detect alarm and fear chemical factors within thirty to forty seconds. How long it takes a child to drown in a pool is not something that has been subject to controlled experiments, unless those plucky Nazis got around to it way back when. We were never going to be able to give a guarantee, but then we never had (as a couple of lawsuits over the years had confirmed), and we'd already missed one product release cycle, and couldn't afford to do it again.

A week ago I decided we'd done as much as we could. We needed some real world testing.

This morning Ray came to live with us.

RAYiOS b0.8
I have power.
All components are functioning.
Next scheduled task: twice-delayed 7:00 P.M. chemical check.
Monitoring for task override . . .
!!! Target child remains in pool
//OVERRIDE.
Delay task additional 15.00 minutes.
!!! CAUTION: chemical factor recognized . . .
//EMERGENCY.
CATEGORY A OVERRIDE.

Three hours ago I was feeling as at one with the world as I had in quite some time. I was in the kitchen, enjoying a large drink. I could hear the child splashing in the pool, with Ray poised to one side, constantly monitoring visual, audio and most of all, chemical broadcasts. I could see Laura lounging on a deck chair, in the twilight. I felt exhausted but buoyed up, ready to tackle the next level, as I always do when a given stage has been passed. But . . .

I could also see that Laura wasn't watching the kid.

Sure, Ray was there to do that, though it was day one of testing and he was still in beta, so a good mom might want to keep at least half an eye out. And that wasn't the point anyway. The point was she was looking at her phone.

The *point* was I saw her furtively glancing up toward the kitchen window, before settling down to type something, a sly little smile on her face.

I'm not a fucking moron.

I knew what was going on right away.

But . . . I should have been smarter. I should have waited. I should have calmed down. I should have thought about something else for long enough to settle my body, and allow it to back off on the signals it was broadcasting.

I did not.

I threw down the rest of my drink and went storming out there. Laura heard the kitchen door slamming. She sat up, hurriedly stuffing her phone into the pocket of her robe and freezing a fake smile onto her face.

"Hey, honey," she lied.

The kid splashed on, oblivious—until he too saw me storming down toward the pool. I've almost always stayed my hand with him, despite everything, but he's still seen enough to tell when daddy has realized there's work to do in ensuring people understand and stick by his rules.

He froze, too.

Ray, though . . . he didn't freeze.

He was on it. Fast, and decisively.

He sensed fear in the creature he was designed to protect, capturing the sharp chemical signals of alarm. At the same time, he caught the anger broadcast from one he had no feeling for, despite me being more his father than I've ever been of Laura's child. Her brat's not mine, you see, except in that I paid for it, like everything else. My seed wouldn't plant, or maybe Laura's body rejected it out of pure spite. So we used a donor.

So Ray has a feeling for him, and her, but not me.

Machines are simple things. They make quick, simple decisions.

They're also powerful. And in Ray's case, now so sophisticated that I'm not sure of his boundaries any more. I thought I'd understood them, but then—when I saw him turn and move quickly from the pool area toward me—I realized perhaps not.

I turned and walked quickly back to the house and went inside.

Ray came right up to the house, roving back and forth outside the kitchen, trying to get at the source of the anger. Behind him, back at the pool, I saw Laura pull out her phone and make a call. In other relationships it could have been a call to the police, or someone else who might help. It wasn't.

Forty minutes ago I heard a car pull up outside the front of the house. She and the kid are now gone.

For now. But when I've got out of this situation, I'm going to go and find them.

Oh yes.

For the moment though it's just me and Ray, and it's dark. I tried moving around the house for a while, crawling under window height so he couldn't see me, hoping to wait it out until he'd lost the scent, or else some other task override cut in. It hasn't worked. Strength of purpose, a determination to succeed, has evidently been passed on from me to him. He's locked on one particular course of action.

I eventually retreated back to my study area.

I locked all the doors, outside and in. But this is a nice house. Half those doors are made of glass.

I'm pretty sure I just heard one of them break, quietly, downstairs.

And dear god he moves fast.

RAYiOS b0.8
I have power.
All components are functioning.
Source of anger factor eliminated.
Compact and evacuate complete.
Standby.

BRIDGE OF SIGHS

KAARON WARREN

10 A.M./ Client: Mr. P/ Subject: His son (16) Overdose

Terry needed a fresh ghost, so he dressed warmly and headed out, camera around his neck, syringes safely packed into the bag over his shoulder.

There were many places to look. People committed suicide in surprising places sometimes, such as a change room in a large department store, or the car park at a primary school, or under the pier at the beach, but more often they jumped from the tops of buildings, from bridges, from dams.

They jumped from the hospital roof too, staff as well as patients. But security could be tight, and once he'd been locked on a roof overnight and didn't want to repeat that experience.

He drove to Culver's Dam instead. Some nights he had a feeling for where the ghosts would be; other times it was research and asking questions.

He loved the hunt. He loved that there was a purpose to it but more than that, it proved time and time again that there was something BEYOND. That his mother did not blink out into nothingness.

Terry parked his car near the entrance to the dam bridge, water noise nearly deafening him. There was one car already parked there; a purple sedan. The bonnet was damp with water spray and cold to the touch so it had been there for some time. It could belong to a hydro engineer, manning switches, checking equipment, or to a sightseer (although in this cold no one would stay so long), or the car was abandoned, its driver over and into the hydrodam.

Feeling the cold, he gathered his camera and syringe bag and trekked to the bridge where he climbed the many stairs, feeling the tension in his thighs. A thick mist settled over the dam and in his hair and on his face. His hands felt frozen so he stuffed them into his pockets but found little warmth there.

Reaching the bridge, he could barely see three steps in front of him. Here, the water roar was so loud he could scream and no one would hear.

He set up his camera and looked through the view finder, seeking features amongst the water droplets.

He didn't think much of those who killed themselves here. Poisoning the water supply, hurting others. Like those who threw themselves in front of a train, or over a wall at a shopping mall, or onto a busy street, it caused trauma to strangers that surely eased no passing and perhaps led to further suicides among those who saw or who felt responsible.

He saw nothing, so walked farther along, gazing through his viewfinder until he saw a middle-aged man, soaked to the bone, shivering with cold. Bare feet. Once their shoes were off it was too late to do anything.

"It's an amazing view, isn't it?" Terry said.

"Yeah, nice view," the man said, glancing out as if seeing it for the first time. "Peaceful."

"It's like the end of the world, isn't it? As if all life ends here," Terry said. "As if nothing matters, no one cares." His voice was gentle but it carried.

The man closed his eyes, gripping the railing. Terry hoped he wouldn't have to get close to the edge. There was a chest-high fence, but he still felt vertigo at the thought.

"You like taking photos?" the man said. He squeezed his eyes shut, as if instantly realising the stupidity of the question.

"Yeah. It's the one thing that keeps me going some days."

The man leaned forward, looking over the edge. "I don't really have anything like that. Are you a drinker?"

"Depends on what it is."

"Whisky my dad left me. Last drops. He was an alcoholic."

"Mine shot himself in front of me."

They exchanged glances; both shrugged. "Go grab it for us? You've got shoes on."

The man threw him the car keys.

Terry took a warm winter coat that was lying on the back seat of the purple car but could find no flask. The car was dirty, uncared for, and it smelt of pizza. Nothing in the glove box beyond official papers. No music, no letters, no photos, no devices.

When he returned to the top of the dam the man was over, so he had wanted privacy in his last moments and had gained it by sending Terry to look for the flask. The mist was thicker, more dank.

There. There it was. His flash was powerful and froze the ghost in place so he could suck up the mist into his syringe.

He stowed his equipment in the backseat, a sense of wellbeing overtaking him. It was always this way. Taking the spirits filled him with grace and kept him from going over himself, some days.

Terry didn't want the man's car, but was glad to have the coat.

His Aunt Beryl called up the studio stairs. "Are you decent?" She'd caught him once, shirt off, and she'd never forgotten it. "Come on up," he said.

She appeared behind a bunch of purple hydrangeas, holding them out like an offering.

"This'll bring a glow to your cheeks, you beautiful man. Although look at you! Picture of health!"

"You know I want pink or red flowers," he said. He said it most times. "Purple gives off the wrong colour."

She was a stupid woman. She understood him though, accepted him, and she had been his mother's best friend. Her bright red fingernails were so long they curled down over the tips of her tanned, crooked, wrinkled fingers. She wore a lot of rings (including an ostentatious engagement ring, although her fiancé had died decades before), smelled of cigarette smoke and used Tabu perfume that made his studio reek. Her toenails were brightly painted as well and she wore sandals too small for her. Her cracked heels hung over the back and her toes stuck out the sides.

She owned the florist shop in the nearby mall. She wore a floral coat that she never washed, over a miniskirt far too short for her. Tabu perfume and old, old sweat. She collected unused flowers from the hospital and turned them into bouquets, charging full price, sometimes selling them to people who would take them back to the hospital.

He liked lots of flowers for his photos. They gave the impression of warmth and life and they provided a focus, a discussion point.

The funeral director texted >>We're heading up now.<<

Terry had Aunt Beryl hide behind the black curtain and climb into the Mama Suit, black gloves stitched into the black curtain, so that she could hold the dead boy up without being seen. She hated it, she said. Hated it when they were cold, hated it when they got warm. But he needed her there, to hold the chin up, keep the shoulders back.

Teenagers often needed help sitting up.

It was good to meet clients at the entrance, not leave them waiting in the hallway with the dead loved one. Terry stood in front of the magnificent trompe l'oeil of The Bridge of Sighs, the concealed doorway leading not to a Venetian prison but to his studio.

"Here we are," the funeral director said. Terry modelled the timbre of his own voice on this man's; it was so perfectly kind, honest, and masculine. The funeral director's judgement was excellent in deciding the level of service to be provided, but the final decision was Terry's. "This is Mr. P. The father." They never shared full names. "I've told him of the comfort you can bring him, in the fullest terms."

"The mother?" Terry asked quietly.

"At home. Inconsolable."

Terry's mother would have been the same. She would not have functioned again, if he'd died before her.

"Come on, then," Terry said. He led the man by the elbow, leaving the funeral director to roll in the trolley with the dead boy.

He gently lifted the boy into the chair in front of the black curtain, then nodded to the funeral director, who whispered, "You're doing a good thing," to the father and left.

Aunt Beryl took grip on the boy.

The father stood close, nervous, hesitant.

"You hold his hand while I set up," Terry said. "Strong boy, wasn't he? What did he like most? Was he a burger lover? Or a vegetarian? A lot of kids are these days." Putting the client at ease was part of the job.

Terry pulled on some gloves, opened the fridge. There was champagne, cold, but not for this shoot or any like it. He took out the recently filled syringe. The ghosts leaked out of the needle if he left them in the fridge too long, forming yellow, viscous puddles on the shelf, like spilled egg yolk.

The father noticed nothing.

Terry bent over the boy and injected the syringe into the corner of his eye.

The boy twitched, and his cheeks reddened, chasing away the blue tones the overdose had given him.

Terry stepped behind his camera and took a quick dozen shots.

"Hold him if you like. Take him in your arms."

Hesitantly, Mr. P stepped forward. "He's warm. He feels warm."

"It won't last long. Make the most of it."

Mr. P held his son close. Beryl knew to let go at that point, take her arms away.

"Say your goodbyes, then. Make him sigh."

Mr. P whispered in his son's ear until the coldness began to creep back. Terry took the boy and settled him into the chair.

"There."

Mr. P was pale. "God. I don't know if his mother would have wanted that or not."

"But you got to say goodbye."

"But it almost feels like . . . that empty feeling of fullness you get from eating a packet of potato chips."

"The photos will make it worth it. You'll see."

"But he's still dead, isn't he?" Mr. P said.

Terry, a professional, kept his emotions in check. He would have given anything to have that moment with his mother, yet this man didn't seem to appreciate what he'd been given.

It helped that he felt as if his mother was beside him, whispering in his ear. "Oh, you angel. Oh, such a good man." This was what he worked for, beyond all the other benefits. This sense of benefaction.

Terry had been sixteen the first time he saw a ghost in the mist. His mother and Aunt Beryl ran the florist together then, and he helped with deliveries. This one was a rooftop memorial to a suicide. Terry's father was long dead by then; "I love you son," and then a deep sigh, then the gunshot, with Terry sitting beside him. Terry couldn't remember a mist forming, but later, it was there. He knew that.

"Be careful near the edge," his mother said. "Even an accident might be considered suicide if you deliberately put yourself in harm's way."

It was misty on the roof, rendering his vision unclear, and he rubbed at his eyes, the bouquet wedged under one arm. He squeezed his eyes tight, opened them, but the mist seemed even thicker. He saw a slumped figure, dejected, so very sad, and reached out to it, thinking to comfort this loner, this apparent outcast.

As he touched it, it seemed to snarl, to reach for him, and he jumped back, landing on the feet of the mourners behind him. Like many in grief, they were disconnected to their bodies and didn't react.

Later, he managed to get hold of some CCTV footage of this suicide, and he watched it over and over again. The moment he looked for, beyond what the others saw (the death of a woman with post-natal depression) was the mist forming, like a small cloud rising from the ground and hovering on the rooftop. As he told his mother, "If I stare for long enough without blinking, I see a face or a figure."

She was arranging flowers in a cut glass vase, her taste impeccable. She was like a delicate flower herself, Terry thought, pink and easily damaged. His father had been like a stick insect, attached to her, always wanting to draw her nectar. She said, "Oh, that poor woman, stuck in limbo. No heaven, no hell." She was a great believer in such things. She liked to remain in a state of grace at all times, just in case she was taken suddenly.

"What about Dad? Is that where he is?"

"He didn't die that way," she said, in denial, always in denial, but Terry still had the tiny blood-spattered t-shirt he'd been wearing that day.

No one else could see what he saw. He read about a group of people who lived by diving and fishing, who trained their eyes to see better underwater, and he took up swimming, long laps along the bottom of the pool, eyes open. His mother on the side, holding a towel, terrified of not seeing his head bob up again.

Eventually he trained his eyes to look through the water and thus the mist, to see clarity beyond it.

He would use this skill to prove to himself that his mother's death was accidental.

She and Beryl had always wanted to travel, especially once they were both widowed. They saved for years, then hired someone to take over the shop when they flew to Europe with their hair done, their lipstick on, their matching suitcases packed neatly, their promises to write often. He didn't see them off. He was deep in a world of buying sex and selling drugs, where stories of his childhood meant nothing.

He sold dreams to people, sold calm, sold respite, and lived well off the proceeds.

Two weeks later, Beryl called him, hysterical, the line bad, voices behind her that she tried to shush. His mother had drowned in a Venice lagoon, off the Ponte dell Liberta. Beryl said, "Come get us, Terry. Come bring us home," but he was in no state to fly. In the end Beryl did it on her own. He'd sobered up by the time she landed.

It wasn't until he saw his mother's body he believed she was gone, and even then, he couldn't reconcile what lay in the coffin with the woman he knew.

"It was an accident, wasn't it?" he asked Beryl. "Tell me she didn't want it."

Because otherwise she'd be stuck there in the mist, graceless. She'd said to him, "Always resuscitate. Even if I'm a vegetable. I don't ever want to be one of those people you see." She was the only one he'd told about the mist.

"No, no, she didn't want it! We were walking with all the other tourists. One minute we were talking, next minute she was over. She did not want it, Terry. All she talked about was the future, and you, and wanting to see how you fared. She wanted better for you."

He drew a line then, under the man he was and the man he would be.

Beryl sat with him and held his hands at the funeral. There were so many flowers people sneezed uncontrollably, but Beryl said, "This is what she would have wanted."

She handed him a camera. "Your mother took lots of photos, Terry. I know she'd want you to have this. Next up was the Bridge of Sighs. There's proof she didn't want it. She was so keen to see that place, and we never made it." Beryl cried then, great snuffling sobs, and he left others to comfort her.

He had the photos developed and he saw what his mother had given him.

Photos of mist, in many of the places they travelled in Europe. "Here there are ghosts," she was saying to him. "And here, and here."

Would he find her there, in the mist? He had to know.

He travelled to Venice, to the Ponte dell Liberta where to his great relief there was no mist, no matter how much he squeezed his eyes and squinted. So he travelled to the Bridge of Sighs, because he wanted to finish her voyage for her. He would look out as those long-ago condemned did, and he would listen for their sighs echoed in the walls.

He heard nothing, but he did see the mist, and flying in the mist, ghosts.

He knew about the belief that suicides did not pass over, that they were confined to the earthly plane. Terry thought it was the embodiment of the sigh that stayed behind. The last sigh so many made before jumping.

The window was like a slice of pizza. He could see the canal, buildings on either side. In the distance, another bridge, laden with tourists and beyond that; more buildings, so much water. He thought, "They're out there."

He began to follow the trail of suicides: the tallest buildings, the bridges, and he found the mist each time.

It was on the Nusle Bridge, in Prague, where he stood transfixed but somehow lost, that he understood what he could do. A young woman, shoes held by the straps, her lips red, her blonde hair wild and wispy around her head, said, "I feel as if he's here. Don't you? Stuck there, in the mist."

He squinted and did see a face.

"Your husband?" he said.

She nodded. "If only you could capture him. Give him to me." The woman ran her hand through the mist and shivered. "You might give him a second chance. Them."

He took a photo, wanting to capture her grief, the moment she reached for the husband she thought waited there. The flash froze the mist and, within the mist, a face. He reached out to touch it, thinking it would disperse, but he could run his fingers through it and feel it, wet.

If only he could capture it.

The widow watched him, her cheeks flushed, and soon they were sharing wine, she was laughing with her head thrown back and he knew that she was using him but that made it even better.

Back home, he established his photography studio above the funeral parlour. Beryl and his mother had long supplied flowers to the parlour, and Beryl was the one who made the suggestion. "You have such an affinity with the grieving. An understanding. You'll be wonderful," she said, and the funeral director agreed.

It took experimentation to discover that syringes worked best to capture the ghosts, but it was not time wasted. Every capture gave him strength. Among the first was his father, trapped in a small wet mist in the backyard over the swing chair. Terry flashed the photo, froze him, syringed him. It was a gift he didn't think his father deserved, but he wanted the mist gone.

His father became one of the yellow stains. Terry soaked it up in a napkin and he kept that with his mother's water-stained Italian silk scarf and his own tiny t-shirt.

He wasted many this way until he remembered the words of his lover in Venice (*You could give him a second chance*), but what led him to make that first injection? He liked to think it was his mother, helping him as he pressed the needle, unseen, into a deceased elderly woman and watched her cheeks colour.

He didn't know what happened to the spirits next. His studio was always cold and sometimes, he thought, misty. But a flash revealed no ghosts there. He liked to think he freed them, but truly he didn't care.

12 P.M./ Client: Mr. S/ Subject: His Fiancée (29) Car Crash

Terry walked into the forest; it was a favourite hunting ground, when he was in the mood for a hike and the fresh air. He loved the smell of pine, and the crunch underfoot of growth and of insect bodies.

The mist was thick at the base of a massive tree, and he took his photos, gathered his spirit, before pausing for a quick sandwich and coffee from his thermos.

The funeral director came out with him once and while the man saw the mist, he did not see the faces within, although he did feel chilled to the bone and a sense of the "Heeb Jeebs," he said.

Terry turned on soft lighting and played romantic music. He threw a satin sheet over the couch and added Erotica to the oil burner.

Mr. S was in his mid-30s. His hair was a mess and his clothes dishevelled and there was a furtiveness about him. The dead woman lay on a trolley, covered by a soft blanket.

"Slight rush on this one. Her parents hate him," the funeral director said in Terry's ear as he passed the trolley over. "Apparently a restraining order on him, hush hush."

"No worries, we're good to go."

"Enjoy," the funeral director said.

"It's a sad name for a photography studio," Mr. S said. The light from the stained glass windows in the foyer bathed him in a deep, colourful glow.

"Kind of," said Terry, "But I also think of the last sigh as both a release and an acceptance. It tells you your loved one was ready to move on. That they are okay." He loved this metaphor, having once read a description of Franz Mesmer's studio as being "filled with the sighs of sweet music and soft female voices."

He settled the dead girl onto the couch, arranging her so she appeared to be resting. Aunt Beryl was at the florist; he didn't need her for this one.

As Terry worked, he asked, "How long had you been together?"

"Two years. But I dumped her. It wasn't working out, so I dumped her. She went out and got blind drunk. This is my fault, I shouldn't have dumped her." The body was severely damaged; broken limbs, deep bruising. Her flesh was spongy in places.

"It's not your fault. You loved her dearly. I can see that. She was a lucky woman." Terry's sleeves were rolled up high around his triceps. He knew he shone under the lights and that the life in him, the brightness, contrasted starkly. He was a handsome man and he knew it, square-jawed, wild-haired, and he was always flicking it out of his eyes. Women shifted it for him sometimes, tucking it behind his ears. He knew he had them when they did that.

"God, look at her," Mr. S said. "Can't you cover that up so she looks normal?"

The whole back of her head was dented. The funeral director had done his best cosmetically, and they nestled her head in cushions, hiding the damage.

Terry pulled on gloves, walked to his bar fridge and removed a syringe.

He'd scratched himself before, raising blisters which were filled with tiny growths, so he always wore gloves now.

"What the fuck is that?"

"It's going to help us make her look better in the photo. Trust me. It's an element of the universal fluid that runs through us all, even your beautiful girl. Her flow has been interrupted, but I can get it going again very, very briefly."

Terry emptied the syringe into the corner of her eye. Stepped back. Waited for the moment. That sudden flare of colour in the cheeks, as if the flesh was infused with dye. This he needed to capture.

A twitch. The glow. "There it is!"

"Is she alive?"

"Just for a moment."

He heard a soft sighing and it was so sweet it made all else seem empty. The smell was ammoniac, though. It made his eyes water.

He took some shots. "Touch her. Go on. She's warm."

There was no personality in the revival. It was the physical body alone that reanimated. No conversation, no thought process.

Still, Terry said, "Say goodbye. *I love you* always feels good. She might hear you. Think of her as in a coma. Your voice might pass through to her. And hold her while she's warm. She'll feel good."

"I'm sorry," Mr. S said to her. "I'm sorry I made you die. If you hadn't left it wouldn't have happened."

Mr. S touched her.

"Go for it," Terry said. "Most people do."

"Really?"

Terry showed him some photos. "Really. Look. I can take a record if you want. Just for your private viewing. You have to be quick, though."

Grief sold. Grief-struck fucking even more so.

The woman blinked. Her mouth opened.

Terry took the photos then printed them out while Mr. S went to the bathroom. He added his special touch to them, the colours he loved. Split lip red, vagina pink. All shoots excited him, but these ones in particular. He didn't relieve himself though; he had a date that evening and looked forward to it. The only dead one he'd ever been tempted by was an actress. The funeral director alerted him, describing her wild bush, her protuberant labia, her large and obvious clitoris. There were no loved ones but that didn't matter.

Terry took photos anyway.

They say a photographer (pornographer) should never star in his own work and Terry agreed. He took plenty of photos, though. She was a beautiful woman.

He presented to Mr. S, now waiting in the viewing room, flicking through magazines. Terry liked his clients to sit with him at the large desk on the comfortable chairs. He made coffee or cocoa or he poured wine and he had chocolate truffles to eat.

"You're a magician. How do you do it?" Mr. S said, surprised even though he had seen the body, felt the warmth.

"I treat each photo like a work of art. Sometimes I have to add a little here, a little there."

"You're a genius."

Another high-paying happy customer. Terry loved to help.

He sprayed air freshener around the studio to absorb the odours. His nose was sensitive to the smell of decay, although he was far more used to it today than he once was. He burned incense by the handful and people liked it. It made some of them think of church, which was a comfort for most.

2 P.M./ Client: Ms. T/ Subject: her daughter (stillborn)

He didn't take bookings too far in advance. He needed to be ready to move, ready to snap on an hour's notice or less. The funeral director kept him updated with lists and he watched the papers, so he could vaguely estimate his day if he wanted to. There was never a dull day, never a quiet one. He sold dreams in a different way now, but he still sold calm, respite and comfort.

Aunt Beryl took a call from the hospital. "Can you go? There's a lady there who needs your help."

"It's better to do it here." She knew that.

He'd never tell the truth of it.

The mother arrived, supported by her sisters. Hair drawn back into a loose, messy ponytail, done by someone else, he thought. Her face washed clean—the sisters again, he thought, and the clothes were her pregnancy ones, as if by wearing them she could pretend she hadn't had the baby yet.

"Come in," he said. He asked the sisters to wait downstairs. Before Aunt Beryl went back to her shop she filled the place with yellow roses and they brought a deep warmth. He took the dead baby gently. "So beautiful, so pure," he said. He nestled her sideways on the soft cushions.

He syringed the mist into her small, clouded eye.

Her cheeks flushed.

"Oh!" Ms. T said. "Look! She's alive, she is! I told them. Those doctors." She picked her baby up, held her close. Shucked off her shirt, engorged breasts leaking colostrum.

He snapped, filmed, clicked, close up of her stretched skin, the bluish nipple moist and dripping.

The baby didn't suckle.

"She's warm. She feels warm. Why doesn't she drink?"

He took photos of the baby before the warm flush faded.

"She doesn't have the strength, poor darling."

The baby lost her warm colour. The spirit had departed. She looked greyer than before, like marble, and so cold his fingers chilled touching her. He placed her in a basket and covered her head.

He laid roses around her. "Such a beautiful girl."

He called for the funeral director to collect her. Ms. T sat slumped in the corner, her shirt still unbuttoned.

"That was amazing," she said. "I don't know what you did."

He showed her the photos on his camera.

"She looks alive. She really does. Doesn't she? I'm not imagining it."

He didn't show her the shots of her tits. He'd cut her head off for those, no need for permission.

She stood up shakily. He took her arm, held her steady. "It's okay. This is difficult for you. It's the worst thing you'll ever have to go through. No one else can imagine it."

Mothers were so grateful they often wanted to do him right there, by the cash register, as if he could make them another baby.

This one didn't have sex with him and he didn't want it, anyway. She'd be all messed up down there after giving birth, he knew that, but he wouldn't mind sucking on those milky tits.

"Do it again, what you did," she said, her voice throaty with grief.

"I can't do it again. I only do it once. I'm sorry."

"Oh, God, please. Please. I'll give you all I've got. Have you got a girlfriend? A wife? One day you'll have a baby and you'll know what it's like."

He had girlfriends, but not the kind she meant.

She fell to her knees, her arms around his shins, begging, weeping. He was glad his mother had died first because he'd hate her to suffer like this.

He wasn't sure how well it would work a second time. Oddly, no one had ever asked him before.

"This has to be the last time. We'll take one last photo so that you'll never forget your beautiful girl."

5 P.M./ Client: Ms. T/ Subject: Her daughter (stillborn)

Terry dressed in a pale blue t-shirt, some lightweight pants. He didn't have time to enjoy this hunt, so drove to the city's tallest building where he climbed to the roof and took out his camera.

He thought of the woman in his studio with her milky, firm tits, and her needy lips, and her gratitude. And he thought of the baby and how much he loved to see them revived, how godlike he felt when that movement came to them.

He patrolled the roof until he found it, a small patch of mist. One two three ghosts there, a family, perhaps.

His studio was always cold.

Ms. T waited, sleeping on the couch. He took a few photos, wondering if she'd notice if he moved her around, shifted her arms and legs.

She stirred. She could almost be one of his subjects, he thought.

"Come on," Ms. T said. She sat rocking her baby; it had a glossy sheen to it now. He couldn't call it a girl anymore; it had moved beyond anything very human.

He bent over the child. Ms. T saw him this time and gasped to see what he was doing, but then the child stirred, sighed, and the mother cooed and sang.

Ms. T danced around with her baby but then started to sob as the body cooled again. Held her up in the air, hoping to revive her. Her daughter's mouth fell open.

"You killed her! What did you do! What did you do?"

"This beautiful soul has left now. Didn't you hear her sigh? She's done. She was ready." He walked to the door, looking for the funeral director.

"Yes," she said. She rolled her shoulders. He'd heard that breast-feeding woman were easily sexually stimulated and he wondered if that was happening here. He gave her his charming smile, the one women liked and thought was only for them.

"Let me help, then," she said. "Let me be part of it."

2 P.M./ Client: Mrs. J/ Subject: Her husband (heart attack)

Ms. T (he called her Mama T. She loved that) proved adept at wearing the Mama Suit, happy to sit sheathed in the black curtain for hours. Sometimes he forgot she was there as he went through his routines, but always they shared a glass of champagne afterward.

She never went with him on a ghost hunt; in fact to him she seemed only to exist in his studio.

He captured this ghost at the hospital, locked roof or not, after hearing a report of the suicide on the radio. On the way back to the studio he'd stopped by Auntie Beryl's shop and bought some roses for his Mama T.

She cooed. "From the hospital?" she said. "Did you collect my baby? Is that who you've got in that syringe?"

"No. It couldn't be," and her mouth formed a sweet moue that made him want to touch his fingers to her lips.

"Sit with me," she said, and he sat beside her. She lifted his chin, kissed his neck. He wouldn't say no, never did, birth-mess or not.

"Close your eyes," she said, and she kissed him on the side of the mouth. His tongue flicked out, catching her lip, and she kissed him harder.

"Wait there," she said. He liked surprises. "Eyes closed," she said.

She opened his fridge and scrabbled in there. "Champagne," she said. "We need champagne."

"After the client," he said.

"Now. I can't wait."

She popped the cork. Sat on his lap and swallowed some from the bottle, then poured some into his mouth.

She held his eyelid open. "Such beautiful eyes," she said. It was gentle, aggressive, made him itch to get at her. It felt as if she was looking deep inside him.

"Here's my baby," she said, purring like a mother cat, but she didn't mean him. She meant the syringe she held. "Here she is," she said, as she injected his eyeball. "Here she is. I've been watching you. I've figured it out."

But she hadn't. Of course she hadn't. When had he ever injected into a living person?

He was instantly filled with despair and a sense of . . . the opposite of vertigo. He wanted to fall, to fly then fall and land and he wanted oblivion desperately.

His skin formed large, pus-filled blisters like spiders under the skin, and moving hurt. The blisters leaked clear fluid and he wondered: Is that him leaving me? That poor sad suicide who had nowhere to die but the hospital?

He reached for his phone to call Aunt Beryl; she'd save him. Instead, he slumped to the ground. As the blisters opened, the heat of him and the cold of the studio formed a subtle mist, but he could not see anyone in it. He heard the funeral's director's deep and comforting voice as he ushered the client in, felt Mama T rocking him like a baby, cooing, and he thought he remembered his mother singing to him that way.

His skin was so puckered, so painful, each time she rocked him he wanted to scream but there was no sound beyond her sweet whispering comfort.

"... filled with the sighs of sweet music and soft female voices" from *Harper's Weekly*, February 1873, "Delusions of medicine. Charms, talismans, amulets, astrology, and mesmerism" by Henry Draper.

THE WORMS CRAWL IN,

LAIRD BARRON

the worms crawl out. The worms play Pinochle on your snout.

We chanted that at mock funerals when I was a kid. Shoot your sister playing cowboys and Indians and she fell dead, that's your dirge. The playground bully challenges you to a duel after class, that's the ditty your friends hummed as the hour of doom approached.

Hadn't heard the worm song since I was twelve, but it's coming back into style, thanks to my wrath. I've been done a great wrong, you see. Done a great injustice by a man named Monroe. However, I've come to think of him as Fortunato. It makes me smile to do so.

He "tricks" me into going on the hiking trip. I've always had a hate-hate relationship with the great outdoors. Bad enough I'm stuck working nine to five in the weather; camping is a deal breaker. My feelings don't matter. He's as slick as a magician or a shrink: talks about one thing, shows you one thing, but there's always something up his sleeve. He knows his con, short or long. Can't dazzle 'em with brilliance, baffle 'em with bullshit, is his motto. Much as the hand is quicker than the eye, Monroe's bullshit usually defies my perception of it until after the fact when it's time to cry.

Phase one of the scam, he invites Ferris and me over to the house for a barbeque. Optimistically, I assume that's merely a cover to regale us with his latest sexual exploits, and yep, Monroe does chortle over a couple of girlfriends he has squirming on the hook, each completely ignorant of the other. But it turns out that this gloating is actually a pretext to maneuver me into a conversation about Moosehead Park and its fabulous game trails.

So, Elmer, you hunt, right? You lived in the woods when you were a kid. The only way he could know that, since I've never mentioned it, is from Ferris. And of course, I correct him. My dad had been the big white hunter in the family; the rest of us were simply dragged along for the ride. Nonetheless, Monroe believes in education via osmosis. It isn't hunting that intrigues him. He is far too much of a wilting flower to lay hands on a rifle, much less put a bullet into the brainpan of some hapless animal. He needs street cred, as it were, wants to butch up his resume with the ladies, and a brief foray into the swamps of south central Alaska is just the ticket. First rule of disappearing into the wilderness is, always bring a buddy.

We chew some ribs, toss back a few brews, and thus plied with meat and drink I agree to tag along this very next Saturday for an overnight campout. It has to be me. Not a chance any of his colleagues will blow a perfectly good weekend with the shifty motherfucker. Plenty of them will gather for a free feed and trade shop gossip, but that is the extent of it. Dude probably thinks he's really clever, manipulating his lummox of a pal, albeit pal might be too strong a word.

Joke's on him. I'm not as dim as I pretend. The trip is exactly what I want. It's my big chance to settle the score.

Ferris doesn't say anything. She *looks* plenty worried. I pretend not to notice. Can't have her suspecting that I suspect she suspects I *know* there is something going on between her and Monroe. In that unguarded moment, her expression says she thinks her boyfriend is out of his gourd, putting himself at the mercy of a paranoid husband who can load a six-hundred-pound engine block barehanded. Alas, Monroe's downfall is his unremitting narcissism. He doesn't want to get away with snaking my wife, he wants to rub my nose in it.

If Ferris were to get a whiff of my true mood she'd forbid Monroe's excursion under no uncertain terms and spoil everything. Although, even in her most febrile visions, it's doubtful she could imagine I plan to off him in some devious manner and drop the body into a deep, dark pit. One of my flaws is jealousy. Not the biggest of them, either, not that she has the first inkling. We've been together since our late twenties. Going on fifteen years, and parts of me remain Terra Incognita to my lovely wife.

See, there are some things you should know about me, things I should get out in the open. I won't, though. Not until later.

Ferris worked as an administrative assistant at the high school where Monroe taught English. Fancied himself a poet, did our man Monroe. A skinny, weepy fella who preened as if his scraggly beard made him kin to Redford's liver-eating-Johnson and that his sonnets were worthy of Neruda.

Yeah, sonnets.

Ferris started bringing the shit home in a special folder, wanted my "professional" opinion. I'm no expert, I drill wells for a living. But yeah, I published a few pieces in lit journals over the years, had one chapbook about blood and vengeance picked up by Pudding House when I was younger and angrier. I read Monroe's poems, told her what I thought of them, which wasn't much. Classic poseur artiste. The kind of asshole who upon learning he can't strum a guitar to any effect minors in poetry or fiction to impress the doe-eyed girls who hang around coffee houses and the bored ones at faculty parties. One of those *I'm writing a book* shitheads who isn't really doing any such thing.

Yeah, everybody hates those guys.

Guys who kiss married women on the mouth aren't too popular either. Even though I was likely the last to know, I'd finally gotten wise at Monroe's Fourth of July house party. A fateful glimpse of him and Ferris in a window reflection was a splash of cold water for sure. Shielded by an open refrigerator door, both of them leaning in for a beer, and by god, Monroe laid it on her. The door swung closed and they acted casual. Cheeks a bit rosier, laughter a notch too sharp, and that was all. I played the oblivious fool. Wasn't tough; waves of numbness filled me, that big old local anesthetic of the gods. It was as if the enemy had dropped depth charges. Those bombs sink real deep before detonating. First time I'd ever thought of Ferris as an enemy.

I didn't fly into a rage or fall into despair. Nah, my reaction was to get chummy with Monroe. I fucked my wife more often and a lot more vigorously than was my habit. Also, I took some dough from a rainy day account and paid a private eye to tail those lovebirds for two weeks. The results were inconclusive. No motel rendezvous, no illicit humping in their cars, but they did frequently meet for drinks at the tavern on

89 when she told me she was shopping for office supplies or groceries. Practically mugging each other in the photos. The detective offered me a cut-rate package to tap their phones and intercept email communications. I declined, paid him, and sent him on his way. He'd shown me enough. My imagination would do the rest.

Then I took that thumb drive of photos and locked myself in a room and brooded. As my dad would've said, I went into the garden and ate worms.

Moose have learned to steer wide of Moosehead Park. Hunters and redneck locals blast the poor critters the second one pokes its muzzle out of the woodwork. The park isn't all that park-like; really just an expanse of marsh and spruce copses in the shadow of the Chugach Mountains that got designated public use. Basically, the feds looked around for the armpit of the great outdoors and said, Fine, peasants. Enjoy! Thanks a lot, Jimmy Carter.

The government hacked a path through it, east to west. Take a step left or right and you're ass deep in devil's club or bog water. You would not believe the mosquitoes that rise in black and humming clouds. Spray on the chemicals, layer your clothes, throw netting over that and spray it too for good measure, and you're still fucked. Those tiny stabbing bastards will find a way to your tender flesh.

I stop by Monroe's house at dawn, load him and his gear, and then drive us to the trailhead. My truck is the only vehicle in the lot. Camping season is kaput and man-eating bug season has begun. This is early fall before the first hard freeze or fresh termination dust on the mountains. Any second now for one or both, however.

Monroe is a willowy fellow of Irish descent, so he slathers his pale skin with sunblock, then slips on a fancy vest he probably snagged off the rack the night before, and squeezes himself into a high tech pack with a slick neon yellow shell and enough elastic webbing to truss a moose, if we see one. It looks heavy and probably is since he's stuffed all of the camping gear in there. I carry my meager supplies, including a sixer of suds, in a rucksack. In my left hand I heft a fishing rod. Trout run in the streams yonder and I've a mind to hook a couple for dinner if the opportunity arises.

Ominous clouds sludge in from the east as we begin our trek. The plan is to hike a few hours, pitch the tent, and maybe recon the surrounding area. In the morning we'll head home. Nothing fancy, nor prolonged or grueling.

We rest periodically. I slug water from my dented canteen and lover boy pops the top on a wine cooler. The trail winds through barren hills and stands of black spruce. Gloom spreads its wings over the land. The air tastes damp, and yes sir, the mosquitoes and the gnats taste us.

No point in making this an epic: At last we reach a patch of dry ground on a hill and set camp. Tent, fire pit, the works. Monroe asks about bears, and he asks about them a lot. I'm not too worried as they tend to be fat and complacent this close to winter. Spring, when the beasts emerge lean and starved, is the dangerous time.

Nonetheless, I tell Monroe that dearie-me, we'd best be on guard against those man-eaters. I instruct him to keep trash and scraps in a sealed container to minimize ursine temptation, which is a sound idea, but fun to watch him perform as he casts worried glances into the underbrush. I scan the horizon and judge that indeed a storm was approaching, although the weather forecast has made no such mention.

I grab my fishing rod and tell him to fall in.

"Fishing? In this weather?" He cups his hand to catch the first raindrops.

"Morning is better. But it's okay. A little rain won't keep them from biting."

His expression is glum as he zips his fancy yellow pastel slicker that matches the glaring yellow backpack shell. The idea of hooking a fish doubtless hurts his tender feelings. I try not to sneer while thinking that Ferris had certainly gone the whole nine yards to find my opposite.

The map indicates a creek within a mile or so and I wade into the bushes, hapless Monroe on my heel. The possibility of a fresh trout fillet appeals. Moreover, it amuses me to let branches whip back at his face and hear his muffled exclamations. I chuckle and think of the skinning knife strapped to my hip. It's the journey, not the destination, right?

I almost trip headlong into the hole. Monroe saves me. He snatches my belt as I teeter on the crumbling brink, and yanks me back. Faster reflexes than I'd have guessed. He has to use his entire bodyweight, and thus counterbalanced, we fall awkwardly among the alder and devil's club.

"What the hell is that?" he says.

"A hole in the ground," I say. Thorns in my shin, rain trickling down my neck, mosquitoes drilling every available surface, all conspire to provoke my ire. Not just a hole. Not a sinkhole, or an animal burrow, or anything of nature. Upturned clay rings the pit. Water seeps gray and orange from its rude walls.

"You know, it looks like a grave." He gains his feet and peers into the hole. "Holy shit. Somebody dug this thing not too long ago."

"It's not a grave. The shape is fubar."

"Yeah? That a rule? Gotta be six by six on the nose? Maybe they were in a hurry. Digging around big rocks. I'm telling you."

"Maybe a retarded hillbilly dug it."

Sarcastic as I might be, he has it right. This is a grave, albeit an oblong, off-kilter grave, six or seven feet deep and freshly dug. It doesn't matter that the shape is wrong; the hole radiates unmistakable purpose. I don't see a shovel or tracks. The latter bothers me. Should be tracks in the wet dirt. Should be more dirt. Should be broken branches. Anything. I'm not a tracker. Still the consistency of the clay, the wisps of steam, convince me that the mysterious digger did the deed and left within the past hour or two.

"Man, what do you think?" Monroe says with less worry and more eagerness than I like.

"I think we should mind our own business and get back to camp. Call it a day."

"Hold on." He swats away a cloud of mosquitoes. "I'm curious. Aren't you?"

"No, Monroe, not really. Either it's a grave, or it's not. If not, then who gives a shit? If it is, then presumably someone will be along presently to dump a corpse. I'd prefer to be elsewhere." I don't wait around to hold a debate. Hell with fishing. Nightfall looms and I want to put distance between us and that site. The need to get away is overpowering.

We make it back to base without incident. I feel Monroe's sulky gaze the whole way. I consider pulling stakes. The idea of folding the tent is unappetizing and impractical. Blundering through the forest in darkness is how tinhorns and Cheechakos wind up with busted legs or lost for a week. No thanks. I light a fire and boil water for the MREs I brought. Keep my trusty .9mm pistol handy, too. Rain starts pissing down for real. We huddle under a makeshift canopy of spruce boughs and a tarp. Blind and deaf, and choking on campfire smoke.

Isn't until after supper and a third brew that I realize I've forgotten about my half-assed plan to kill my little buddy.

Late that night I wake to the drum of rain on the tent fabric. Pitch black.

"Elmer," Monroe says. He sounds tense.

"Yeah?"

"Why'd you bring me here?"

"I didn't. You wanted to."

"Uh-uh. *You* wanted this."

"Monroe, shut the fuck up and let me sleep."

"Something occurred to me when I saw that grave. You made it. You made it and then brought me to it."

I lie very still. I smell the fear on his breath.

"Elmer?"

"Yeah?"

"Great minds think alike. This is for Ferris."

He sighs heavily next to me in the dark before smashing the rock down on my head.

You are stripped utterly naked when confronted by your own mortality. You are stripped utterly naked when you are dropped to the bottom of a hole and buried in the mud, handful by handful, and left to rot. The worms crawl in.

Two items from the grim days of my youth.

Dad and his brothers were into cockfighting. Many a blue-collar paycheck was won and lost on his prize Lubaang and Asil warrior birds. My people spent generations in El Paso and they'd picked up the sport from the Mexicans. Gorgeous destroyers, our fighting roosters. These weren't simple chickens like you see on a farm. A damn sight bigger and meaner than their domestic kin. Orange and black and sheened emerald, tall as a man's knee, and eager for violence. One glimpse and you could see the devil in them, you could trace the line of descent back to dinosaur raptors.

Dad taped razorblades and jags of glass to their spurs and turned them loose in a killing pit. Hell of a lot of blood and feathers, afterward. I liked the blood and the smell of the blood. The black feathers were my favorite. I gathered a bunch and made a war bonnet. A boy at school offended me and I pursued him in my war bonnet of orange and black feathers and threw him down and rubbed his face in the playground dirt.

In retrospect, Mom and little sister flying the coop, so to speak, when I was four, the cockfighting, boozy gambling, and a procession of whores that followed my dad around might've had an effect on me. Also, we relocated from Texas to Alaska. The main difference between the two states is the distinct lack of an electric chair in the Land of the Midnight Sun.

The other thing is, I could do a weird trick with my mind. Got hooked on the idea of telekinesis after reading an old science fiction novel called *The Power* about some dude with superhuman abilities. God alone can say how many hours I spent squinting in concentration. And it worked, sometimes. I tipped water glasses and caused electronic devices to go haywire without touching them. I could stop a clock by beaming death-thoughts at it. Once I concentrated hard enough to levitate a cinderblock about six inches above the garage floor. Dad stumbled upon me; I was out cold, bleeding from my nose and ears. A three day coma followed; doctors diagnosed it as epilepsy. Dear lord, the apocalyptic nightmares I suffered: oceans of blood, rivers of maggots, the damned leading the damned across plains of fire and ash. The damned pointing their crisped, skeletal fingers at me and wailing in unison.

Shot a silver streak through my hair. At least the girls thought it cute. I was too scared to screw around with ESP and telekinesis after that. Set it aside with other childish things.

There's nothing dramatic about the transmogrification of lowly Elmer D. from dead meat into a walking and talking abomination unleashed upon the hapless people of the Earth. It occurs between one drip of rain from a spruce bough and the next. An owl glides in and snatches a squirrel. A cloud smokes across the face of the moon. The night takes a long breath, and then I am among all that is.

I have no memory of clawing up out of the muck, although it would be keen if my cadaverous hand had thrust free of the soil like in all those hoary old movies. One moment I lie interred in smothering blackness, the next I find myself striding through a twilight forest where mist hangs from evergreen branches. Gray upon gray. In this instant, I question nothing, I ponder nothing. My only goal is to plow forward into the infinite grayness.

A strange sensation to be plugged into every birdcall, every snapped twig, every stir of grass in the breeze, the scents of dead leaves, loam, and moose droppings; yet disconnected, numb. My body is a lead float, adrift. It oscillates between here and there, fat and thin. Hideously immense, yet helium light. I lurch, dragging my left foot. My power is enormous. I brush tree trunks and they crackle and uproot and crash.

Flames leap from a pile of logs. This clues me in to the fact it isn't sunset or dawn, but rather the dark of night. My sight penetrates spectrums beyond the human norm. Constellations flare, white against gray. I *hear* the stars as a celestial chorus, molten atoms colliding and chiming.

Three hunters squat around the fire as men have done since saber tooth tigers prowled the land. A motor home is parked nearby. Electric light streams from the windows. I've crossed many miles in a blink to arrive in the parking lot. Sweat, beer, gun oil, I smell it all. Seven hundred yards to my left, an owl regurgitates the pellet of the squirrel it gobbled for dinner. I smell that too.

None of the hunters notice my apparition at the edge of the cheery circle of their fire. Unlike me, they can't see in the dark. Soap bubbles form above the head of the nearest man. The bubble shimmers and expands. It contains images of a blue-collar truck commercial: happy children, barking dogs, muddy Fords, him sighting down on a bighorn ram and blasting it off a ledge. Him plowing his stolid wife, blowing out the candles on a cake. That sort of deal. Once glance tells me the life story of Hunter Numero Uno.

A phantom approximation of his face swells the bubble. It whispers to me in the language of electron particles, "Master!"

I nearly swoon in an ecstasy of desire and my tongue lolls to my grimy navel. I am starved.

One by one, I seize them and crack their skulls and scoop out the brain matter and gulp it whole. Sparks sizzle and drip down my chin, light me up from the inside. For a few moments, before the incredible rush fades, I, as Whitman said, contain multitudes.

This transformation started long before the inciting incident in the hole. Maybe it had been occurring my entire life. Ten bucks says Dad's sperm was already mutating when it plowed into Mom's egg. He'd gotten spritzed with Agent Orange during his tour in Vietnam and suffered all kinds of health problems afterward. He drank, and so did Mom. There was also a sense of cursedness haunting the family line. Dad went in a wreck. Dad's cousin was an ace Alaskan bush pilot who death-spiraled his Cessna into Lake Illiamna. An uncle was eaten up by cancer despite living a clean, Presbyterian life, no smokes, no booze. An aunt did ten years in the pen and got hit by a motorcyclist three days after her parole. Somebody else got shanked in a brawl at the Gold Digger, back when it *really* was a saloon with sawdust and a mechanical bull and full of motorcycle club thugs and crankheads looking to stab you in the kidney. My sister, she joined the FBI. Her name was Jeanie and last I saw her she was eighteen months and counting. Rumor is she went down in a corruption sting and sliced her wrists.

Dumb luck I didn't pop out of the womb with two heads.

I like the idea that death is a transitory state; my passage from pupa to final instar. I'm a whole new insect. While the notion I've become posthuman sends my nerves a twanging, I'm not exactly afraid, or even concerned. Oh, a tiny fragment of the old me mewls and screeches in its cage, but to no greater effect than the whine of a fly under glass.

The Usurper deigns to answer my imprecations at one point.

We are the next big thing. This whisper issues from inside me; it oozes forth. The whisper is blood welling from a puncture. Sexless, dispassionate. *We are Omega, we are Kingdom Come. We have always been, we will always be.* I receive a picture, muddy and flickering, of warm seas and green light, of trilobites and worms and moss. Dinosaurs have not been invented, but the devil is everywhere.

We are the apparatus. We are the apex. We are first.

I cannot reply. I'm trying to decide if apex means precisely what it intimates and if it's something I want to be (*of course you do, you ninny!*). Again, images coalesce from the ether, like bursts of speech through shortwave static. The future unravels in an arc of projectile vomit from the jaws of Saturn: an approaching tsunami of blood and peeled flesh and more blood. A thousand feet tall, rolling at a thousand miles per hour. The first of many such waves. Wave after wave of carnage, and me in gigantic repose atop a heap of bones. My friends and foes, beneath me at last!

Ferris is fucking Monroe. We don't have to take that kind of bullshit. We should fix their wagons. We are the apparatus. We are the way.

That sounds reasonable. A man should attend his priorities. Family comes first.

I loved monster movies as a kid. Don't all boys love monster movies?

Dawn of the Dead. Evil Dead. Reanimator. From Beyond. The Fly. The Thing. Right on. I dug it, especially zombie flicks. The shambling undead did it for me.

Had my first hot and heavy teen make out session with Julie Vellum during a screening of *Night of the Living Dead* at her dad's split-level Girdwood house. I'd seen the movie plenty of times, but this was super-fucking-hot cheerleader Julie Vellum, shag rugs, a leather couch, and her pop's brand new Magnavox television we were talking about. That's why Mr. V tolerated me sniffing around his princess that lost summer of my junior year in high school—like me, he was a devout fan of classic fright features. Val Lewton and George Romero were unto gods in Mr. V's estimation. Death gods, I thought, but kept such smart-ass observations to myself by concentrating upon the sky-high hemline of his daughter's skirt.

The three of us camped on that giant couch. Me on one end, Julie on the other, her dad, larger than life, occupying the middle. We kids sipped bottles of Coke while Mr. V blasted his way through a fifth of Maker's Mark and talked over all the good parts. Soon, he slurred and blessedly lengthy gaps interrupted his monologue. He rose and staggered toward the kitchen in quest of more booze. There followed a series of thuds and then a crash that shook the living room.

"Holy shit!" I said.

"Oh, don't worry. That's just him passing out. He does it all the time." Julie gave me a cat-eyed look. Two seconds later we met in the middle. She kissed me as my hands went roaming places they had no business, and then she jacked me off like she'd done it before.

I made it with Julie a half dozen times before school started again. Once the frost set in, she dropped me like a bad habit. Despite my momentary anguish, it was for the best. White trash, both of us. However, she had a little money, and that made all the difference. She also carried a torch for the quarterback on our football team. Beating his ass wouldn't have been a problem; I was really good at inflicting pain by then. Size and meanness were on my side, although I made certain to keep the latter under wraps. My gambit was to smile and keep my mouth shut whenever possible. Didn't matter. Most everyone was piss-scared of me for reasons they couldn't express. The assholes voted me most likely to wind up in prison or in an early grave.

This was why I suppressed my rage, and why I let JV saunter into the sunset with her trophy jock. The things I envisioned doing in the name of love would've landed me in Goose Bay Penitentiary or a nuthouse. Instead, I went into the garden and ate worms and went quietly mad exactly as the moldy poets from pen and quill days had done.

Nightmares afflicted me with a vengeance I hadn't experienced since adolescence. Who knows what precipitated them. Stress? Hormones? Whatever the case, these were the stuff of legends. Imagine being trapped inside a waxworks dedicated to atrocities, and all the doors sealed. Horrors from pre-adolescence reinvented themselves into subtler, more sophisticated iterations freighted with guilt and shame. My nightmares had *matured* and they took a cat-o'-nine-tails to my psyche. I was visited every night for several months.

The phenomenon leaked into waking life. I became gaunt, pallid, and terser than ever. I forced myself to wear a shit-eating grin while secretly worrying that I'd gone around the bend. I began to hallucinate. At school I caught glimpses of my classmates and teachers wearing death masks. Some were pale and serene, others contorted and agonized, and still others dripping blood, or caved in, or sheared away entirely to expose the cavern of the mind.

The unexpected result of this being that I got better with my own mask, more scrupulous about tightening the bolts. Even so, it's a miracle I kept a straight face while gazing at exposed brains or punctured eyeballs. I got good at nodding and smiling.

Nonetheless, a particular incident almost undid me. One morning during passing period Julie's locker door was open and for some reason, don't know what the hell I was thinking, I eased on over to chat her up. Second week of school, me being lonely and horny, not in my right mind, which covers any teenage boy, but me more so. The door swung shut and there she stood, enfolded in the jock's arms, playing tonsil hockey. The bell broke up their tryst and they sauntered away, not acknowledging my presence as I stared after them.

I didn't feel anything, the exact same way I didn't feel anything the time Dad got drunk and slugged me in the jaw and laid me on my ass. The same lights flickered in the dark regions of my mind, the same roar of distant wind rose in my ears. The locker and a section of the concrete floor dissolved as if by acid. A hole bored into the earth and I had an erection that nearly split my pants. No nosebleed this time around. I was afraid, though. Terrified enough that I got away and got drunk on Dad's stock of Old Crow, damn the consequences were he to discover the theft, and I made myself forget. But the nightmares. Jesus. Jesus.

Dogged, simpleminded stubbornness got me though the autumn more or less intact, and largely unscarred.

What *scarred* me was getting ejected face-first through the windshield of Dad's 1982 Chevy that winter. He hit a patch of ice and left the road doing around sixty-five and smacked a berm of snow packed tight as concrete by the state road graders. Never a compulsive buckler of seatbelts, I flew over the berm and burrowed into the virgin snow beyond. Dad burned up with the Chevy. Odd, how of all the folks that were rendered a horror show in my visions, I hadn't ever seen his death mask until I glimpsed him through the flames and melting glass.

No more nightmares for a long, long time after that incident. No dreams of any kind. Sleep became a chrysalis.

) ❩ ❫ ● ❪ ❨ (

Apparently, a side effect of apex prowess is peckishness. The Glenn Highway spreads before me, a glistening buffet table strung with cozy sodium lights for mood.

Whatever manipulates me is not traveling of its own volition so much as being pulled as a steel filing by the mother of all magnets. The delays and digressions are but zigzag deviations of a neutron star as it's dragged into a black hole.

In any event, I zig through a rest stop near Eagle River and am compelled to annihilate the dozen or so inhabitants. Well, I *say* compelled—it's not as if I require much arm-twisting.

I wrench doors from semi-trucks, and peel the roofs off compact cars. I am a beast cracking oyster shells. My need is overwhelming, my appetite is profound. I lick eyes from sockets, then the brains, the guts, the cracked-from-the-bone marrow, and even swallow a few bones whole. I expand and contract, I divide and reform. I squirm and slash. I am a pit that is everywhere. Light bends around me, or it is consumed.

A handful of survivors flee into the dour Plexiglas and cement octagon with a stylized eagle blazoned on the sloped roof. My reflection warps against the glass, or perhaps warps the glass itself. A cockscomb of jagged flint erupts from the sundered dome of my cranium. Spurs of razor-tipped basalt extrude from my wrists, elbows, and knees. Even as I take in its ghastly splendor, my physiognomy alters and is transfigured into something far worse, something that overwhelms my capacity to articulate its awfulness.

I am resplendently dire. I am a figure of awe. I am a horror.

They barricade the entrance with soda machines and that delays me for a few seconds once I finish outside. I find them cowering and gibbering prayers under Formica tables and in bathroom stalls. Somebody stabs me with a hunting knife, somebody else plugs me with a small caliber handgun. Six or seven teeny popgun flashes in the dark among the roaring and screaming. It hardly matters.

Toward the end, I flop, maw agape, on the concrete floor at the end of the demolished gallery and let that sweet hot stream of blood and viscera roll down my gullet. Overhead, the lights flicker crazily and shadows rip themselves apart.

When it's finished, I shamble forth from the despoiled building. Pasted in gore and excrement, crowned by a garland of intestines, I strike a Jesus Christ pose in the center of the highway.

Traffic routes around me, makes me consider the legend of the stampeding buffalo herd breaking around a man if he remains motionless and tall in his boots. The sun arcs across the sky four times, and so swiftly it sheds tracers of flame. A green-gold ball of bubbling gas, a bacterium in division. The amoeba sun segments in rhythm with my own squamous brain cells. The sun strobes and vanishes. The sliver moon swings down and sinks into my breast, cold as a fang of ice. That which nests within my DNA blooms and reticulates as it rewrites parameters of operation.

The city awaits.

I project myself forward along a corridor of alternating light and darkness, contract through a crimson doorway, and into a dance hall. My need to gorge is satiated and replaced by an urge I don't recognize. A wormhole opens behind my left eye. The void shivers and yearns; it lusts for sensation.

Music dies as the DJ apprehends me with his bemused gaze. Then the dancing. All heads turn toward my dreadful countenance.

What happens at the Gold Digger Saloon. I cannot speak of it. The ecstasy is the sun going nova in my brain. Nova, then collapsing inward, a snow crystal flaking, disintegrating, and then nothing left except a point of darkness, the wormy head of a black strand that bores its way to the core of everything.

We aren't rich. The pool house is our compromise—as long as Ferris didn't push for a mother-in-law cottage, I'd see she had herself a full-length heated pool to do laps. Ferris was on the swim team in high school and college and she's tried valiantly to maintain her form. The YMCA is a no go. Too many sluggish old people in the lane, too many screaming kids, too many creepy dudes in the bleachers. Thus, the pool house. A gesture of defiance in the face of brutal Alaska winters.

I enter through the skylight. A long dead star field turns and burns over my shoulder. The coals that were stars sigh.

Ferris lies naked and icy pale against the dappled green water. Her eyes are closed. Occasionally her arms and legs scissor languidly. Beneath her, is her seal shadow and the white tile that slopes away into haziness. Vapors shift across her body and carry its scent to me, sharp and clean amid the faint tang of chlorine. She daydreams on the cusp of sleep and I taste the procession of phantoms that illuminate her inner landscape. Mine is not among them.

I descend as if a great spider on its wire, then stop and hang in place. This thing that has hijacked and reconstituted my body, reduced my consciousness and placed it in a bell jar, is drawn to her. More specifically, that which I have become is drawn to something *within* her. I don't comprehend the intricacies. I can only bear mute witness to the spectacle as it unfolds.

A black spot stains at the bottom of the pool. The spot spreads across the white bed, a ring of darkness widening as pieces of tile crumble into the depths. It is a pit, slackening directly below my lovely, frigid wife. My betrayer wife, my arm extending, my claw, hollow as a siphon, its shadow upon her betrayer's face, and the abyssal trench an iris beneath. Wife, come along to Kingdom Come, come to the underworld.

Her eyes snap open.

"I didn't fuck him," she says. "I fantasized about it, plenty."

Monroe is absent from the scene, and that's a shame. Every pore in me longs to drink his blood, to liquefy him, fry him, to have his heart in my fist. To ram his heart down her throat.

"I didn't fuck him. Elmer, I didn't. I should've."

Her blood. His blood. Their atoms.

I open my mouth (maw) to accuse, to excoriate, and the dead song of the dead stars worms out. But she doesn't blink, she repeats that she hasn't fucked him, hasn't fucked him. She projects her innocence in an electromagnetic cone meant to kill. She is entirely too composed, this fragile sack of skin and water.

She says, "Are you here to hurt me, Elmer?" Her smile is pitiless, it cuts. "The time you came home drunk and forced me? There's a word for you, hon. Don't you remember what you've done?"

I don't remember. I seethe.

Difficult to concentrate through the interference of her thoughts that explain via pointillism how Monroe opportunistically slaughtered me and then so much like the narrator of "The Tell-Tale Heart" had succumbed to guilt and paranoia and eventually fled the country. The FBI hunts him in connection with my disappearance. He could be anywhere. She suspects Mexico. Monroe always had a romanticized notion about Mexico and what he could do there, a super gringo lover man.

The little shit swallowed her teary stories of my cruelty and violence. He'd done me in as an act of vengeance. An act that only earned Ferris's contempt. She is utterly my creature and let no man cast asunder what all the powers above and below had seen fit to forge.

I convulse with a complicated longing and snatch for her. She's too quick. She rolls, sleek and white, and flashes downward amid a cloud of bubbles into the pit. Fool that I am, I follow.

We meet in darkness, each illuminated by a weak spotlight that dims and brightens with our breathing. I sense immense coldness and space pressing against the bubble where we reside. I am whole. My cloven skull and rotting flesh are restored. My mind is papered over with gold star stickers and crepe.

She points an automatic pistol at me. I understand that it's a present from her would-be lover. The barrel aligns with my eye. I have traveled through the barrel and been deposited in this limbo.

"I warned him. Told him he'd never succeed. If I couldn't kill you, then there was no hope for him." She laughs and shakes the wet hair from her eyes. "Arsenic in your coffee every day for three months. Nothing. For God's sake, I frosted your birthday cake with rat poison."

Now that she mentions it, now that her thoughts bleed into mine, I recall the bitter coffee, the odd aftertaste of the icing on my last cake. A skull and crossbones has hung over our marriage for years. Yet, I remain. What does it mean?

"I hurt you, but I couldn't kill you. Monroe couldn't. Nobody can. You died in childhood. Maybe you were never born. Maybe the parasite that fruits your corpse is the only true part of you that existed."

Am I merely a figment? If so, I am the most rapacious, carnivorous, and vengeful figment she will have the misfortune to encounter. I strike aside the gun and reach for her. A black halo of light manifests around Ferris. Her arms spread wide and she becomes the very figure of a dread and terrible insect queen. The enormity of her eclipses my own.

She clutches me and the sting slides in. "It was always here, love. In all of us, always."

It's apparent that I've miscalculated again.

Reality has bent and bent. I look past the nimbus of black flame into her cold eyes. Reality just goes right ahead and comes apart.

Darkness rolls back to daylight. It's spring and balmy. The breeze is redolent with sweet green sap and the bloom of roses. Guests and children of the guests clutter a lawn that's too bright and too green to be real. "Death to Everyone" by good old Will Oldham crackles over the speakers.

I'm stuffed into a poorly fitted tux. At my side, Ferris shines as radiantly white as the Queen of Winter.

I have seen this, relived this, in a thousand-thousand nightmares.

My hand overlaps hers as we saw the blade into that multi-tiered cake. She opens her mouth and bites through the icing, the bunting, and my brittle soul. I shudder and kiss her. It feels no different than kissing ice bobbed up from the bottom of an arctic lake. She inhales my heat and my vitality before I can inhale hers. She's always been stronger, in the only way that counts. She always will be stronger.

Oldham's voice fades and the guests stare at us in hushed expectation.

Nearby, a little girl in a black funeral dress begins to sing the "Hearse Song" to the boy she's tormenting with malice or affection, take your pick:

"They put you in a big black box
And cover you up with dirt and rocks.
All goes well for about a week,
Then your coffin begins to leak.
The worms crawl in, the worms crawl out,
The worms play pinochle in your snout,
They eat your eyes, they eat your nose,
They eat the jelly between your toes."

This time around, I do what I should've in the first place all those lost years ago. Instead of cutting a piece for the first guest in line, I grip the knife and slice my throat. Blood fans the cake and Ferris's white dress. She throws back her head and laughs. I sink to my knees in the thirsty grass. The sun pales and contracts to a black-limned ring. Red shadows pour through the trees, drench the lawn, and reduce the paralyzed spectators to negatives. I try to speak. Worms crawl out.

Ferris's parents loved me. I first met them during Thanksgiving when she and I stayed over at the family casa—Ferris slept in her old room with the Prince poster and a mountain of heart-shaped pillows and teddy bears while I bunked in the basement on a leather sofa between her old man's pool table and a gun safe.

There was a tense moment when she removed her shades and revealed the Lichtenburg flower of a purple knot under her eye. Ferris was so very smooth. She spun a story about getting kicked in the face during swim practice, and her family bought it. She wasn't speaking to *me* except as required, probably hadn't even decided whether to stay with me or toss her engagement ring into the trash.

Hell of it was, at that early stage in our romance I didn't care much either way.

Turkey, gravy, pumpkin pie, and afterward, a quart of Jim Beam passed around a circle of a half-dozen of Ferris's menfolk. Salt of the earth bumpkins who raised coon dogs and revved the engines on four-wheelers at the gravel pit and picked through piles at the dump for fun.

You like John Wayne? one truck-driving uncle wanted to know. Shore as hail, I love the Duke! And with that, I was in like Flynn. My lumberjack beard, plaid coat, and knowledge of professional football didn't go amiss, either.

Her dad welcomed me to the family with teary eyes and a bear hug. I wasn't "nothin' like them pussies she usually brings home from college." How right my future in-law hillbillies were! Not three days before that Clampett-style feast I'd beaten a UAA fraternity brother within an inch of his life for giving me the stink eye as I staggered home from the Gold Digger Saloon. I made the letter-sweater-wearing jock try to eat a parking meter. The whole time Ferris's family exchanged jocular crudities at the supper table, my hand was in my pocket, caressing the frat boy's braces, with a few teeth still stuck in them, like a God-fearing Catholic fondling his rosary. It was the only thing that kept me from stabbing one of those bozos with a steak knife.

I gave the lot of those silly, inbred bastards my best aw-shucks grin, and daydreamed about how lovely and charred their slack-jawed skulls would shine from the cinders of a three A.M. house fire.

Aided by booze and a vivid imagination, I survived dinner and into the following day. Driving home, the stars were blacked. Snow fell like a sonofabitch. Every now and again the tires slipped against ice and the truck shook. Dad's ghost muttered in my ear. My heart knocked and I forgot to blink for at least forty miles. The high beams carved a tunnel into the blizzard. Patsy Cline came on the radio out of Anchorage. Patsy sang "Crazy" and that was our song, all right.

Ferris reached across the gulf from the passenger side and held my hand. Her fingers clamped cold and tight over mine. In the rearview there was nothing but darkness, snowflakes endlessly collapsing in our wake, and a black slick of road painted red in the taillights' glow.

THE ATTIC

CATHERINE MACLEOD

Most of Micah's funeral is a merciful blur now, a hundred odd moments of my life gone and good riddance. But not all of it.

I remember the startled looks I got, walking into the Church of the Risen alone for the first time.

Old Maisie Langan bleating, "What's *she* doing here?" and Davena Simon hissing back, "Hush! She doesn't know any better."

I remember wondering where they thought I should be, if not at the funeral for my husband and his parents, who'd burned in the car with him.

But valley people don't use the word *funeral*. The service is called *acknowledgement of death*. I never understood all the local expressions, any more than I understood why Pastor Vance read from The Book of Corinthians at every service. I remember him droning on about our Lord rising from the darkness on the third day, and how we awake to righteousness, and come forth in perfection.

I remember praying he'd run out of breath.

And a remark that should've felt as if it had just come out of the blue, but didn't. As I shook hands at the door—some of the grips disturbingly limp, a few uncomfortably hard, and all of them too quick for good manners—Maisie, smelling of that morning's diaper, tottered over and said, "I suppose now you'll want the key to the attic."

"Hey, we're here. You want to get some coffee?"

"Yes, please." I shake myself awake, groggy and stiff. It's dark. I check the road signs and the map crumpled in my lap, and see that I've travelled eight hundred miles today. "Are you stopping for the night?"

"Yeah. What about you?"

"I need to keep going."

I hop down from the passenger seat and watch as he backs his truck into an impossibly narrow parking space. His name is Chook Travis. I wait for him at the diner door.

"Thanks for the ride. I'm sorry I wasn't better company."

"That's okay. Tell you the truth, you looked as if you needed the sleep."

"Tell you the truth, you were right. Here, let me buy you some supper."

I hold out two twenties. He takes one with a grin. "Thanks." I wait. It happens. His smile fades, and, like every trucker I've ridden with today, he takes another look at my bruised face and my wedding ring, and holds out his cell phone. "Sure you don't want to call someone?"

"No, thanks anyway."

Like all the others, he doesn't ask any more questions. Probably wouldn't answer any, either—truck drivers are, by and large, a chivalrous lot.

I can't tell them I have no one to call. Anyway, the only phone number I've ever memorized is Grayman's, and the way my luck is running he'd probably answer.

The diner is busy, even this late. It's nice to be on familiar ground again, but I keep to the corners as I wait for my sandwich, just in case someone recognizes me. It's a long shot, and maybe it wouldn't matter, but I don't want anyone from the valley to hear tell of me. I eat outside, watching the lot lizards in their high heels trolling for business.

A big man exits the diner and makes a beeline for me. I immediately wonder where I should hit him to bring him down the fastest. "Excuse me? My friend in there says you need a ride north." I glance back through the diner window. Chook sees me looking, nods toward my companion, and gives me a thumbs-up. I tip him a two-fingered salute.

"Thanks. I'd appreciate it."

Truckers travel a different line of sight than other drivers, seen but only briefly noticed. Few people could describe a rig a minute after passing it, even fewer could identify the driver. I don't think they're supposed to carry riders; something about insurance. But it's a different world up here. Different rules. The trucker who picked me up at dawn passed me on to another when he stopped, and they've been moving me north ever since.

Grayman was a big fan of hiding in plain sight. I didn't think much of the old sayings he liked to spout, like *The more things change, the more they stay the same* and *All good things must end*, but *People don't notice what's right in front of them* was disturbingly true.

Ten miles up the highway, Chook's friend offers me his cell. "You want to call someone?"

"No, thanks anyway."

He lets it go, thank God. I have no answers for either of us. I don't know what to do except get as far away from Riser's Valley as I can.

The trouble is, part of me never left.

A flurry of whispers blew around the pastor's drawing room as I entered. Apparently I shouldn't have been at the reception, either. Then Bryce Simon said, "Would you like a cup of tea, Nell?" The offer was more than kind—he didn't expect me to know rules no one had taught me. He didn't think the dancing bear actually knew the minuet.

"That would be nice."

What I really wanted was a glass of the sherry Mrs. Vance knew better than to serve with Davena around, and what I wanted more a moment later was to throw it in Davena's face. Even for her, it took a lot of gall to yank the hair-stick out of my bun, letting my hair fall down my back. She waved it in front of my face and said, "You don't have the right to wear this now."

There was an appalled gasp from my neighbours, who knew that a decent woman doesn't wear her hair down in public, and another as I snatched the stick back with one hand and cracked her across the mouth with the other. Watching her stagger back, pale with shock, I think I might have smiled.

A soft voice beside me said, "Nell, you must be tired. May I drive you home?"

"Please."

Bryce walked out without a look at his wife. He didn't speak again until we'd passed the place where Micah's car had gone off the road the day before. The skid marks were black and ugly.

"She doesn't always think before she acts," he said. I noted he hadn't actually expressed regret for her behaviour. "Josie should've told you, but I suppose she didn't think you'd need to know for a while. The hair-stick comes out as soon as you hear of your husband's death. You braid your hair until you come out of mourning."

"Oh." I'd never noticed that. But then, I'd never seen anyone actually *mourn* in the valley.

"Just keep it in mind." As he pulled up to the house he asked, "Will you be all right here alone?"

"I'll be fine. I just need some rest." I turned to thank him for the ride, and caught him eying my hair like most men would bare breasts. I got out and hurried inside, locking the door as he drove away.

The quiet was a relief. I was glad for the bed of coals in the kitchen stove, and the wood fire snapping in it a minute later. The fridge was stuffed with food the neighbours had brought that morning, far too much for one person. I ate a sandwich; then, when it stayed down, I ate another. It wasn't the time to let myself get weak.

I left the lights off, knowing the neighbours were watching the house. I didn't even have to wonder about it. Most of the women would have known that Josie had the house keys on her when she died, including the one for the attic door. I wondered if any of them had ever been told they had no right to wear their husband's hair-stick.

I braided my hair then, combing my fingers through it as Micah used to do. He'd been a good husband to me. He'd never thought of me as an outsider. But sitting there in the dark, I realized he'd been the only thing protecting me from those who did.

I'm sorry to have left Emery. Sorry I'll never go back to that little town. It's funny, I guess, that I arrived there wanting more than anything to keep moving. But, sitting on the bench outside the grocery store, waiting for the next bus that would take me farther away from Grayman, an accident happened: I noticed my surroundings.

The closest I'd ever been to the country was robbing a house with a back yard. I was a city girl, raised in a puzzle of alleys and shortcuts. No photo had ever prepared me for Emery—I could see for miles just by moving my eyes. The distant mountains were green-turning-gold, the sky an unnameable blue.

Whether I was simply starved for beauty, or exhausted from being on high alert for too long, my sudden yearning for peace and quiet was stronger than my fear of Grayman.

I wanted to stay there; the waitress I replaced at the truck stop wanted out. Her job was nothing new to me, and I liked the boss. Ace gave his girls one free meal a day and kept his nose out of our personal lives. Most of the customers were nice enough, and I could handle the ones who weren't—there are ways to show a predator which of you has the sharpest teeth, and I know most of them.

I rented a small trailer across the road. The owner said, "It's nothing fancy, but it's clean and in good repair." I checked the door locks. It would have taken me at least three minutes to pick them, which meant it would take most other thieves longer. There was hot and cold running water, just enough furniture, and a place to hide my exit bag. I paid for three months in advance, thinking two might be the longest I could resist the urge to keep running. But I stayed put. I liked tuning my radio to the Top 40 instead of the police report. I liked wandering up the highway to take in the scenery, and the occasional drive to the nearest big town with the cook, Shana, when we had an afternoon off.

During one of those drives I noticed the road sign for Riser's Valley.

"What's down there?" I asked.

"Not much. I went down one evening, just to sightsee, you know? Six o'clock and there was nobody on the streets. You could see them through the windows, having supper. A few of them come into the stop once in a while, but they don't say much. They don't seem to know how to talk to outsiders."

Quite a few of our customers fit that description. Some were just shy. "A valley? Sounds pretty."

"I guess."

I tried out the free internet at the town library. There were no hits for Riser's Valley. That seemed just about quiet enough.

I didn't think about being lonely. I'd never had real friends; I'd never known any real love but my mother's. I thought you couldn't miss what you'd never had.

Until the day Micah walked into the diner.

In the valley, on the day before his wedding, the groom gives his intended a wooden hair-stick. The bride twists her hair up into a bun and inserts the stick to hold it in place. Her husband takes it out on their wedding night, knowing that from then on he's the only man who'll see her hair down.

Micah made mine from oak, a splinter of a pew from an abandoned church. He and his father, Ben, had torn the building down for the new property owner, who didn't care what happened to the wood as long as they hauled it off his land.

He drove me past the site as he took me to meet his parents. "I thought it was a handsome building," he said, "even if it *was* old and weathered. I'm glad you have a piece of it now."

"So am I. Thank you, dear."

He blushed when I called him *dear*. He was a year younger than me, but sometimes it might as well have been ten. I'd always thought of myself as cold, had never been in love to know how it should feel. But I did love him, I think. He was soft-spoken and steady. He'd never been anywhere near the world I'd escaped. In the year he was courting me, he brought me trinkets and wild flowers. He waited until I finished my shift and walked me home. He barely touched me for the first three months, until I said, "Micah, will you *please* kiss me now?"

Even then he hesitated. He combed his fingers through my hair, almost as dark as his, as straight as his was curly. Ran them over my face until we were both breathing hard. But his kiss was gentle and tentative, and he backed away first. I wondered if he'd ever touched a woman before.

But he didn't speak to me much beyond placing his order when he came in the diner with Ben. After a while I realized his father didn't know about us. I didn't ask Micah why; I had too many secrets of my own to criticize his. He was getting ready to start his own life, I thought. I was his first big decision.

Not knowing who my own father was, I liked watching Micah with his. Hearing them talk about their work. Like most good carpenters, they were in demand. They built furniture, gazebos, and park benches, and rough boxes for every undertaker who asked. They built whatever they could turn their hands to, and sold it all.

Micah told me this when he gave me my hair stick. "You'll never go hungry, I promise. I can keep you well." He didn't ask about my past, or why I had no photos of my family. He just said, "We're going to have a long time to get to know each other," as if it explained everything.

He was young and hopeful for the future. I didn't know any better. Eloping was a romantic notion.

Grayman would've laughed his head off.

) ❩ ❫ ● ❪ ❨ (

On my last day at the diner Ace said, "Did you tell the other girls you're going?"

"No."

"Going to?"

"I don't think so." I hadn't even told Shana I was getting married—I didn't want her throwing me a bridal shower with presents and guests and a photographer from the local paper.

"You want me to give them your goodbyes?"

"If you would."

"No problem. Take care."

I stopped in the ladies' room to twist up my hair and shove the stick into place. Outside it was already dark, a fall rain promising to get harder. The back lot was empty, but that would change as visibility worsened.

Micah was waiting in my trailer. We had an hour to get to the courthouse. I pulled the diner door shut. Cold metal tapped the back of my neck.

"Hello, Nell."

"Hello, Grayman."

"I'm disappointed in you, leaving me like that. I thought you loved me." There was no right answer for that. "Turn around, slowly."

I don't think about that moment often, but when I do I almost think he might have been proud. He did train me, after all. I raised my hands and clasped them loosely behind my head, hearing his soft chuckle of approval. "Good girl."

I drove my hair stick into his eye.

He hadn't tracked me all that way for an apology.

I was glad of the rain as I put his wallet and gun in my purse. Moving on autopilot, I hefted him into a low wooden dumpster and rolled the trash bags down on top of him. I stood in the rain a moment longer, trembling. I'd never killed anyone before. A random thought came to me—that I wasn't a machine after all, that I could actually feel something. And then another—that this wasn't how I'd wanted to find out.

Trembling turned to shivers as the rain picked up. I remembered that someone could walk out the kitchen door at any time. I remembered that Micah was waiting.

I remembered my hair-stick was still in Grayman's eye.

I washed it off and threw up in the same puddle. Wound my hair up again, and waited for the guilt that was bound to surface. But it didn't. Surely Grayman hadn't expected honour from a thief.

We made it to the courthouse in time. I was the only one surprised by my tears as I signed the register. Micah and I spent the night in the trailer. The next morning he loaded my few belongings in the truck and drove me down to the valley.

I probably shouldn't accuse Davena of gall.

But I had nowhere else to go. I wanted to be with Micah. I wanted the peace I was sure awaited. And, at long last, I was grateful to be safe.

Ben said, "I knew Micah was sweet on someone," and shook my hand politely. His wife Josie didn't say anything as she followed suit. I felt a little gap of missing fingers on her right hand. She broke the following silence by offering me a cup of coffee.

"Thank you, I'd love one."

I'd never seen a real wood stove, much less basked in its warmth. Never been in a real country kitchen that smelled of meat pie and gravy. Never been inside a house with three storeys and a stained glass window under the front peak. And I'd never had coffee before—all my caffeine had come from a soda can—but after the first taste I understood how people became addicted. Josie smiled at my obvious enjoyment.

My nerves settled after that day. Neither Ben nor Josie scolded Micah for bringing home an outsider, at least not in my hearing, and I thought that unless I proved unfaithful, they'd give me the benefit of the doubt.

Although that first evening I heard Ben ask her, "How long until she can join The Risen?"

"I'll have her ready in about a year."

Thinking they were talking about taking me into their church, I backed away from the door. I was rocky on the subject of religion; my mother's bible had been stolen property. Josie would talk to me about it in her own time, I thought. It would be rude of me to ask first, like asking how she'd lost her fingers.

I expected that one day Micah and I would have a home of our own. Meanwhile, Ben and Josie used half of theirs and left the other for us.

We didn't use much of it except the bedroom.

That first winter was the best time for me. Not minding the cold seemed to earn me some respect from the neighbours, and the snow was beautiful. When Ben and Micah took the neighbour's dogs out bow-hunting, I helped cut and wrap the meat they brought home. I smiled for a whole day when Josie said I was a good worker.

She had a thing for jigsaw puzzles. There was usually one scattered on the end of the dining room table. She said, "I love that *crunch* when the last piece goes in." She didn't seem to mind me helping with them, or the careful questions I sometimes asked. She was a woman of many talents, among them painting wonderfully detailed landscapes. When I asked if she'd ever wanted a career, she said, "I thought about being an artist once."

"And, what . . . it just didn't happen?"

"I met Ben, and Micah came along. They came first."

"Did you ever regret giving up your chance?"

"Not really. You never know when there might be another. And anyway, you're supposed to make sacrifices for your family, aren't you?"

She did that every day, I thought. She worked for them constantly. "Yes, they have a pretty comfortable life here."

"Well, making a life *is* a woman's work, after all." She said it as if I should've known without being told. I wondered if maybe I should.

I wondered about a lot that year. The town fascinated me. I admired what I thought were just the ways of an old country society—how people looked out for each other, and pulled together to get things done. I liked the way everyone knew your name, and how the mail driver honked going by.

But I also wondered why so many people were missing fingers, hands, even a couple of feet. I could understand a certain measure of clumsiness, but this seemed well above the norm. I couldn't make myself ask anyone about it, though, not even Micah. I had a feeling that certain questions wouldn't be well-tolerated.

I remember how surprised I was the one Sunday Elton Carlyle missed church, and how I didn't know what to think the next week when he and his wife were in their usual pew. I whispered to Ben, "Davena said Elton's tractor rolled over on him."

"Yes, it did."

"It must not have been as bad as I heard."

"Oh, no, it was plenty bad." And Elton's wife was missing a thumb.

I didn't even comment when Mrs. Mary Studevan had a severe heart attack in the post office one Monday, then showed up at that weekend's bake sale. For the first time since I'd known her, she had all her fingers. But her husband was missing one of his.

I wondered about the small number of stones in the valley cemetery, and why the dates indicated all the dead were *old*. But when I said,

"There aren't many grave markers here, are there?" Micah looked genuinely puzzled.

He said, "Why would there be? We know where everybody is."

A year to the day after I moved in, things went bad. Maybe I should have seen it coming—I knew secrets were dangerous, and curiosity even worse—but I wasn't quite paranoid enough. Grayman would've said I'd lost my edge.

I wanted to see the attic. Before coming to the valley, I'd never been in a house *with* one, and wondered what it looked like. Such a silly thing. By then I was used to having the run of the house, and didn't think anything of trying the door handle, until Josie said behind me, "It's locked." It was. "And why would you want to go snooping?"

"Snooping?" The chill in her voice set me back on my heels.

"Shoving your way into a place you have no business being."

I couldn't have been more amazed if she'd hit me. It was the first time she'd shown me any hostility, and there was no need of it—just telling me the attic was off-limits would have been enough. But apparently I'd crossed a line I hadn't known about. Stung, I snapped, "Are you talking about the attic or the house?"

She blinked. "What?"

I avoided her for the rest of the day. For a few foolish moments I thought that everything had been fine until I'd tried the attic door, but no, it hadn't been fine at all. She hadn't forgotten I was an outsider; she just hadn't seen me as a threat until I'd tried to go upstairs.

Ben came looking for me that evening. He said, "Josie tells me you tried to go into the attic." I nodded. "Why?" His voice was as hard as hers.

I'd already thought of a reasonable lie. Curiosity didn't seem like a good excuse. "I wanted to see the windows up close."

He blinked. "What?"

"The stained glass windows. Micah said you made them yourself, and I always thought they were beautiful."

"That's all?"

"That's all."

"Well, I'm working on a new window out in the shed. Do you want to see it?"

I didn't. "Yes, please." All the time he was talking, I thought of his unexpected coldness, of Josie's sudden about-face. The secrets in their attic were none of my business.

I stayed away from the door after that. They didn't mention the incident again.

But while they weren't mentioning it, I got my edge back.

Arthur Grayman was my mother's boss. She'd been his lock-pick since before I was born. When she was shot and killed just after I turned eighteen, he was the first visitor to the funeral home.

My childhood wasn't what you'd call normal, but it wasn't bad, either. I remember bedtime stories and birthday presents, and the occasional trip to the beach. Mom taught me her craft instead of her favourite recipes. She left enough money to put me through college, if I'd thought to go, but I was young and adrift, and in need of the familiar even if it meant trouble. Grayman, knowing I was in need of a niche, offered me hers.

I never knew the name of the man he killed to keep me there.

He took me to one of his warehouses the day I joined his crew. His personal driver was already there, standing over a man stretched out on the floor, wrists and ankles tied to two posts. Grayman picked up a double-bladed axe and said, "I want you to see this, Eleanor. This man betrayed my trust."

When he was done, the thing on the floor was nothing you'd recognize.

Grayman said, "Do you know what a blood price is, Eleanor?" I shook my head. "It's a very old expression. It's the cost of an extraordinary privilege. You can ask all kinds of favours, as long as you remember that you might have to pay for them in blood." He leaned too close. "The greatest privilege you can claim now is my protection. In return I expect your loyalty."

I looked at what was left of the man, and didn't ask what he'd done. Grayman followed my gaze. "I think he was confused," he said. "I believe the act of treachery comes from not knowing what you really want." I nodded, not understanding at all. "Do *you* know what you want, Eleanor?"

"Yes." To forget I'd ever seen this. To be anywhere Grayman wasn't.

"What?'

"I want to die of old age."

He patted me on the head, leaving the man's blood in my hair, and walked away.

I did my best for him, knowing anything less would get me killed. Knowing there were things no one said out loud that you were just supposed to understand, and that not understanding could get you killed, too. I listened to him go on about how his crew were his children, and how family love was like no other, and wondered how my mother had stayed as sane as she had.

He gave good advice, though. The best he gave me was, "Read and get a job." He thought people were less likely to be suspicious of someone who was well-spoken and legally employed. I got a library card and a job waiting tables at an upscale restaurant, and spent my evenings waiting for his call.

I couldn't bank much of the money he gave me—no tax accountant would believe a waitress got those kinds of tips—but I could stash it, and did. Because Grayman had taught me something else—always know when to get out.

He'd been talking about break-and-enter at the time, but it was still a good lesson. He said it the morning I realized that someday he'd probably kill me anyway, for some imagined slight. That maybe the man on the floor hadn't done anything at all.

I planned. I waited. I didn't have to wait long.

Grayman had been following a woman named Brenda Keven for a month. She lunched with the ladies a couple of times a week, shopped a lot, drank a little too much. She had time on her hands. Grayman said the diamonds on them glittered like stars.

I don't know if they glittered when she pulled the trigger. I don't know who she shot first, or who the second bullet was meant for. I was too busy jumping through my window of opportunity.

Grayman kept a cheap apartment for when a job went bad. If we had to scatter we could meet back there and decide what to do next. But sometimes getting there took a while—he wouldn't think anything of me disappearing for a few hours. I left my purse and cell phone in my apartment, hoping that when he finally came looking he'd think I was still around. He'd check the hospitals and the morgue, and, if I was lucky, decide I'd met with an accident somewhere. Or maybe he'd never realize I'd run.

But no, with Grayman you couldn't count on luck. It was best to use the time until he figured it out putting miles behind me.

The small knapsack I'd stashed in the bus station locker held a change of clothes and an obscene amount of cash. There was just enough room left for my tool case.

There were a few things in the apartment I'd miss, but they would've been no good to me dead. I wished I could've taken the photo of Mom and me on the boardwalk on my eighteenth birthday. As the bus pulled out I wondered who she'd seen hacked to death.

I've seen enough hard deaths that shock doesn't come easily to me. When the constable told me about Micah's car crash, I just kept thinking I should have been more surprised. I didn't even cry—Grayman had trained all the tears out of me.

I thought of him as I went up to bed. I set the alarm clock for dawn, and dreamed of Micah. But the next morning, unlocking the attic door, the only husband on my mind was Bluebeard. He told his wife not to go into the attic, but sharpened his knife behind her back, knowing that eventually he'd find a reason to use it. I worried about squeaky steps as I climbed. But Josie's attic was surprisingly unscary, just an unfinished room with exposed ceiling beams and a rough floor. There were no cobwebs, no dust. The windows were clean. I stayed away from them.

There were a few pieces of furniture, a box of old china. A big trunk full of neatly folded clothes, smelling of mothballs. Nothing looked like anything that needed to be hidden. It was all familiar junk; I recognized everything. Even the four rough boxes behind the old bookcase didn't surprise me at first glance.

The second glance set me on my heels.

I didn't want to open the boxes, but reached for the nearest even as I decided not to. I needed to know who was inside.

I was.

No one came to the house that day. Nobody phoned. The mail driver didn't honk going by. I spent the morning worrying at Josie's last jigsaw, and as the pieces fell into place, the pieces fell into place.

I don't know how long I stood staring at the me in the coffin, at the perfect skin and lashes, and the expression more peaceful than any I'd ever seen in the mirror. Neither of us breathed. Finally I had to.

I lifted all the lids. The light through the stained glass cast a yellow glow across Micah and his parents. Josie had all her fingers. I made myself touch her. There was no pulse. In any good horror novel that would have been when they all opened their eyes and sat up, but they didn't. Their skin was smooth and warm. I thought about cutting it to see if they bled, but even my curiosity has limits. I brushed my fingers over Micah's face as he'd once run his over mine, and closed the cover.

I knew they'd burned in the car wreck; the constable had been only too willing to give me the details. Nobody had spared me those. But no one had told me any secrets. No one had warned me about the attic people.

There was a faint *crunch* in the back of my mind as I caught a glimpse of the big picture. It wasn't anything I recognized. Sudden panic grabbed me, making me turn away too quickly. I yelped as I banged my face into a ceiling beam.

Downstairs, I locked the door behind me, sure there would be nails clawing the other side at any moment. When there weren't, I caught my breath.

Josie's jigsaw was one of the few things I understood that day. I was sure she'd made the me in the attic—making a life is a woman's work, after all—but couldn't imagine how. *Why* made a disturbing amount of sense, though. I thought of her frightening devotion to her family. Of Pastor Vance's obsession with The Book of Corinthians. Of the too-small number of stones in the graveyard.

I thought of Grayman's blood price.

Finally, when it was dark, I went upstairs and packed my knapsack again—a change of clothes, an obscene amount of cash, and my tool case. And Micah's hair-stick, which I'll never wear again. The radio said the night would be cloudy, with light snow toward morning.

As I ate another sandwich, fuelling, it occurred to me the neighbours might be expecting me to run. I wanted a cup of coffee, but skipped it—not a good idea when they might set the dogs after me. I put Grayman's gun in one coat pocket, spare gloves and more money in the other.

I didn't even think of using the door.

Shimmying out a narrow cellar window, keeping low, I made the short sprint into the woods, needing to be long-gone by sunrise. If I could just get to Ace's, I thought, I could hitch a ride.

I did.

Another hundred miles north, another takeout coffee. It's not as good as Josie's.

"You're awfully quiet over there," the driver says. "Sure you're okay?"

"I'm fine. Just thinking."

About Elton Carlyle's bad-enough accident. How he was up and walking three days later, his wife missing her thumb. About Mary Studevan's heart attack, and how, when I saw her again, she had all her fingers and her husband didn't.

About families making sacrifices for each other.

That maybe Pastor Vance's platitudes weren't. In all the sermons I heard him give, he never read the Psalms. He never once talked about the valley of the shadow.

That instead of going to the funeral, I was expected to be home with my family, waiting for them to draw breath. That by the time I got to Emery, at dawn of the third day since the accident, the neighbours would have been arriving at the house to make sure I brought my family back.

Beyond that, there are too many things I don't know, and more I don't want to. Like how much flesh and blood I'd have to lose to raise three people from the dead, and if they can rise without it. If anything happened to me now, would I end up back in Josie's attic, and would Micah still love me enough to sacrifice me back to life?

Would my resurrection finally erase my alien status?

Would I still have the right to wear my hair up?

I think of the things no one said out loud, that you were just supposed to understand, like knowing that people only had to stay dead if they died of very old age. Like the cost of an extraordinary privilege being part of a greater mystery, and how there are some things even I can't unlock.

I wonder if I'm being selfish, not giving of myself as Micah expected. But I didn't marry him in The Church of the Risen. When I promised *till death do us part* I didn't specify how many times.

Part of me thinks that if I loved him enough I'd go back. But part of me has had enough of that kind of love.

It's a relief when the driver interrupts my thoughts again. "Hey, I never asked. Where are you headed?"

I can't very well say, "Someplace where the houses don't have attics."

So I lie, because my answer is something I've been wrong about before.

I tell him, "I'll know when I get there."

WENDIGO NIGHTS

SIOBHAN CARROLL

DAY ELEVEN

Lately I've been thinking about eating my children.

When Olivia tugs at her glossy curls, I think about her hair in my mouth. Paper-dry, tasting of smoke and strawberry shampoo. The strands would break between my teeth. The sound they'd make—a tiny crunch, like a foot falling through snow—that sound would fill me. I would not be so hungry after that.

I allow myself the hair. It is better than the other things I imagine eating.

Macleay says, "I'm going to try again this afternoon. I think today's the day." We nod as though we believe him.

I study Macleay's hands. They're large and dirt-streaked. I imagine crunching through his knuckles and rolling the tattered joint on my tongue like a marble.

"What about you, Hui?" Sanderson's tone is a bit too casual. "Any news on that canister?"

I shrug. I don't want to open my mouth. I'm afraid of what might happen.

The arctic wind howls through our silence. It's blizzarding outside the research station, -36 Celsius by the thermometer, god-knows-what once you factor in wind chill. The kind of weather even the locals complain about.

"They'll send a plane as soon as the weather clears," Bannerjee mutters. She's been saying the same thing for a week now.

"Yeah." Macleay doesn't look at her. "I'll try again this afternoon."

"You okay, Hui?" I can feel Sanderson's eyes on me. He knows something's off.

Carefully, very carefully, I part my lips. Not much. Just enough to reply. And I know this is my chance—maybe my last chance—to warn them.

Olivia giggles in the corner. The thought darts into my head: *If not Macleay, then her.*

"Fine," I mutter. "I'm fine."

After a moment, Sanderson nods.

That was on day eleven.

DAY NINE

They say people who've received a terminal diagnosis brood over history. They go looking for mistakes: theirs or someone else's. They try to identify the moment things started to go wrong.

I can think of two possibilities. In my mind, I flip them like a coin.

The first possibility: eleven days ago.

Bannerjee set something dull and gray on my work bench. "Check this out." She looked flushed, proud as an angler who's caught his first salmon. "It was in the ice, about a meter down."

I picked it up. A gray canister, about the size of a paint can, weighing about two kilos. It was made out of a clouded, dull metal, striated with rings.

"What is it?" I wasn't interested, just being polite. Nothing about the canister suggested danger.

"No idea." Bannerjee leaned forward. "But I saw another can down there. And clothing." She was practically squirming with excitement.

"Clothing?"

"A wool coat." She grinned. "I stopped drilling. Shifted the borehole. We need to call this in." Seeing my confusion, she added: "Could be old."

Now something connected. "How old?"

"Dunno. But . . . it could be old."

I turned the canister over. Once, maybe, we'd have shrugged our shoulders over a frozen coat. But not these days. The scramble for the melting Arctic is on, and governments look to history to strengthen their territorial claims. Canada has resumed the nineteenth century's search for Franklin. Hell, a few years ago, Russia planted a flag on the seabed beneath the North Pole. A *flag*. Like in the Eddie Izzard skit. Everything old is new again.

"Franklin et al.," I said. "They wore wool coats, didn't they?" Like me, Bannerjee wore Canada Goose, the unofficial uniform of the frigid zone. Her coat was blazing red; a slot for the Arctic Rescue tag gaped emptily on her back.

"Yeah." Bannerjee's eyes glittered with what I assumed was excitement.

Now, looking back, I wonder if I was wrong about the look in Bannerjee's eyes. If, like the slow crack of lake-ice underfoot, things were already getting out of hand.

DAY TWELVE

"We need to talk about Bannerjee," Sanderson says in a low voice.

I grunt. So far I have managed to get through the morning without opening my mouth. I am thirsty, but the hunger is much, much worse. It claws at my insides like a wild animal stuffed in a cage. If I open my mouth, I fear it will get out.

"I can't find her anywhere," says Macleay of the edible fingers. "I thought . . . I thought she might have tried for the mine. But when I checked the snowmobiles I found this." He opens his dirty hands to reveal a tangle of black wires.

"She butchered the machines." Sanderson's voice sounds wet and heavy, like warm-weather snow.

It takes me a moment to register what they're saying. I raise my eyebrows at Macleay.

"I can't repair this," Macleay says in disgust. His eyes are frightened. "We're stuck here until the plane comes. Or until the satellite phone starts working again." He makes no mention of trying the phone again this afternoon.

The blizzard moans through our walls. Out of the corner of my eye, I see Ethan and Olivia watching us. *Dohng, Suug Yee*, I would say, were I to call them by their Cantonese names. Unlucky names. I try to smile at the children reassuringly, but my heart is sinking.

We are in more trouble than I can bear to think about. Some facts I can face head-on: the damaged snowmobiles, the missing plane. Others I can only sneak glances at.

Fact: *I was the first person to touch the canister after Bannerjee.*

Fact: *Something is wrong.*

Fact: *I do not have, and never have had, any children.*

"Well," Sanderson says eventually. "Keep an eye out for her." He looks deflated, as though he has finally realized what I have suspected for eleven days now.

Escape is no longer an option.

DAY NINE

The second possibility: five years ago.

My then-girlfriend, Anna, wanted to see the Anthropology museum. One of her college friends was in Vancouver for a conference. So I drove her and the other folklorists to the weird borderland-city of UBC.

I circled the Bill Reid sculpture while Anna and Joel reminisced about grad school. I've always loved wood, and the honey-glow of the giant raven appealed to me. Not so the rest of the museum. A bunch of masks with distorted faces and stringy grass hair.

"The last murder was in the 1960s," Joel said.

That jerked my attention back to their conversation. "What?"

"Creepy," Anna agreed. Her skin was almost the same colour as the yellow cedar. Ethereal.

She turned to me. "They left the uncle to babysit their kids." Her words were aimed in my general direction, but her eyes drifted past mine. Another one of the disconnections that had become common between us. "When they came back, he'd built a fire on the lawn. He was roasting his nephew's body. And crying about it."

The mask that reared up behind them was ugly. Lips peeled back from red-lined teeth. Black eyes staring nowhere.

"Did you hear about that bus murder in Winnipeg?" Joel said, out of nowhere.

Anna grimaced. The news was full of the Greyhound murder, which fascinated and repelled us. It was the sort of thing our Vancouver friends avoided talking about.

But Joel was from New York. "Beheading and cannibalism," he continued, staring at the mask. "I'm just saying. Maybe wendigo psychosis is still with us."

"Wendigo?" I could feel the conversation rushing past me, the way they usually did when Anna and her grad-school comrades got together.

"Yeah." Joel's face got the bright, careful look I imagined he must wear when teaching. "You've heard of the wendigo?"

And that was it. The moment of infection.

DAY ???

I am finding it difficult to keep track of time.

This is a common complaint in the Arctic. The land of the midnight sun. It disorders everything.

Still. Time is becoming difficult. I watch the old plastic clock on the wall to make sure the seconds are still advancing.

I hear sounds from the kitchenette. But I will not get up. I will not investigate.

Things must be kept in order. Or else.

DAY TWELVE

My children are playing with leftover office paper. Olivia is showing Ethan how to fold the green-and-white sheets into dolls. They decorate their creations with pencil: people don't bring pens to our latitude.

Ethan batters the dolls against each other, making them fight. It disturbs me, but I don't know why.

Outside the wind is raging. I try not to think about Anna's description of a deranged uncle roasting kids on the lawn. I don't even know the whole story. The gaps in my knowledge make it worse, somehow.

"Hui."

I hear Ethan drop his pencil. Olivia's eyes widen and I follow her gaze to where Bannerjee stands, dripping and wide-eyed. Dried blood cakes the side of her head.

The sudden, frozen silence of my children's fear gives me the strength to take Bannerjee gently by the arm. I steer her out of the small dorm room.

"*What are you doing?*" I spit through clenched teeth. I want to rip her throat out. "*What have you done?*"

Bannerjee shakes her head. She's always been a small, anxious woman. Now she's trembling like someone's running a current through her.

"Macleay," Bannerjee manages. There's something wrong with her eyes. "I found him by the snowmobiles. He . . . was tearing them apart. He tried to *kill* me, Hui."

I feel the same way I did in the museum all those years ago. Things are rushing past me faster than I can handle.

"Macleay?"

Bannerjee nods. She's crying now, big, fat tears that track mascara and blood down her face. "You have to help me. He's looking for me."

I feel dizzy. I can't remember the last time I ate. I feel my mouth move—"How can I help?"—although I'm not sure I trust Bannerjee. I'm not sure I trust Macleay either. Something about the way he held those wires.

Here's a question I never thought about when I flew up here: *If the world goes haywire, is there anyone in this station you can trust?*

"It's the canister," Bannerjee says hoarsely. That look in her eyes. "We need to get it out of here. We need to give it back."

I nod as though this makes sense. Part of me—a part I can barely keep track of right now—agrees, but wants to warn her. Because here's the thing about extracting resources. It's always easier to take something out of the land than it is to put it back.

But suddenly I am too tired to say anything.

"Sure," my mouth says. And I watch myself follow Bannerjee down the hallway. She keeps glancing back at the way we came. She's dragging her left leg a little.

As we enter the field lab, Bannerjee whispers something that gives me pause. "We've angered the *vetala*."

"The what?" I hear myself say. An echo of a museum long ago.

Bannerjee looks at me strangely. "The air is full of ghosts." She delivers this information as though it were an ozone reading: a fact, visible to us all.

Later I wish that Bannerjee had explained herself. If I could have heard her version of the last twelve days—maybe I could have altered something.

But maybe not. "Come on," Bannerjee says and pushes the door open.

I don't like to think about what happens next.

DAY ONE

"Is that it?"

Sanderson is framed by the doorway, a big, burly man who likes to wear his beard long and curly. He's typical of a certain kind of Arctic visitor: the geologist who thinks of himself as a frontier throwback. And like a lot of geologists, he's a bit odd.

Automatically I've thrown a cloth over the canister. For some reason I don't want people to see it. Now, reluctantly, I remove the cloth.

Sanderson snorts. "Doesn't look like much. Thought it might be the Holy Grail the way Bannerjee's been carrying on."

My stomach grumbles, and I am suddenly, painfully hungry. But I've already eaten three meals today. It isn't even noon yet.

"Has she got through?"

Sanderson shakes his head. "Coms are down. Murphy's law. Bannerjee makes a find and she can't tell anyone. It's driving her nuts." His shoulders shake as he laughs. Sanderson prides himself on being laid-back. He finds the high-strung Bannerjee amusing.

"Do you think the plane will come through?"

Our station gets a bi-monthly supply drop. The pond-hopper that visits us and the southern Inuit villages is a tough little bird. It might be able to get through in this weather. But I'm not surprised to see Sanderson shrug.

"Maybe." He sounds bored. "Wind's bad. Don't blame them if they postpone the drop. It'll drive Bannerjee extra nuts though." He chuckles.

I wonder now if Sanderson remembers this moment. I wonder if he appreciates the irony.

The pond-hopper never arrives. Normally I mark a missed drop with a minus symbol in my diary: -1 day of supplies. But that evening, I write "Day One" at the top of the page. Because that is what it feels like. Like something has begun.

DAY TWELVE

The day she left, Anna and I argued in the parking lot. She said I was incapable of love. Worse, she said it sadly, as though it was something we both knew and had just been too polite to mention until now.

I protested, but words have never been my strong point.

If I could talk to Anna right now—if we could get a line out, if I could feel confident about baring my teeth to the air—I'd tell her that she was wrong. That what I find difficult isn't love, but expressing it.

If she could see me now—the way I'm trying to shelter the children from danger, the way I'm trying to protect them from myself—I think she'd think differently.

At least, I hope she would.

"Tell us a story," Olivia begs. I look away from her dark curls and Ethan's bright, plump cheeks. The only stories in my head are awful ones. Franklin and his men staggering in the dark. Starving men cutting up their comrades for cooking pots. And the story Joel told me all those years ago.

"No," I mumble. "No story tonight." Olivia wails. Ethan bounces up and down.

"Fine," I say. "Once upon a time there was . . ."

"A canithter," Ethan lisps.

It takes me a moment to respond. I am tired. So very tired of fighting. And I really can't think of anything else to say.

"A canister." My voice sounds dull, even to my ears. "Buried in ice."

"And then one day . . ." Ethan prompts. They look at me expectantly, with glittering eyes.

"One day," I agree.

"One day," Olivia says, her voice rising with excitement, "it gets *out*!"

FIVE YEARS AGO

Joel turns to me and says, "You've heard of the wendigo?"

I shake my head. Out of habit I want to stop him; I tend to be bored by Anna's descriptions of legends and tale-types. But she is watching me closely.

"'*This is the blue hour / The ravenous night* . . .'" Joel quotes. He pauses, looking at me. When I show no sign of recognition, he moves on. "It's a Native American legend." (Anna winces at his word choice.) "A cannibal spirit that possesses a person and makes him want to feed on human flesh. Particularly friends and family members."

"We always hurt the ones we love." Anna is smiling sadly to herself.

"Vampire and werewolf stories are similar that way," Joel reflects. "But I think the wendigo's scarier."

"Why?"

"Because of the way it's transmitted."

Joel smirks and preens a little. I know he wants me to ask him about the transmission. I don't want to ask him. I try to catch Anna's eye, but she isn't looking at me. And I can't figure out a way to exit this conversation. So I turn back to Joel, and ask him, "How?"

This, ultimately, is my tragedy. I go along with things.

"Anyone can become a wendigo," Joel says. "It's a culturally transmitted madness. That's actually documented, by the way. Wendigo psychosis."

"Which means?"

"As soon as you learn about the wendigo, you can turn into a wendigo." He grins triumphantly, haloed by the amber light of the museum. "Just by listening to this, you've been infected."

I feel a flash of anger. Even now, all these years later, I still want to punch him.

I think I could forgive Joel for telling me about the wendigo. But I can't forgive him for that grin.

Me, I apologize. I don't know if that makes it any easier. I was just trying to make sense of things. And it was easier for me to do that on paper.

Even in reading these words, you have been infected.

DAY ???

This is the blue hour. The ravenous night.

I find Macleay in the kitchenette. His body is bent like a broken straw. He looks dead. But I can hear his breath, even above the sound of the wind. The slow pump of blood in his veins.

His eyes slide open as I approach. Puppet's eyes.

"Still alive, Hui?" He gives a mad, wet giggle.

I sink down in a crouch before him. I'm salivating at the metallic taint of blood in the air. This disgusts me. I wish I didn't know what was going to happen next.

"It's the canister," Macleay says and smiles. His face slides into the same holy-fool expression that Bannerjee's wore at the end. "Not from this planet after all."

His smugness irritates me. Like Bannerjee, he thinks he has found an explanation. Bannerjee blamed ghosts. Macleay wants aliens. I suppose it does no harm to let them believe they figured it out at the end. That there was an answer.

"What happened?" I rasp, trying to delay the inevitable.

"Sanderson," Macleay whispers. He smiles a red smile. "I thought he was all right. But he fooled me. The son-of-a-bitch."

"Where is he?"

Macleay rolls his eyes towards the door. *Outside. In the death-storm.*

I hear a gasp behind me and know that Olivia has trailed me into the kitchen. I motion her back with my free arm. I don't want her to see my face.

"Get him for me, will you?" The shred that remains of Macleay wants vengeance. I nod, to keep him happy.

The crunch of bone fills my mouth and I try to think about other things. About the line I once came across in an old explorer narrative that Bannerjee had picked up in Anchorage. "The North has induced some degree of insanity in the men."

The North has induced some degree of insanity in the men. It's untrue, of course. One of those annoying stories that southerners like to tell about the Arctic. But we bring those stories with us when we come up here.

My opinion? I don't think there was anything in that canister. There didn't need to be. All it needed was our stories.

"Sanderson's putting gasoline around the building," Olivia announces in a detached voice. I nod. I can smell it, an ugly, thick stench that corrupts the taste of blood in my mouth. I clamber to my feet, ignoring the stickiness on my hands and face.

I've always been good at ignoring uncomfortable truths. The wariness in Anna's eyes. Macleay's corpse at my feet. The children.

The only excuse I can make is that, when things descend into nightmare, you cling to the parts of the story you want to believe in.

"Hui!" Somewhere, Sanderson is screaming my name. He wants to test his story against mine. I grin a death-mask grin and click my nails together. I can feel my body stretching to accommodate the life it has devoured.

"Don't worry," I tell my silent, ghost-faced children. "I'll protect you."

I put my hand on the howling door. I pull it open.

This is the blue hour. The ravenous night.

EPISODE THREE: ON THE GREAT PLAINS, IN THE SNOW

JOHN LANGAN

"Oh bury me not on the lone prairie"
—"The Cowboy's Lament"

"It's like I told you last night son. The earth is mostly just a boneyard. But pretty in the sunlight," he added.
—Larry McMurtry, *Lonesome Dove*

I

The two ghosts—*impressions*, Lynch corrected himself, that was how Melinda insisted on referring to them—stood considering the wreck. It was some kind of van: Lynch didn't recognize the make; although its snub-nosed front put him in mind of the space shuttle (time was, he'd known cars as well as anyone). The vehicle had been bulled off the road onto the frozen ruts of the field beside it. It had been struck on the left side. You could see where the doors had buckled under the force of the blow. Funny that it hadn't rolled, or at least tipped, over. Probably had something to do with the height at which the object that had collided with it had done so (time was, he would've known why that was, too, understood the underlying principle if not the exact equations demonstrating it). The roof had been peeled open; rudely, he thought, the way a child tore the foil off a piece of chocolate. Long gouges grooved the van's crumpled side, its hood. The windshield was a frozen explosion. Scattered around the van were shredded pieces of its seats, a white and red cooler apparently intact, half of a heavy blanket—a quilt, maybe—and assorted articles of clothing: sweatshirt, snow boot, baseball cap. Balanced on the hood, rocking slightly in the wind that whistled like a child trying to find a tune, was a squarish block of plastic. Lynch couldn't identify anything more than its geometry, wasn't sure—

"It's part of a car seat," Melinda said. She'd noticed him staring. "A child's car seat."

Ah, that was why he hadn't placed it sooner. His own children were . . . Anthony was twenty-four, wasn't he? He had been at some point. His memory was particularly bad, this moment, the worst it had been in the last three weeks. He tried to concentrate on his family, his children. Anthony the oldest, twenty-four. Katie was . . . what was she? Twenty-one? Maureen . . . Eighteen? Seventeen? Regardless, his children were all long past the age of car seats. (Though hadn't there been a grandson? Anthony's—Jordan, perhaps? He had a sudden vision of a little boy wearing a red sweatshirt and hugging a toy dinosaur.)

"Shall we take a closer look?"

"What for?" he said.

"I don't know. Isn't that what you're supposed to do?"

Wasn't it? "In TV shows," he said, "in TV shows about the police." He turned to her. "Were you a member of the police?"

"No."

"Then we might as well stay here until the real police arrive. Maybe we'll learn something, then."

"You just want to stand here?"

"The wind isn't bothering me."

"The wind—I'm going to check this out."

"Wait." But she was striding away from him towards the—what had been the van.

"It isn't as if I'll disturb anything," she called over her shoulder.

Not because he shared her desire to view the carnage up close, but because he didn't care to stand over here, across the road, by himself, with nothing but miles of empty field around him, Lynch hurried after her. It was strange to find himself squeamish, now, past the point of all hurt, but he was sick with dread at the prospect of seeing what might be left of the car seat's former occupant. He had been fond of violent movies, horror movies, war movies—had been watching one when Anthony was born, he remembered, something with Vincent Price, lurid Technicolor—but this: there was blood everywhere, splashes on the hood and roof, streams down the windshield and sides, puddles cupped by the frozen earth. It was as if someone had sprayed the scene with a fire hose of the stuff. He had been the one to tend the kids when they injured themselves, or were vomiting-sick (he had a flash of a nail embedded in the spongy sole of a flip-flop, weeping blood), but who knew, who knew the human body had so much blood in it?

Not to mention, the things he tried to confine to the corners of his vision as he came up behind Melinda, a rope of what might have passed for sausage, a carmine slab of something, a scattering of pale chunks. Could he pass out? He wasn't sure, but this seemed like the test. He looked at Melinda, who had stopped beside the driver's door and was leaning forward, attempting to peer around the splotch of blood in the middle of the window. Voice thick, he said, "See anything?"

"Only what you do. How many do you think there were?"

"I don't know. What does a van like this hold? Four, five, six?" There had been five people in his family.

"You can squeeze eight people into one of these things," she said. "Two in the front, three in the middle, three in the rear." She glanced at him, at his expression, and added, "But I don't think there were eight people in here. Four, five tops."

"It's enough."

"Yeah."

The air was full of snowflakes, again, which, he'd noticed, was how it started snowing out here. No gradual increases, no few flakes leading the way down for more and more after that: this was like being inside a giant snow globe you hadn't felt being shaken. The air was clear, and then it was thick with snow that didn't fall so much as swirl into existence. These flakes were small, almost freezing rain. Faintly, a siren wailed.

"Finally," Melinda said. "That guy in the Saab must've called them, after all."

"Let's stand back," Lynch said, "and let them do their job."

"Why? Don't you want to know what they find?"

"To be honest, I don't think they're going to find much. Not any more than we have."

"You never know."

"Can we please move away?"

"All right, all right, no need to raise your voice. We're all on the same side, here."

"Thank you."

Through the snow, the source of the siren appeared, a police car, its roof rack strobing red.

Lynch said, "That's it?"

"What were you expecting?"

"More than a single car. An ambulance, at least."

"He was probably closest. Besides, what good do you think an ambulance would do?"

"Suppose someone—"

"Someone isn't."

He had nothing to say to that.

They watched the police car roar up to the site, its brakes screeching at the last minute. It was a local unit, its driver so overwhelmed by what was visible to him from inside his car that he forgot to shift into Park before opening his door. The car stuttered forward, almost spilling him out of it. He lunged inside, threw the transmission into Neutral, and yanked up the parking brake. For a moment, he sat with his head on the steering wheel, no doubt telling himself that he could handle this. He raised his head and reached for his radio. Lynch could hear him reciting the string of codes that shorthanded the situation. He thought the cop sounded about sixteen. Once he had completed the call, the cop replaced the radio, reached for his hat, and stepped out into the snow. Lynch was surprised to see him wearing a baseball cap instead of the wide-brimmed quasi-cowboy hat he'd assumed was part of the general police uniform in this neck of the woods. The cop had his hand on his gun; although he hadn't drawn it. He called, "Hello? Can anyone hear me?" as he advanced across the road towards the van, his face draining of color. He started to identify himself, then caught sight of something on the ground before him and threw up.

"Very nice," Melinda said.

"He's just a kid."

To his credit, the cop wiped his mouth with the back of his hand and continued forward on shaking legs. “Hello?” His voice so tremulous a strong gust of wind might have carried it away. “Is anyone . . .” Obviously, he couldn’t decide how to finish the question. Alive? Here? In one piece? As he neared the van, he unholstered his gun.

“Oh, right,” Melinda said. “As if the bad guy’s waiting to jump out at him.”

Gun in his right hand, right wrist grasped by his left hand, both hands out in front of him, down but not too low, the cop surveyed the van’s interior, then began to circle it, stepping left foot across right. His eyes were cartoon-wide. Lynch guessed he was telling himself to focus on the details and finding that none too easy. By the time he had completed his circuit of the van and was backing away from it, new sirens were audible.

“The cavalry arrives,” Melinda said.

There were three more police cars—two local and one state—and an ambulance. The trooper, a wide brim over his startled face, practically leapt out of his car shouting questions and commands. The first cop croaked answers, the remaining two returned to their cars and sped off up and down the road to block it. A pair of EMTs, a tall man with a beard and an even taller woman with a ponytail, emptied from the ambulance and started arguing with the trooper about whether they should approach what he was insisting was a crime scene, what they were calling an accident. The first cop told the trooper to let them have a look, then told the EMTs they weren’t going to find anyone. They didn’t. After they’d made their search, they retreated to the ambulance, on whose hood the woman placed her gloved hands and leaned over, while the man walked into the field on the other side of the road. He walked as if he had someplace to be, some destination in mind, and did not stop walking when the woman raised her head, caught sight of him, and called his name. She abandoned her spot at the front of the ambulance to run after him, reaching him in long strides and catching him in a bear hug that he did not return.

“I see what you mean,” Melinda said. “Just look at the difference they made.”

Without answering her, Lynch turned away and began walking north along the road, towards the town. The fear, horror, that had flared in him had burnt out, leaving ashy sadness. Right now, he wanted nothing more than to put as much distance between himself and the blood and ruin that had been a family on their way somewhere. Was it Christmas? Were they driving to a grandparent’s house to exchange presents? He hadn’t noticed anything that resembled wrapping paper, boxes . . . while it was snowing, he didn't think it was Christmas. He thought the snow was more because of where they were, which he couldn't quite name but which he was pretty sure was somewhere in the broad middle of the country, someplace like South Dakota or Wyoming, a state where they had snow more often than they didn't.

Melinda followed him. "Hey," she said. "Where're you going? The professionals are here. Don't you want to watch them work, see what we can learn?"

He kept walking. He had a feeling he had been the one to do the teasing in his family. He recalled Anthony, frustrated to the point of tears because the zipper on his jeans was stuck open. They were cheap jeans—K-Mart special, or maybe Marshall's—but Lynch hadn't been able to resist cracking wise about his oldest's inability to zip his pants. How old had his son been? Thirteen? Fourteen? The years of maximum self-consciousness. No surprise to find it wasn't as pleasant on the other side of the barb.

"Ah, never mind," Melinda said, falling into step beside him. "We already learned what we needed to."

He couldn't help himself. "What was that?"

"You tell me. What did you notice?"

"Notice? You mean, aside from the blood, the carnage, the parts of people I don't have names for?"

"I'm sorry. It was pretty rough, wasn't it?"

"Pretty rough, yeah."

"So what did you notice?"

"What . . ." He stopped. "What—all of it. I saw all of it."

"Then you saw what was missing."

"Besides whoever did this?"

"They're long gone. I told you that."

"I don't know, nothing."

"Nothing's right."

Tumblers fell into place. "They were. The family . . . their ghosts."

"Impressions, and they weren't. They should have been there, all of them. We shouldn't have had to speculate about how many of them there were. We should've been able to count them, ourselves. Don't know that they would have been all that much fun to talk to. Anyone who's gone through something like that—well, sometimes they never come out of it. But even if every last one of them had been standing there screaming, we should have seen them."

"What does that mean?"

"It means things just got a lot more serious."

II

The bar, whose name hadn't registered, had a plain wooden floor scattered with sawdust, onto which patrons at the dozen or so tables around it dropped the broken and empty shells of the peanuts they scooped from the bowls in front of them. Lynch was fascinated by this, didn't think he'd seen anything like it before. A jukebox whose contours were drawn in yellow and red neon finished singing in the big voice of a man who kept insisting that ladies love country boys and switched to the softer, slower sound of a woman wrapping her rich voice around her funny Valentine. Lynch sat up straighter.

"What is it?" Melinda asked.

"I know this."

"What?" She nodded at the jukebox. "Ella?"

"Yes," he said, "Ella. Ella Fitzgerald."

"Funny, I didn't tag you as a jazz fan."

"Yes."

"Not that I figured a jukebox in here would have Ella Fitzgerald on its play list."

Lynch supposed she meant the men with their cowboy hats and boots, the women in their flannel shirts and jeans, but the contrast that impressed Melinda skated over him. His wife had given him an Ella Fitzgerald CD for Valentine's Day, a compilation. He could see the picture of Ella on its front, a sepia photograph that showed her from the waist up, wearing an off-the-shoulder gown, her generous mouth open to utter the lyrics of some song or another, the members of a big band out of focus on the risers behind her. Had he freed it from its plastic wrapping? He couldn't recall, didn't think so. He was going to wait until he was home from the hospital, wasn't he?

Melinda remained silent for the rest of the song, while Lynch drank in Ella's almost-girlish voice, the saxophone tracing her words, the steady whisper of the brushes across the drums. How long ago . . . he had been standing in a friend's basement den; the friend's name was a blank but his almost comically broad face, broad forehead, curly hair, square jaw, and square glasses were vivid in his memory. The two of them—three,

Anthony had been there, too—the three of them had stood in the dim den in the late afternoon light while Lynch's friend, who seemed like an old friend, someone he'd known for decades, eased a record from its sleeve, positioned it on his turntable, and lowered the needle into place. The hiss of the needle tracing the vinyl had given way to a brash, bright trumpet, which had yielded to a man's voice, deep as a well, rough as gravel, which had been succeeded by Ella's (*I Got Plenty o' Nuttin'*)—Armstrong, Louis Armstrong, Louis and Ella. Anthony had surprised him by turning to show a huge grin. "This is great," he had said, and Lynch had felt suddenly, unexpectedly close to his son.

With a shimmer of cymbals and a flourish of notes from the saxophone, the song on the jukebox ended and was replaced by the vibrating twang of a guitar set to a country complaint. Lynch looked at Melinda, who was surveying the rest of the bar, and said, "Thank you."

"It's important to do stuff like that when you can. It helps you stay . . . coherent longer."

"Maybe I should wait for it to come on again."

"Some do," Melinda said. "Not that they hang around jukeboxes for that special song, but they attach to places that, you know, had meaning for them."

"But you didn't."

"No, I didn't. For that matter, neither did you."

"No."

"You sound less than happy. Is that what you would've wanted, hovering over their shoulders, watching them grieve?"

"I . . ."

"Worse, watching them stop grieving, get on with their lives."

"It would have been something."

"It would have been nothing. You would have drifted off to the basement, attic, some corner of the house or another, and sat there moping. Every now and again, when everyone was asleep, you'd have gone for a walk, wandered from room to room feeling miserable, spooking the cat."

"We didn't have an attic. Just a crawl space."

"Oh. How about a cat?"

"Yes. A white cat, with a black mark on her forehead. The kids named her—"

"Spot?"

"Ashley. For Ash Wednesday, you know."

"Not really. Anyway, the point is, it wouldn't have been long until you'd faded to next to nothing, just a tissue of a couple of unconnected memories. A year, two at the outside. And not long after that, you wouldn't have been anything more than a cold spot, a disturbance in the atmosphere. Your wife, kids, would've walked through the space that was you and shivered, rubbed the goosebumps on their arms and wondered if they'd left a window open. You can't honestly tell me you would've wanted any of that."

"I would have been with them."

"No, you wouldn't. You think you would have, but trust me, that kind of situation—the inertia—it sticks to you. I've seen it, seen guys who had the same idea as you reduced to a single word they keep whispering as they melt into the wall. Not pretty. Believe me—this is better, way better."

"This?" Lynch raised a hand to the room. "This place? I can't even remember its name."

"It's not much on the ambiance, I'll give you that. But they do have Ella on the jukebox."

Despite himself, Lynch smiled. "Yeah."

"Hey—remember when you got here and you thought it was heaven? I guess it kind of made sense, what with all the white around, but still."

"Well, I revised my assessment the minute I met you."

"What are you talking about?" She sounded almost aggrieved. "You count yourself damned lucky if I'm the angel waiting at the end of your tunnel of light. Just see how well you do on your own. Five minutes, and you'd be roaming the streets, scaring people half to death with your moaning."

"'Half to death': very funny."

"Whatever."

The jukebox exchanged one country song for another that Lynch knew, Kenny Rogers rasping "The Gambler." After a moment, he said, "So what about this van?"

"What about it?"

"What happened to it?"

"That's what we're trying to figure out."

"That's what I'm trying to figure out. I'm the new one, remember? I think you know exactly who did this."

"You're wrong."

"Then you have a very good idea."

"No, nothing that would count as very good."

"Stop playing word games."

"I'm not. The most I've got is a couple of facts I don't like very much."

"There was no one, no *impression*, at the accident scene. We already said that."

"Yeah," Melinda said, "but what it means . . . the thing that did this—you figure it has to be some kind of animal, right?"

"I don't know about that," Lynch said.

"Have you ever seen a collision between two cars that looked like that?"

"I haven't seen many—any accidents at all, if that's your reference point. Bad as it was, though, if another car had been involved, I can't imagine it would have been in any kind of shape to drive away."

"Yes, exactly."

Lynch held up his hand. "But there's no animal that could have done that to a van. Maybe a bunch of tigers, or polar bears, only those things don't hunt in groups, do they? Not to mention, they're pretty scarce in these parts. No, I think what happened to that family was the fault of people, some kind of gang, or a cult, maybe."

"How do you explain the damage to the van? You saw the shape that thing was in, like a bag of potato chips that'd been torn open. Not to mention the family—their physical remains. I saw you trying not to look too closely, but you know what I'm talking about. There's a gang of super-strong cannibals on the loose, waylaying hapless motorists?"

"It's better than rabid polar bears."

"Not by much."

"What, then?"

"Something that makes me uber-nervous. Something strong enough to push a decent-sized van that must have been going a decent speed off the road, get into it, and devour the passengers, body and soul."

"I thought we weren't souls."

"Figure of speech. Something that can consume their flesh and their impression on the quantum subjectile—their ghosts. Better?"

"What can do that? You're describing a monster."

Melinda nodded. "I am."

"And you're serious."

"It's what fits the facts."

"A monster?"

"For all intents and purposes, yes."

"And this is better than the super-strong cannibals how?"

"Would it help if I called it a self-precipitating and -perpetuating anomaly that's accumulated sufficient energy to allow it to pierce the ontological membrane?"

"Monster it is, then."

"Don't look so offended. You can't tell me you never saw this kind of thing on the way here. It hasn't been that long since I made the Walk; I know what it's like. There's that long, blank time when you don't know anything. Then you realize you're moving, shuffling along a road, which looks an awful lot like one of the main roads you live near, except that it's colorless, not white or gray so much as *faint*, a pencil drawing done on cheap paper. Whatever lies to either side of you is too vague for you to make out, but you don't worry about that very much, if at all. You're surrounded by people all around you, some heading in your direction, the rest bound for God-knows-where. Just about everyone's dressed in one version or another of normal clothing; although maybe you see an old woman over there who's in her nightgown and slippers, a guy over here who's too old and fat for the baseball uniform he's squeezed into. To your right, there's a kid—you thought he was a kid, sixteen or seventeen, but when you turn your head again, you see he's fifty if he's a day. That's a little strange, but it isn't as bad as the woman ahead who keeps *flickering*. While you watch her, she goes from being stick-legged twelve to broad-hipped thirty, like a jump-cut in a movie. You look down, and maybe the hand you hold up looks a little rough at the edges. A few folks try to walk together—could be you're one of them—but it doesn't last long. For one thing, you can't hear each other too well. It's as if your ears are clogged. Even your own voice sounds as if it's coming more from inside your head than your mouth. For another thing, you can't stay focused on what anyone else is saying long enough for a meaningful exchange. Your mind keeps returning to this question, to the Question: What happened to me?

"But it's a question that isn't really a question. It's a placeholder for an image. You, stomping the brake and steering hard to the right as the truck backs out of the alley directly ahead of you. Or you, lying in a hospital bed wired to a host of machines, a ridge of bandages rising over the fresh scar up the center of your chest. Or you, stepping backwards as the kid holding the gun sweeps it in your direction, this lavish gesture that he probably picked up in a movie he watched in rerun on Channel 9. You see his index finger tightening on the trigger, and then—

"That's just it, though: there isn't any *then*. There's that moment, then this moment, this place that looks vaguely familiar, but it's like looking through a lens smeared with Vaseline. The only thing that seems one hundred percent, undeniably real is the compulsion that's drawing you forward, step-by-step, east west north south. You don't have a way to describe it. It's like nothing you've felt before, as if you're an iron filing and the biggest magnet in creation is saying, *Come to me*. What can you do? So you walk.

"And on the way to wherever it is you're bound, there are these people. A man wearing a black suit fifty years out of date, the collar of his shirt open, the ends of an actual bowtie flapping out from under the collar in the wind that blows up as the guy approaches you. From his thin hair, the lines of his face, you take him for an old man, until he draws near enough for you to tell that he isn't, he's maybe the same age as you, he just has one of those old faces, and probably has since he was in his twenties. It's the kind of face he would've spent all his life trying to catch up to. There's about two days' worth of blond stubble on his chin, his long cheeks, which is odd—not that you've made a survey or anything, but the other men you've noticed so far have been by and large clean-shaven. Even the couple of guys with beards you've run across have been pretty well-groomed.

"The man comes closer to you—he staggers, lurches, as if his legs don't work properly, the knees stiff, the hips locked. It's like when you're a kid and you play at being Frankenstein's monster, those same exaggerated motions. All he needs is both arms held out in front of him. They aren't, though. His arms weave and windmill to either side of him, trying to help his balance. He draws closer to you, bringing with him this smell, a thick stink like milk well on its way to becoming cheese. You would think the wind that surrounds him would clear the air, but it's as if the smell is threaded through it. Right before this guy reaches you, clamps one hand on your shoulder, leans toward you, so that you can see his eyes are the same blank color as the road—right then, you realize that this is the first thing you've smelled since—since the scorched rubber of your tires scraping over the blacktop; or the flat, antiseptic hand-sanitizer that your family has to rub over their hands when they enter your cubicle in the ICU, and that clings to their fingers as they slide chips of ice between your lips; or the thick grease the man pointing the gun at you applied to it before he left his apartment to walk to the little bodega you like to stop at for a glass bottle of Mexican Coke.

"When the man, this old-young man in the black suit that has a vest, too, speaks, his voice is a distant shriek, as if the wind around him is carrying it from a long distance. You can't understand everything he's saying, but you hear words like, 'Over here,' and, 'Please,' and, 'Salvation.' The man is gesturing for you to follow him, to leave the road for a place off to one side. The terrain in that direction does seem to be a little more distinct. There are other people there, a surprising number of them. They're standing around a huge bonfire—it's orange, the brightest color you've seen since you started walking. You can't believe how good it feels to see something that vivid. It's almost enough to send you off the road into this . . . pocket.

"What stops you is the figure on the opposite side of the fire from you. You have a hard time seeing it clearly, because the fire's giving off a lot of heavy, black smoke, but it looks enormous, far taller than anyone you've met, and wider, too. Its proportions are wrong, the arms too long, overdeveloped, the chest massive. Its head is narrow, rising almost to a point, as if it's wearing some kind of helmet, and you have the absurd thought that this is no person: it's an ape, a gorilla; although it's nothing like the animals you've stared at in zoos or watched in nature documentaries. This is something that pulls itself up skyscrapers with one hand while swatting airplanes with the other. You're afraid, because how could you not be? But you're fascinated, too, by the sight of something so fantastic. There's still a chance you'll go with the man in the black suit, follow his distant scream, until, trying to peer through the smoke, you see that what the fire's burning are bodies, men and women who continue to move as the flames roar over them. You have the impression that the smoke is being inhaled by the thing on the other side of it—that maybe the smoke *is* it—but you're already moving away from the place, running along the road, in terror that whatever you've witnessed is going to abandon its spot and come after you.

"You wonder what all of this is. It's a question you'll have the chance to ask yourself several more times on your way to whatever your destination is. If you're lucky, you'll be pulled in the direction of one of the major currents, and once you enter it, you'll be whipped along at what feels like a thousand miles an hour. If you're less fortunate, there's more walking in your future; maybe a lot. Either way, in the course of your journey, you'll see a number of other pockets, some of them pretty elaborate, all of them presided over by huge figures that seem as if they were dreamed up for a Hollywood soundstage."

As ever, Melinda told a good story. It shared enough details with Lynch's actual experience to have him nodding. "Yes," he said, "but I thought you told me the creatures in those pockets were confined to them. Also, that they were made up of the people in the fires, that the men and women in the pockets surrendered themselves to the flames to keep the creatures going."

"That's not the point," Melinda said. "The fact is, there's a whole lot of weird shit out there, so don't be too surprised that we're dealing with some more of it."

Lynch's reply was swallowed in the wave of sound that swept through the bar. It came from his right, where the wall behind the jukebox burst inwards in a spray of wood and drywall. Dust swirled across the floor, blown by the freezing air that rushed into the room. For an instant, the jukebox gave voice to a man insisting that he was so much cooler online, and then a second wave of sound surged through the room. It was a roar, though such a roar as Lynch could not remember ever having heard. Half freight-whistle and half avalanche, it shook the glasses on the tables, clattered the liquor bottles against one another. At the bar, someone screamed, and that solo noise swelled to a chorus when the author of the roar thrust its great head through the breach it had forced.

What Lynch saw reminded him of an alligator, if that alligator's head had been as long as a tall man. Jaws lined with fangs like carving knives thundered together as the head swung right and left, chasing after the women and men who scrambled out of its way. An eye the size of a saucer rolled in its socket. Lynch could see the thing, its pebbled flesh, which appeared feathered in a few places, but he could also see through it, to a bleached skull that would have been at home in a museum display. *Tyrannosaurus Rex*, he heard Anthony's voice say. *King tyrant-lizard*. He shook his head. The beast sucked in a mighty breath, and unleashed a fresh bellow. Lynch backed into the booth. A busboy who had dropped to the floor when the wall exploded slipped as he scurried to his feet, and the monster darted its head to catch him as he fell. Its teeth scissored him in half with a wet crunch that vented blood into the wind. Droplets spattered Lynch, who cried out and rinsed his arms against them.

Melinda seized his hand. "Come on," she said, "while it's occupied."

Lynch didn't argue. Still holding her hand, he bolted for the door, past the enormous head jerking towards the ceiling as it gulped the busboy down.

Outside, the early evening was full of snow and screaming and the distant whine of sirens. Melinda steered them to the extended porch of the second building up the street from the bar. Lynch flattened against the space between a pair of windows. Melinda remained at the edge of the porch.

"Come back!" Lynch hissed. "It'll see you."

"Hear that?" Melinda said. Through the screams and the approaching sirens, Lynch heard the crack of timbers snapping, the rattle of debris on the ground. "That's it leaving."

"Leaving? Where's it going?"

"Back out there," Melinda said, nodding towards the plains. "It's moving fast. I figured we'd have at least a few days before it tried the town. Then again, who knows how long it's been on the loose, already?"

"Okay," Lynch said. "Okay." If he acted as if he were calm, maybe he would be calm. "What now?"

Melinda had no answer.

III

On what Lynch thought was the north side of town, a solitary black mailbox stood on the street side of a large, vacant lot. Lynch was reasonably sure there had been a house and barn here at some point; on a couple of his and Melinda's previous stops at the mailbox, he'd had the impression of a pair of large, boxlike structures, one closer to the road, the other farther back, neither quite visible, both more like the smudges left after an eraser has cleared the blackboard. Each time, he had intended to ask Melinda about the phenomenon, but the message she'd read on the letter she withdrew from the mailbox had pre-empted his question. This morning, nothing was visible in the lot except a few tufts of scrub grass poking through the crusted snow. Lynch supposed this was for the best. He hadn't appreciated how exposed this location was: only one more street of small warehouses separated the mailbox from the expanse of the plains, dazzling white under the early sun. He didn't need any distractions from the vigil he was doing his best to maintain. Had he been a soldier, once? He thought so; though it was more of the obligatory-duty variety, not the active-wartime type. Hard to imagine that combat experiences, however intense, would have prepared him for the beast that had thrown the jukebox crashing over.

After a restless night spent within the bland confines of a modest Protestant church, Melinda had set out for the mailbox. Lynch had started to protest the recklessness of her decision, but she had cut him off, asking, "What makes you think we're any safer inside? That thing didn't seem to have any trouble breaking down the wall to that bar." All the same, Lynch wanted to say, there was a difference between the beast coming looking for you and you putting yourself out where it could find you. But already, Melinda was out of earshot.

Lynch didn't understand the black mailbox. Aside from the two of them, he doubted anyone could see or touch it, but with its chipped black paint and flag broken at the base, it had a strangely substantial feel, as if whoever had leveled the house and barn it served had intended to remove it, as well, but failed to complete the job. Once a day, he accompanied Melinda to it so that she could lower its front door and check its oblong interior. There was almost always something inside, usually a letter in a denim-blue envelope whose flap Melinda split with her thumb. She would read the letter twice, return it to its envelope, and replace the envelope within the mailbox, which she shut. As yet, she had not shared any of the messages with Lynch.

Instead, presumably following directions she'd received, Melinda led them to a different part of the town or its surroundings. There, they performed a task whose significance was generally lost on Lynch. A day or two after he arrived here, they ventured to the dirt alley separating a pair of houses, where Melinda handed him a shovel he hadn't noticed her carrying and directed him to dig at a spot a foot and half away from one of the houses. Lynch, who would never be sure of the exact relationship between his present form and the world he continued to inhabit, took the shovel and sank it into the ground. About two feet down, the blade rang on metal. Working more slowly, Lynch cleared the dirt from a bronze disk the diameter of a dinner plate. Its surface was incised with tiny symbols that Lynch didn't recognize. He pried the disk loose and raised it on the shovel to Melinda, who took it with heavy gloves he hadn't seen her tug on. After he refilled the hole, and leaned the shovel against the house where she told him to, Lynch returned with Melinda to the mailbox. He guessed its opening would be too small to fit the bronze plate, but Melinda angled the disk and the mailbox accepted it without difficulty.

On another occasion, they passed unhindered and unchallenged into the recesses of the town jail. On the wall of one of its cells was an elaborate graffiti that Melinda copied onto a slip of paper whose destination was the mailbox. A third time, they made their way into the large rest home on the west side of town in order for Melinda to stare at an old woman whose face had so many lines, it was difficult to pick out her eyes and mouth among them. Of course, Lynch had asked what the purpose of their actions was, but Melinda had deflected his questions with one of her own: "You had plans?" If he persisted, she told him that what he was asking was above his pay grade, and refused to be drawn any further. Her answer was the same when he asked who, exactly, was sending the messages.

Today, the mailbox yielded a padded envelope whose contents jingled as Melinda tore it open. She removed a letter and a pair of keys from it. Lynch watched her face as she read and reread the letter, but could discern nothing from her features. She replaced the letter in the mailbox, and held onto the keys. "This way," she said to Lynch, and started in the direction of the next street and its warehouses and, beyond, the open plains. Lynch had no desire to walk any distance out of town; in retrospect, their trip to survey the remains of the van the previous day seemed to him the height of recklessness. Neither did he want to abandon Melinda; in the time that he'd been here, she had been essential to him adjusting to . . . everything, to all of it. He wasn't sure she was an irresistible force, but he was no immovable object. Following arguments with his wife, hadn't he apologized first? After confrontations with the kids over infractions of the house rules, hadn't he sought them out in their rooms, mock-bullying them into reconciliation? Nonetheless, the white expanse sparkling in the distance made his throat constrict with dread.

Melinda led them into the shadowed space between a pair of darkened warehouses. Some kind of car sat in the middle of the passageway. Eyes dazzled by the sun, Lynch did not register the vehicle as anything more than smallish, low to the ground. Melinda stopped beside the driver's door. Bending at the waist, she slotted one of the keys she'd received from the mailbox into the lock. She swung the door wide and surveyed the car's interior. "You drive?" she said.

"Yes."

"Stick?"

"Uh-huh."

"Okay, then." Straightening, she snapped her wrist. The keys arced through the air. Lynch lunged at, caught them. He said, "Hang on. We have cars?"

"Car," Melinda said. She was circling to the passenger's door. "Chop chop."

A two-seater, the car's age was apparent in the rips in its buckets seats, the roughing of the steering wheel and dashboard. Surprisingly for this location, it was a convertible. Lynch leaned over to unlock Melinda's door, then slid the key into the ignition and turned it. The engine came to life with a coughing growl. Something about the deep rumble felt achingly familiar. Lynch put in the clutch, pushed the gearshift into first, and let the clutch out slowly. The car eased along the passageway into daylight. As it did, Lynch saw that its hood was white, its fenders a burnt-orange that might have faded from red. He jerked his foot off the clutch. The car lurched and stalled.

"Is there a problem?" Melinda said.

"This car," Lynch said. "I know this car."

"Okay."

"No, you don't . . . it's an MG—I can't remember the model, has a V8 engine. It was my, my fantasy car, you know? For when I won the lottery. One summer—we were on vacation—we used to vacation at a little lake somewhere north—the Adirondacks, I think. We rented a cottage just up from the beach. The couple who owned the place had a son who was the same age as my boy. Their youngest. Most days, the boys hung around together, building sandcastles, catching bullfrogs, going on hikes around the lake. The mother and father were nice enough. I can't recall their names. I talked cars with him a couple of times each trip. Nothing too involved, but he knew I liked the MG. One afternoon, he came down to the cottage and asked my wife if he could borrow me for a little while. She said, Sure, take him.

"I couldn't figure out what he wanted me for. He was big into his beer, too—thought of himself as a connoisseur. I wasn't, not really, but I'd traveled for work, places like Germany and Belgium, where I'd tasted some decent beer, so this man liked to share whatever beers he'd discovered with me. It wasn't beer, though: it was this." Lynch spread his hands to take in the car. "Somehow, he had found an MG for sale at a price he was willing to afford. He knew I'd appreciate the purchase. The car looked a little worse for wear, but the engine ran fine. We popped the hood to check it. Anthony, my boy, was around, playing with the man's son. Both boys came over to admire the car. The man turned to me, and asked if I wanted to take the car for a run. At first, I thought he was saying that he was going to try out the car and was inviting me to come along—which would have been fine. But no. He handed me the keys and told me the car could use a good run.

"It was so unexpected, so . . . generous. I felt the way you do when something good just happens to you, out of the blue. I asked Anthony if he wanted to go for a ride. He did. We belted in, and off we went. The top was down, which made it hard for us to have much of a conversation. But I could see the expression on his face. He wasn't that old, maybe eight or nine. He was putting on his best serious face. I'd never included him in anything like this, before, and he was trying to show he understood it—its importance. The sheer pleasure lit up my face. I loved to drive. I didn't get my license until I was in my twenties, but the minute I did, it was as if the driver's seat was where I was born to be. My son had a toy: I can't remember what it was called, but it was a kind of a space-age centaur, except, instead of horse's legs, it had four tires. My wife said that was me.

"Anyway, I took the car to a highway and went all the way up to fifth. Probably too fast. Definitely too fast. If there had been a cop there, he wouldn't have had to use his radar gun. There weren't any cops. I don't think there was anyone on our side of the road. To the left, there was a mountain, leaning back to a round peak. On either side of us, the scenery whipped by, but in the distance, that mountain turned very slowly.

"I could have kept going, would have driven all the way to Canada and back. I wonder if Anthony remembers it." Lynch shook his head. "What is this car doing here?"

"Waiting for you to drive it," Melinda said.

"You know what I mean."

"I can't tell you."

"More information that's above my pay grade?"

"Probably, but that isn't why. I don't know why this particular car was waiting for us. I do know that we don't usually use cars because of the risk of drawing undue attention to ourselves. We exist beyond the limit of most people's perceptions. Give us a car to roar around in, and we move that much closer to visibility, which causes all kinds of complications. That we're sitting in this vehicle tells me how serious the situation with this creature has become."

"All right," Lynch said.

"I heard a theory, once," Melinda said, "that your impression on the subjectile can form a kind of bond with other impressions. Doesn't work for people, otherwise, you'd be surrounded by your loved ones, right? But maybe it applies to objects."

"Huh," Lynch said. "It's a pity I never owned a bazooka. You?"

"Closest I came was a shotgun, which, I think you'd agree, is not up to the task."

"No," Lynch said. "Where are we going?"

"The battleground. Think you can find it?"

"We'll see." He let out the clutch, and steered onto the street.

IV

What Melinda called the battleground was a shallow bowl in the landscape maybe five hundred yards across. It was five miles north-northeast from town, along a narrow road that followed the twists of a wide creek. Melinda had taken Lynch to the place the third day after his arrival, as a lesson in blending in with the living. A small tour bus ferried interested tourists out to the site, waited a couple of hours for them to wander its grounds, read the plaques positioned around it, and visit the gift shop, then carried them back to town. The bus was never full, Melinda said, which allowed the two of them to steal aboard and take one of the seats at the rear, where they found it relatively easy to escape detection, except for a toddler, a girl in blue overalls, who would not stop staring at them.

Not to worry, Melinda said, kids—little kids—saw all kinds of things adults didn't.

When he and Melinda had exited the bus, Lynch had been struck by the noise, a cacophony of screams, shouts, cracks, and booms, which none of the other passengers appeared to notice.

It filled the air this bright morning, as he and Melinda stepped out of the MG. Per her instructions, he had driven the car to the far end of the parking lot—empty at this early hour—then up the access road that led the short distance to the bluff that overlooked the large dip in the earth. Lynch parked there; though he observed that a dirt version of the road continued down into and across the snowy expanse.

"Well," Melinda said, "what do you think?"

Lynch couldn't remember what the name of the battle was. It was part of the larger struggle between the United States Army and the natives of the northern plains that had flared in the decade following the Civil War. Some thirty or forty cavalry had ridden straight into a significantly larger contingent of Lakota and Cheyenne. The physical engagement between the forces was over in less than an hour, and resulted in the devastation of the Army forces. Its place in the history books had been overshadowed by the events at the Little Big Horn, a short while after. Here, however, in this intermediate existence, the battle had not ended. Lakota warriors, their bodies dyed yellow and red, their feathered headdresses streaming behind them, rode their horses between cavalry officers who struggled to draw a bead on them with their long pistols. A handful of soldiers fired their rifles from behind the barricade they had improvised of their dead horses. A trio of Cheyenne warriors shot the soldiers who were attempting to position a pair of small cannons near the top of the slope opposite. Men shouted commands and obscenities. Clouds of gray smoke floated across the ground, over puddles and pools of blood. Holes burst open in men's heads, their chests, where bullets struck them. Arms, feet, hung dangling from where they'd been shot. Unhorsed Native warriors swung heavy clubs at the soldiers who swung the butts of their rifles at them. Men screamed in exultation and agony. Rifles snapped. The cannons thudded. In ones, twos, more, men died—then continued the battle, rising unwounded to attack one another anew. Above the scene, the smoke gathered in a great knot whose contours suggested a fist.

The first time Lynch had seen this place, had watched the tourists wandering its grounds, blissfully ignorant of the horror continuously unfolding around them, he had demanded an explanation from Melinda. For once, she had answered him directly. Some events, she had said, were sufficiently traumatic that their participants remained caught in them, long after they occurred. War, violence, tended to produce that result. Did that mean these men were trapped here, like this, forever? he'd asked. Melinda had shrugged. They'd been here this long.

The cannons boomed, dirt geysered, and Lynch understood what Melinda was proposing. Here was an army for them to employ. "Would that work?" he said.

"If we could lure it here, maybe."

"But," he gestured at the combatants. "It hasn't stopped any of them."

"That's because they're caught in this event. Bring someone, or something else into it, and the situation becomes a lot more dangerous."

"What about all of them?" He nodded to the men.

"I suppose it'll rip most of them to shreds; though the horses might help. I'm not sure how fast the thing can run."

"What'll happen to them?"

"They'll cease to exist," Melinda said. Before Lynch could voice the objection forming on his lips, she added, "Which is harsh, yes. But is it any more so than what they're trapped in, now? Who was it said that hell is repetition? What do you think this is for these guys?"

"And who says you get to make that decision?"

"If you have a better idea, I'm all ears."

A half-dozen proposals flitted through his mind, each relying on a crucial detail whose impossibility rendered the rest of the plan useless: he and Melinda revealing themselves to the town's authorities; those men and women understanding and accepting what actually was happening; detonating the fuel tanks of one of the gas stations in the center of town; procuring an M1A1 Abrams tank. He shook his head. He'd already figured out who was going to be leading the beast here, too.

V

As he turned out of the parking lot, Lynch said, "I'm pretty sure I know what this creature is."

"A Tyrannosaurus, right?"

He nodded. "T. Rex."

"It looked different in the movies. Less of those little feathers. What makes you so sure?"

"Science projects. For school: my kids."

"Huh," Melinda said. "Okay."

Science projects: the words were keys, unlocking the padlocks on a cache of memory. He had helped all of his children with their annual entries for the school science fair, which he recalled describing (to whom?) as the bane of his existence, elaborate posters and models whose design and construction were inevitably delayed until the night before the event. (One of the girls—Katie?—had been somewhat more responsible, beginning her projects a weekend or two early.) Anthony, in particular, had little interest in science proper. Hadn't Lynch encouraged him to build a basic pulley, and hadn't he rejected the idea through his apathy towards it? The topics in which his oldest was interested: The Loch Ness Monster, UFOs, Bigfoot, had skirted the edge of legitimate science, to put it mildly, and while Lynch had built models for him in his basement workshop out of Plaster of Paris, he'd done so with a dull annoyance souring the process.

A patch of ice on the road ahead burned phosphorous-bright with sunlight. Lynch squinted and eased off the gas.

The exception had been Anthony's third grade project, when he had selected dinosaurs as his topic. Lynch had known his son was interested in the great beasts; the enthusiasm appeared general amongst the boys his age. Certainly, Lynch had purchased enough plastic and rubber replicas of the creatures for Anthony to have a plentiful supply with which to populate the diorama they fashioned on Lynch's workbench. What he hadn't counted on was Anthony's passion for actual dinosaurs, which had resulted in his son attaining what seemed to Lynch an encyclopedic level of knowledge of the vanished animals, from their Latin designations to their habits to the precise eras during which the various species had roamed the planet. A pair of figurines he'd assumed showed the same bipedal carnivore did not: the one with the slightly more-developed forelegs was Allosaurus, who had lived tens of millions of years before the larger-headed Tyrannosaurus Rex. Lynch had held Tyrannosaurus up for inspection as Anthony described its six-foot skull, its long jaw lined with six-inch fangs. Believe it or not, Anthony had said, paleontologists weren't sure if T. Rex hunted its prey, or if it was a gigantic scavenger, like a vulture or hyena.

The monster whose teeth had bit a man in two was Anthony's Tyrannosaurus, and from the way it had snapped at the men and women fleeing from it, it had no trouble chasing its meals down. "How is this even possible?" Lynch said.

"You do realize the irony of your question," Melinda said.

"By that logic, this place should be overrun by thousands more creatures like that one. Not to mention, all the animals that have lived here since then."

The road veered towards the creek, whose surface consisted of thousands of shards of light. Lynch accelerated through the curve.

"Touché," Melinda said. "From what I understand, the subjectile consists of layers. It's like the bottom of the sea: things drift down and settle there and, over time, you wind up with this stratified structure. What belongs to a particular era tends to remain at that approximate level, so to speak. There's some movement possible between levels if they're relatively close, but beyond a certain, limited range, you're pretty much stuck where you are."

"So eventually we'll become what? Fossilized ghosts?"

Melinda looked away. "Not exactly. It's more a case of, we'll be sealed off within our layer."

"That doesn't sound much better."

"Don't worry about that. What matters is, this is why you haven't been chased by hordes of hungry velociraptors, or stalked by a saber-toothed tiger."

"However," Lynch said, "I have seen more than I would have liked of a Tyrannosaurus." The things you'd never think you'd say.

"True," Melinda said. "There are fissures in the subjectile, cracks that extend deep—very deep, in a couple of cases—into it. They're dangerous—unstable—but if you could navigate one, you might be able to cross a tremendous part of the structure."

"That would have to be a pretty significant break, for a dinosaur to come up it."

"There are a couple that go back a ways, and a new one could have formed. It's also possible the T. Rex found its way along a series of smaller cracks, like a rat solving a maze."

"What happens if we don't stop it?"

"It continues to chow down on the living, gaining strength as it does."

"But eventually, the Army—the modern Army—will come in and blast it."

"Eventually," Melinda said. "In the meantime, people continue to die horribly, deprived of any chance of a continuing existence. Even after the Army shows up, depending on when exactly this is, they may find it harder to deal with the thing than they'd expect. By then, the T. Rex will have ingested a lot of energy from its victims, which will tend to make it more resilient."

"You make it sound like some kind of vampire."

"That isn't too far off."

"That . . ." In front of him, the road wavered, as if a sheet of water had slid over the windshield. Instinctively, he downshifted, tapping the brake as he did. The engine whined at being forced into lower gear. "A . . ."

As clearly as if he was standing beside them, he saw Anthony and his son, Jordan. They were in a narrow room, its walls peach, its floor carpeted (cream), one end occupied by a small bed whose blue frame was the shape of a sports car—Jordan's bed—they were in Jordan's bedroom, in the house Anthony and his wife were renting in that village with the French name (Arles? St. Marie? Lyon?). Anthony was lying on the floor, on his left side, his head supported with his left hand. Jordan was sitting across from him, all of his five-year-old's attention focused on the assortment of toys spread out between them. Lynch saw rows of plastic cowboys and Indians, all cast in the same bright red and yellow. Opposite the figures, a handful of Matchbox cars and trucks lay overturned. Jordan's small hands gripped a plastic Tyrannosaur that was almost too big for him. It was painted red, with almost fluorescent purple stripes wrapping its back. Between its shoulders, a rectangular button protruded which, when Jordan pressed it in, opened the toy's mouth and caused it to emit an electronic roar. Anthony held a Matchbox car between the thumb and index finger of his right hand that he drove in circles over the carpet, making revving-engine and squealing-tire sounds as he did. "I'm gonna get you!" Jordan shouted, shaking his dinosaur.

"No way, man," Anthony said, grinning. "This is an MG, the fastest car ever made."

"I have T. Rex!" Jordan said. "Rawr! Rawr!"

"MG's faster than T. Rex," Anthony said.

"Oh no he isn't," Jordan said.

"Oh yes he is," Anthony said.

"Well—he's a vampire!" Jordan shouted.

"A vampire?" Anthony said. "Uh oh . . ."

"LYNCH!" Something slapped his right cheek, hard. "We're in the middle of the freaking road!"

"What?" He turned, and, for a moment, did not know the woman sitting next to him. Face stinging, he closed his eyes, certain that, when he opened them, he would be someplace else: a hospital bed, most likely, wired to a dozen different devices charting his steady decline, surrounded by his wife and children, their faces forecasting the grief due to arrive. But the sight that greeted him was the same as the one he'd left, the woman he knew was Melinda facing him across the interior of the MG whose engine was rumbling away, while the air outside filled with snow.

The expression on Melinda's features blended concern with irritation. "Whatever's happening to you," she said, "can it wait long enough for you to move us out of the path of any oncoming traffic?"

Already, this existence had settled upon him like a cat that rises from your lap, only to position itself there more comfortably. "It's—I'm fine," he said, and put in the clutch.

VI

Here the road ran straight through the plains. Had the remainder of the drive to the town been longer, Lynch supposed Melinda might have spent more of it quizzing him about what had happened. As it was, he answered the single question she put to him by saying he'd just remembered something—a memory he didn't care to discuss, he added—and that seemed to be enough for her. It was far from sufficient for him, in no small part because it wasn't true. Enough of his life, his previous life, his living life, remained opaque for him not to be sure, but he didn't think he'd witnessed the scene of Anthony playing with Jordan. It didn't have the familiar, the comfortable feel of his actual memories. At the same time, some quality of the exchange he'd observed struck him as authentic. Which meant what, exactly? That his son and grandson were aware of the posthumous drama in which he found himself an actor? Or that Lynch was in some way playing out the situation they were enacting? It could be a coincidence, but if so, it was such a one as to push the idea past the point of breaking.

Ahead, on the right-hand side of the road, sat the single trailer that marked the farthermost limit of the town in this direction. Although the snow had picked up, the great rent in its middle was clearly visible. A ribbon of black smoke wound up from the trailer's interior to the clouds assembling overhead. Lynch slowed, glancing at Melinda.

"There's no point," she said. "We know what we'll find."

"All right," he said, "where to, then?"

"The Highway. Maybe someone will have seen something."

What Melinda called the Highway ran due north out of town. The name was as much metaphor as description. A path wide enough for a half-dozen people to walk abreast, the Highway rode the contours of the land out to a junction that was lost in the distance. An irregular but unceasing flow of people left the town walking the route, most of them finding their way to it from the rest home on the west side. Their ultimate destinations were unknown to Lynch and, so she claimed, to Melinda. It was the Highway that had brought him to this place that, yes, he had mistaken for Heaven, because where else could the journey he'd taken have led? In the days since, he had avoided the path, half-afraid that, were he to stray too close to it, he would be caught by it and find himself embarked on a fresh odyssey.

Given what Lynch recalled of his early moments on the road that had led him away from the place of his decease, he was skeptical of Melinda's plan. On the other hand, he hadn't encountered any dinosaurs on that route, so maybe it was worth a try, after all. He turned right at the first intersection.

To his left, a dozen streets deeper into the town, the firehouse's siren sent up its mournful call. The falling snow seemed to dampen it.

"The trailer," he said.

"You hope," Melinda said.

A left onto a side street, a right onto a road that ran between rows of weather-beaten houses, another left onto a long driveway that dead-ended in a small parking lot, brought them there. The Highway commenced at the other side of the parking lot, a flat path whose dull white surface appeared to consist of some kind of rock. Lynch did not see anyone in the parking lot, nor on the road. He pulled the parking brake, went to turn the key.

Melinda said, "Wait."

He did. "What?"

"Take us out there," she said.

"Is that allowed?"

"Is there anyone stopping us?"

"That's not the same thing," he said, but he released the brake and rolled the car onto the Highway. The snow was streaming down, large white flakes whose individual designs he could almost pick out. Although they eddied around the car, none of them landed on the windshield, the hood, or stuck to the windows. On either side, the plains were veiled by white.

Lynch felt the dash for the controls to the radio. "What are you doing?" Melinda said.

"Trying to find the radio."

"You want to listen to music, now?"

"It calms—"

"Hang on," Melinda said, "what's that?"

"What?"

"That." She pointed at a spot on the road maybe ten feet ahead on the right. Lynch slowed the car to a crawl as he followed the direction Melinda indicated. For a moment, he could pick out nothing except snow falling behind snow, then the shape Melinda had noticed came into focus. The size of a small bird, it appeared to be floating a couple of feet off the ground with a lazy motion that reminded Lynch of a balloon. Which was ridiculous. He brought the car to a stop and flipped on the headlights. The snow caught most of the light and flung it back, but the shape did not. By the glow of the headlights, Lynch saw that it was a human hand, an adult's, most likely, severed at the wrist. Palm up, fingers outstretched, it rotated in a slow circle.

Nor was it alone. Suspended at different heights along the road in front of them, a variety of body parts formed a grisly constellation: a pair of hands, one clenched, one open; a foot, toes pointed down as if for ballet; an arm and part of a shoulder, ribbons of blood trailing from its ragged edge; and a head in the approximate center of everything, the open eyes reflecting the headlights, the mouth slack, the heavy white hair swaying around it.

"God . . ." Stunned, Lynch did not register the massive shape looming behind the carnage. When the Tyrannosaur lunged forward, sending body parts spinning off like marbles, its vast jaws open, he hesitated, shocked, before dropping the car into reverse. The MG jolted to the right as the beast's jaws smashed the windshield and tore the roof. Lynch cried out and threw his arms in front of his face. With a shriek of torn metal, the T. Rex pulled its head up, taking the roof and half of the windshield with it. Snow rushed into the car. Lynch simultaneously let out the clutch and floored the gas. The car lurched backwards, heading for the edge of the road. He caught the steering wheel, cut it to the right, and once the car was in the center of the Highway, straightened out. He half-turned in his seat, to see the direction he was reversing. As he did, he saw Melinda's seat empty, the top half of it bitten away.

VII

Lynch crested the bluff overlooking the battlefield, downshifted into second, and plunged down the dirt road that led into the thick of the continuing battle. The road was smoother than he had anticipated; though not enough for him to shift to third. At least the snow seemed to be abating. Hooves thudding on the ground, a brown horse carrying a painted Sioux warrior galloped in front of him. A trio of soldiers fired their rifles after the man, and Lynch heard the bullets zip overhead. The stink of gunpowder clotted the air. A Cheyenne warrior aimed his rifle at the three soldiers, and his shot struck the MG's trunk with a hollow ping. On the left, a pair of cavalry officers, their pistols held out in front of them, raced past.

He had been hoping to cover half the battleground before the Tyrannosaur arrived. He was maybe a third of the way when its roar split the air. A glance over his shoulder showed the creature already rushing down the road after him, its great head swaying from side to side as its powerful hind legs propelled it forward, its tapered tail out behind it as ballast. *Big.* It was so big. He had never appreciated how stupendously big these animals had been. He heard young Anthony's voice saying that a full-grown T. Rex would have been longer than a city bus, but that had been an abstraction, an illustration on a page, two-dimensional. In no way had it prepared him for the beast in 3-D, its bulk, black and yellow, the back ornamented with what appeared to be feathers, its mouth jammed full of razored fangs, its sheer, relentless vitality. He had assumed he would have to drive slowly enough for the Tyrannosaurus to keep up with and keep its interest in him. He had been wrong. From the start, the creature had moved with a speed and stamina that had required what skill he possessed as a driver to outrun, even as he steered the road winding out here. Now, hampered by this dirt road he was struggling not to skid along, he was losing the slender lead he'd maintained on the animal.

A bullet chipped a piece off what was left of the windshield. Lynch flinched. A Cheyenne warrior leapt his horse across the car. The Tyrannosaur's roar drowned out the rifles cracking around him. He looked back, saw its jaws almost at the trunk. He stomped the gas, heard the bite crash where he'd been. He shifted to third, fighting to hold the car to the road as it bumped and bounced over it. Bullets rang on the passenger door. With a thunder of hooves, half a dozen cavalry flanked the car, keeping pace with it. Lynch saw the men looking at him, seeing him, attempting to fit him to the scene in which they'd acted for so long. In a few of their expressions, a terrible knowledge hovered. One man waved his pistol at Lynch, who couldn't tell if the gesture was intended as threat, or request for him to pull over. The T. Rex bit the man off his horse, taking a chunk of the horse's back with him. The horse screamed and thrashed, mortally hurt. The other riders peeled away, only to circle around and begin firing their guns at the creature. In an instant, it was off the road and among them, knocking one soldier and his horse to the ground with a blow from its head, then falling on them. A swipe of its tail took the legs out from under another horse, rolling it over on top of its rider. A quartet of soldiers bunkered behind the carcasses of their horses shifted their aim from the Sioux warriors racing past them to the beast and delivered a volley into its flank. It wheeled and leapt at them. For their part, the Sioux swung their rifles away from the soldiers and sighted on the thing's head.

Halfway across, the access road leveled off and ran straight to the foot of the slope where the twin cannons were positioned. Lynch saw the soldiers stationed at them pause in their duties to consider the situation unfolding below them. To either side of him, Native warriors and U.S. soldiers had stopped their bloody routine to observe the monster fighting their colleagues. A few were riding or running in the direction of the new threat. The MG's engine whined as Lynch raced the remaining distance to the bluff. Behind him, the Tyrannosaurus roared in answer to waves of gunfire. Funny, he thought, how in movies, you were supposed to find these creatures sympathetic, even root for them against the humans—whereas his sole desire at present was to return this example of the species to the extinct category.

When the road climbed the far slope, Lynch put in the clutch and let the car's momentum carry it part of the way up; then, before it slowed too much, he dropped into second and closed the rest of the distance to the cannons. Once he was beside the artillery, he braked hard, letting out the clutch too fast and stalling the car. It didn't matter. He flung open his door and ran to the handful of men in sweat-stained blue shirts and grimy grey pants. They watched him approach, their eyes enormous. Young—most of them were Anthony's age, younger; the oldest couldn't be more than thirty. *Orders*, he thought. *These boys are soldiers. They need orders.* "Who's in charge, here?" he said.

A fellow with yellow sergeant's chevrons on his sleeve stepped forward. He had a long nose, a droopy mustache, a checkered bandana knotted around his neck. Voice raspy, he said, "I am."

"How good is your aim?" Lynch said.

"Good enough."

Lynch pointed toward the T. Rex. "If you can hit the head, do it. If not, the chest. I don't know how fast you are; I do know how fast that thing is. If you miss the first time, you might have a second. The beast won't give you a third."

The sergeant nodded. Turning, he said, "All right: you heard the man."

While the soldiers prepped and aimed the guns, Lynch surveyed the battlefield. As far as he could see, every last man on it had forsaken the round of actions that had occupied him the last century and a half to join the attack on the Tyrannosaur. Sioux, cavalry, Cheyenne rode this way and that around the animal, weaving in and out of one another's paths as they emptied their rifles and pistols into its hide, searching for weak spots. From positions farther out, men on foot maintained a steady stream of fire at the animal. For its part, the Tyrannosaurus ranged amongst its attackers, darting its head to bite the head from a horse, catching a man under one of its rear legs and crushing him to the ground, spinning and knocking a pair of men from their mounts with a blow from its tail. In the short time it had been on the field, the creature had cut the number of men on it in half. Bodies and pieces of bodies lay strewn across the earth. Overhead, the low, dark cloud that Lynch had observed during his previous visits to the site seemed to draw down closer to the earth.

Someone tapped his shoulder: a private, his features waging their own struggle to keep up with what was happening. "Sir?" he said. "Sarge says you may want to cover your ears."

Lynch clapped his hands to his head a second before the cannons erupted, venting fire and smoke in a pair of blasts that buffeted him. One shot went wide, but the other struck the T. Rex on the right hip, staggering it almost off its feet. Enraged, the creature swung in the direction of this new assault. Sighting the soldiers hurrying around the cannons—as well, Lynch thought, as the car it had chased here, in the first place—the thing bellowed and began a halting run towards them. What men remained on the battlefield, realizing the hurt that had been done the Tyrannosaur, renewed their efforts. A group of Sioux and Cheyenne ran at the animal's wounded leg, long clubs and knives out in their hands. A cavalry officer shot close enough to the dinosaur's left eye for it to whip its head around and bite him in half. Next to Lynch, the soldiers loaded the cannons. A Sioux warrior drove his knife into the creature's right foot; it jerked the foot up and out, impaling him on its claws. Despite its injuries, the beast was almost at the start of the bluff. It was met there by the dark cloud, which had been descending from its place above, drawing in on itself as it went, gaining in definition, until what crashed into the T. Rex was almost the same size, a smoky assemblage of limbs that reminded Lynch of nothing so much as a great hand, seizing the Tyrannosaur in its outsized grip.

A vision of Anthony and Jordan at play flickered before his eyes. Anthony was on his back, laughing, the Matchbox MG held aloft in his left hand, his right hand grabbing Jordan's toy Tyrannosaurus, which Jordan, who was sitting on Anthony's stomach, was pushing forward with both hands.

The cannons boomed, the slap of sound deafening. The first shot punched through the cloud-thing and the Tyrannosaur's chest behind it. The second shot struck the dinosaur high in the throat, blowing out the back of its skull. The combined force of the impacts toppled it onto its side. The cloud-creature fell with it.

VIII

Afterward, there was no cheering, no celebration. Looking as if they had awakened from a particularly savage nightmare, the few men who remained began to walk in the direction of the town and, Lynch supposed, the Highway. His hearing had not returned to normal, so he was startled by the soldier who appeared beside him. His mouth moved, and Lynch heard his words as if through ears stuffed with cotton. “Sir,” the young man said, his eyes darting between Lynch and the MG, “are you an angel?”

What would Melinda have said to that? The memory of her stilled his urge to laugh. Instead, he shook his head. “Just a man.”

“This,” the soldier said, the word straining to carry the weight of the men lying in whole and in part across the landscape, the enormous ruin of the Tyrannosaurus, the cloud-thing draining into the earth, even Lynch and the car. “What is all this?”

How should he answer? A game played by his son and grandson? A dying hallucination? The posthumous firing of a few, random brain cells? He considered the soldier standing there, swaying as if drunk. Whatever fantasy this might be, Lynch decided, he could remain loyal to it.

“I suppose,” he said, “you could call it an exorcism.”

For Fiona, and for Nick Langan

CATCHING FLIES

CAROLE JOHNSTONE

Sometimes I pretend I'm a Roman lady in my Roman villa in a countryside which has got long pointy trees and marching soldiers and wide tinkly rivers with ducks and swans. I used to spy on mum watching a TV show called *Rome* and that's where I got the idea. There was lots of blood and guts and sex in it and mum's face went pink when she found my hiding place behind dad's armchair and she told me to close my mouth and sent me to my room and told me never to spy on her watching it again.

But sometimes when mum's busy with Wobs I sneak into the kitchen and pour some of her baking raisins into the bowl that she grinds stuff up in and then some Ribena into the chipped wine glass next to the sink cause I can't reach the good ones. I get the old dust sheet from under the stairs and wrap it round me as many times as I can and still breathe and sometimes I try to pile my hair up on top of my head using string or elastic bands but it doesn't usually work.

There's an old shezlong in the living room that came in a van after granny M died. It's just a couch really—with a low back and only one side—but after I asked mum if granny M died on it and she said no it became the thing that I sit on all the time. Especially when I'm being a Roman lady.

That was what I was doing when mum shouted on me. When she screamed.

Now I'm scared. I'm *more* scared. I'm in a strange room in a strange place and there's people outside it but I don't know who they are. I think they might be policemen and policewomen but they don't have uniforms on.

I don't know where mum is. I don't know where Wobs is. But all the people outside want to know is where dad is and I don't know that either. On Fridays after school he and Sadie-who-tries-to-make-me-call-her-mummy wait outside our house in their car to pick me up. Mum doesn't come out and she thinks I don't know it's 'cause she hates them and then they take me to their house and it takes a while to get there. Their house is much bigger than ours is but I don't like it as much. But I like my room okay. It's painted with big yellow daisies.

I don't like this room. It's wee and white and it smells like the stuff mum puts on my cuts. In it is a bed and a table and a chair and a window that doesn't open 'cause I've tried. I don't like the bed. It's metal and cold. Even the bit where my head goes when I'm sitting up. My bedroom at home is yellow and green and the window opens and has Angelina Ballerina curtains (I've told mum I'm a bit old for them now). My bed is soft and squishy all over and I've got a really cool Lord of the Rings light that stays on all night 'cause I still don't like the dark. There's only one light in here and it's just a bulb hanging from the middle of the ceiling.

I hear the door creak and I open my eyes and swing my legs round so I can get up off the bed. My knees are shaking but I pretend they're not. I close my mouth and make sure with my fingers. A man comes in. He's fat and hairy and he's wearing a stripy jumper that's too small. He's got a white something over his arm. He says "hello, Joanne" and then "can I sit down, Joanne?" and then he does it anyway when I don't say yes.

"Where's my mum?"

"I'm not here to talk about your mum just yet, Joanne."

"Where's my mum? Where's Wobs?" I put my hands on my hips and pretend to be mad. Mum says I'm a stroppy little madam but she smiles when she says it so I think it's a good thing. And sometimes it gets me what I want.

The man tries to smile but his lips won't stretch right. I think there's something wrong with his nose 'cause he sounds coldy and I can hear his breath. I can see his teeth. I can see his *tongue*. It's got white bits on it.

"Let's get you sorted out first, Joanne. I've got you some new clothes to get changed into." He shows me the white things: a T-shirt and joggy bottoms.

"Where's my mum? Where's Wobs?" I'm starting to get scared again. I keep checking my mouth in between speaking 'cause I have to open it to do that.

The man makes a big rattly sigh that makes me feel a bit sick. His eyes look red like dad's used to when he came home late from work. "Wobs is Colin, yes?" He doesn't wait for me to say yes. "He's okay, Joanne. He's in the room right next to you, snug as a bug. He got changed into his new clothes without any fuss at all."

I roll my eyes and forget to be scared. "He's a baby."

The man blinks and tries to smile again. I can't stop hearing his horrible breath. I think I can hear a buzzing noise too and my heart gets jumpy. "Nevertheless—"

"Where's my mum?"

"Joanne." He screws up his fat hairy face. Now he looks the same as dad did when he lied and said he had to go away for a bit. He uses the same kind of voice too. "You *know* what happened to your mum, sweetie."

I shriek when he gets up off the chair and starts coming towards me and then remember to clap my hands over my face. I step backwards and the bed bangs cold at the back of my legs. I think the buzzing is getting louder. Nearer. I look at his horrible tongue and his horrible teeth.

"You should shut your mouth," I say through my fingers.

"We'll talk about your mum soon, I promise, sweetie." His fat face looks worried like he's done something wrong. "Just not yet."

"Shut your mouth!"

"Joanne—"

I'm angry and hot and scared and the backs of my legs are cold *cold* against the bed. "You'll catch flies," I whisper.

He doesn't listen. He keeps on breathing his horrible breath through his horrible mouth and I can tell that he's getting angry now too. He throws the white clothes on the white bed. "You need to get changed, Joanne. You don't have to do it now while I'm here, but you—"

"I've got clothes on!" I shout and one of my fingers slides over my teeth.

He steps back away from me and folds his arms. "But they're dirty, aren't they, Joanne?" he says in dad's voice again. "Look at them. They're dirty."

I look at them. I have to take my hands away from my mouth or else I can't see. I've got on a pair of jeans and my favourite yellow jumper. It's got daisies on it. And blood. Lots of blood. Even though it's dried and even though it's nearly brown. I still remember that it's blood.

I didn't cry when granny M died even though I think I was supposed to. Granny M was mum's mum but she was very strict and very cross and very ugly. When she came round to visit she sat at the table in the kitchen with her cross face and a china cup of tea. She had no lips and lots of wrinkles so her mouth looked all sewed up like a scary puppet.

When she saw me or heard me she'd say to mum "you let that child get away with far too much, Mary." To me she always said "you'll catch flies, girlie!"

Mum said that to me too—all the time in fact, ever since I could talk I bet—but she didn't *just* say that and nothing else. She was fun so it was okay. She let me paint flowers on the walls in our garden and we had Mad Hatter tea parties and when I helped her with dee-I-why and other boring stuff she said things like "hi-ho, hi-ho, it's off to work we go" and "triumph begins with try and ends with umpf!" just to make me giggle I think. Sometimes we danced around the living room to loud music with the curtains shut and she laughed and went pink and forgot to look scared. Sometimes when she tucked me into bed and switched on my Lord of the Rings light and stroked my hair and whispered "I love you, Jojo" I wanted to cry. But it was a nice kind of wanting to cry.

When she shouted for me—when she screamed for me—I got off the shezlong and ran to the stairs. My heart was beating very fast but I still stopped at the bottom to unwind the dust sheet before going up. I wondered if I was in trouble—if she'd heard me saying things like "bastards of Dis!" and "you piss-drinking sons of circus whores!" while I'd been pretending to be a Roman lady. I knew it wasn't that though. I was just trying not to be scared.

Mum had stopped screaming when I got to the landing. I went into Wobs's room on tiptoe though 'cause I was still scared. She was standing next to his cot and her hands were over her mouth. I started to do the same but then she took hers away.

"It's okay now, I think. I'm sorry, Jojo, I didn't mean to frighten you again."

The sun was going down to sleep and the room was full of yellow. It made mum look like an angel. Her face was bright and her hair was glowy like my nightlight. Wobs was still sleeping in the cot like always. His fuzzy hair was sticking up and his dummy tit was taped to his big pink cheeks so I couldn't see the rubber sucky bit inside his mouth.

Colin is a really stupid name for a baby. Before dad left to make new babies with Sadie-who-tries-to-make-me-call-her-mummy he'd give me piggybacks around the landing and dangle me upside down till I screamed "uncle!" and then he'd laugh and say "Joanne has got the Collywobbles! Wobbles have her Colly got!" I didn't know what it meant but he laughed even more when I started to call Colin Wobs. Mum didn't like it at first but now she calls him it too.

"Is Wobs okay?" I whispered.

"Yes, sweetie, he's okay." Mum looked like she was going to cry again and I didn't like that. I hate it when she cries. Me and Wobs are the ones who are supposed to cry. After dad left she was sad a lot. We didn't have many Mad Hatter tea parties anymore and she got scary letters that she tried to hide and she thought I didn't know what all the brown boxes full of our stuff in the hall meant but I thought I did. "Thank you for coming when I called you, Jojo."

"That's okay," I said. "Can I go away now?"

Mum smiled but I saw her closed lips wobble. "Can you stay here for a wee while maybe?"

I wanted to ask why but I didn't 'cause I thought I knew anyway. I was thinking about the last big time she cried—more than when granny M died or dad went away—the day when the Really Bad Thing happened to mister and missus S next door. Their house is all boarded up now and the for sale sign has fallen over but lots of people still come and point and stare. "Okay."

She left Wobs to come over and cuddle me. My nose went funny when I smelled her—it was like the smell in dad's tool shed: like the big metal vice on the wooden bench. The big metal vice with its wide wide teeth. Mum usually smelled like the flowers in our garden.

"What would you have done if it wasn't okay, sweetie?"

"Mum—"

She pinched my arms till it hurt a bit.

"I know it!" I said. "I know what to do!" 'Cause then I knew for sure she was talking about mister and missus S and I didn't want to talk about it back. It made me think about all the screams and then the quiet and the policemen and the black trolleys on wheels that dripped black stuff down the path like the slime behind a slug.

"I know you do, Jojo," she said and she let me go and went down on her knees to give me a proper cuddle. "I'm sorry, sweetie, I'm sorry."

I cuddled back but I could still smell that nasty smell and she felt funny too. Cold but wet. And I knew what both those things meant. It meant mum was still scared.

"It's just that it's getting worse, sweetie. It just keeps on getting worse." Her breath tickled my ear but I didn't want to laugh. She'd said that a lot since granny M died. She'd said it nearly every day and every night.

I wake up and it's night time again. The horrible hard bed creaks as I sit up and then stand up. The floor is cold. The stupid white clothes don't fit me. The T-shirt is too tight and the joggy bottoms are too long—they swish on the floor as I creep to the door.

There's a funny feeling in my tummy. Mum said I would feel it one day and now I do. It's not horrible like I thought but fluttery like there's birds inside me. Which there isn't.

The fat hairy man said dad's coming tomorrow. He'll take me and Wobs to his and Sadie-who-tries-to-make-me-call-her-mummy's big house and I won't be able to dance around the living room with the curtains shut or have Mad Hatter tea parties or pretend to be a Roman lady in her Roman villa anymore.

Mum always says that I'm older than my age but I don't think anyone else thinks so. Whenever something went wrong (usually during dee-I-why cause I'm clumsy mum says) I'd shout "fils de pute!" or "me cago en todo lo que se menea!" and mum would laugh and choke and tell me never to say things like that in front of any other grownups or else they'd take me away. And now they have.

I push down the handle and pull open the door. It creaks again but not too much. When I'm in the corridor I let the door go slowly till it stops moving and then I roll up my joggy bottoms to my ankles. The corridor is cold and shiny. I know Wobs is in the room next to mine but I don't know which one. I tiptoe left and my tummy is flapping and flapping inside. Before I can try the black door next to mine I hear voices and freeze.

"It's a crying shame" a lady says. "An absolute crying shame."

I can hear other people muttering and yes-ing but they don't get closer.

I hear the roll of a chair on wheels and look at my room door and pretend I can't feel the birds inside me.

"We think there's abuse." It's the fat hairy man—I can tell by his wheezy nose. "I phoned the school, spoke to the girl's teacher. It runs in the family. Apparently she refused to speak at all for the first three years."

"A crying shame," the lady mutters again like it's the only thing she can say.

They're talking about me and mum and Wobs and maybe even granny M. Bastards, cunts, and short-arsed shits. I think it inside my head just like mum told me to. The fat hairy man is the son of a Narbo scrotum. My tummy jumps and flutters and then I remember that I'm trying to find Wobs.

I turn round and go back past my horrible room. The door on the other side of mine has a little window in it. I try to look inside it but it's dark. I try the handle and the door opens with no creak. I put my hand over my mouth and I go inside but it still stays dark. I don't like the dark. I wait till the door shuts again and then whisper "Wobs?"

I don't hear anything back. It's stupid that I wanted to—he's just a baby. But that fluttery funny feeling in my tummy is getting worse and I know it's cause he's in here. I know it's cause he's in here and the flies are coming and there's no mum to look after us anymore. No mum to feel a fluttery funny feeling in her tummy and know what to do about it. Or to tell me what to do about it.

"Wobs?" I slap the hand that's not on my mouth against the wall 'cause there must be a bulb hanging from the middle of the ceiling and so there must be a light switch.

And then I find it. The light is very bright. I move my hand from my mouth to my eyes till I can see right. Wobs is lying in a cot just like the one in his room at home. He's wearing white pyjamas and lying on his back with his legs and arms out but he doesn't have a dummy in and his mouth's wide open.

That fluttery feeling in my tummy gets worse and now I can hear the buzzy sound again too. The buzzy sound that keeps on getting louder and louder even though the other window in Wobs's room is just like mine: mean and wee and locked. There's a funny mini room in the other corner—it's made of glass and has a little door in the side. Someone's left a cup of coffee on a table inside it but there's no one there to drink it.

My legs get shaky when the buzzy sound gets even louder and my knees smack against the cold floor before I know I've fallen down. I keep whispering for Wobs even though he's a baby—a baby who slept all the way through his mummy dying and me and him getting taken away to here.

They're coming. *They're coming.* I'm older than my age. I'm clever. I'm nearly a grownup really. I keep thinking these things as the fluttering gets harder and the buzzy sound gets louder. But I don't believe them. I'm just really *really* scared. And I want my mum.

And then the light buzzes too and then it goes out. The dark is darker. The buzzy sound is so loud I can't hear anything else. I think of mum saying "I love you, Jojo." I think of her pinching my arms till it hurt and asking "what would you have done if it wasn't okay, sweetie?" And I think of all our practicing after mister and missus S and the screaming and then the quiet and all the policemen in uniforms who came to ask us questions 'cause mum said she'd been too scared to stop the Really Bad Thing. And then dad lying to me like mum lied to them when he took me to see the monkeys in the zoo and said he had to go away for a bit.

I march into the middle of the room and I reach out into the dark till I feel the bars of Wobs's cot. And then I think of mum smiling in the living room with the curtains shut and the stereo on and whispering in my ear "come on, Inch-high Private Eye, what's your plan?"

Keep your mouth shut, I think. Or you'll catch flies.

I thought everything was okay again till I was halfways down the stairs looking at the messy sheet on the floor. This time mum didn't scream my name—she just screamed and screamed. And then she stopped. I turned round and ran back up but I didn't want to. Wobs's room was dark 'cause the sun had gone away behind the wall at the end of our garden.

Mum stood in the middle of the room. Her face looked strange. Fat and black and full. When she saw me she shook her head from side to side and her eyes were wide. She closed them once and then waved a hand over her face.

"Mum!" I shouted and I didn't care that my mouth was open 'cause I knew that they'd come back and I was scared. They'd come back 'cause of granny M and dad and Sadie-who-tries-to-make-me-call-her-mummy and their new baby and the scary letters and the brown boxes. And I was scared the most 'cause mum had done the thing she'd always told me not to—the thing she'd been too scared to do too.

She put out her hands to stop me running to her and then covered her mouth with her fingers till I remembered I was supposed to do that too. I could hear Wobs trying to cry but he couldn't cause of the taped-up dummy.

Mum ran out the door and onto the landing. I saw her eyes fill up black when she turned round to check I was coming and then she stopped and pulled open the cupboard door next to the stairs and ran inside.

When I got there she'd shut the door already but she'd pulled the string that lit the bulb so I could see her through the little slats. Her face was still fat and black and full and her eyes were still wide and her fingers were still over her mouth. She banged at the door till the key fell out onto the floor and I remembered what I was supposed to do and picked it up and put it in the lock and turned it till I heard the click just like we'd practised.

I saw mum fall a bit when she heard the click too and then she couldn't hold her breath in anymore. She let a bit of it out and some of the flies came out too. They buzzed black at the slats. I heard her scream a bit and then she waved her hands about trying to make them go back into her mouth. She was crying but I could only tell 'cause her face was all wet when she looked at me through the slats.

"Mummy, make it stop! Make them go away! Make them go away, please!" I wanted her to stop crying and holding her breath too. I wanted that the most.

She stared at me till her eyes went as black as her face and I couldn't see them anymore. And then she smiled. I think she smiled 'cause I saw the white flash of her teeth before I heard her twist the stick that closed the slats and then I couldn't see anything anymore.

The light on the landing got dim but it didn't go out. I heard the buzzy sound get louder and louder and I heard mummy scream and scream and kick and punch and rattle the door and I ran back into Wobs's room and sat on the floor and cried and cried and held his pudgy hands till it all stopped.

The fluttery feeling in my tummy and chest is starting to hurt now. I don't like it. I didn't like it anyway but now I really don't. The buzzy sound is so loud it's like it's *inside* my ears and I've got one hand over my shut mouth but I don't think they're here yet. Wobs's cot isn't just like the one at home 'cause I can't fit my arm through the slats to cover his mouth too and when I stand up I'm too short to reach over the top.

They're coming. They're coming. My heart is banging really hard and really fast in the wrong place—I don't like that either. I try not to cry 'cause mum says that doesn't ever help but I'm scared. And I need to look after Wobs but I can't 'cause he doesn't have a dummy and the cot is different and I can't fit my arm through.

The flappy feeling in my chest is in my throat and it and the buzzy sound nearly make me scream till I remember to keep my mouth shut. Something fizzes the back of my tongue like sherbet and then I start to gag like when I have a tummy bug and then it all comes up out of me in a big chokey rush.

And then the light comes on again. It buzzes buzzes buzzes and then goes on completely and it makes me blink.

The room is full of black. It's filled up with it. Black that came from *me*. I put my hand over my mouth again and I want to scream and cry but then I remember Wobs. He's still lying on his back with his legs and arms out and his mouth wide open.

"Mummy, make it stop. Make them go away, please!" I whisper into my sweaty and wet hand.

But mum is dead.

After the screaming and punching and rattling and buzzing stopped I went back out onto the landing and stood at the cupboard door and stared at the key. After nothing happened I turned it till it clicked again and pulled it slowly open.

Mum was curled up on the floor like we used to do in the garden when it was too sunny for dancing. There was no buzzy sound and her face wasn't black anymore but she was covered in blood like the dead provocators in gladiator munera and most of it was coming from her mouth and nose and ears. Her eyes were staring up at the ceiling and her tears were red too. Her hands were like claws and some of her nails were gone I think.

I went down the stairs really slowly cause my knees felt funny and then I picked up the dust sheet and then I climbed back up. At the top I listened again but I couldn't hear Wobs and I couldn't hear the buzzy sound so I went back in the cupboard and lay down next to mum and pulled the dust sheet over us both and waited for dad.

He didn't come but other people did. And they took me and Wobs away and left mum behind.

I'm older than my age. I'm clever. I'm nearly a grownup really. And I have to be brave. Mum always said that I have to be brave. No matter what.

I look down at Wobs. The buzzy sound is making him twitch and breathe faster. I think he's about to wake up.

The room is still black and buzzy and full of flies. Our bit of room is the only bit left.

I take my hand away from my mouth but it's very shaky and my mouth is shaky too. I Have To Be Brave. I look down at Wobs again and hope his eyes won't open. I try to reach him over the top of the cot but I still can't do it.

"I'm sorry, Wobs," I whisper. "I've got to go away." I look at his pudgy fingers and red cheeks and silly fuzzy hair. "I've got to catch them so you don't."

And then I leave our bit of the room and run into the black buzzy noise. I put my hands over my mouth again and hold my breath and close my eyes and pretend I'm not crying. I pretend I'm not scared and my heart isn't banging really hard and really fast in the wrong place.

And then when I think I'm far enough away and when it feels right—which means when it feels really really *wrong*—I take my hands away and I open my mouth. Wide. Wider than a tinkly river with ducks and swans. Wider than the throwing net of a retiarius. Wider than the teeth in the big metal vice on the wooden bench in dad's tool shed. And then I breathe in.

It hurts. The things I breathe in hurt. Much more than when they came out. Much more than I thought they would and I'd thought they would. I nearly scream as they rattle and buzz in my ears in my nose in my mouth in my throat in my tummy. They scrape and scratch and flap and buzz 'cause now they're angry. I keep breathing in and in and in till the room stops being black and I've got no breath left and then I clap my hands over my mouth and stop breathing anything at all.

I run to the little door in the glass room and when I let one of my hands go to try the handle it opens. I run inside and turn around and shut it again. I can see Wobs's cot through the fuzzy glass but I don't think I'm far enough away yet for him to be safe.

It's hard to hold your breath. It's even harder when you're scared and your mum's dead and you're trying to be brave but you don't know what to do. And when angry things are scraping and scratching and buzzing and trying to get out again. I hit my leg against the table with the coffee cup and it topples over spilling everywhere. My spare hand hits the window and bounces back to hit my face. Letting some flies out before I manage to breathe them back in.

I'll be able to get back out too. When my eyes go black and I start to scream and punch and kick and rattle like mum did I'll still be able to escape. I'll be able to run to Wobs's cot and let all the black out. I'm scared and I'm sore and my heart's still wrong and I'm full of flies but I'm still Brave like a Gladiator. I still remember what mum said. I've got to have a plan. After mister and missus S we always *always* had A Plan.

I look back at the door and there's a card sticking out of a slot like a key. I don't know if it's the same thing but while I can still hold my breath I pull it out and drop to my knees and push it as far under the door as I can till it's gone and I can't see it.

And then I have to breathe out. I can't hold it anymore. I feel sick and scared and hot and sore and all I can see now are black spots. The flies buzz and buzz and fill the mini room black but I can breathe again and when they push me into the door it doesn't open.

I think of Wobs's room when it was full of yellow. I think of mum when she looked like an angel. Her face bright and her hair glowy like my nightlight. I cough and choke and breathe.

I look at Wobs through the fuzzy glass. I can see his pudgy arms waving through the bars of the cot as he starts to cry. I can see the fat hairy man and maybe the lady who kept saying "it's a crying shame" barging through the door with the window in. But I keep looking at Wobs.

"I love you" I think inside my head cause I think that's what mum was thinking inside hers when she looked at me before her eyes went black and she twisted the stick that closed the slats in the cupboard door. And I hope it won't ever be the same for him. The same as for granny M and mum and me. I don't think it will be.

I try to smile again before I forget how to. Wobs *will* call Sadie mummy. But I don't mind. And I don't think mum will either.

The fat hairy man and the crying shame lady run out into the corridor with a screaming Wobs between them. The flies turn back from the fuzzy glass and the locked door. They fill me with black and angry. They choke till I can't remember being scared or sore or me.

☽ ☽ ☽ ● ☾ ☾ ☾

And the flies. Filled with fury and stymied grief. Anomalies. The divine and diabolical; the magical and humoural. The obtuse, the diseased, the misunderstood. Never any of it more than flies.

And now, an opportunity too many lost. Finally, an end. We know it's over. And so we stop flying.

SHAY CORSHAM WORSTED

GARTH NIX

The young man came in one of the windows, because the back door had proved surprisingly tough. He'd kicked it a few times, without effect, before looking for an easier way to get in. The windows were barred, but the bars were rusted almost through, so he had no difficulty pulling them away. The window was locked as well, but he just smashed the glass with a half brick pried out of the garden wall. He didn't care about the noise. He knew there was only the old man in the house, the garden was large and screened by trees, and the evening traffic was streaming past on the road out front. That was plenty loud enough to cloak any noise he might make.

Or any quavering cries for help from the old man, thought the intruder, as he climbed through. He went to the back door first, intending to open it for a quick getaway, but it was deadlocked. More afraid of getting robbed than dying in a fire, thought the young man. That made it easier. He liked the frightened old people, the power he had over them with his youth and strength and anger.

When he turned around, the old man was standing behind him. Just standing there, not doing a thing. It was dim in the corridor, the only light a weak bulb hanging from the ceiling, its pallid glow falling on the bald head of the little man, the ancient slight figure in his brown cardigan and brown corduroy trousers and brown slippers, just a little old man that could be picked up and broken like a stick and then whatever pathetic treasures were in the house could be—

A little old man whose eyes were silver.

And what was in his hands?

Those gnarled hands had been empty, the intruder was sure of it, but now the old bloke held long blades, though he wasn't exactly holding the blades . . . they were growing, growing from his fingers, the flesh fusing together and turning silver . . . silver as those eyes!

The young man had turned half an inch towards the window and escape when the first of those silvery blades penetrated his throat, destroying his voice box, changing the scream that rose there to a dull, choking cough. The second blade went straight through his heart, back out, and through again.

Pock! Pock!

Blood geysered, but not on the old man's brown cardigan. He had moved back almost in the same instant as he struck and was now ten feet away, watching with those silver eyes as the young man fell writhing on the floor, his feet drumming for eighteen seconds before he became still.

The blades retreated, became fingers once again. The old man considered the body, the pooling blood, the mess.

"Shay Marazion Velvet," he said to himself, and walked to the spray of blood farthest from the body, head-high on the peeling wallpaper of green lilies. He poked out his tongue, which grew longer and became as silver as the blades.

He began to lick, tongue moving rhythmically, head tilted as required. There was no expression on his face, no sign of physical excitement. This was not some fetish.

He was simply cleaning up.

"You'll never guess who I saw walking up and down outside, Father," said Mary Shires, as she bustled in with her ludicrously enormous basket filled with the weekly tribute of homemade foods and little luxuries that were generally unwanted and wholly unappreciated by her father, Sir David Shires.

"Who?" grunted Sir David. He was sitting at his kitchen table, scrawling notes on the front page of the *Times*, below the big headlines with the latest from the war with Argentina over the Falklands, and enjoying the sun that was briefly flooding the whole room through the open doors to the garden.

"That funny little Mister Shea," said Mary, putting the basket down on the table.

Sir David's pencil broke. He let it fall and concentrated on keeping his hand still, on making his voice sound normal. He shouldn't be surprised, he told himself. It was why he was here, after all. But after so many years, even though every day he told himself this could be *the* day, it was a terrible, shocking surprise.

"Really, dear?" he said. He thought his voice sounded mild enough. "Going down to the supermarket like he normally does, I suppose? Getting his bread and milk?"

"No, that's just the thing," said Mary. She took out a packet of some kind of biscuit and put it in front of her father. "These are very good. Oatmeal and some kind of North African citrus. You'll like them."

"Mister Shea," prompted Sir David.

"Oh, yes. He's just walking backwards and forwards along the footpath from his house to the corner. Backwards and forwards! I suppose he's gone ga-ga. He's old enough. He must be ninety if he's a day, surely?"

She looked at him, without guile, both of them knowing he was eighty himself. But not going ga-ga, thank god, even if his knees were weak reeds and he couldn't sleep at night, remembering things that he had forced himself to forget in his younger days.

But Shay was much older than ninety, thought Sir David. Shay was much, much older than that.

He pushed his chair back and stood up.

"I might go and . . . and have a word with the old chap," he said carefully. "You stay here, Mary."

"Perhaps I should come—"

"No!"

He grimaced, acknowledging he had spoken with too much emphasis. He didn't want to alarm Mary. But then again, in the worst case . . . no, not the worst case, but in a quite plausible minor escalation . . .

"In fact, I think you should go out the back way and get home," said Sir David.

"Really, Father, why on—"

"Because I am ordering you to," snapped Sir David. He still had the voice, the tone that expected to be obeyed, deployed very rarely with the family, but quite often to the many who had served under him, first in the Navy and then for considerably longer in the Department, where he had ended up as the Deputy Chief. Almost fifteen years gone, but it wasn't the sort of job where you ever completely left, and the command voice was the least of the things that had stayed with him.

Mary sniffed, but she obeyed, slamming the garden gate on her way out. It would be a few years yet, he thought, before she began to question everything he did, perhaps start bringing brochures for retirement homes along with her special biscuits and herbal teas she believed to be good for reducing the chance of dementia.

Dementia. There was an apposite word. He'd spent some time thinking he might be suffering from dementia or some close cousin of it, thirty years ago, in direct connection to "funny old Mister Shea." Who was not at all funny, not in any sense of the word. They had all wondered if they were demented, for a time.

He paused near his front door, wondering for a moment if he should make the call first, or even press his hand against the wood panelling just so, and flip it open to take out the .38 Colt Police revolver cached there. He had a 9mm Browning automatic upstairs, but a revolver was better for a cached weapon. You wouldn't want to bet your life on magazine springs in a weapon that had sat too long. He checked all his armament every month, but still . . . a revolver was more certain.

But automatic or revolver, neither would be any use. He'd learned that before, from direct observation, and had been lucky to survive. Very lucky, because the other two members of the team hadn't had the fortune to slip in the mud and hit themselves on the head and be forced to lie still. They'd gone in shooting, and kept shooting, unable to believe the evidence of their eyes, until it was too late. . . .

Sir David grimaced. This was one of the memories he'd managed to push aside for a long, long time. But like all the others, it wasn't far below the surface. It didn't take much to bring it up, that afternoon in 1953, the Department's secure storage on the fringe of RAF Bicester. . . .

He did take a walking stick out of the stand. A solid bog oak stick, with a pommel of bronze worked in the shape of a spaniel's head. Not for use as a weapon, but simply because he didn't walk as well as he once did. He couldn't afford a fall now. Or at any time really, but particularly not now.

The sun was still shining outside. It was a beautiful day, the sky as blue as a bird's egg, with hardly a cloud in sight. It was the kind of day you only saw in films, evoking some fabulous summertime that never really existed, or not for more than half an hour at a time.

It was a good day to die, if it came to that, if you were eighty and getting tired of the necessary props to a continued existence. The medicines and interventions, the careful calculation of probabilities before anything resembling activity, calculations that Sir David would never have undertaken at a younger age.

He swung out onto the footpath, a military stride, necessarily adjusted by age and a back that would no longer entirely straighten. He paused by the kerb and looked left and right, surveying the street, head back, shoulders close to straight, sandy eyebrows raised, hair no longer quite so regulation short, catching a little of the breeze, the soft breeze that added to the day's delights.

Shay was there, as Mary had said. It was wearing the same clothes as always, the brown cardigan and corduroy. They'd put fifty pairs in the safe house, at the beginning, uncertain whether Shay would buy more or not, though its daily purchase of bread, milk and other basics was well established. It could mimic human behaviour very well.

It looked like a little old man, a bald little man of some great age. Wrinkled skin, hooded eyes, head bent as if the neck could no longer entirely support the weight of years. But Sir David knew it didn't always move like an old man. It could move fluidly, like an insect, faster than you ever thought at first sighting.

Right now Shay was walking along the footpath, away from Sir David. Halfway to the corner, it turned back. It must have seen him, but as usual, it gave no outward sign of recognition or reception. There would be no such sign, until it decided to do whatever it was going to do next.

Sir David shuffled forward. Best to get it over with. His hand was already sweating, slippery on the bronze dog handle of his stick, his heart hammering in a fashion bound to be at odds with a cardiopulmonary system past its best. He knew the feeling well, though it had been an age since he'd felt it more than fleetingly.

Fear. Unalloyed fear, that must be conquered, or he could do nothing, and that was not an option. Shay had broken free of its programming. It could be about to do anything, anything at all, perhaps reliving some of its more minor exploits like the Whitechapel murders of 1888, or a major one like the massacre at Slapton Sands in 1944.

Or something greater still.

Not that Sir David was sure he *could* do anything. He'd only ever been told two of the command phrases, and lesser ones at that, a pair of two word groups. They were embossed on his mind, bright as new brass. But it was never known exactly what they meant, or how Shay understood them.

There was also the question of which command to use. Or to try and use both command phrases, though that might somehow have the effect of one of the four word command groups. An unknown effect, very likely fatal to Sir David and everyone for miles, perhaps more.

It was not inconceivable that whatever he said in the next two minutes might doom everyone in London, or even the United Kingdom.

Perhaps even the world.

The first command would be best, Sir David thought, watching Shay approach. They were out in public, the second would attract attention, besides its other significant drawback. Public attention was anathema to Sir David, even in such dire circumstances. He straightened his tie unconsciously as he thought about publicity. It was a plain green tie, as his suit was an inconspicuous grey flannel, off the rack. No club or regimental ties for Sir David, no identifying signet rings, no ring, no earring, no tattoos, no unusual facial hair. He worked to look a type that had once been excellent camouflage, the retired military officer. It still worked, though less well, there being fewer of the type to hide amongst. Perhaps the Falklands War would help in this regard.

Shay was drawing nearer, walking steadily, perfectly straight. Sir David peered at it. Were its eyes silver? If they were, it would be too late. All bets off, end of story. But the sun was too bright, Sir David's own sight was not what it once was. He couldn't tell if Shay's eyes were silver.

"Shay Risborough Gabardine," whispered Sir David. Ludicrous words, but proven by trial and error, trial by combat, death by error. The name it apparently gave itself, a station on the Great Western Line, and a type of fabric. Not words you'd ever expect to find together, there was its safety, the cleverness of Isambard Kingdom Brunel showing through. Though not as clever as how IKB had got Shay to respond to the words in the first place. So clever that no one else had worked out how it had been done, not in the three different attempts over more than a hundred years. Attempts to try to change or expand the creature's lexicon, each attempt another litany of mistakes and many deaths. And after each such trial, the fear that had led to it being shut away. Locked underground the last time, and then the chance rediscovery in 1953 and the foolishness that had led it to being put away here, parked and forgotten.

Except by Sir David.

Shay was getting very close now. Its face looked innocuous enough. A little vacant, a man not too bright perhaps, or very short of sleep. Its skin was pale today, matching Sir David's own, but he knew it could change that in an instant. Skin colour, height, apparent age, gender . . . all of these could be changed by Shay, though it mostly appeared as it was right now.

Small and innocuous, old and tired. Excellent camouflage among humans.

Ten paces, nine paces, eight paces . . . the timing had to be right. The command had to be said in front of its face, without error, clear and precise—

"Shay Risborough Gabardine," barked Sir David, shivering in place, his whole body tensed to receive a killing blow.

Shay's eyes flashed silver. He took half a step forward, putting him inches away from Sir David, and stopped. There was a terrible stillness, the world perched on the brink. Then it turned on its heel, crossed the road and went back into its house. The old house, opposite Sir David's, that no one but Shay had set foot in for thirty years.

Sir David stood where he was for several minutes, shaking. Finally he quelled his shivering enough to march back inside his own house, where he ignored the phone on the hall table, choosing instead to open a drawer in his study to lift out a chunkier, older thing that had no dial of any kind, push-button or rotary. He held the handset to his head and waited.

There were a series of clicks and whines and beeps, the sound of disparate connections working out how they might after all get together. Finally a sharp, quick male voice answered on the other end.

"Yes."

"Case Shay Zulu," said Sir David. There was a pause. He could hear the flipping of pages, as the operator searched through the ready book.

"Is there more?" asked the operator.

"What!" exploded Sir David. "Case Shay Zulu!"

"How do you spell it?"

Sir David's lip curled almost up to his nose, but he pulled it back.

"S-H-A-Y," he spelled out. "Z-U-L-U."

"I can spell Zulu," said the operator, affronted. "There's still nothing."

"Look up my workname," said Sir David. "Arthur Brooks."

There was tapping now, the sound of a keyboard. He'd heard they were using computers more and more throughout the Department, not just for the boffins in the back rooms.

"Ah, I see . . . I've got you now, sir," said the operator. At least there was a "sir," now.

"Get someone competent to look up Shay Zulu and report my communication at once to the duty officer with instruction to relay it to the Chief," ordered Sir David. "I want a call back in five minutes."

The call came in ten minutes, ten minutes Sir David spent looking out his study window, watching the house across the road. It was eleven A.M., too late for Shay to go to the supermarket like it had done every day for the last thirty years. Sir David wouldn't know if it had returned to its previous safe routine until 10:30 A.M. tomorrow. Or earlier, if Shay was departing on some different course . . .

The insistent ringing recalled him to the phone.

"Yes."

"Sir David? My name is Angela Terris, I'm the duty officer at present. We're a bit at sea here. We can't find Shay Zulu in the system at all—what was that?"

Sir David had let out a muffled cry, his knuckles jammed against his mouth.

"Nothing, nothing," he said, trying to think. "The paper files, the old records to 1977, you can look there. But the important thing is the book, we . . . I must have the notebook from the Chief's safe, a small green leather book embossed on the cover with the gold initials IKB."

"The Chief's not here right now," said Angela brightly. "This Falklands thing, you know. He's briefing the cabinet. Is it urgent?"

"Of course it's urgent!" barked Sir David, regretting it even as he spoke, remembering when old Admiral Puller had called up long after retirement, concerned about a suspicious new postman, and how they had laughed on the Seventh Floor. "Look, find Case Shay Zulu and you'll see what I mean."

"Is it something to do with the Soviets, Sir David? Because we're really getting on reasonably well with them at the moment—"

"No, no, it's nothing to do with the Soviets," said Sir David. He could hear the tone in her voice, he remembered using it himself when he had taken Admiral Fuller's call. It was the calming voice that meant no immediate action, a routine request to some functionary to investigate further in days, or even weeks, purely as a courtesy to the old man. He had to do something that would make her act, there had to be some lever.

"I'm afraid it's something to do with the Service itself," he said. "Could be very, very embarrassing. Even now. I need that book to deal with it."

"Embarrassing as in likely to be of media interest, Sir David?" asked Angela.

"Very much so," said Sir David heavily.

"I'll see what I can do," said Angela.

"We were really rather surprised to find the Department owns a safe house that isn't on the register," said the young, nattily dressed and borderline rude young man who came that afternoon. His name, or at least the one he had supplied, was Redmond. "Finance were absolutely delighted, it must be worth close to half a million pounds now, a huge place like that. Fill a few black holes with that once we sell it. On the quiet, of course, as you say it would be very embarrassing if the media get hold of this little real estate venture."

"Sell it?" asked Sir David. "Sell it! Did you only find the imprest accounts, not the actual file? Don't you understand? The only thing that stops Shay from running amok is routine, a routine that is firmly embedded in and around that house! Sell the house and you unleash the . . . the beast!"

"Beast, Sir David?" asked Redmond. He suppressed a yawn and added, "Sounds rather Biblical. I expect we can find a place for this Shea up at Exile House. I daresay they'll dig his file up eventually, qualify him as a former employee."

They could find a place for Sir David too, were the unspoken words. Exile House, last stop for those with total disability suffered on active service, crippled by torture, driven insane from stress, shot through both knees and elbows. There were many ways to arrive at Exile House.

"Did you talk to the Chief?" asked Sir David. "Did you ask about the book marked 'IKB'?"

"Chief's very busy," said Redmond. "There's a war on you know. Even if it is only a little one. Look, why don't I go over and have a chat with old Shea, get a feel for the place, see if there's anything else that might need sorting?"

"If you go over there you introduce another variable," said Sir David, as patiently as he could. "Right now, I've got Shay to return to its last state, which may or may not last until ten thirty tomorrow morning, when it goes and gets its bread and milk, as it has done for the last thirty years. But if you disrupt it again, then who knows what will happen."

"I see, I see," said Redmond. He nodded as if he had completely understood. "Bit of a mental case, hey? Well, I did bring a couple of the boys in blue along just in case."

"Boys in blue!"

Sir David was almost apoplectic. He clutched at Redmond's sleeve, but the young man effortlessly withdrew himself and sauntered away.

"Back in half a mo," he called out cheerfully.

Sir David tried to chase him down, but by the time he got to the front door it was shut in his face. He scrabbled at the weapon cache, pushing hard on a panel till he realized it was the wrong one. By the time he had the revolver in his hand and had wrestled the door open, Redmond was already across the road, waving to the two policemen in the panda car to follow him. They got out quickly, large men in blue, putting their hats on as they strode after the young agent.

"Not even Special Branch," muttered Sir David. He let the revolver hang by his side. What could he do with it anyway? He couldn't shoot Redmond, or the policemen.

Perhaps, he thought bleakly, he could shoot himself. That would bring them back, delay the knock on the door opposite . . . but it would only be a delay. And if he was killed, and if they couldn't find Brunel's book, then the other command words would be lost.

Redmond went up the front steps two at a time, past the faded sign that said, "Hawkers and Salesmen Not Welcome. Beware of the Vicious Dog" and the one underneath it that had been added a year after the first, "No Liability for Injury or Death, You Have Been Warned."

Sir David blinked, narrowing his eyes against the sunshine that was still streaming down, flooding the street. It was just like the afternoon, that afternoon in '43 when the sun had broken through after days of fog and ice, but even though it washed across him on the bridge of his frigate he couldn't feel it, he could only see the light, he was so frozen from the cold Atlantic days the sunshine couldn't touch him, there was no warmth that could reach him. . . .

He felt colder now. Redmond was knocking on the door. Hammering on the door. Sir David choked a little on his own spit, apprehension rising. There was a chance Shay wouldn't answer, and the door was very heavy, those two policemen couldn't kick it down, there would be more delay—

The door opened. There was the flash of silver, and Redmond fell down the steps, blood geysering from his neck as if some newfangled watering system had suddenly switched on beside him, drawing water from a rusted tank.

A blur of movement followed. The closer policeman spun about, as if suddenly inspired to dance, only his head was tumbling from his shoulders to dance apart from him. The surviving policeman, that is, the policeman who had survived the first three seconds of contact with Shay, staggered backwards and started to turn around to run.

He took one step before he too was pierced through with a silver spike, his feet taking him only to the gutter where he lay down to die.

Sir David went back inside, leaving the door open. He went to his phone in the hall and called his daughter. She answered on the fourth ring. Sir David's hand was so sweaty he had to grip the plastic tightly, so the phone didn't slip from his grip.

"Mary? I want you to call Peter and your girls and tell them to get across the Channel now. France, Belgium, doesn't matter. No, wait, Terence is in Newcastle, isn't he? Tell him . . . listen to me . . . he can get the ferry to Stavanger. Listen! There is going to be a disaster here. It doesn't matter what kind! I haven't gone crazy, you know who I know. You all have to get out of the country and across the water! Just go!"

Sir David hung up. He wasn't sure Mary would do as he said. He wasn't even sure that the sea would stop Shay. That was one of the theories, never tested, that it wouldn't or couldn't cross a large body of water. Brunel almost certainly knew, but his more detailed papers had been lost. Only the code book had survived. At least until recently.

He went to the picture window in his study. It had been installed on his retirement, when he'd moved here to keep an eye on Shay. It was a big window, taking up the place of two old Georgian multi-paned affairs, and it had an excellent view of the street.

There were four bodies in full view now. The latest addition was a very young man. Had been a young man. The proverbial innocent bystander, in the wrong place at the wrong time. A car sped by, jerking suddenly into the other lane as the driver saw the corpses and the blood.

Shay walked into the street and looked up at Sir David's window.

Its eyes were silver.

The secure phone behind Sir David rang. He retreated, still watching Shay, and picked it up.

"Yes."

"Sir David? Angela Terris here. The police are reporting multiple 999 calls, apparently there are people—"

"Yes. Redmond and the two officers are dead. I told him not to go, but he did. Shay is active now. I tried to tell you."

Shay was moving, crossing the road.

"Sir David!"

"Find the book," said Sir David wearily. "That's the only thing that can help you now. Find the leather book marked 'IKB.' It's in the Chief's safe."

Shay was on Sir David's side of the street, moving left, out of sight.

"The Chief's office was remodelled last year," said Angela Terris. "The old safe . . . I don't know—"

Sir David laughed bitter laughter and dropped the phone.

There was the sound of footsteps in the hall.

Footsteps that didn't sound quite right.

Sir David stood at attention and straightened his tie. Time to find out if the other command did what it was supposed to do. It would be out of his hands then. If it worked, Shay would kill him and then await further instructions for twenty-four hours. Either they'd find the book or they wouldn't, but he would have done his best.

As always.

Shay came into the room. It didn't look much like an old man now. It was taller, and straighter, and its head was bigger. So was its mouth.

"Shay Corsham Worsted," said Sir David.

ACKNOWLEDGEMENTS

Thanks to all who read submissions during the open reading period: Klaudia Bednarczyk, Samantha Beiko, Bob Boyczuk, Felicia Di Pardo, Chris Edwards, Brent Hayward, Sandra Kasturi, Barry King, Matt Kressel, Helen Lee, Kari Maaren, Michael Matheson, Kerrie McCreadie, Matt Moore, Kelsi Morris, Tehani Wessely, and Sam Zucchi. Another thank you to Matt Kressel for his advice, and for setting up and wrangling the submissions system.

A big thanks to Hank Schwaeble.

ABOUT THE AUTHORS

Nathan Ballingrud is the award-winning author of the short story collection *North American Lake Monsters*, from Small Beer Press. He lives with his daughter in Asheville, NC, where he is at work on his first novel.

Laird Barron is the author of several books, including *The Croning*, *Occultation*, and *The Beautiful Thing That Awaits Us All*. His work has also appeared in many magazines and anthologies including *The Magazine of Fantasy & Science Fiction*, *Lovecraft Unbound*, and *Haunted Legends*. An expatriate Alaskan, Barron currently resides in Upstate New York.

Pat Cadigan is the author of fifteen books, including two nonfiction books, a young adult novel, and the two Arthur C. Clarke Award-winning novels, *Synners* and *Fools*. She has also won the Locus Award three times and the Hugo Award for her novelette "The Girl-Thing Who Went Out For Sushi." Pat lives in gritty, urban North London with the Original Chris Fowler and Gentleman Jinx, coolest black cat in London. She can be found on Facebook and tweets as @cadigan. Her books are available electronically via SF Gateway, the ambitious electronic publishing program from Gollancz.

When not globetrotting in search of dusty tomes, **Siobhan Carroll** lives and lurks in Delaware. She wrested her Ph.D. and B.A. in English Literature from the twin ivory towers of Indiana University and the University of British Columbia, respectively. Her fiction can be found in magazines like *Beneath Ceaseless Skies*, *Realms of Fantasy*, and *Lightspeed*. Sometimes she writes under the byline "Von Carr." Both versions of herself firmly support the use of the Oxford Comma. For more, visit voncarr-siobhan-carroll.blogspot.com/.

Ellen Datlow has been editing science fiction, fantasy, and horror short fiction for over thirty years as fiction editor of *OMNI Magazine* and editor of *Event Horizon* and *SCIFICTION*. She currently acquires short fiction for *Tor.com*. In addition, she has edited more than fifty science fiction, fantasy, and horror anthologies, including the annual *The Best Horror of the Year, Lovecraft's Monsters*, a reprint anthology of stories, each involving at least one of H. P. Lovecraft's creations, the six volume series of retold fairy tales starting with *Snow White, Blood Red*, and *Queen Victoria's Book of Spells: An Anthology of Gaslamp Fantasy* (the latter anthologies with Terri Windling).

Forthcoming are *Nightmare Carnival, The Cutting Room,* and *The Doll Collection.*

She's won nine World Fantasy Awards, and has also won multiple Locus Awards, Hugo Awards, Stoker Awards International Horror Guild Awards, Shirley Jackson Awards, and the 2012 Il Posto Nero Black Spot Award for Excellent as Best Foreign Editor. Datlow was named recipient of the 2007 Karl Edward Wagner Award, given at the British Fantasy Convention for "outstanding contribution to the genre" and was honored with the Life Achievement Award given by the Horror Writers Association, in acknowledgement of superior achievement over an entire career.

She lives in New York and co-hosts the monthly Fantastic Fiction Reading Series at KGB Bar. More information can be found at www.datlow.com, on Facebook, and on twitter as @EllenDatlow.

Terry Dowling is one of Australia's most respected and internationally acclaimed writers of science fiction, dark fantasy and horror, and author of the multi-award-winning Tom Rynosseros saga. He has been called "Australia's finest writer of horror" by *Locus* magazine, its "premier writer of dark fantasy" by *All Hallows* and its "most acclaimed writer of the dark fantastic" by *Cemetery Dance* magazine. His collection *Basic Black* won the 2007 International Horror Guild Award for Best Collection. London's *Guardian* called his debut novel *Clowns at Midnight* "an exceptional work that bears comparison to John Fowles's *The Magus*." Terry's homepage can be found at www.terrydowling.com.

Brian Evenson is the author of over a dozen works of fiction, most recently *Immobility* and *Windeye*. His novel *Last Days* won the American Library Association's RUSA Award for Best Horror novel of 2009, and his story collection *The Wavering Knife* won the International Horror Guild Award. His novel *The Open Curtain* was a finalist for an Edgar Award and he is the recipient of three O. Henry Awards. He lives in Providence and works at the college that served as the model for Lovecraft's Miskatonic University.

Formerly a film critic and teacher, award-winning horror author **Gemma Files** is probably best known for her Hexslinger Series (*A Book of Tongues*, *A Rope of Thorns*, and *A Tree of Bones*), which has been collected into a Hexslinger Omnibus Edition that includes almost 50,000 words' worth of new material. Her stories have been published in the anthologies *The Grimscribe's Puppets*, *Clockwork Phoenix 4*, and in the webzine *Beneath Ceaseless Skies*. It has been collected in *Kissing Carrion* and *The Worm in Every Heart*. She has also published two chapbooks of poetry. Her next book will be *We Will All Go Down Together*, from ChiZine Publications.

Jeffrey Ford is the author of the novels, *The Physiognomy*, *Memoranda*, *The Beyond*, *The Portrait of Mrs. Charbuque*, *The Girl in the Glass*, *The Cosmology of the Wider World*, and *The Shadow Year*. His short fiction has been published in numerous journals, magazines, and anthologies and has been collected in *The Fantasy Writer's Assistant*, *The Empire of Ice Cream*, *The Drowned Life*, and *Crackpot Palace*.

Carole Johnstone's short stories have been published in numerous magazines and anthologies, have been reprinted in Ellen Datlow's *The Best Horror of the Year* series and *The Best British Fantasy*, and are being collected in the forthcoming *The Bright Day is Done*. *Frenzy* and *Cold Turkey*, two of her novellas, have been published as individual chapbooks. She is currently working on her second novel while seeking fame and fortune with the first—but just can't seem to kick the short story habit. More information on the author can be found at carolejohnstone.com.

Stephen Graham Jones is the author of thirteen novels and four collections. Most recent are *The Gospel of Z*, *States of Grace*, and *Not For Nothing*, and up next are *Floating Boy and the Girl Who Couldn't Fly*, with Paul Tremblay, and *After the People Lights Have Gone Off*, a horror collection.

Jones has some two hundred stories published, many reprinted in best of the year annuals. He's been a Shirley Jackson Award finalist, a Bram Stoker Award finalist, a Colorado Book Award finalist, and has won the Texas Institute of Letters Award for fiction, the Independent Publishers Award for Multicultural Fiction, and an NEA fellowship in fiction. He teaches in the MFA programs at CU Boulder and UCR-Palm Desert. He lives in Colorado, and really like werewolves and slashers and hair metal. For more information: demontheory.net or @SGJ72.

The New York Times recently called **Caitlín R. Kiernan** "one of our essential writers of dark fiction" and S. T. Joshi has declared "hers is now *the* voice of weird fiction." Caitlín's novels include *The Red Tree* (nominated for the Shirley Jackson and World Fantasy awards) and *The Drowning Girl: A Memoir* (winner of the James Tiptree, Jr. and Bram Stoker awards, nominated for the Nebula, World Fantasy, British Fantasy, Mythopoeic, Locus, and Shirley Jackson awards). Her short fiction has been collected in thirteen volumes, including *Confessions of a Five-Chambered Heart, Two Worlds and In Between: The Best of Caitlín R. Kiernan (Volume One)*, and, most recently, *The Ape's Wife and Other Stories.* Currently, she's writing the graphic novel series *Alabaster* for Dark Horse Comics and working on her next novels, *Cherry Bomb* and *The Dinosaurs of Mars.* She lives in Providence, Rhode Island.

John Langan is the author of two collections, *Mr. Gaunt and Other Uneasy Encounters* and *The Wide, Carnivorous Sky and Other Monstrous Geographies.* His first novel, *House of Windows*, was published in 2010 and he is currently working on a second. He co-edited the anthology *Creatures: Thirty Years of Monsters* with Paul Tremblay. He lives in upstate New York with his wife, younger son, and a menagerie.

Catherine MacLeod's publications include short fiction in *On Spec, TaleBones, Black Static*, and several anthologies, including *Horror Library #4, Tesseracts Seventeen*, and *The Living Dead 2*. Her attic is a wonderfully boring place.

Helen Marshall is an award-winning Canadian author, editor, and bibliophile. Her poetry and fiction have been published in *The Chiaroscuro, Abyss & Apex, Lady Churchill's Rosebud Wristlet, Tor.com* and have been reprinted in several Year's Best anthologies. Her debut collection of short stories, *Hair Side, Flesh Side* was named one of the Top Ten SF/F Books of 2012 by *January Magazine*. It was nominated for the Aurora Award and won the British Fantasy Society's Sydney J. Bounds Award. When not writing, she spends her time studying medieval manuscripts in Oxford, England. You can find more information here: //www.manuscriptgal.com/.

Bruce McAllister's science stories have been published over the years in the science fiction/fantasy/horror field's major magazines and many "year's best" volumes (including *Best American Short Stories: 2007*, Stephen King ed.). His short story "Kin" was a finalist for the Hugo Award; his novelette "Dream Baby" was a finalist for the Hugo and Nebula awards; his novelette "The Crying Child" was a finalist for the Shirley Jackson Award. His short fiction has been collected in the career-spanning *The Girl Who Loved Animals and Other Stories*. Three of his short stories—science fiction and horror—are currently under option, in development or in production as films. He is the author of three novels: *Humanity Prime*, *Dream Baby*, and most recently *The Village Sang to the Sea: A Memoir of Magic*. He lives in Orange County, California, with his wife, choreographer Amelie Hunter, and works as a writer, writing coach, and book and screenplay consultant. For more information: www.mcallistercoaching.com/.

Gary McMahon is the acclaimed author of nine novels and several short story collections. His latest novel releases are *Beyond Here Lies Nothing* (the third in the acclaimed Concrete Grove series) and *The Bones of You* (a supernatural mystery). His recent short stories have been collected in *Where You Live*, and some of his short fiction has been reprinted in various "Year's Best" volumes. Gary lives with his family in Yorkshire, where he trains in Shotokan karate and likes running in the rain. More information can be found at: www.garymcmahon.com.

Garth Nix was born in Melbourne, Australia. A full-time writer since 2001, he has worked as a literary agent, marketing consultant, book editor, book publicist, book sales representative, bookseller, and as a part-time soldier in the Australian Army Reserve. Nix's books include the award-winning fantasy novels *Sabriel*, *Lirael*, and *Abhorsen*, and the science fiction novels *Shade's Children* and *A Confusion of Princes*. His fantasy novels for children include *The Ragwitch*; the six books of *The Seventh Tower* sequence; *The Keys to the Kingdom* series; and the *Troubletwisters* books (with Sean Williams).

More than five million copies of Nix's books have been sold around the world, his books have appeared on the bestseller lists of *The New York Times*, *Publishers Weekly*, *The Guardian*, and *The Australian*, and his work has been translated into forty languages. He lives in Sydney, Australia.

Robert Shearman has written four short story collections, and between them they have won the World Fantasy Award, the Shirley Jackson Award, the Edge Hill Readers Prize and three British Fantasy Awards. The most recent, *Remember Why You Fear Me*, was published in 2012. He writes regularly in the UK for theatre and BBC Radio, winning the *Sunday Times* Playwriting Award and the Guinness Award in association with the Royal National Theatre. He's probably best known for reintroducing the Daleks to the twenty-first century revival of *Doctor Who*, in an episode that was a finalist for the Hugo Award.

Michael Marshall Smith is a novelist, short story writer, and screenwriter. Under this name he has published over seventy short stories, and three novels—*Only Forward*, *Spares*, and *One of Us*—winning the Philip K. Dick, the International Horror Guild, the August Derleth Award, and the Prix Bob Morane in France. He has also been awarded the British Fantasy Award for Best Short Fiction four times, more than any other author. Writing as Michael Marshall, he has published six internationally-bestselling thrillers including *The Straw Men*, *The Intruders*—currently in pre-production as a miniseries with the BBC Worldwide—and *Killer Move*. His most recent novel, *We Are Here*, was published in early 2014. He lives in Santa Cruz, California with his wife, son, and two cats. More information can be found here: www.michaelmarshallsmith.com/.

Shirley Jackson Award winner and World Fantasy nominee **Kaaron Warren** has lived in Melbourne, Sydney, Canberra, and Fiji. She's sold many short stories, three novels (the multi-award-winning *Slights*, *Walking the Tree*, and *Mistification*) and four short story collections. Three of her collections have won the ACT Publishers' and Writers' Award for fiction including her most recent, *Through Splintered Walls*, which also won a Canberra Critic's Circle Award for Fiction, two Ditmar Awards, two Australian Shadows Awards and a Shirley Jackson Award. Her stories have appeared in Australia, the US, the UK, and elsewhere in Europe, and have been selected for both Ellen Datlow's and Paula Guran's *Year's*

Best Anthologies. She was shortlisted for a Bram Stoker Award for "All You Can Do is Breathe," and was Special Guest at the Australian National Science Fiction Convention in Canberra 2013. You can find her at http://kaaronwarren.wordpress.com/ and on Twitter: @KaaronWarren.

COPYRIGHT ACKNOWLEDGEMENTS

KICKSTARTER BACKERS

We are tremendously grateful to everyone who backed the *Fearful Symmetries* project on Kickstarter. We would never have been able to produce this wonderful anthology of original horror fiction without your support.

A couple of notes:

1. We have attempted to contact all backers with regard to our acknowledgement of their generosity but could not track down a few people.

2. We would also like to thank those backers who asked not to be named, for their generosity.

Thank you!

ChiZine Publications & Ellen Datlow

PRINT BACKERS:

@solardepths
Adam Israel
Allen W Snyder
Andrew Springer
Anthony R. Cardno
Arachne Jericho
Arinn Dembo
Bear Weiter
Brian Grindey
Bruce McAllister
Carrie Laben
Cary Meriwether
Chris Bauer
Chris Fielding
Chris McLaren
Chris Rochford
Christopher L. Irvin
Christopher Reynaga
Christopher Stout
Crystal Leflar
David Hoffman
David Rheingold
E.L. Kemper
Erin Hawley
Frederick Foy
Gary M Dockter
Gord Sellar
Gordon White
Greg Gbur
Hari Sue Seldon
Helen Marshall
James Thomas
Jason Andrew
Jennifer Brozek
Joanne Austin
Jon Lasser
Jon Weimer
Jules
Justine Musk
K. Luis
Kate Heartfield
Kate Kligman
Kate Moore
Ken Janzen
Kevin McAlonan
Kimberly Kefalas
Laurel Halbany
Linda D. Addison
Louise Christine
Lucas K. Law
Lucy Taylor
M. Huw Evans
Marcel O. Philipp
Mark Carroll
Marlyse Comte
Mekenzie Larsen
Mia Nutick
Michael H. Hanson
Mike Rimar
Nancy Baker
Niels-Viggo S. Hobbs
P. Gelatt
Patricia Lynne Duffy
Paul Roberts
Peggy Hailey
Peter Straub
Rebecca M. Senese
Remmik Petra
Richard Wright
Robert Joseph Levy
Ronald L. Weston
Samuel Holden Bramah
Sean R. Padlo
Soban B.
Sonika Edwards
Steven Kaye
Suzanne Church
Terry D. England
Terry Weyna
Usman T. Malik
V. Critchley
Victor LaValle
Walt Boyes
Willa McCafferty
williamcookwriter.com

EMB
RACE
THE
ODD

DEAD AMERICANS
BEN PEEK

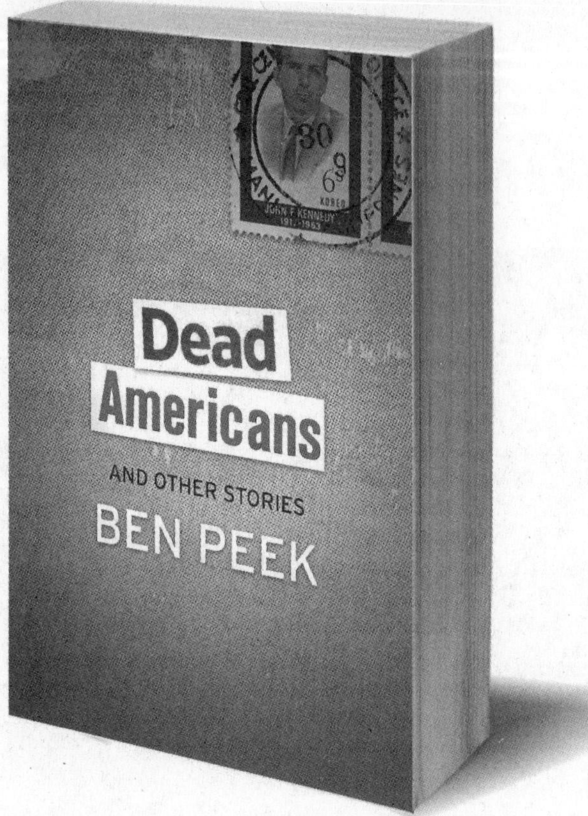

A collection of the critically acclaimed surreal short fiction of Ben Peek. Welcome to the dark, weird worlds imagined by one of the finest writers of short fiction in English:

A world where bands are named after the murderer of a dead president, where the work of Octavia E. Butler is turned into an apocalypse meta-narrative, and John Wayne visits a Wal-Mart. A world where a dreaming Mark Twain has visions of Sydney, where a crime that begins in a mosque, and answers are given to a questionnaire you never read. Where a dying sun shines over a broken, bitter landscape, and men and women tattoo their life onto their skin for an absent god.

AVAILABLE NOW

978-1-77148-172-4

ALSO AVAILABLE FROM CHIZINE PUBLICATIONS

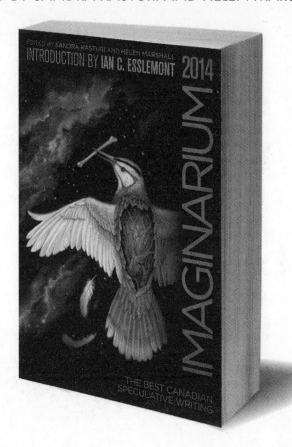

GIFTS FOR THE ONE WHO COMES AFTER

HELEN MARSHALL

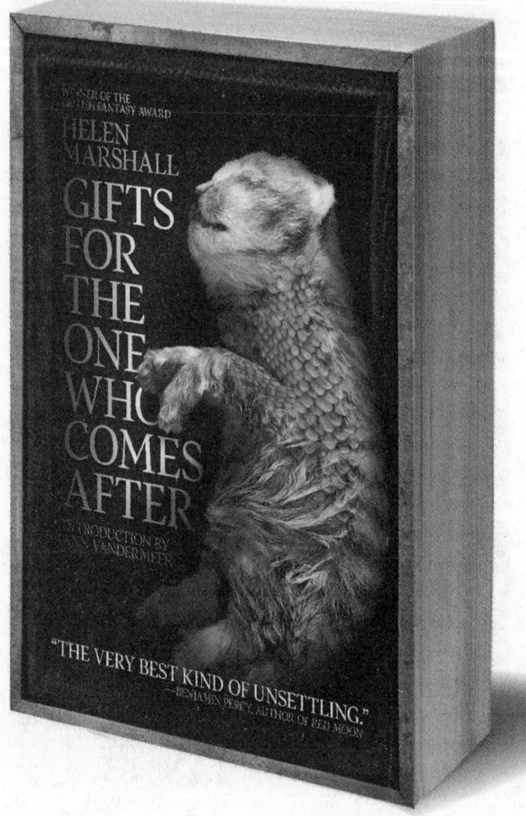

Ghost thumbs. Miniature dogs. One very sad can of tomato soup . . . British Fantasy Award-winner Helen Marshall's second collection offers a series of twisted surrealities that explore the legacies we pass on to our children. A son seeks to reconnect with his father through a telescope that sees into the past. A young girl discovers what lies on the other side of her mother's bellybutton. Death's wife prepares for a very special funeral. In *Gifts for the One Who Comes After*, Marshall delivers eighteen tales of love and loss that cement her as a powerful voice in dark fantasy and the New Weird. Dazzling, disturbing, and deeply moving.

AVAILABLE SEPTEMBER 2014

978-1-77148-303-2

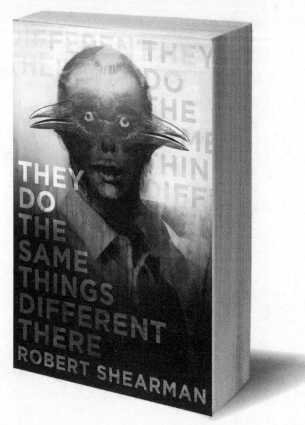

CZP

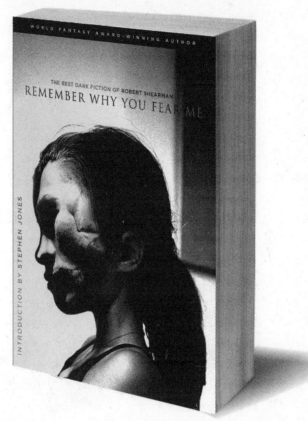

WE WILL ALL GO DOWN TOGETHER

GEMMA FILES

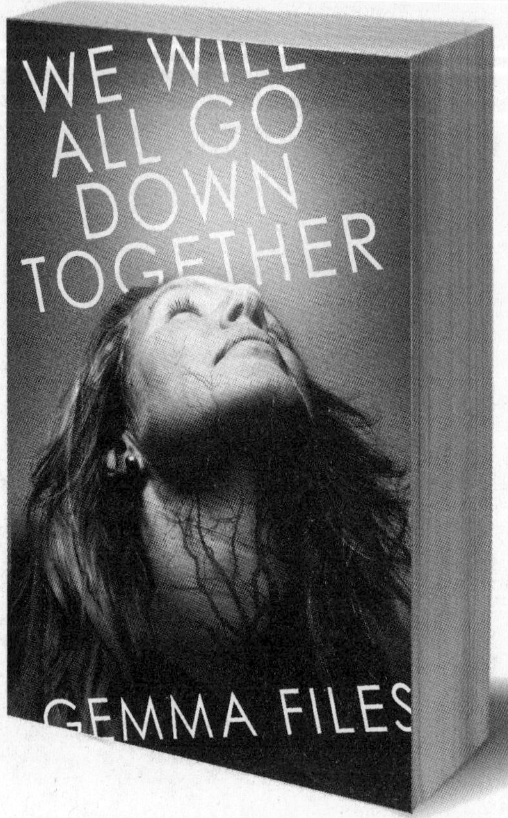

In the woods outside Overdeere, Ontario, there are trees that speak, a village that doesn't appear on any map and a hill that opens wide, entrapping unwary travellers. Music drifts up from deep underground, while dreams—and nightmares—take on solid shape, flitting through the darkness. It's a place most people usually know better than to go, at least locally—until tonight, at least, when five bloodlines mired in ancient strife will finally converge once more.

AVAILABLE AUGUST 2014

978-1-77148-202-8

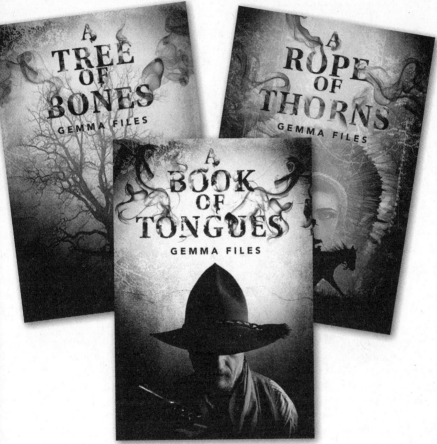

FLOATING BOY AND THE GIRL WHO COULDN'T FLY

P.T. JONES

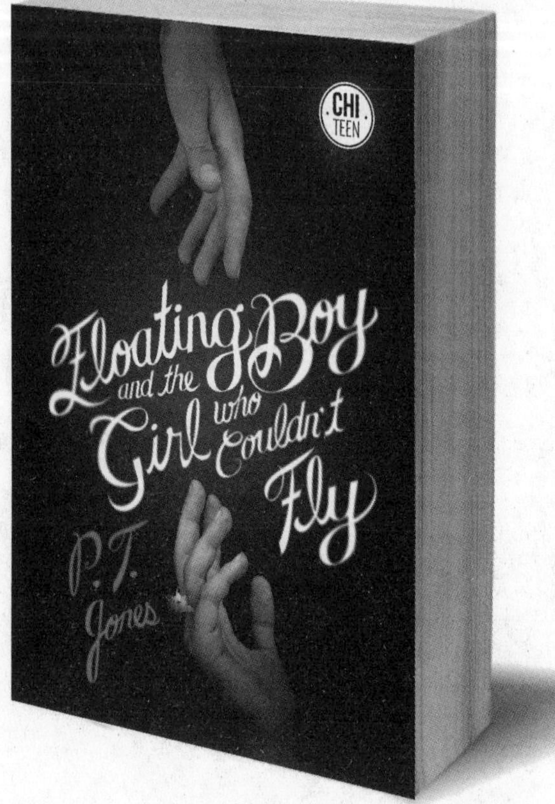

Things Mary doesn't want to fall into: the river, high school, her mother's life.

Things Mary does kind of want to fall into: love, the sky.

This is the story of a girl who sees a boy float away one fine day. This is the story of the girl who reaches up for that boy with her hand and with her heart. This is the story of a girl who takes on the army to save a town, who goes toe-to-toe with a mad scientist, who has to fight a plague to save her family. This is the story of a girl who would give anything to get to babysit her baby brother one more time. If she could just find him.

It's all up in the air for now, though, and falling fast. . . .

AVAILABLE OCTOBER 2014

978-1-77148-174-8

ALSO AVAILABLE FROM CHITEEN

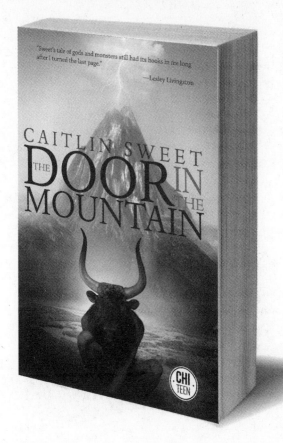

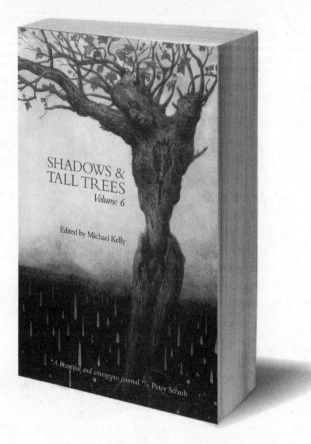

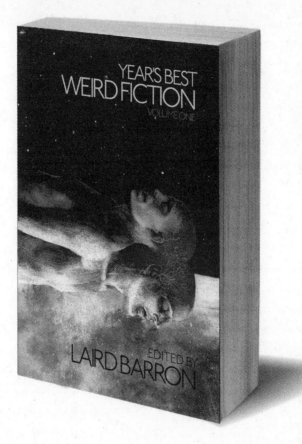